MW01195702

DARCY'S MELODY

A PRIDE AND PREJUDICE VARIATION

JENNIFER REDLARCZYK

Sallianne,
Thanks so much for participating
in my giveaway. I'm
thrilled you won a copy
of my book —
Happy Reading!
Jennifer Redlarczyk

REDLARK PRESS

Jennifer Redlarczyk

Darcy's Melody ~ A Pride and Prejudice Variation

Copyright © 2018 by Jennifer Redlarczyk

Cover Art by Daniel Ichinose ~ Atomatron Designs

Cover Image ~ Wikiart.org ~ Young Girls at the Piano by Pierre-Auguste Renoir

Interior Design by E-book Formatting Fairies

Published by Jennifer Redlarczyk ~ Redlark Press

Redlark Press

This is a work of fiction. Names, characters, places, brands, and incidents are either the product of the author's imagination, or are used fictitiously. Any resemblances to actual persons, living or dead, events, business establishments, or locales are entirely coincidental with the exception of those taken from Jane Austen's novel, *Pride and Prejudice.*

ISBN-13: 978-1544102788

ISBN-10: 154410278X

August 2018

With fond memories of my sister, I would like to dedicate Darcy's Melody to Melody Ann Ferree, who was the inspiration for this story.

ACKNOWLEDGMENTS

Being a moderator on the Private JAFF forum DarcyandLizzy.com, I would like to thank Brenda Webb, my fellow moderators and of course so many readers who have been very encouraging of my work. In addition, many thanks go out to my Beta team: Lorena Alberni, Kathryn Bigley, Jessica Ferree, Wendy Delzell, Betty Jo Kennedy, Jacqueline Wade, and special mention of Carmalee Mitchell and Jessica Moynihan Washer who served as cold readers. I would also like to thank my son, Daniel Ichinose, who offered his creative talent in creating the cover design for my book and to my husband Greg who always puts up with my JAFF obsession.

Thank you all! ~ Jennifer Redlarczyk ♬

CHAPTER ONE

UNDER THE COVER OF BOOKS

London
Tuesday, 21 May 1811
Early afternoon

*B*allard's was an eclectic treasure trove of rare first editions and unusual books located on the thoroughfare of Piccadilly. Although it appeared somewhat dingy and dimly lit from the outside, inside the ageing building the atmosphere was inviting, and a vast array of literature beckoned lovers of the written word.

Promptly at one o'clock, Fitzwilliam Darcy entered the bookshop and walked directly towards his favoured section. While paging through a military war journal, he instinctively glanced toward the back of the shop. Even with several patrons milling about the establishment today, Darcy's eyes were drawn to a young lady who appeared to be examining a small book in the poetry section.

Closing the journal, Darcy ambled over to where the woman stood and began perusing the titles on a nearby shelf. After taking a book in hand, he purposely turned his head towards the young lady. Captivated by her large, dark emerald-green eyes sparkling with mischief, he felt his lips curve into a half smile when she spoke.

1

"Pray, sir, may I trouble you to hand me the book of Cowper poetry on the upper shelf?"

Darcy nodded. "With pleasure. Cowper is an excellent choice."

As he reached for the book, she continued, "One poem in particular reminds me of Oakham Mount in *Hertfordshire*. I find I am rather desirous of its solace today if only through the eyes of the poet."

Handing her the book, he answered in kind. "I understand your sentiments for I, too, am from the country and have longed to return to *Derbyshire*."

Arching an eyebrow in his direction, she inclined her head and said, "I thank you, sir."

"You are most welcome."

As she turned the pages of her selection in search of the poem, Darcy heard the young lady gasp when both of her books slid out of her hands and onto the floor. "Oh dear," she sighed, stooping down to retrieve them.

"Allow me," he immediately offered. Both reaching for the books, Darcy felt her small, warm hand carefully slip a folded piece of paper into the palm of his own. The young lady had not replaced her glove after perusing her own book, and her skin was soft to the touch. Leaning closer, the faint scent of lavender seemed to strengthen, causing his chest to tighten and his heart to quicken in response.

Feigning innocence, she looked up at him and said, "Again, sir, I am in your debt. Perhaps I should make my purchases before I have another mishap."

"Permit me to carry these to the desk for you."

Acknowledging his offer with a slight curtsey, the young lady whispered, "Sir, I think we are being observed." Then speaking louder, she added, "Thank you again. You are most kind."

"Your servant." He bowed. With his senses heightened from being forewarned of impending danger, Darcy spoke softly in return, "How did you come? I would not have you leave here unescorted."

"There is a carriage waiting, sir. A manservant is nearby and a maid is within."

"Then leave now and be careful."

2

After he placed the books on the counter, the young lady thanked Darcy, made her purchase, and quickly exited the shop. From where he stood, Darcy watched the footman assist her into the carriage. Assured of her safety, he abruptly turned and faced the observing patron who had folded his newspaper and was preparing to leave the shop.

"Excuse me, have we met?"

The man was obviously confused and stammered, "I ... I think so. You are Mr. erm.... "

"Fitzwilliam Darcy. And you are?"

"My name is ... is Gerard Mooreland, and if I remember correctly, my son, Jonathan, was a classmate of yours at university some years back."

Darcy furrowed his brow for a moment in thought. "I do not seem to recall the name. Do you care to refresh my memory?"

"My ... my son was a master with the blade and was an active participant in the fencing club," Mooreland boasted through a somewhat crooked smile.

With no recollection of either man, Darcy made further inquiries after which he gave Mooreland his card and requested his son pay him a visit when he was next in Town. Concluding their conversation, Darcy made his purchase and left the bookshop being rather unsettled.

~ ♫ ~

Darcy House

Upon returning home, Darcy strode into the study to wait for Colonel Fitzwilliam's imminent arrival. Shaking his head, he tried to make sense of what had transpired. Earlier in the day, Darcy received a message from his cousin requesting his services. Colonel Fitzwilliam was a military officer by profession. Lately, he had been employed as an intelligence agent with his Majesty's newly formed *Secret Guard*. With the concept of the guard being proposed by Lord

Matlock, a personal friend of the Prince Regent, it was only natural for him to recommend his son who had been highly decorated during the Peninsular Wars to assist with this group. When residing in Town, Darcy occasionally assisted the colonel's efforts by taking on the minor role of courier.

Such had been the case with today's activity. Shortly before his departure, however, he had received further instructions stating there had been a change in plans. Instead of meeting his usual contact, he was to exchange watchwords with a young woman who would give him the coded message.

"What could Richard have been thinking? How could he possibly have involved a young lady in this type of activity?" Gripping the window sash, Darcy blankly stared into the courtyard. While reflecting, he could not help but be reminded of what had happened when he last assisted his cousin. "I loathe to think what might have been lost had I not done his bidding last time."

~ ♫ ~

Kent
Friday, 15 March 1811
Two months earlier

Dark clouds loomed overhead as Darcy attempted to peer out of his carriage window. A light drizzle had begun to fog the glass, but as long as the weather held, he could continue his journey without delay. Being a short distance from the eastern coast, one was never sure if a squall might blow in off of the North Sea, yielding a heavy rain.

Knowing the seaside village of Broadstairs was less than two miles from Ramsgate where his sister was currently residing, the colonel had no trouble convincing Darcy to make a confidential delivery on this particular occasion. Upon completing his task, he looked forward to arriving at Georgiana's establishment and surprising her with a visit.

Reaching into his satchel, Darcy took out a small miniature of his sister and smiled with affection. "Dearest Georgiana," he murmured to himself. Lifting a book from the carriage seat, he removed a letter which she had sent him several months prior. Turning to the end of the second page, he began to read.

As you know, my music master, Herr Schneider, will be removing to Ramsgate near the end of December. Having made such excellent progress under his tutelage, it pains me to think I shall no longer be able to profit from his guidance and expertise.

After much discussion with Herr Schneider, I am asking you to consider my request and allow me to finish my musical studies with him in Ramsgate rather than remain at school. Be assured, this request is not something I have taken lightly, as I have prayed about it for many weeks now. If it pleases you, perhaps you might find a capable companion who would oversee my academic lessons as well. I promise you I shall not remain idle, and if you could but find it in your heart to grant my petition, I shall be eternally grateful.

Your loving sister,
Georgiana

Refolding the letter, Darcy let out a soft chuckle. *My little sister is growing up. As much as I love her, it is good she is learning to be independent of me.*

Georgiana had only been residing in Ramsgate for two months, yet Darcy missed her and was anxious to see how she was getting on for himself. Exiting the carriage, he proceeded directly to the house. Entering, his senses were heightened when he noticed a man's outer garments hanging in the receiving area. Upon hearing a familiar male voice coming from the sitting room, Darcy hastened forward with anxiety.

"Georgiana, surely you know how much I care for you, my love. May we not make a few changes in our plans? I find I cannot wait until next week to make you mine."

"George, I would like nothing better, yet … I am so uncertain. Could we not inform William of our...." Her voice trailed off at the sound of heavy footsteps echoing in the hallway. Suddenly, the door swung open so hard it hit the wall with a thud.

"Wickham, what the devil are YOU doing here? And Georgiana, where is Mrs. Younge?"

"Brother, I.... William, we are to be married. I had hoped you would be pleased," she quietly offered, looking scared and confused.

The colour immediately rose on Darcy's face as he sought to control his temper. "Georgiana, leave us at once. Send Mrs. Younge here, and remain in your room until I come for you."

"Ye … yes," she stammered, leaving the room in tears.

Mere minutes later, Mrs. Younge glided into the sitting room, her expression unapologetic and disdainful. Closing the door with an almost inaudible click she asked, "What may I do for you, Mr. Darcy?"

Darcy could control his anger no longer, his voice rising as he began to question the two. Wickham, who refused to be intimidated, sarcastically scoffed at Darcy's interrogation before blurting out his heartless words.

"Me? Am I in love with your spoiled little sister? Surely, Fitzwilliam, you must know by now what type of woman I prefer." He laughed. "Your precious Georgiana was merely a means to an end. I simply came for what I was due. As usual, you have cheated me, and I insist you at least pay for my silence if I am to leave here without her portion."

Darcy was furious. He could not believe the cruelty and arrogance displayed by a man who was once his childhood friend and a favourite of his father. It took all of his mental fortitude to restrain himself from inflicting bodily harm on Wickham for his contemptible behaviour.

"Pay for your silence? Consider yourself lucky I do not run you through. YOU are the one who chose to ignore the generous living left by my father. You were amply compensated and will not be given another farthing for your misconduct. Furthermore, you will say NOTHING which might harm my sister's reputation. You and Mrs.

Younge will leave this place immediately, and if one word reaches me of Georgiana's disgrace in this affair, the two of you will have to endure my wrath.

"Be forewarned, Wickham—if you cross me in this, you will also have to deal with my cousin. Believe me when I say Colonel Fitzwilliam will not be as kind to you as I have been today. Do I make myself clear?" There was silence. "Be gone! And let me NEVER see your loathsome faces again!"

Watching Wickham and Mrs. Younge exit the room, Darcy's heart sank when he recognised Georgiana's hurried footsteps running down the hallway and up the stairs. The minute the two conspirators had gone from the house, Darcy went to his sister and found her collapsed on the bed, crying uncontrollably. Taking her in his arms, he offered comfort and reassurance, not knowing how his dear sister would handle the humiliation and disappointment which had befallen her on this day.

"I am so sorry, my darling girl. We shall get through this together. I promise."

~ ♪ ~

The present

Not long after returning to London, Darcy had quietly procured the services of Jean Annesley, a recently-widowed matron, who would provide companionship for Georgiana and help oversee the remainder of her studies. Once the two women established a rapport, Georgiana's activities slowly returned to normal even though her emotional state remained in turmoil.

While Darcy resumed his business affairs in Town, he continued to be concerned about Georgiana's despondency. This prompted him to curtail many social engagements including his annual spring visit to Rosings Park where he often assisted his aunt, Lady Catherine de Bourgh, with estate matters. For Darcy, this altered routine resulted in a rather dull Spring Season—until today.

It was nearly six o'clock when Colonel Fitzwilliam finally appeared at Darcy's door. His butler, Benson, escorted the colonel to the study and retired with a bow.

"Sorry, Cousin. My meeting ran late, and I could not get away as quickly as I wanted. How about drinking a little of your smooth brandy to soothe my weary soul while we talk? I suppose you are in need of some explanation for the sudden change in plans."

Darcy retrieved the bottle and two glasses from the cupboard. Setting the tray on the table, he abruptly said, "I have been waiting. When I read your directions earlier today, I was astonished to find you were sending a *young lady* to deliver your precious message."

"Yes." The colonel blew out a long breath. "I knew you would not like it, but the decision was not mine to make." He picked up a glass and poured himself two fingers of the amber liquid before continuing. "My father's contact in Cheapside was responsible for *that* decision."

"Cheapside?" Darcy scowled.

"Cheapside. Apparently, there was a last minute problem with his usual man, and for the sake of security and time, the gentleman sent his niece."

"His niece!"

"Yes. And from what my father says, she is quite pretty," he chuckled.

"Humph!" Darcy grunted and took a sip of his drink, refusing to comment on the young woman. "It may have been her uncle's decision; nevertheless, it was highly improper."

"Father says we are not to worry as she can be very discreet and clever."

"Well, with that I should agree."

"Oh?"

"Yes, she observed an older man watching us and alerted me to his presence."

"Are you certain?"

"Undeniably. I decided to confront the man myself before leaving the shop. He told me his name was Gerard Mooreland, and while I do not recall the acquaintance, he implied he met me through his son,

8

Jonathan, at university. The man appeared uneasy when we spoke, which makes me doubt his claim. I do believe he warrants some further investigation."

"Definitely. If you do not mind, I shall send one of my aides here in the morning to interview you."

"Yes, yes, of course."

"Are there any more questions?"

"No, I think not," grumbled Darcy.

"Good! Now, tell me, how is our dear, sweet Georgiana faring? What has it been, five or six weeks since Ramsgate?"

Darcy's eyebrows narrowed slightly. "It will be ten weeks on Friday to be more precise," he said before downing the rest of his drink.

"Hopefully, she is no longer pining over that scum Wickham. All I need is for you to say the word, Cousin, and I shall delight in calling him out."

"If only it were so simple." Darcy reached for the decanter and refilled his glass.

"How is she managing with her new companion?"

"Actually, the two of them are getting along quite well under the circumstances. Once again, please extend my gratitude to your mother for her recommendation. Mrs. Annesley has proven to be steady and has done much to encourage Georgiana in resuming her studies."

After taking another sip of his drink, Darcy looked up and continued, "I wish I could say the same for her mental state. In general, Georgiana's emotions remain unstable, and she refuses to talk about what happened. Thankfully, she has begun practicing her music again. Small as it may be, I do count it as another positive step in her recovery. Mrs. Annesley has also suggested my sister become involved in some kind of charity work in an effort to refocus her attentions and possibly lift her spirits."

"I see." The colonel nodded. "Well then, it seems our girl may become rather busy in the near future." Darcy raised his brows in questioning.

"Mother has sent me with a request. While she knows nothing of the unfortunate events at Ramsgate, she did notice how withdrawn Georgiana was when she visited here last week. Consequently, Mother would like to take our Georgie under her maternal wing by including her in some aspect of her current charity project. If Georgiana were to volunteer on this project, she seems to think it would give her more purpose and possibly help her to overcome some of her reserve."

"I wonder if Georgie would entertain the possibility." He paused to contemplate his aunt's proposal. "Frankly, Richard, I would give anything for my sister to feel better about herself. Still, the decision to participate must come from her."

"I agree. You know, Cousin, to be truthful, I am heartily tired of this whole blasted hospital project. It has turned out to be one of Mother's most elaborate undertakings. Mind you, she talks of nothing else. I trust you have been solicited for funds?"

"To be sure." Darcy smiled. "Raising money for the construction of an additional building at the London Hospital which will service our military is admirable."

"I never expected her to put forth such fervour with this project. Why, *the Committee* has been extended well past her usual circle of friends and continues to grow daily. I swear nothing will stop her at this point."

"You must admit your mother's efforts can be attributed to her devotion and concern for you as an officer."

"I suppose it to be true. Yet, in some ways, I think this latest undertaking has provided her another way of diverting her frustration over my elder brother's shortcomings. Not being able to control Reggie's bad habits with her ultimatums, I suspect exercising complete authority over every aspect of the project has given her new purpose. Sometimes, I wonder if her committee functions more out of fear than anything else. All in all, I have actually come to the conclusion my mother would make an *excellent officer* for the Crown should women ever be permitted to serve."

Darcy could not help but chuckle when the colonel suddenly

snapped to attention and pretended to salute his mother. "Richard, *you* are incorrigible! Now, if you could please be serious for a moment, I would like to know exactly what Aunt Eleanor has in mind for Georgiana. Your mother is well meaning, yet I would not wish for my sister to be subject to one of her moods."

"To begin with, you do remember both you and Georgiana are invited to Mother's little dinner party on the seventh of June?"

"Richard, nothing your mother ever does is by any means *little*. And yes, we are coming. In fact, I was surprised to learn the Bingleys and the Hursts were also invited."

"I suspect it is more of an endeavour to combine business with pleasure. One of the hospital's physicians, Mr. Stephen Madison, who has been working closely with the board of directors for the project, will be available to speak with patrons along with several committee members. Both Bingley and Hurst were among those who made substantial contributions and were thus included. In point of fact, you may be interested to learn Lord Ellington and his lovely wife and daughters will also be in attendance." Darcy stiffened at the mention of their names. "If I recall, is not their younger daughter, Lady Lilyan Ashbourne, acquainted with Georgiana?"

"Yes, they were friends at school."

"I trust then you *do* remember her older sister, the very beautiful and captivating Lady Clarissa?" He smirked.

Clearing his throat in discomfort, Darcy responded, "Yes, how could I forget? Her parents invited me to countless outings during her first season. Nevertheless, because of Georgiana's situation, I have been unavailable for many of their recent gatherings. Oh, I admit Lady Clarissa is pleasant to look at and can be a rather charming partner at the theatre or the opera, but...." He trailed off, raking his hand through his hair in frustration and donning a frown.

"Just what are you implying, Cousin? She is one of the most sought after women of the *ton* and has a marriage settlement of forty thousand pounds to boot!"

"Richard, if she had twice the amount, I would not be interested in courting her. To be sure, she is well enough impressed with tales of my estate, and I do admit she plays and sings divinely, yet...." He let out a sigh of exasperation. "Lady Clarissa can scarcely engage my mind with all of the absurdities she constantly expels concerning fashion and local gossip. I doubt if the woman has ever read a book in its entirety since she surpassed the need for a governess. In general, I have nothing against the lady except she is far too possessive of my meagre attentions and even more impressed with her own consequence."

With this, the colonel could no longer contain himself and broke into a hearty laugh. "Darcy, you have so much going in your favour and could have any number of women. Why is it you continually find fault with each and every lady you meet? Oh, to be in your shoes! A second son of an earl is a true death sentence when it comes to beautiful, wealthy women."

Darcy rolled his eyes and retorted disdainfully, "Frankly, Richard, you need to come up with a better statement. Now, if you do not mind, please get to the point and tell me what all of this has to do with Georgiana becoming involved with your mother's charity."

"I am getting there. Be patient, Cousin." He purposely took his time, swirling the amber liquid and taking another sip. "At Mother's party, there will be four more people in attendance who I believe will pose a greater interest to you." Darcy raised a brow expressing curiosity.

"A Mr. and Mrs. Edward Gardiner and their nieces, Miss Jane Bennet and Miss Elizabeth Bennet, have also been asked to dine with us. Have you never heard of the gentleman?"

"No, I cannot say I have. Let me think ... Edward Gardiner, ah ... would this be the same Gardiner whose warehouses monopolise trade in the finest textiles throughout the merchant district?"

"Yes, he is one and the same. And as a point of interest to you, his wife was born and raised in Lambton." Darcy acknowledged this information with a nod, prompting the colonel to continue. "Edward Gardiner has the reputation of being a shrewd tradesman, and his integrity and fairness as a business leader are well received. The majority of his warehouses are in Cheapside."

"Cheapside?" Darcy questioned with apprehension.

"Yes," he drawled, giving Darcy a moment to ponder. "I did say Cheapside, did I not?" Darcy furrowed his brows and gestured for his cousin to finish.

"With Gardiner being one of the more prominent leaders in trade, his wife often represents that particular faction in charity endeavours like the one my mother is now sponsoring. From what I hear, I do believe Mrs. Gardiner and Mother present quite a formidable pair."

"Go on."

"At this point in time, Mother is nothing but complimentary of the woman and has developed a partiality for her nieces. Interestingly, my father and Gardiner have *also* been associates in certain business ventures not to mention more discrete matters, if you catch my meaning." Darcy made no comment.

"In fact, according to the earl, I believe you met one of Mr. Gardiner's nieces earlier this afternoon." His look was smug. *"Miss Elizabeth?"*

"You cannot be serious!"

"The Bennet sisters have been in Town assisting their aunt since the beginning of January, and Mother thinks Georgiana would greatly benefit from contact with Mrs. Gardiner and her nieces in this instance."

"Richard, I do not know if I can agree to this. Miss Elizabeth Bennet was involved in a clandestine transaction today. Furthermore, I am not sure I care for my sister associating with women who are from Cheapside."

"The young ladies are from *Hertfordshire* where their father is a country squire. According to Mother, Miss Elizabeth has an overflowing enthusiasm and passion for this project. Her elder sister is remarkably patient and is always cheerful despite the many frustrations the committee often encounters. Mother may fault these women for their lack of fortune and their connection to trade; yet for the sake of her project, she has decidedly overlooked those issues.

"Personally, I cannot wait to meet them." He flashed a grin at Darcy before adding more seriously, "Listen, can you not trust

Mother on this one? She will make the introductions at her dinner party, and if you still have reservations, we simply shall not encourage any further contact between Georgiana and the young ladies."

"Dinner...." Darcy rubbed his chin. "Well, assuming I go along with your suggestion, I am not sure Aunt Eleanor's dinner party would be the best setting for Georgiana to become acquainted with these women. If my sister *is* to meet Mrs. Gardiner and her nieces with the prospect of discussing the charity, I would prefer the women come here for their initial introductions and make their presentation. Assuming all goes well, it will be easier to continue the connection at your mother's party. Do you think it can be arranged?"

"Certainly! Mother will be pleased. Moreover, with your reservations, it will give you the opportunity to make your own evaluation." He patted Darcy on the back. "Now, having exhausted that topic, shall we go see our dear Georgie? And while we are at it, may I ask what is on the menu for dinner this evening? With all this talk of dining, I am absolutely starving," he snickered.

The two proceeded to walk to the drawing room where they met Georgiana before going into dinner. Allowing his cousin to present Lady Matlock's request, Darcy was pleased when Georgiana did not reject the idea and was willing to meet with Mrs. Gardiner and the Bennet sisters privately. Despite being somewhat cautious about the connection, for his own part, he would not mind seeing the young lady from the bookshop for a second time.

CHAPTER TWO

A BEGINNING

Darcy House, London
Thursday, 30 May 1811
The following week

*S*itting on the tufted seat in front of her upper-story bedroom window, Georgiana gazed through the glass onto the dreary courtyard below. After an early morning downpour, the pathways were strewn with mud and debris and in much need of attention. A small, curious bird landed on the windowsill, eager and unaffected by what had passed merely hours before. Gently fingering the misty glass, Georgiana smiled momentarily, wondering if she could ever be so carefree. When the small bird flew off, she was again faced with the reality of her current despair and involuntarily shivered in response.

"If only I could disappear as easily as you," she murmured.

It seemed nothing could lift her forlorn spirits since returning from Ramsgate. With remorse and humiliation remaining her constant companions, Georgiana wondered how she would be able to face her aunt's committee members later in the day. Yet, for her brother's sake, she knew she must try. Endeavouring to calm her nerves,

Georgiana closed her eyes for a moment before retrieving a fresh handkerchief from her nightstand. A single tear rolling down her pale cheek was accompanied by a nearly inaudible sob.

"I loved him. I trusted him," she whispered, going through the motions of blotting her eyes and returning the handkerchief to her pocket. She had not been at Ramsgate much more than a month before George Wickham appeared, changing her life forever.

Closing the drawer, Georgiana reached for a small ornamental box resting on top of the table. Her long, slender fingers slowly caressed the curves of the tiny shells imbedded in the lid. Carefully opening the box, she examined each item. Seeing the smooth, pearl-like shell taken from the beach where they had strolled arm in arm, every detail came rushing back.

The day had been brusque and windy. Murky waves swelled toward the shoreline, beneath the clear, blue sky of the eastern coast. In the distance, the continuous sound of shrieking seagulls permeated the air with their discordant pitches. Even with the cool air, Georgiana had never felt chilled. First, she was warmed by the heat of Wickham's passionate words, and later by his body when he broke with all propriety and drew her into a secure embrace. During that precious sliver of time, she had felt safe and wanted. It was then Wickham had kissed her with a hunger which awakened her soul.

Closing her eyes, Georgiana touched her lips with the back of her hand. Trembling, she relived the fire of her first kiss, a kiss which had left her breathless and totally within his power. After several seconds had passed, Georgiana forced herself to look back into the box. More tears were shed as she took out the broken pieces of a tiny glass figurine Wickham had bought for her at a village shop. Holding them in her hand, she slowly turned each piece, remembering how the object had shimmered in the light.

"You said it sparkled like my eyes," she whispered.

Returning the pieces, Georgiana next took out the beautiful gold locket displaying Wickham's likeness and held it to her breast. He had given her this token after making his declaration of love and asked her to come away with him so they might marry in Scotland. In her mind, she could still see his hazel eyes, his dark brown hair, and his warm smile as he embraced her.

"*Dearest Georgiana, you are the angel of my dreams. I cannot live another day without you. I pray you will make me the happiest of men and accept my hand in marriage. Why, we could leave for Gretna Green as early as next week and no one would be the wiser.*"

"George," she hesitated. "*I ... I do wish to accept your offer, for I dearly love you. It ... it is William I worry about. He has no knowledge of our attachment, and I fear he will be sorely distressed if we marry without first seeking his permission.*"

"*My dear, you worry unnecessarily. How could Fitzwilliam possibly object to our marriage? Do you not remember your father was always very fond of me?*"

"*Yes, George, I do.*"

"*Your father was my godfather. He cared for me as though I was his son, and he treated me with respect. He provided me with the education and the means to better my position in life—a life I wish to share with you.*" He warmly caressed her cheek before touching his lips to hers. "Georgiana," he whispered. "*You must trust me. Do you not see it is our destiny to be together?*"

"*I ... I do.*"

Trembling with great anxiety, Georgiana suddenly found it difficult to breathe. Having overheard his hateful exchange with her brother at Ramsgate, she knew everything George Wickham had said to her during their time together was a lie. "Oh, how could I have been so blind?"

Inadvertently, the little box slipped from her hands to the floor, splitting apart and scattering the contents. Repulsed by the locket, she threw it to where the rest of her broken treasures lay and immediately dropped onto the bed, sobbing in earnest. Consumed with anguish, she cried for some minutes before sliding off the edge of the bed and onto her knees, where she began to pray in earnest. "Please, dear Lord, help me! I am so lost. I beg of you...." Pulling herself back onto the bed, Georgiana buried her face into the soft pillows and continued to cry until she fell asleep, completely exhausted.

~ ♫ ~

Gardiners' Carriage
The same day

Early in the afternoon, three modestly dressed ladies left Gracechurch Street bound for Grosvenor Square, located in the fashionable Mayfair district. The day was pleasant and sunlight filtered through the glass windows of the carriage which jostled back and forth down the uneven dirt road. Time passed quickly, and before long, the vehicle turned onto a cobblestone drive which would eventually lead to Darcy House.

For the most part, when entering the district, Elizabeth could not help but be fascinated by the unbridled display of wealth. The lavish homes and surrounding gardens were impressive to say the least. Yet, today, she could not fully attend to everything she saw. Instead, her mind was drawn back to a conversation she had with her uncle.

"I understand you will be visiting the Darcy townhouse tomorrow."

"Yes, Lady Matlock has requested we be introduced to Miss Darcy. She is hopeful our presentation will encourage her niece to participate in some aspect of her current charity project."

"So I have heard. Well, Lizzy, I shall come to the point. It is very likely you will also be introduced to the young lady's brother, and I wanted to put you on your guard."

"Oh?"

"As you know, I generally do not discuss information about your contacts when you assist me. Nevertheless, in this case I should tell you Mr. Darcy was the gentleman you met while delivering my latest communication. On that particular day, he happened to be assisting his cousin, Colonel Fitzwilliam, just as you have done for me on occasion. I expect you to use discretion when meeting him, and under no circumstances are you to make any reference to our more clandestine activities."

"I understand."

"Very well, I shall depend upon your good judgement."

Thinking back to their brief encounter at the bookshop, Elizabeth had no difficulty bringing to mind the unknown person to whom she delivered her charge. The well-ordered, impeccably-dressed man was very tall, and his demeanour suggested he was a gentleman of the upper class. Suppressing an urge to giggle, she wondered if his curly black hair ever gave him trouble in maintaining his proper, meticulous appearance. The man's noble face was enhanced by a well-formed jaw, revealing two prominent dimples when he smiled, and his deep voice was quite pleasant. The moment their hands met and he looked at her with his crystal-blue eyes, she nearly lost her breath. Yes, Mr. Darcy was indeed handsome, and the thought of meeting the gentleman again caused Elizabeth to smile with anticipation.

Breaking her reverie, she enquired, "Aunt Gardiner, please tell us again what you know of the Darcys."

"Yes," seconded Jane. "I hope they are pleasant people. I would not wish to relive any of what we experienced last week at Bromewell House, especially for Lizzy's sake."

Remembering the offensive encounter with Lord Bromewell, Elizabeth stiffened for a moment before playfully shrugging it off and expressing her sentiments with a sense of drama. "In truth, with the exception of His Lordship *accidentally* pinching me in the hallway and accosting me with his foul breath, it was not so disagreeable. Of course we did have to endure Her Ladyship speaking indirectly to us through her personal maid. Then, there was that one little unpleasant remark between her two lovely daughters concerning our dress. Thankfully, she did pledge a donation in the end, did she not?" The three women exchanged knowing glances and immediately found themselves laughing out loud.

Calming herself, Elizabeth added, "In all seriousness, I do have the greatest respect for Lady Matlock and should never disparage her efforts. It is a pity so many in her circle are superficial and in want of compassion when it comes to people of lesser consequence. I know it is unfair of me to make these generalities, but having been insulted on numerous occasions—I can find little excuse for such behaviour.

Mrs. Gardiner reached for her nieces' hands. "Lizzy dear, Jane dear, I am truly sorry for what the two of you have endured at the whims of the upper class. Your efforts have meant much to me, and I am more grateful than words can ever express.

"Girls, we must keep our eyes on the end result and not despair over the path which takes us there. Once the construction of the additional building for the London Hospital is completed and ready to service our injured soldiers, it will benefit so many. Our own discomfort is insignificant when compared to what these young men have suffered for England."

"It is true, Aunt," Elizabeth agreed. "I am sorry if I let my wounded sensibilities get the better of me. Please forgive my complaints. I agree this work far outweighs our trials, and I shall endeavour to humble myself for the sake of our project."

"I am sure you will." Mrs. Gardiner smiled in return. "Now, with regard to the Darcys, Mr. and Miss Darcy are from Derbyshire as I previously mentioned. If you will recall, Pemberley, their great estate, is very close to Lambton where I grew up. In my day, I do remember the estate itself was vast and must have provided work for some two hundred of the neighbourhood locals, possibly more."

"So many?" Elizabeth questioned.

"Yes, I believe so. You can well imagine the prosperity of such a large estate sustains much of the entire region."

"Do you know anything more specific of Miss Darcy or her brother?" Elizabeth continued to prod.

"From what Lady Matlock intimated, apparently the Darcys tend to be more reserved and somewhat quiet."

"Reserved?" This information surprised Elizabeth since she had found Mr. Darcy to be rather engaging during their brief encounter.

"Yes, from what Lady Matlock said, I suspect Miss Darcy is particularly shy and resists being drawn into conversations. I assume this is why we have been invited to speak with her in a more private setting. Her Ladyship believes Miss Darcy's participation in some aspect of our goings-on might help to build her confidence. It is also my understanding she will not be sixteen years-of-age until late August."

"Aunt, why do you suppose the Darcys exhibit such reserve?" Jane questioned.

"Other than what Lady Matlock has mentioned, I know little more of Miss Darcy. In the case of the elder brother, while Mr. Darcy's reputation in Lambton is exemplary, in Town there it is said he is proud and tends not to associate with people of lesser consequence. I fear it is often the way with those who have grown up in a more privileged society. On the other hand, it is possible Mr. Darcy's reserve may have also resulted from the circumstances surrounding the death of his parents.

"You see, Lady Anne, his mother, was taken ill following Miss Darcy's birth. She never fully recovered and died when the child was not yet four. I understand Miss Darcy has been raised by several governesses and is currently under the guardianship of her brother and Colonel Fitzwilliam, Lady Matlock's second eldest.

"Following his wife's death, it is also well known the elder Mr. Darcy retreated from society. He only survived his wife by some five or six years, leaving the younger Darcy to become the master of a very large and demanding estate at the young age of one or two and twenty."

"Oh my," said Jane, distressed by what she had heard. "It is too sad. Lizzy, I do not know how we would endure it if both of our parents were no longer living."

"Dearest Jane." Elizabeth gently squeezed her sister's hand. "Aunt, it is good you told us of these circumstances. Without ever meeting Miss Darcy, I cannot help but have compassion for the dear girl. I promise you we shall do whatever we can to encourage her and to help her feel more comfortable in our presence."

"Thank you. I can ask no more."

~ ♫ ~

It was not long before the carriage entered Grosvenor Square and stopped in front of the entrance to a large three-story, white limestone building sporting stately Greek columns. Within minutes, the three women were shown into the drawing room where Miss Darcy and her companion awaited their presence. With her radiant blond hair and fine features, Miss Darcy presented a picture of innocent beauty. Except for her blue eyes, Elizabeth could not detect any resemblance to her elder brother. The young lady appeared to be exceedingly shy as her aunt had predicted and obviously struggled in addressing her guests. Following the initial introductions, Mrs. Gardiner took a seat nearer to Mrs. Annesley, allowing Elizabeth and Jane to position themselves on either side of their hostess. Moments later, light refreshments were served, and the servants were dismissed.

"Mrs. Gardiner, Miss Bennet, and Miss Elizabeth, I … I wish to thank you for waiting on me this afternoon," Georgiana quietly offered.

"Miss Darcy," Mrs. Gardiner responded. "Let me assure you, the pleasure is ours."

"Thank you. My … my aunt has spoken quite favourably of you and has commended your continued efforts with … within the various charities she sponsors."

"Lady Matlock is very kind. Indeed, I have known your aunt for nearly five years now, and I must contend her energies outmatch my own on our current project."

Forcing a little smile, Georgiana responded. "Yes, I agree, my aunt can be rather formidable when she has resolve. I … I must confess, however, I am unfamiliar with the procedures of charity work and … and I do not know what to expect in this instance."

Before continuing, the ladies were interrupted by the entrance of Mr. Darcy. "Please forgive my intrusion. I mean no imposition but am merely curious to hear your presentation this afternoon as a passive observer."

With the presence of her brother, Georgiana sat taller and tried to exert herself a little more while introducing him to her new acquaintances. Following a brief exchange, Darcy removed himself to the other side of the room where he stood near the mantelpiece and remained in silence.

Elizabeth could not help but discretely watch Darcy as the ladies resumed their conversation. Interestingly, the gentleman bore an unexpected air of superiority and did not exhibit one trait of the man she had met at the bookshop.

Mrs. Gardiner was the first to speak in earnest. "Miss Darcy, we are delighted to present you with information regarding the hospital charity and our committee work." Georgiana demurely nodded in acknowledgement. "Our current project was proposed to members of the hospital board of directors by Lady Matlock more than a year ago. Soon after, your aunt invited me to assist with this project, and I have since enlisted the help of my nieces.

"At present, the accommodations for our soldiers at the London Hospital are very confined, limiting the treatment and recovery of the wounded. The possibility of creating an additional facility which will service so many more has been highly motivating.

"Thus far, we have raised a substantial amount of the needed funds through private donations. Even so, we have decided to expand our efforts by including a variety of activities which will give more public notice to the project. Many of these events will take place during the upcoming seasons."

"My aunt has mentioned the Military Ball, but I have not been made aware of any other events."

At this point, Elizabeth reached into her satchel and took out a list detailing the various offerings which had been planned to date. Handing it to Georgiana, she took over the narrative.

"The Military Ball, which will be given next month, in mid-July, is the first of our larger events. As with the ball, most of the following proceedings such as the Twelfth Night Ball, the Opera Gala, and an extensive concert series will be put forth through patron subscription. With regard to the *Autumn Festival*, that event will be available to the general public for a very minimal admission fee and is scheduled for late September. It should be a lovely celebration and will take place at Green Park where a variety of musicians and artisans are to be featured."

Envisioning some of the proceedings, Georgiana's face took on a childlike glow. Clearly allowing her curiosity to outweigh her reserve, she responded with eagerness, "Brother, I do hope we shall be able to attend some of these events." Darcy acknowledged her with a nod but gave no verbal comment.

"Through Elizabeth's suggestion, Lady Matlock was able to secure the assistance of Mr. Henry Bishop who has agreed to be our musical advisor for the duration of our project," Mrs. Gardiner offered. "Being the newly appointed director and composer in residence at Covent Garden, we are honoured to have his support."

"Mr. Bishop has been extremely helpful," Elizabeth added. "He has not only assisted with our proposed concerts, but has personally contacted musicians on our behalf who have agreed to perform.

"Miss Darcy, Her Ladyship has spoken of your own proficiency on the pianoforte." Georgiana blushed profusely in response to being praised. "If you happen to be in Town when we present our chamber music concerts, I am sure you will want to hear the evening of Bach. According to Mr. Bishop, much of Bach's instrumental music has been greatly neglected since the composer's death and is, for the most part, unknown to the London audience."

"Brother and I attended a patron's forum and were introduced to Mr. Bishop shortly after he was appointed to his post," Georgiana shyly remarked. "Herr Schneider, my … my former music master, was very fond of Bach. At school, I accompanied my friend, Lady Lilyan Ashbourne, who plays the flute. Together, we studied the most beautiful sonata composed by Bach. The accompaniment was originally written for the harpsichord. With the help of Herr Schneider, I … I arranged it for the pianoforte." Looking to Darcy, she hesitantly asked, "William, do you not think we could … in … invite Lady Lilyan and her family to join us for the chamber music concerts if we are able to attend?"

"Why, yes, of course, Georgiana. I am sure they would welcome our invitation."

She nodded in appreciation. "Mrs. Gardiner … I am awed by all I have heard this afternoon. Still, given I have no experience with charities, I am curious to know in what capacity I might be able to offer … my assistance."

Mrs. Gardiner smiled reassuringly. "To begin with, Miss Darcy, we thought some of our less demanding projects might be of interest to you. These activities are ongoing, and you could participate whenever it was convenient. For example, my nieces began a volunteer activity in which women from both the *ton* and merchant communities have been assisting patients. We call this *Correspondence Hours*. Within this endeavour, volunteers assist by reading and writing letters for those who are physically impaired due to their wounds. Perhaps this activity might prove enjoyable to both you and Mrs. Annesley." Georgiana looked to her companion who in turn gave a nod of approval.

"Please, may we hear more?"

In her gentle demeanour, Jane took up the conversation, detailing how the activity came about and how it currently functioned. "You see," she continued. "Our hospital wards are often short on attendants and cannot consistently offer the service which we can so easily provide."

"Jane, dear, I wonder if you and Lizzy could relate the story of Mr. Blakemore."

"Miss Darcy, this story is truly a remarkable," Jane continued. "Shortly after we established the *Correspondence Hours*, my sister came upon an unfortunate officer who was disoriented and suffered from memory loss because of a severe head injury. Lizzy...."

Eager to relate the tale, Elizabeth continued, "The young man in question had no difficulty conversing. Unfortunately, he did not know his name nor was he able to recount any details of his regiment or his past. Based on his arrival date at the hospital and some enquires we made, we suspected Mr. Blakemore became separated from his unit which was stationed near Cadiz, Spain. It was there during the Battle of Barossa, fought on the fifth of March, that he was injured. At the time, casualties were very high on both sides with our British troops losing some twelve hundred men."

Georgiana shuddered when she heard the numbers. "So many." Her voice was timid.

"It is not uncommon in war, my dear," remarked Darcy. "Please go on, Miss Elizabeth."

"Mr. Blakemore did not arrive back in London until the first week of April, and with very little paperwork, I might add. After meeting the gentleman, I found I could not rest until we knew more of him and were able to secure information about his family.

"I began researching Mr. Blakemore's case with the help of a military aide from the War Office here in Town. Once he determined which units were in Cadiz at the time, we searched through a seemingly endless list of recruits, officers and missing persons. It appeared two units comprised of men primarily from Kent were stationed in the vicinity where Mr. Blakemore was found. From there, we proceeded to compile a list of soldiers who were presumed missing in action from those units."

"Oh, do tell me you were able to find his family."

"Indeed! There is much more to this story, Miss Darcy. You will not be disappointed. Since we had no specific identity of Mr. Blakemore at the time, we had small likenesses drawn of him for distribution purposes. Jane and I sent out numerous letters along with the sketches to various church parishes in Kent. Our hope was to gain some assistance in contacting his family."

At this point in the story, Elizabeth shared a knowing look with Jane and could not help but smile as she continued. "Not long after we made our initial inquiries, we received a reply from the newly appointed Rector at Hunsford, who coincidentally happens to be a second cousin of our father."

"Hunsford?" questioned Darcy and Georgiana simultaneously.

"Yes," affirmed Elizabeth. "Our cousin, Mr. William Collins who is the Hunsford Parish Rector of the village, was instrumental in finding Mr. Blakemore's family and establishing the man's identity. We understand his patroness, Lady Catherine de Bourgh, is your aunt."

"You are correct," confirmed Darcy.

"Because of Mr. Collins' devotion to your aunt and her being the sister of Lady Matlock, our cousin was allowed to make very detailed inquiries of other clergy throughout the county on our behalf. Furthermore, I am more than happy to report as a result of our combined efforts, Mr. Blakemore will be returning home shortly."

Georgiana clasped her hands together. "Oh, it is too much! They must all be so very happy."

"Yes, finding the family was truly a blessing," Jane added. "Had we not been able to locate Mr. Blakemore's loved ones, the poor man might have ended up in the asylum at Bethlehem Hospital in Moorfields."

"Oh my," Georgiana gasped.

"We understand his family is eager to help with his rehabilitation and will care for him at his parents' home. With stimulation from his past environment, the physicians believe it will be the best situation for him to try and regain his memory."

Hearing this, Georgiana began to wring her hands and could no longer contain her emotions. "Oh, William," she nearly sobbed unable to hold back her tears. "I … I had no idea our men could suffer in such a way. Suppose it had been our dear Richard? I … I simply must try to help, should I not?" Elizabeth reached over and touched Georgiana's forearm while Jane handed her a handkerchief.

"I am so sorry, Miss Darcy," offered Elizabeth. "We had no intention of distressing you."

"I am fine," she whispered, desperately trying to regain her composure.

Darcy approached the women and knelt directly in front of Georgiana. Taking her hands in his, he smiled and lovingly said, "Dearest, I shall be most supportive and proud of any undertaking you care to make for this worthy cause."

"Thank you, William," she softly responded.

Darcy arose. "Georgiana, I believe some additional refreshments are in order." He rang for a servant. "Please continue your visit and I shall see to it." Motioning to a maid who promptly appeared at the doorway, Darcy quietly began issuing instructions and left the room.

After he was gone, Elizabeth remarked to Georgiana, "Miss Darcy, it seems you have a very attentive brother."

"Oh yes," she nearly whispered. "He is the kindest, most generous brother although I fear I do not always deserve him." She dropped her eyes again, causing Elizabeth and Jane to look at each other in bewilderment.

"On the contrary, I am sure you do," Elizabeth contended. "From his remarks, it is evident your brother thinks highly of you and believes you are most deserving."

Nodding in agreement, Jane added, "Truly, Miss Darcy, your brother's devotion pays you the greatest compliment."

"Thank you," Georgiana quietly replied.

In an effort to lighten the girl's mood, Elizabeth proclaimed, "We should have dearly loved to have had a brother. Is that not so, Jane?"

"Oh yes. We have no brothers at all and are the eldest of five sisters."

Georgiana shyly replied, "I would like to have had a sister."

"Well, if we told you how silly the three youngest in our family can be, you might *possibly* change your mind," Elizabeth teased. She then began a light-hearted discourse on the unusual merits of their sisters.

A few minutes later, a servant brought in an ample tray filled with cakes and various fruits, followed by another with beverages. Not long after, Darcy himself returned. Stopping in the hallway, his heart was warmed by the sound of his precious sister giggling in response to the humorous remarks shared by the Bennet sisters and their aunt. To his astonishment, he realised Georgiana had not talked this much since they returned from Ramsgate.

Darcy could not help but take pause and wonder. *These three women are nothing like most ladies of the 'ton.' They have not been raised in opulence, nor have they been given the advantages of a more prestigious society. Mrs. Gardiner is the wife of a successful merchant in trade, who lives in Cheapside. Yet, her manners are refined and she is dedicated to promoting the same charitable causes as my aunt, a member of the 'upper tier.'* In his mind, all three women were refreshing, and they seemed to be very supportive of his sister and her needs.

Darcy found himself wanting to let down his guard and partake in their conversation. Listening, he felt a sense of warmth and contentment. This was something he had not experienced in a very long time, perhaps not since the death of his mother.

Yet, despite their charm, these women were significantly beneath him. In the back of his mind, he could hear his father telling him a gentleman of his station was expected to limit his personal acquaintances to those of a similar standing. True, he had made some allowances when it came to assisting Bingley in his quest to embrace a higher society, but could he do so in this instance? His father's directives had been laid out for him from the time he was a mere lad.

"Fitzwilliam, you are a Darcy! You must adhere to what our society expects of a gentleman and never disgrace our family or what we stand for. You have been given certain privileges and great responsibilities which come with our wealth and heritage. Therefore, I expect you to represent our family with proper pride and regulation."

The memory prompted Darcy to rake his fingers through his hair in frustration. Despite their kindnesses to Georgiana, for the present, he would remain apart.

Walking back into the room, Darcy returned to his former position near the mantelpiece, where he quietly resumed his previous demeanour. Taking note of him, Elizabeth retrieved a large envelope from her satchel and excused herself from the rest of the group.

"Mr. Darcy, may I have a moment of your time?"

"Miss Elizabeth Bennet." He nodded.

"Sir, at your aunt's suggestion, I have prepared some documentation detailing our proposals and projected expenditures to date. May I leave them for your perusal?" Holding out the envelope which he promptly took, Elizabeth gifted him with one of her mischievous smiles. Then quickly donning a more serious face, she whispered, "Sir, I must warn you, it might be a rather boring read since it does not contain any errant pages from my uncle's *War Journals*."

Momentarily caught off guard, Darcy purposely scowled at her tease. Even though he had avowed to remain distant, he could not resist challenging this self-assured young lady from Cheapside. In response, Darcy decided he would purposely provoke Elizabeth, testing her ability to hold her own against his remarks.

"Frankly, Miss Elizabeth, I find it rather odd a young woman with so little formal education could have much knowledge of the financial workings in matters such as *these.*"

Elizabeth, obviously surprised by his response, squared her shoulders and looked directly into his eyes. "Mr. Darcy, in Hertfordshire, where I come from, I am considered to be my father's son with regard to *these* types of matters. I must inform you I have been thoroughly trained in the affairs of my father's humble estate, having assisted him since the age of sixteen."

Darcy schooled his face into an expression of disbelief. "Come now, Miss Bennet. Surely you do not expect me to believe such assertions."

"Sir, I have often acted as my father's secretary, studying his financial ledgers and formal documents. With his encouragement, I have settled disputes with our tenants and attended to their needs. I can assure you I *do* comprehend a great deal in this respect."

Yes, that did raise her ire, he thought with the intent of continuing to annoy her. "I must confess I am curious to know what sort of *man* your father is. It is highly unusual for any gentleman to entrust the running of his estate to his young daughter."

"Mr. Darcy." She glared at him in defiance. "My father may not have had the means to educate me in the manner of the more affluent, but I must defend him in saying I was given every advantage a young man under his care and tutelage would have had."

While she waited for his response, Darcy studied Elizabeth's face, taking delight in the fire he saw in her eyes. "You are very singular, indeed!"

"Pray, Mr. Darcy, have you never encountered any ladies of the *ton* who are bold enough to invade a gentleman's domain in this fashion?"

Rubbing his chin for a moment before responding, he finally answered, "With the exception of my aunt, Lady Catherine de Bourgh, I would definitely have to say ... no." Then giving her a patronizing grin, he continued, "Where many ladies of my acquaintance are well educated, I find most *accomplished* women choose to devote their time to more *refined* activities, such as music or drawing. They have studied the modern languages and have sought the improvement of their minds through extensive reading. They do *not* take pleasure in the invasion of a *gentleman's domain* in this manner, as you have intimated."

"An accomplished woman!" declared Elizabeth, looking rather indignant.

Before she could further respond, he put the envelope on the mantelpiece and said with another attempt to provoke her, "I must say I *am* looking forward to examining your work, Miss Elizabeth, and I shall bring forth any pertinent comments, should I find something amiss."

"*Amiss?*" Her eyes sparkled as though she were accepting his unspoken challenge. "Mr. Darcy, I shall eagerly await your evaluation. Of course, I should warn you, sir, all of my efforts have been reviewed and met with the approval of your aunt's very own solicitor." Turning up the corners of her mouth in a self-assured smile, she attempted to mock him.

Darcy was exhilarated by her response, but continued to give the appearance of indifference. "So be it, Miss Elizabeth, I shall endeavour to give these documents my full attention."

"Thank you, Mr. Darcy." Elizabeth curtseyed then turned with the intention of re-joining the ladies.

"Miss Elizabeth," he said, halting her with his words. She boldly looked back at him arching her brow. Darcy would not placate Elizabeth with an apology for annoying her since he had purposely meant to unnerve her and she bore it well. He would, however, offer up his thanks where Georgiana was concerned.

"If I may, I would like to extend my gratitude for the kindness you, Miss Bennet, and Mrs. Gardiner have shown to my sister this afternoon." His face relaxed, revealing a half smile. "It is greatly appreciated." He bowed.

Surprised by his sincerity, Elizabeth softened her own expression and replied, "Mr. Darcy, your sister is a lovely, sensitive, young woman. It has been our privilege to speak with her today. I beg your forgiveness for having caused her undue distress during our earlier conversation."

"Thank you." He spoke in earnest. "I regret to say she experienced an emotional disturbance some months ago and thus far has not fully recovered. At present, her sensibilities are ... fragile." He looked away in reflection. "I confess I have been at a loss as to what course I should take." Looking back at her, he continued, "Nevertheless, I am hopeful my aunt's suggestion will prove to be helpful. From what I have seen today, I *am* encouraged."

Elizabeth smiled reassuringly. "Mr. Darcy, my sister and I are well versed with the emotions of a younger sister, three to be exact. If you will allow us, we shall do what we can to assist Miss Darcy."

"Thank you again, Miss Elizabeth."

"Sir, if I may, we do have one other proposal to present to Miss Darcy which may prove to be of interest. My sister and I coordinate a series of musical concerts on Tuesday afternoons. We are assisted by the wife of Mr. Stephen Madison, who is the principal physician assisting the hospital board on behalf of our charity. These modest recitals are prepared for the entertainment of those patients who are able to attend and take place in the dining hall of the hospital. Occasionally, Lady Matlock encourages prospective donors to join us. At such times, Mr. Madison avails himself on behalf of our committee by giving an informational talk about our project. If you think it would be appropriate, I would like to invite you and Miss Darcy to attend next Tuesday. We have heard much of your sister's musical abilities and hope she might one day be willing to participate, provided she would feel comfortable in doing so."

He nodded. "I believe we have no fixed engagements for next Tuesday. Please feel free to extend your invitation."

Elizabeth beamed. "Thank you, Mr. Darcy." A few minutes later, Mrs. Gardiner informed her nieces their carriage would return shortly. Before taking their leave, Elizabeth formally invited the Darcys and Mrs. Annesley to join them on the following Tuesday at the hospital for their concert and Mr. Madison's presentation. Once Georgiana accepted, it was agreed the Bennet sisters would meet the Darcy party fifteen minutes prior to the start of their concert near the dining hall entrance.

~ ♫ ~

Gardiners' Carriage

Somewhat perplexed by everything which had taken place at Darcy House, Elizabeth wondered what her next encounter with the Darcys might yield. Based on Lady Matlock's assertions, she had expected Miss Darcy's shyness, yet not to the extent she would be so easily distressed. Mr. Darcy only added to the mystery with his puzzling behaviour.

He was nothing like the charming gentleman I met at Ballard's. In truth, I believe he took a particular delight in vexing me, but for what purpose? Had his arrogant manner persisted, I could have easily assigned him to the same category occupied by many of the other ill-mannered members of the 'ton,' but....

It was Mr. Darcy's relationship with Miss Darcy which contradicted those opinions. The bond existing between brother and sister was endearing. With Miss Darcy, he let go of his hauteur, reserve and pride. Speaking in a gentle, supportive tone, his eyes softened, and he became more like the man she had previously met.

Interrupting her musings, Mrs. Gardiner asked, "Well, girls, how did you find the Darcys this afternoon? I believe our meeting went quite well, did you not think so?"

"On the whole, I agree," Jane remarked. "Of course, I was surprised Miss Darcy was not able to maintain her composure while we spoke of Mr. Blakemore. I cannot help but wonder what might have caused her such distress."

"Well," said Elizabeth. "When Mr. Darcy and I were conversing, he mentioned his sister had recently suffered an emotional upset."

"I do not suppose he gave any of the particulars," wondered Mrs. Gardiner.

"No, he did not."

"I see." Mrs. Gardiner nodded. "I have the greatest respect for Lady Matlock, and I think we should try to support Miss Darcy in whatever way we can. Lizzy, it was good of you to suggest the Tuesday afternoon concert."

"I thought if Miss Darcy could personally see how valuable these offerings are for the patients, she might at some point be able to overcome her fears and wish to participate. Of course, we shall have to go slowly for it must be her decision."

"I agree." Mrs. Gardiner smiled. "Well, my dears, I believe we accomplished much today. Lady Matlock will be pleased. Miss Darcy is fortunate to now be in possession of *two* elder sisters who intend to look out for her best interests and give her encouragement."

"Yes, Aunt, I trust Jane and I shall be able to manage with yet another sister. But please, do not tell Mama. Her nerves might not be able to handle the thought of one more unmarried daughter."

~ ♫ ~

Darcy's Study

Later that evening, Darcy sat at his desk examining the documents given to him by Elizabeth, making notes in the margins as he saw fit. In his opinion, the woman was not only confident, independent, and clever, but she had a good head for business matters.

Recalling her sparkling eyes and beguiling smile, his mind raced on. During the course of her conversation with Georgiana and the other women, he found himself frequently staring at her. She was pretty and from where he stood, he could smell the faint scent of lavender, which had only served to increase his heightened senses. In reviewing their lively discussion, he found Elizabeth challenged him in a way no other woman ever had. Surprisingly, she did not back down when he provoked her with his responses. Not to mention she did not go out of her way to flatter or impress him. *In short, Miss Elizabeth Bennet was ... remarkable.*

Admittedly, his attraction to Elizabeth had grown. Yet, because of her situation, Darcy also knew it would be unacceptable to act upon those feelings. Still, he was determined to promote the connection for the sake of his sister. It had been an emotional afternoon for Georgiana, but Darcy was encouraged by her interaction with Mrs. Gardiner and her nieces. For the first time since his sister had returned from Ramsgate, Darcy felt it might be possible for her to begin a more positive recovery.

In anticipation of the hospital outing, Darcy encouraged Georgiana to invite Lady Lilyan, her friend from school, to spend the day and accompany them. He also made a similar request of his good friend, Charles Bingley. In the end, Fitzwilliam Darcy was looking forward to what might be a very pleasant day.

CHAPTER THREE

A MUSICAL INTERLUDE

London Hospital
The following Tuesday, 4 June 1811

*I*n anticipation of Tuesday's afternoon concert, all parties had been looking forward to their outing at the London Hospital. Noting their arrival, the Bennet sisters were pleased to see the Darcys and Mrs. Annesley who were accompanied by two additional guests. Once Lady Lilyan Ashbourne and Mr. Charles Bingley were introduced, the sisters directed everyone to the visitors' section of the Dining Hall, where Mr. Stephen Madison and his wife were waiting. Promptly at two o'clock, the three women were introduced to the audience, and Elizabeth stepped forward to preside over the musical offerings.

"Good afternoon. Today I shall begin with a well-known Scottish marching tune. But first, I would like to single out one of our patients, Lieutenant Charles Overton, who has so graciously volunteered to assist me with the song. If an attending orderly would be so kind as to bring Mr. Overton forward, I shall begin directly."

Minutes later, Mrs. Madison, who was seated at the pianoforte, started playing the introduction to the song with a vigorous drumlike rhythm in the lower register of the instrument. Upon hearing the higher repetitive melody characteristic of the fife, Elizabeth tilted her head and began the song with energy.

Oh! Charlie is my darling, my darling, my darling,
Oh, Charlie is my darling, the young chevalier.
'Twas on a Monday morning, Right early in the year,
When Charlie came to our town, the young chevalier
Oh! Charlie is my darling, my darling, my darling,
Oh! Charlie is my darling, the young chevalier....

Jacobite Marching Tune, 1775

Since many of the soldiers were very familiar with this song, it was not long before the audience began to clap in rhythm and voluntarily joined in on each chorus. Meanwhile, Lieutenant Overton periodically responded to Elizabeth's subtle teasing with humorous facial expressions, rousing his fellow soldiers to laughter every time he did so. Upon finishing, the audience extended their appreciation with an enthusiastic round of applause.

Next, Elizabeth called on Jane to join her in a traditional ballad, *Greensleeves.* One could not help but notice the favourable response from the young men in the audience when Jane stepped forward to offer her lovely lyrical verses against Elizabeth's richer alto harmony. Jane's beauty, elegance and serenity presented a vision that was soothing to their weary souls.

Similarly affected was Charles Bingley. "Darcy, why did you not tell me I would be entertained by an angel this afternoon?" he whispered. "She is the most beautiful creature I have ever beheld."

"Bingley, you are hopeless." For those who knew Charles Bingley, it was not uncommon to hear him express those same sentiments whenever he met an attractive woman.

Greensleeves was all my joy,
Greensleeves was my delight;

Greensleeves was my heart of gold,
And who but my Lady Greensleeves....

Elizabethan, 1580s

After finishing their duet, Elizabeth announced she would sing one last selection while Mrs. Madison prepared her violin for the remainder of their recital. This time, her song was a mellow Scottish ballad which she performed unaccompanied. Assuming a more refined attitude, Elizabeth began the simple tune in her lower range where the melody ebbed and flowed before ascending to the more dramatic higher phrases. Singing tender words for a love who had parted, the listener could not help but be drawn into the imagery painted by the poetry and Elizabeth's soothing voice.

O, my love is like a red, red rose,
That's newly sprung in June;
O, my love is like a melody
That's sweetly played in tune.
As fair art thou, my bonnie lad,
So deep in love am I;
And I will love thee still, my dear,
Till all the seas go dry....

Robert Burns, 1794

If anyone had observed Fitzwilliam Darcy during her singing, they would not have missed how he, too, was affected by her performance. Despite his good intentions to remain apart, Darcy's resolve proved insufficient once Elizabeth began to sing. The melody itself was haunting and the heartfelt emotion with which she sang drew him into her world of song. Upon finishing, not a sound could be heard in the hall until Elizabeth humbly dropped her head, signalling the end.

Next, Mrs. Madison came forth and concluded the afternoon's entertainment with several lively Scottish folk tunes. Lastly, Elizabeth thanked the audience for attending and wished them well. Once the room had cleared, the three women returned to their guests who greeted them with enthusiasm.

"Mrs. Madison, Miss Bennet, Miss Elizabeth." Darcy offered a slight nod. "I must commend you for your excellent presentation today. Without question, your concerts fill a vital need for the patients here, and I speak for all of us when I say we were thoroughly impressed with your efforts." His sentiments were enthusiastically echoed by the rest of the party.

As expected, Mr. Madison invited the group to join him for a brief discussion and overview of the project. Madison's presentation proved to be very informative, and at the conclusion, Darcy singled out the man for some further discussion. At the same time, Bingley took the opportunity to engage Jane in conversation while Mrs. Annesley asked Mrs. Madison about the Scottish folk tunes and Elizabeth entertained the younger women.

"Lady Lilyan, Miss Darcy tells me you are very proficient on the flute," Elizabeth remarked.

"Thank you. With our family being so very fond of music, I was fortunate to begin my studies at a young age. Although my father does not play, my mother is skilled on the harp and my elder sister, Lady Clarissa, excels at the pianoforte and sings. Her talent is exceptional and she is always asked to perform whenever we attend parties."

"Your sister must be very accomplished, and I do hope to one day have the pleasure of hearing her."

"Thank you."

"Miss Elizabeth…." Georgiana hesitated for a moment. "Could you please tell us a little more of what is expected from the performers who assist with the hospital concerts? We very much enjoyed your presentation this afternoon, and wondered … that is if you think we might be of service…. We … we would like to perform together on one of your future concerts."

Delighted by Georgiana's request, Elizabeth could not contain her joy and clasped her hands together with enthusiasm. "Miss Darcy, Lady Lilyan, what a lovely surprise. We would be honoured to have the two of you perform. While I would not care to rush you, it is my understanding we are in need of performers for the next two Tuesdays. Assuming you will have enough time to rehearse, would you perhaps consider performing in two weeks?"

The girls briefly conferred before Georgiana responded, "While we have not played together in some months, we believe with sufficient practice we shall be ready to perform at that time."

"Splendid! I shall make the arrangements with Mrs. Madison. May I ask if either of you have a particular selection in mind?"

"We are considering a piece which was arranged for us by Miss Darcy's music master when we were at school and possibly one other."

"Miss Elizabeth, the composition was written by a woman composer, Maria Theresia von Paradis who is a personal friend of my cousin, Lady Helmsley. They met in Vienna when she and her husband were lately there in residence."

"A woman composer? Why, she must be extraordinary!"

"I believe she is." Georgiana smiled. "According to my cousin, Miss Paradis became blind at a very young age. Yet, despite her affliction, she is an accomplished musician and has not only performed in Vienna but has toured throughout the continent."

"Truly, I am in awe of her abilities and determination," Elizabeth remarked.

"Miss Paradis is currently residing at the summer home of my cousins in Brighton. They will be hosting a large house party there in August, and I ... I shall be introduced to her when my brother and I join them at the end of July."

"Miss Darcy, what good fortune! I am quite envious. You have much to look forward to, and I shall wait with anticipation to hear both of you play her composition."

Conversations continued for the next ten minutes or so. When their time drew to a close, Darcy took the lead in thanking the Bennet sisters and the Madisons for a very enjoyable afternoon. Goodbyes were exchanged, and the little party looked forward to renewing their acquaintances later in the week at Matlock House.

~ ♫ ~

Gardiners' Residence

Arriving home, Elizabeth and Jane were greeted by their aunt, who was eagerly awaiting their return. As soon as they were divested of their outerwear, the women joined their aunt for a cup of tea in the parlour.

"Aunt, I wish you could have been with us this afternoon," Jane began. "Our concert was well received, and we had such a pleasant time."

"I am glad to hear of it. May I enquire of Miss Darcy?"

"She was definitely more at ease this afternoon," remarked Elizabeth. "To our delight, she invited her friend, Lady Lilyan Ashbourne, who happens to play the flute."

"May I assume she is the younger sister of Lady Clarissa Ashbourne?"

"Yes, she is. Miss Darcy and her friend were very cordial and seemed to be taken by our presentation. So much so, that they have volunteered to perform with us in two weeks."

"Remarkable! I surely did not expect Miss Darcy to contribute to our endeavours so soon, especially after witnessing her shyness the other day."

"I, too, was surprised. Apparently, they often played their instruments together while they were in school. I believe their contribution will make an excellent addition to our musical entertainment, and I look forward to hearing their music."

"My dears, Lady Matlock will be extremely pleased."

Elizabeth teasingly arched a brow in Jane's direction then continued, "Aunt, we should tell you there was one additional person who accompanied the Darcys this afternoon."

"Oh?"

"Yes, a Mr. Charles Bingley, who apparently is a close friend of Mr. Darcy." At the mention of Bingley's name, Jane began to blush.

"Jane, what is this?" Mrs. Gardiner questioned, seeing the colour rise on her niece's face.

"Aunt, Mr. Bingley took me quite by surprise. At the conclusion of the concert, he sought me out and complimented my singing. Our conversation was very pleasant. Mr. Bingley's sisters will be accompanying him to Lady Matlock's dinner party on Friday." She blushed again and reservedly said, "He wishes for me to make their acquaintance."

"I see." Mrs. Gardiner continued to study her niece. "Perhaps I should speak with your uncle. Through his business dealings, Edward has knowledge of many influential people and may know something of the young man." She paused for a moment, appearing to be quite serious when she resumed speaking. "While I am not familiar with Mr. Bingley, he *is* Mr. Darcy's friend and, no doubt, is a man of some means. Without question, the worth of both of these gentlemen goes far beyond that of your own family; therefore, neither of you should be encouraged by their attentions.

"Lizzy, I hesitated to say anything the other day, but when we were visiting with Miss Darcy, it became apparent that Mr. Darcy was quite intent in observing you during much of our stay. In truth, from what I observed, his eyes rarely left your person except to attend to his sister. I am not implying an admiration could be formed on such a short acquaintance, but knowing the wishes and expectations of his aunt, I must insist you use good judgement when in the gentleman's company."

Trying to hide her discomfiture at her aunt's implications, Elizabeth responded, "It is true, Aunt. I was also aware of Mr. Darcy's constant gaze, but when we spoke more privately, he was not in the least bit solicitous. His only kind words were spoken of his sister. Had I not been a witness to his affection for Miss Darcy, I would have been the first to accuse the man of being equally as proud and disagreeable as any of the *ton*. Why, even today, he barely spoke two words to me except when he complimented all of us on our performance."

"Very well," replied Mrs. Gardiner. "I shall accept your judgement on the matter for the time being. Girls, your uncle should be arriving home within the next hour. In the meantime, I suggest the two of you take some time to refresh yourselves before we dine."

~ ♫ ~

Darcy House

After saying their farewells to the Bennet sisters and the Madisons, the Darcy party boarded their carriage and proceeded directly to Darcy House. Georgiana told her brother of her offer to perform with Lady Lilyan and had garnered his approval. Upon arriving, the young ladies excused themselves and went directly to the music room in order to search through Georgiana's sheet music. Meanwhile, Darcy's butler informed him Colonel Fitzwilliam had arrived earlier and was currently waiting in the study.

Proceeding through the hallway, Bingley found he could contain himself no longer. "Darcy, did you see her face when she was singing?"

Darcy rolled his eyes, knowing what was to follow. "Yes, I did."

"The lilt of her sweet voice penetrated my very soul. And when we talked, she smiled at me as though I were the only man in the room. I could hardly bear it. And did you see her beautiful golden hair? I had to restrain myself from touching her long curls." Darcy opened the door to his study while Bingley continued to enumerate the many charms of Miss Bennet.

"Darcy, I would certainly like to call on her!" he exclaimed.

"What is this?" questioned the colonel with a look of curiosity.

"Bingley is besotted with Miss Jane Bennet after only one meeting," Darcy grumbled. "She was introduced to my friend here during one of your mother's charity functions for the London Hospital not more than three hours ago. I tell you, he falls in and out of love faster than any man I have ever met."

The colonel let out a noticeable chuckle. "So I have heard."

"She is an angel on this earth if ever I saw one!" Bingley proclaimed.

"She smiles too much," commented Darcy rather dryly.

"Smiles too much! Why her smile is warm and inviting and her...."

"Richard," interrupted Darcy. "Before Bingley pledges his undying love to Miss Jane Bennet, do you think you could enlighten my friend here on the great disadvantages associated with the pursuit of that particular young woman?"

"Darcy, I protest!"

"Bingley," the colonel began. "As much as I love a pretty face, there is some merit in my cousin's assertion. According to Mother, the Bennet ladies come from a small estate in Hertfordshire which is entailed away to a second cousin of their father upon his death. They have little portion of which to speak and would definitely be frowned upon by any member of the *ton*, given such a situation. If either of these women wishes to secure a future, they must aspire to raise their prospects by aligning themselves with a man of means, which makes *you*, my dear fellow, the perfect prey."

"Not to mention," Darcy added, "an alliance with a woman in such a position has negative consequences which could equally affect your sister's prospects for making a good match."

"Darcy, you are ahead of yourself," stated Bingley. "I certainly have no intention of marrying Miss Bennet after one meeting! I simply found the woman I met today to be quite charming, and I would like to know her better. At any rate, I *shall* see Miss Bennet again at the Matlocks' dinner party, and that is the end of it."

"It appears you are overruled, Cousin. I must confess, I am heartily looking forward to meeting *both* of the lovely Bennet ladies myself."

Darcy muttered, "Shall I call forth the reading of the marriage banns for you as well?"

"Enough! I will not hear any more censure of Miss Bennet or her sister. Gentlemen, I must be off. Caroline is expecting me to join her and the Hursts for an early dinner, to be followed by a viewing of an art exhibit. I shall see both of you on Friday. Darcy, my friend, I thank you for a very delightful afternoon!" Bowing, he finished with a broad grin and left.

Shaking his head, Darcy conceded, "Bingley has no idea what he is about when it comes to making his way in this society. A connection to Miss Bennet or some other beautiful lady in her situation could deter his quest to become recognised by members of the *ton*."

"You have the right of that."

"So … tell me, what brings you here this afternoon besides the hope of a good meal? As usual, I see you have already siphoned off some of my best brandy." Darcy walked over to the tray and poured himself a glass.

"How could I resist?" He grinned. "I shall get to my purpose directly, but first, tell me about Georgie's progress."

"Your mother's intuition has proven to be exceptional in this case. Georgiana responded quite favourably to Mrs. Gardiner and her nieces at their initial meeting. Although it is difficult for me to whole-heartedly approve of the connection, I believe my sister has already benefited from their sincerity and compassion. Today, I was amazed at how relaxed she had become in the presence of Miss Elizabeth, in particular. To see my dearest sister smile and converse with less reserve warmed my heart immeasurably. All in all, I think Georgie has left the worst of her troubles behind, and for that I am grateful."

"Excellent! I could not have wished for a better report."

"There is more."

"More?"

"Yes. In addition to Bingley, we invited Georgiana's friend, Lady Lilyan, to accompany us this afternoon. Miss Elizabeth was absolutely engaging during her presentation, and both girls clearly saw the validity of this type of service. Richard, you will not believe it. Georgie and her friend have volunteered to perform for another such concert in two weeks' time. The girls are currently in the music room looking through sheets of music as we speak."

"Darcy, I am astonished!" The colonel smiled, slapping him on the shoulder. "Cousin, I am very encouraged by what you have just told me. Miss Elizabeth Bennet must be an extraordinary woman, indeed."

"Yes, so it would seem," he dryly answered.

"Speaking of the lady, I shall come to my purpose for calling this afternoon. My man, Morris, has garnered some information, and I would like to put you back to that day at the booksellers."

"Go on," Darcy guardedly replied.

"From what Morris discovered, it seems your mysterious gentleman was not following you at all. He was following Miss Elizabeth."

"What?!" Darcy bellowed. "Richard, I do not like the sound of this, not one bit."

"It appears there is no Gerard Mooreland whose son, Jonathan, attended Cambridge during our time. And … my father assumes the lady was being followed because of her uncle's connection to Lord Wolverton."

"Baldwin Wolverton, the ambassador? What could Wolverton possibly have to do with Gardiner?"

"For one, His Lordship is an intricate part of our group of agents. He has been working covertly for some time now, causing the French a bit of discomfort, to put it mildly." Darcy began to pace as the colonel clarified the connection.

"Apparently, His Lordship invested in some of Gardiner's ventures several years back along with Father. Being in trade has proven very convenient for the *Secret Guard* since Gardiner is willing to relay information back and forth from the Continent on our behalf. As for Wolverton, I am sure you have met him sometime or other at one of my mother's gatherings."

Darcy suddenly stopped pacing and fixed his gaze on his cousin. "Indeed, I have." He scowled. "Not to mention I am *very* familiar with his reputation, both as an ambassador *and* with the ladies. Tell me, Richard, how does this involve Miss Elizabeth Bennet?"

"For one, Wolverton cares little for the unspoken rules of the *ton* and has no qualms with entertaining Gardiner and his family about Town. Apparently, this was the case when he took all of them to the opera on the sixth of May in celebration of Miss Elizabeth's birthday. According to Father, our infamous Lord is quite *taken* with her. Because of Wolverton's attentions at that particular event, it appears the young lady's activities were monitored for several weeks."

Seething, Darcy spat, "Richard, what could Wolverton be thinking?

Surely he would not stoop so low as to seduce the niece of one of his associates?"

"I would think not. To satisfy his more carnal nature, it is my understanding His Lordship recently took a house for two sisters who both lost their husbands in battle." He snickered. "I hear they make a happy threesome."

Darcy's voice grew louder at this point. "Richard, this is not something to make light of. We are talking about a young woman whose reputation and safety may be at risk."

"Forgive me, you are absolutely correct."

"And what of Miss Elizabeth? How does *she* respond to Wolverton's advances?"

"Evidently, she is thoroughly disgusted with His Lordship and pays him little heed. He is only tolerated for the sake of his *unusual* relationship with her uncle."

"To think that Wolverton would even mention his desires to your father is appalling." Darcy began to pace the room as he continued to speak. "What then of Gardiner? After all, she is under his protection. What does *he* do to curb Wolverton's unwanted attentions?"

"Father says Edward Gardiner has the reputation of being a very principled and honourable gentleman. Since Wolverton's flirtations at the opera, he has insisted His Lordship tread lightly where Miss Elizabeth is concerned. Father suspects Gardiner would not hesitate to defend his niece's honour were Wolverton's baser desires made known to him or to the public. With regard to Miss Elizabeth being followed, that is nothing out of the ordinary since all of Wolverton's associates have been under surveillance at one time or another. In this case, Father did not think it was anything out of the ordinary."

"In other words, may I assume Gardiner was *not* informed of the incident?" The colonel shrugged, unable to give a definitive answer.

"Richard, I do not care for this information! Can you not see how this complicates things? If what you say of Wolverton's desires were common knowledge, Miss Elizabeth's attention to Georgiana could put my sister in grave danger by association."

"I have considered as much, and at this time, I beg to differ. Despite His Lordship's discreet admission of lust to my father, he is never in Miss Elizabeth's company without the presence of her family. In his frustration, he occasionally looks for ways to quietly tease or embarrass her for refusing his notice, but so far, that is the extent of it. As for the man you met at Ballard's, the encounter with the imposter was nothing more than a mere reconnaissance which proved fruitless for the opposition. According to Father, she is no longer being followed."

"Humph!" Darcy knitted his brow and continued to listen, unmoved.

"I understand Lord Wolverton is yet in Town and may be for some time. Father invited him to Mother's dinner party. If you like, you can observe the two of them on Friday and make your own judgement concerning His Lordship's attentions to Miss Elizabeth."

"Richard, you know my first obligation is to Georgiana. If you think I am inclined to accept these sorry excuses, you are mistaken. Believe me, I *shall* be taking note of your father's *noble* guest, and I shall unquestionably keep my reservations about his connection with Miss Elizabeth until I am convinced otherwise."

"I have no doubt of that. Listen, Miss Bennet is not even a minor player in the scheme of things. She has merely been a courier for her uncle on a few occasions. We know she detests Lord Wolverton and essentially poses a threat to no one."

Darcy continued to scowl. "I will leave it as you say, for now, but I am not satisfied, not in the least."

"I understand." Attempting to break the tension, he said, "After all of my disturbing news, am I still invited for the evening's meal?"

"Richard, does the military not ever feed you?"

"So it would seem." He snickered. "Say, how about you lighten up and we enjoy a game of billiards until it is time to dine?" Darcy agreed, and the two cousins left the study hoping to dispel the tension they both felt after such a heated conversation.

CHAPTER FOUR

DINNER AT EIGHT

Gracechurch Street
Friday, 7 June 1811
A few days later

*E*arly in the day, the Gardiner home became a flurry of activity as the ladies of the household began their preparations for the party. Even though Lady Matlock had insisted the dinner would not be an elaborate affair, the Bennet sisters knew their apparel would hardly meet with London standards for this function. In desperation, the girls had asked for new laces and ribbons from their uncle's warehouse with the intention of making their gowns look more fashionable.

"Jane, which colour do you think looks better?"

"The gold ribbon is pretty against the pale yellow, but I prefer the dark green. It matches your eyes."

Holding the ribbon next to her face, Elizabeth looked at herself in the mirror and replied, "I also like the green." Then putting it down and holding up her dress she remarked, "It is too bad the hem of this dress is so uneven. I am not sure if this lace will be able to hide all of its flaws."

"Never mind about that, miss," interjected Sophia. "I shall have no trouble attaching the lace and adjusting the hem. Both of your dresses will look newly made when I have finished with them."

Mrs. Gardiner's maid, Sophia, was an expert with a needle and had an excellent eye for dressmaking. She had learned from her sister, Hannah, who was a seamstress at one of the more fashionable dressmakers in Town. Not only was Sophia able to improve their dresses, but she also arranged their hair into styles which were very flattering.

~ ♫ ~

Matlock House

Prominently situated on George Street, in the highly acclaimed Grosvenor Square of the Mayfair district, was the lavish townhouse of the Earl of Matlock and his wife, Lady Eleanor. Like Darcy House, theirs was of a newer style, sporting large Greek columns at the front of the building.

Thus far, Elizabeth and Jane had only been permitted admittance into the small sitting room which was used for their committee meetings. Tonight, however, much more of the house was open for the guests' perusal. The large drawing room, where the attendees initially gathered, was scattered with an array of floral arrangements and luminescent candelabra. The large room bore a resemblance to that of royalty with its deep red carpets and rich tapestries. Adding to the elegant atmosphere, the guests were pleasantly greeted by the lilting melodies of a string quartet playing the music of Haydn in the background.

"Jane," Elizabeth whispered to her sister. "Lady Matlock's dinner party is far grander than anything I could have imagined. "Can you fancy what Mama would say if she were here with us tonight? I sincerely believe Papa would lock himself in his book room for at least two full days in order to avoid her talk of lace and finery."

Noting the arrival of the Bingley party, Elizabeth was not surprised to see Mr. Bingley seek out Jane's company once he and his guests had finished greeting their hosts. Introductions and pleasantries were exchanged with the Bennet sisters and polite conversation ensued. In contrast to Mr. Bingley's amiable personality, his relations were decidedly reserved and gave off an air of superiority. Elizabeth found it rather odd since according to her uncle's information, Mr. Bingley's wealth had come from trade.

A little later, Elizabeth excused herself from the group and after chatting with some of her friends from the committee, eventually made her way to where the musicians were playing. Taking a cool glass of punch from one of the servants, she paused for a few moments and listened with pleasure. Casually observing the various guests, her attention invariably returned to Lady Matlock and her immediate family. Undeniably, her greatest curiosity involved Mr. Darcy, who had escorted Georgiana and was now conversing with members of the Ellington party.

Elizabeth was pleased to see Georgiana and Lady Lilyan enjoying each other's company and suspected they would remain together for most of the evening. As she continued to watch, an unmistakably beautiful woman took up the conversation with Mr. Darcy. Every detail, from her dress to the style of her hair, spoke of perfection. Assuming she was Lady Clarissa, the elder sister whom her aunt had spoken of, Elizabeth was curious to see how the two of them would get on.

Interestingly, there was no apparent admiration on the part of the gentleman. The woman, on the other hand, seemed determined to garner his attention. As they conversed, Lady Clarissa purposely moved closer to Darcy, taking his arm, obviously making candid remarks behind the safety of her silk fan. Instead of enjoying her attentions, Darcy seemed less than amiable. While she could not hear what was being said, his speech appeared to be abrupt and his countenance unyielding.

To Elizabeth's amusement, Darcy's discomfiture became even more noticeable when the couple was joined by Miss Bingley and her sister, Mrs. Hurst. With Darcy being addressed from both sides, he had unknowingly begun to back himself into the wall. In observing the entire group, Elizabeth could no longer suppress her giggles. It was at that very moment Darcy happened to look in her direction clearly noticing her taking delight in his dilemma. Quickly turning to avoid his gaze, she found it difficult to hide the involuntary shaking of her shoulders as she tried to ward off her laughter and compose herself.

Within minutes, the object of her merriment unexpectedly appeared at her side and began speaking. "Miss Elizabeth Bennet, I trust you are enjoying yourself this evening?"

She looked at him and smiled beguilingly. "Why yes, Mr. Darcy. How kind of you to ask. I must confess I *am* enjoying myself."

"You seem to be singularly amused in this corner of the room. May I ask what has caught your attention?"

"At this moment, sir, I have nothing in particular to report. It so happens, when I am not in conversation, I often find myself entertained by observing various situations or trying to make out one's ... *character.*" She arched a brow in his direction.

Not willing to show his own amusement, he seriously replied, "Ah, so you deem yourself to be an expert in the study of character. Pray, Miss Elizabeth, dare I ask what type of person has caught your interest this evening?"

Playfully feigning innocence, she looked at Darcy with her luminous eyes and stated, "Sir, I claim to be no such expert. Sadly, I must confess this evening's findings have proved inconclusive. Yet, since you have asked, I will say that I find ... a *complex* character to be the most intriguing of all."

"I see." He gave her a half-smile. "Since I know you have been in Town for some months now, I suspect it would be better for me to enquire how your studies of city dwellers compare with those who reside in the country."

"I wonder you would ask such a question when city dwellers such as yourself *also* reside in the country."

"True, but could it be your observations are not as *astute* as you led me to believe."

"If you must know, Mr. Darcy, I have found city dwellers to be less...." Stopping mid-sentence, Elizabeth hesitated when she saw Miss Bingley and Mrs. Hurst glaring at her with the most unpleasant expressions. Lady Clarissa was no longer in their midst.

Taking note of the sisters, Darcy stiffened and said rather dryly, "Forgive me. It seems I have been neglecting my duty. Perhaps we shall continue this discussion another time." With a slight bow bidding her farewell, he immediately resumed the task of seeking an attending footman who was circulating about the room with a tray of beverages.

Watching him leave, Elizabeth politely smiled at the women, acknowledging them with a nod of her head and proceeded to seek out the Madisons. At present, they were conversing with an officer in uniform. Upon seeing her, Mr. Madison graciously welcomed her into their group and proceeded to make the introduction.

"Colonel Fitzwilliam, may I present Miss Elizabeth Bennet. Miss Elizabeth, Colonel Fitzwilliam is Lady Matlock's second eldest."

"Miss Elizabeth, the pleasure is mine! Having heard so much about you from my mother, I would like to commend you for all of the effort you have put forth with her committee."

"Thank you, sir. You are too kind." The colonel was amiable, and the two of them struck up a lively discussion over the trials and tribulations of military service.

~ 🎵 ~

Shortly before dinner was to be announced, Lord Baldwin Wolverton made his entrance with an air of distinction. Dressed in clothes easily rivalling those of the Prince Regent himself, Wolverton made it known to all that he was a man of great consequence. Moving casually about the room, it was not unusual to see His Lordship extending his charm with the women and spouting his political knowledge to the men. Wolverton's manner was to be expected, but Elizabeth had never seen him more forward than on this particular evening.

Because he was a close business associate of her uncle, Elizabeth had first met the ambassador in late January when he invited her family to be his particular guests at a vocal concert which was given at St. James. From the very beginning of their acquaintance, she had found the man to be overbearing and flirtatious. During each subsequent meeting, his resolve to unsettle her continued.

When seeing the man move in her direction, Elizabeth's heart began to quicken, and her palms grew moist within her thin gloves. Her efforts to control her physical response proved useless knowing how much Lord Wolverton thrived on pushing the boundaries of propriety. In the past she had not backed down from his challenges, but in this particular setting, his presence was most disturbing.

"Miss Elizabeth." The man bent over her hand and held it in such a way that she could not withdraw it as he prolonged a kiss. "I have not seen you since we all attended the opera on the sixth of May. I trust you have been well?"

"Very well, I thank you," Elizabeth answered with cold civility.

"I have missed you, my dear. You look lovely this evening."

His forward manor prompted Elizabeth to take a step back. "I confess I am surprised to see you here. When we last met, you led us to believe that you would be returning to the Continent." Elizabeth desperately looked about the room in search of her uncle. To her dismay, Mr. Gardiner was facing the opposite direction and would not be able to perceive her predicament. For one brief moment, Elizabeth's eyes met with Darcy's. His brows were furrowed as he stood watching her with Lord Wolverton. Even so, she prayed he might show some compassion and come to her aid.

Purposely trying to unsettle Elizabeth, Wolverton stepped closer and whispered, "Fortuitously, my assignment was recently altered and I now have the opportunity to spend an evening with you, my dearest Elizabeth."

Elizabeth's ire quickly rose with Wolverton's continued forwardness. Facing him, she declared with conviction, "Lord Wolverton, your persistence is not welcome. I know perfectly well what you are about. You *will* refrain from using my Christian name, *and* ... if you continue to embarrass me in this manner, I promise you, sir, I shall have no qualms in letting you feel the wrath of my hand!"

Wolverton let out a hearty laugh and said, "As you wish, *Miss* Elizabeth." He tipped his head in acknowledgement, but continued to look at her in an unseemly manner. "Tell me, my dear, how did you like the selection of sheet music which I recently sent you?"

"You sent music to *me*? I beg your pardon, but I distinctly remember the direction on the parcel being addressed to *Mr. Edward Gardiner*." Again, he laughed.

"Your Lordship, I insist that you send no more gifts. Your business is with my uncle and *not* with me. Proper decorum demands I return anything you send, as you are well aware."

Wolverton could not resist continuing his harassment and pulled out a small book of poetry from his pocket. "Then I suppose this copy of Lord Byron is not to your liking."

"It certainly is not!" She protested, trying to hold her voice in check. "Please, I beg of you. You *must stop* this instant."

While Lord Wolverton was not about to relent, at that moment, Darcy happened to join their group. "My Lord," he began, causing the man to break off his offensive conversation with Elizabeth and acknowledge his presence.

"Darcy." As the two men politely exchanged greetings, Elizabeth briefly closed her eyes then mouthed a simple thank you to the man who had purposely interrupted His Lordship's offences on her behalf.

"My uncle tells me you have spent an extensive amount of time on the continent. I have heard rumours that Napoleon might be readying his armies to invade Russia. I would like to know your opinion on the matter."

Entering into a verbal battle of military policy and war strategy, the gentlemen were promptly joined by several others who enjoyed this type of exchange. Elizabeth immediately excused herself and went in search of her aunt, hoping no further attention would be drawn to her person this evening.

"Aunt Gardiner, His Lordship is positively insufferable! Why did he have to humiliate me in front of all these people?"

"Lizzy, it would be better if you did not let him upset you so. We all know Lord Wolverton has a reputation for the absurd. Your uncle says his work as an Ambassador is invaluable to the Crown, and at times we simply have to overlook his eccentric ways."

"Well, if you must know, I was about to overlook his *eccentric ways* with the back of my hand. Believe me when I say I surely would have, had not Mr. Darcy come to my rescue and diverted His Lordship with talk of the war. Aunt, I owe the gentleman a huge debt of gratitude."

"Take heart, my dear. I promise you I shall ask your uncle to speak with His Lordship before the night is over. For the time being, I think it would be better if you stayed close to me."

"Thank you, Aunt. At the moment, I would like nothing better."

Promptly at eight o'clock, Lord Matlock offered his arm to Lady Eleanor who invited her guests to accompany them into the main dining hall. Elizabeth and Jane joined the Madisons, who were seated close to the Bingleys. To Elizabeth's relief, Lord Wolverton was placed much further away, next to Colonel Fitzwilliam. From where she sat, she could easily attend to and observe several conversations. Still, the one person she wished to speak with was not close enough to do so. Consequently, there would be no opportunity to personally thank Mr. Darcy in this setting.

Following dinner, the gentlemen departed for the library to enjoy port and cigars for a time. In the interim, Lady Matlock invited the women to join her in the large drawing room where they would await the evening's entertainment. Not having conversed since their arrival, the Bennet sisters found a rather secluded spot where they could speak privately for a few minutes.

"Jane," started Elizabeth. "From what I have observed this evening, it seems as though Mr. Bingley is thoroughly taken with you. In my estimation, he rarely conversed with any other person before *or* during dinner."

"Dear Lizzy, he is everything I would expect a young man of

consequence to be. He is knowledgeable, amiable, and handsome. Why, I never saw such complaisant manners. I must confess I do like him very much."

Smiling warmly at Jane, Elizabeth added. "In that case, I shall give you leave to have your preference." Looking in the direction of Miss Bingley and Mrs. Hurst, she added, "It is unfortunate his sisters are not as affable."

"I wonder if you are a little too quick to judge, Lizzy. They were very cordial to me during dinner and mentioned they would like to become better acquainted. The sisters are hoping their brother will take a house in the country during the next several months. Mr. Bingley told me thus far his solicitor has two estates in mind. Lizzy, the estates are in Hertfordshire, and one happens to be Netherfield Park." Jane blushed.

"Jane!" exclaimed Elizabeth. "I cannot believe it. Why, Netherfield Park is but three miles from Longbourn." She smiled in return.

"Mr. Bingley indicated that he would be joining Mr. Darcy at his home on Monday afternoon to go over the particulars. Apparently Mr. Darcy is eager to advise Mr. Bingley since he has never managed an estate."

"Can you imagine what Mama would do if she were here tonight and privy to our conversation? I dare say she would not let the poor man rest until she was assured of his settling somewhere in the neighbourhood." The sisters tried to suppress their giggles, knowing how determined Mrs. Bennet was to secure husbands for her daughters.

"Jane, let us talk more of this later. I have yet to speak with Miss Darcy. Shall we go and see how she and Lady Lilyan are enjoying the party?" Jane agreed, and the sisters walked towards the two girls who were seated next to each other on one of the smaller sofas.

"Lady Lilyan, Miss Darcy," greeted Elizabeth. "I regret this is the first opportunity we have had to visit with the two of you this evening. It is indeed a pleasure to see you again." The girls responded in kind, and the sisters proceeded to take two vacant chairs positioned nearby.

"Miss Bennet, Miss Elizabeth," spoke Georgiana. "We ... we are happy to tell you we have chosen a second selection to play for the hospital concert, and we were wondering if the two of you would be able to … to join us for our first practice on Monday afternoon at my home. Your suggestions would be most welcome."

Elizabeth gave Jane a sly look, remembering Mr. Bingley's plans to meet with Mr. Darcy on the same day. "That would be delightful. We have no fixed engagements for Monday, do we, Jane?"

"No, we do not," replied Jane, with a slight blush rising in her cheeks.

"What time would be convenient?" Elizabeth enquired.

"We plan to meet at two o'clock and hope to begin our practice shortly thereafter."

"We shall be pleased to join you then, and look forward to our own private performance," Elizabeth teased, causing the girls to giggle. The four of them talked on about music until they were joined by Miss Bingley and Mrs. Hurst, who were eager to impart their own knowledge of the subject.

Once Miss Bingley had her say, she decidedly changed the topic, making bold inquiries of Elizabeth. "Miss Eliza, I noticed you speaking rather intimately with Lord Wolverton this evening. I found it very odd the gentleman would take an interest in *your* affairs, knowing you are in Town merely to assist with Lady Matlock's committee."

Elizabeth was not only annoyed at Miss Bingley for using her name in such a familiar way, but also for her rudeness in attempting to embarrass her in front of Miss Darcy and her friend. "Miss Bingley, His Lordship happens to be a business associate of my Uncle Gardiner."

"Mr. Gardiner, the same uncle who is in trade?" She snickered.

"Yes, the very same. Coming from a similar background, surely you must realise it is not uncommon for a man of the *haute ton* to invest in a lucrative business venture upon occasion."

Miss Bingley bristled. "It is true, Miss Eliza, our family fortune *was* made in trade, but that was long before my father's death. Please allow me to inform you we *now* move in very different circles and are fortunate to experience a more *refined* society."

With her next breath, Miss Bingley turned to her sister and began fanning herself. "Dear me, Louisa, I do believe I need a little turn about the room before the entertainment begins. The air in this corner is simply stifling, is it not?"

"Why yes, Sister, it is."

Purposely excluding Elizabeth, Miss Bingley smiled and politely said, "Lady Lilyan, Miss Darcy, Miss Bennet, pray excuse us."

The two girls, who had remained silent throughout the last of the conversation, looked bewildered by what had just taken place. While nothing further had been said, Elizabeth was certain Georgiana's spirits were dampened by the unpleasant exchange, since she had lowered her head and was now looking down upon her folded hands.

Hoping to ease her discomfort, Elizabeth quietly whispered, "Miss Darcy, please do not be disturbed by Miss Bingley's remarks. I was not offended." The two sisters had moved to the pianoforte and seemed to be inspecting the instrument. Motioning in their direction, Elizabeth continued, "Shall we take a guess as to who will be the first to perform? I suspect it will be Miss Bingley for she will not want to be outdone by any of the other ladies. What do you think?"

"I have been acquainted with Miss Bingley for some time and ... and I fear you are entirely correct. Even so, I ... I do not believe she has ever heard Lady Clarissa play. There may be some ... some rivalry." She shyly smiled.

Taking Georgiana's hand, Elizabeth offered, "Then I shall be very happy to sit here with you this evening and listen to the ladies exhibit their expertise. It may prove to be quite entertaining."

During this exchange, the gentlemen had begun to make their way into the Drawing Room. Bingley immediately sought out Jane while Darcy took a place off to the side where he could observe his sister who was sitting near Elizabeth and Lady Lilyan. Noting Georgiana's discomfiture, he wondered what might have taken place while he was absent. Continuing to watch, he was amazed to see how easily Elizabeth's encouraging words could reassure his sister. Within moments, the two women were chatting as though nothing of a disturbing nature had taken place.

When everyone was seated, Lady Matlock openly thanked her guests for attending her dinner party. She then invited them to relax for an hour of music and introduced Miss Bingley who began with a lively Scarlatti selection. This was followed by a Mozart duet which she played with Mrs. Hurst. Although the sisters were technically adept, the judicious listener might not be moved by their performance for it was devoid of feeling.

The next person to perform was Lady Clarissa Ashbourne. Choosing a melancholy movement from a Beethoven Sonata, she sat at the keyboard and began playing *Quasi una Fantasia - Almost a Fantasy*. Like the woman who performed it, the mysterious, haunting melody was breathtakingly beautiful. With her long golden curls draped to one side of her head, Lady Clarissa swayed back and forth, captivating her audience as she flawlessly played a melody filled with longing and desire. Astounded by Lady Clarissa's performance, the audience entreated her to continue. Presenting *Ach ich fühle's*, from Mozart's *Die Zauberflöt -The Magic Flute* which was currently making its London debut at the King's Theatre, her vocal selection proved to be equally impressive.

When she was finished, there was much conversation in praise of her performance, and the room did not quiet for several minutes. During that time, Lady Matlock approached Georgiana and asked her to play next. Taken by surprise, Georgiana's face suddenly lost its colour and her hands began to involuntarily tremble. Asking to be excused, she quietly informed her aunt that she did not feel comfortable playing in front of so many people, particularly after Lady Clarissa's performance. Lady Matlock was not pleased with her niece's response, knowing Georgiana had volunteered to play at one of the hospital concerts.

"Forgive me, Your Ladyship," Elizabeth interjected. "I do not mean to be impertinent, but my sister and I have been working on a duet from *The Marriage of Figaro*. I believe it would do nicely after Lady Clarissa's presentation and wonder if you might allow us to perform next?" Comprehending her niece was obviously not up to the task, Lady Matlock agreed to Elizabeth's proposal.

Like Georgiana, Elizabeth had not wanted to perform after Lady Clarissa, but the necessity of relieving her young friend's misery outweighed her own apprehensions. Without hesitation, she called on Jane and Mrs. Madison to join her.

"Tonight, my sister and I, along with Mrs. Madison at the pianoforte, would like to entertain you with our rendition of the *letter duet* from Mozart's *Le Nozze di Figaro*." Elizabeth could not help but note the look of triumph radiating from the face of Lord Wolverton, since the duet was amongst some of the music he had previously sent to her uncle.

Choosing not to be flustered by him, Elizabeth proceeded by giving a short synopsis of what was to take place at this point in the opera. Singing the role of the Countess, Elizabeth assumed a dignified pose and began the dictation of the letter: *Canzonetta Sull'aria - A little Song on the Breeze*. The two sisters acted out a charming scene which proved to be a delightful contrast to all of the serious music presented thus far.

After finishing the duet, Mrs. Madison offered to conclude with the first movement of a Vivaldi concerto. Having previously accompanied Mrs. Madison at one of their hospital concerts, Elizabeth felt fairly confident, despite the fact she would be in the shadow of the other women who had played so well. Unfortunately, the performance was delayed for a few minutes when Mrs. Madison discovered she had a broken string on her violin and needed to change it. With Elizabeth being seated at the pianoforte, she offered to sing a simple ballad in the interim.

Believe me, if all those endearing young charms
Which I gaze on so fondly today,
Were to change by tomorrow, and fleet in my arms,
Like fairy gifts fading away,
Thou would'st still be adored, as this moment thou art,
Let thy loveliness fade as it will,

And around the dear ruin each wish of my heart
Would entwine itself verdantly still....

Thomas Moore, 1808

Unlike the other offerings of the evening, this particular song stirred something within Darcy. Having recently been given a small book of Moore's poetry, he took delight in the heartfelt words which Elizabeth sang so eloquently. Interestingly, he knew of two rumoured stories which supposedly were the inspiration for the text. One held that Moore had written it for Wellington's wife, who had suffered from smallpox. In the case of the second account, it had been said Moore wrote the song for his own lady fair.

Listening, Darcy reasoned this particular song would give comfort to the recovering soldiers at the London Hospital during one of Elizabeth's concerts. Her presentation was simple and unassuming. Yet, as she continued, he found she touched his own heart in a way no other woman ever had. This realization combined with the kindness which she repeatedly showed his sister gave him pause.

How can Elizabeth Bennet, the daughter of an insignificant country squire, embody nearly everything I desire in a woman? He quietly sighed. *If only her situation was different, I would not hesitate to seek a courtship.* Knowing these thoughts could not be resolved to his satisfaction, he vowed to put them aside and determined it would be in his best interest to avoid all women for the rest of the evening.

Following Elizabeth's song, Mrs. Madison returned and the ladies proceeded as planned. When the entertainment ended, the guests broke up into various groups and continued on in conversation until the close. Altogether, Lady Matlock was very pleased and declared her dinner party a success.

CHAPTER FIVE

THE REHEARSAL

Darcy House
Monday, 10 June 1811
Three days later

*S*tanding in the doorway to the music room, Darcy listened to some of the more difficult phrases in the accompaniment Georgiana was practicing. When his sister first agreed to meet Mrs. Gardiner and her nieces, he never dreamed their influence would be so helpful to her recovery. Her bold commitment to perform with Lady Lilyan in little more than a week warmed his heart immeasurably.

"William." She smiled broadly, looking up from her music.

"Please forgive me for interrupting your practice. It was lovely. Bingley should be arriving shortly, and I shall look forward to hearing some of your rehearsal later this afternoon once we have finished our business."

"Thank you. I would like it if you joined us."

Darcy walked towards the piano and held out a letter as he spoke. "This just came for you from Ellington House. I am assuming it is from Lady Lilyan."

Georgiana eagerly took the note and read its contents. "Oh, dear," she frowned. "Lady Lilyan's arrival will be delayed."

"I hope nothing is amiss."

"She says Lady Clarissa has decided to attend our rehearsal and wishes to offer her musical expertise. Unfortunately, her sister has an earlier appointment which cannot be postponed, thus the delay. William," Georgiana spoke hesitantly. "I ... I do not mean to be ungracious, but sometimes I find Lady Clarissa to be ... somewhat ... condescending, and ... and I fear I may not meet her expectations."

Darcy was not happy with the thought of Lady Clarissa coming to his home uninvited. Knowing she could be manipulative, he tried not to let Georgiana see his displeasure. "Georgie, both you and Lady Lilyan play exceptionally well, and you should view Lady Clarissa's offer to help as a compliment. She is a superb musician and will no doubt have useful suggestions which can only improve your performance."

"I know," she replied, trying to force a smile.

Sympathising with his sister's discomfort, Darcy took her hands in his and spoke reassuringly. "Georgiana, you will be fine. Moreover, with the Bennet sisters here, this afternoon should prove to be not only productive but pleasurable."

"I do look forward to seeing them. Miss Bennet is so kind, and Miss Elizabeth has such an amusing way about her." She shyly smiled. "I cannot help but enjoy myself when I am in their company."

"All will be well." He kissed her on the forehead. "Enjoy your afternoon, sweet one."

"Thank you, Brother."

~ ♪ ~

A little more than an hour later, the Bennet sisters arrived and were shown into the music room where Georgiana and Mrs. Annesley were waiting. Following some light refreshments, Elizabeth remarked on the beautiful pianoforte and asked if Georgiana might play something while they awaited the Ashbourne sisters.

"Miss Darcy," exclaimed Elizabeth after Georgiana finished. "I do not believe I have ever heard a more beautiful instrument! The tone is exquisite and infinitely superior to anything we have ever played on. Is that not so, Jane?"

"Yes, it is. Our pianoforte at Longbourn is quite old and does not hold the pitch well. Here in Town, our aunt merely has a small clavichord."

"Of course, considering how little we practice, we could hardly merit an instrument such as this," Elizabeth added.

"For as long as I can remember, our family has always had the very finest of instruments, and I am fortunate to have had several excellent music masters," Georgiana answered with modesty.

When the hour was nearing three o'clock, Georgiana apologised again and expressed concern that the Ashbourne sisters might not be coming after all. Hoping to put her more at ease, Elizabeth decided to take out some music which was stored in her satchel.

"I had planned to leave this anthology with you so that you might look through it at your leisure, but I wonder if you would care to see it now. This music, along with the Mozart duet which Jane and I recently sang at your aunt's dinner party, was given to my uncle by one of his associates. Since our plans have been altered, I believe this is the perfect time to take a look."

"Miss Darcy, you will love this collection," Jane remarked. "It originates in Vienna, and according to the title page, it was published nearly twenty years ago by Baron Gottfried von Jacquin, a personal friend of Herr Mozart. As you will see, the Baron has included two of Mozart's short songs at the beginning of this publication."

"May I?" Taking the music from Elizabeth, Georgiana eagerly began to play the first of the selections.

"Oh my, the accompaniment is quite dramatic!" she exclaimed. "If I did not know this song was composed by Mozart, I might attribute it to Herr Beethoven. It is nothing like the other Mozart pieces which I have played."

"The text is written by a woman poet, Gabriela von Baumberg," said Elizabeth. "A*ls Luise die Briefe ihres ungetreuen Liebhabers verbrannte* is quite a long title for such a short song."

"*As Louise was burning the letters of her unfaithful lover,*" Georgiana murmured.

"I think you will enjoy this particular passage." Elizabeth pointed to one section of the music where the piano accompaniment was meant to imitate the sound of burning flames. "Sadly, my technical abilities are insufficient to play this difficult passage while singing. The entire song is filled with passion and the end, itself, is heart breaking when she says, '*Doch ach! Der Mann, der euch geschrieben, brennt lange noch vielleicht in mir.*'"

"Alas, the man who wrote you burns much longer within me," Georgiana nearly whispered in awe. "Oh, please, Miss Elizabeth, will you not sing it? I simply must hear this song sung in its entirety."

"I would be happy to; however, I am not proficient in German, as you have just heard. Although I understand enough vocabulary and grammar to translate the text, I have never formally studied the language. After hearing Lady Clarissa and her impeccable German, I am sure her talents would be better suited to the drama of this song."

Sweetly smiling, Georgiana replied, "It is true. Lady Clarissa *is* a most accomplished performer. Still, for the present, I would rather hear none other than you sing this song." Elizabeth nodded, and Georgiana began playing the introduction with great feeling.

By the time they finished, Georgiana could barely contain her pleasure and clapped her hands in response. "Miss Elizabeth, thank you. Your interpretation was perfect. I cannot imagine it sung any other way."

"Miss Darcy, you are too kind."

Georgiana returned to the music and studied the words once again. Moments later, her face paled as she looked up at the two sisters and asked in earnest, "Have either of you ever been in … in love?"

Elizabeth and Jane looked at each other then back at Georgiana and replied in unison, "No!" All three girls began giggling.

"In truth," stated Jane. "Our situation is difficult. We would dearly wish to marry for love, but it is unlikely it will ever happen." Georgiana seemed puzzled by this remark.

"I think I mentioned our father's estate is entailed to our Cousin Collins," continued Elizabeth. "We have no male heir in our family, and while our father is a landed gentleman, our dowries are very modest. Therefore, it is unlikely any man of consequence will make us an offer."

"I see," uttered Georgiana, trying to comprehend the plight of her friends.

"Miss Darcy, please excuse us. We did not mean to distress you with talk of our circumstances. I hope we did not offend you in any way."

"Miss Elizabeth, Miss Bennet, it is I who should beg forgiveness. I merely enquired because I have yet to be presented in court and experience my first season. I fear every young man whom I should meet will only look to my fortune and will have no sincere interest in *me*. Whenever I attend functions with my brother, I often hear people whisper about our estate and how much we are worth. It makes us feel very uncomfortable." She closed her eyes for a moment and then looked up trying to suppress her unshed tears. "I confess I, too, wish to marry ... for love."

The sisters each took one of Georgiana's hands as Elizabeth said, "Miss Darcy, you are beautiful, intelligent, and an exceptionally talented young woman. You must not feel you are at the mercy of every gentleman who may seek out your acquaintance. All you need is more confidence. Your brother seems very devoted to your welfare, and I do not believe he would force you into a marriage which you did not desire."

"We have never spoken of such, but yes, that is my wish."

"Since you are not yet out in society, it is only natural you might feel a bit insecure where gentlemen are concerned," Jane added.

"I admit I do feel rather shy when I attend affairs where many people are present. It is ... difficult for me to converse with persons with whom I am not well acquainted." Without realizing it, Georgiana had begun to twist her handkerchief while speaking of her concerns.

"Then, because I am not out, I am never allowed to dance unless it is with William or one of my cousins at a family gathering. I am terrified of failing in that respect, even though William has promised to provide me with a dancing master well before my presentation."

Having compassion for Georgiana, Elizabeth resolved to lighten her mood. "If such is the case, tis a pity you cannot come with us to Longbourn for you would surely have much practice at our home. Would she not, Jane?"

"Yes, indeed. Our younger sisters live only for the next assembly or ball. Why, they know all of the latest steps and would welcome a chance to impart their expertise to you."

Elizabeth whispered something to Jane and before Georgiana could object, the two women took her by the hands and pulled her up to a standing position. "Mrs. Annesley, if we may impose upon you to kindly assist us by playing the pianoforte, we shall be happy to share our knowledge with Miss Darcy and practice now."

Blushing profusely, Georgiana looked to Mrs. Annesley. "I could not ... could I?"

Giving her a nod of approval, Mrs. Annesley moved to the instrument and began looking for some appropriate music. In the meantime, Elizabeth and Jane explained some of the steps they would be practicing. From there, the sisters guided Georgiana with much enthusiasm and merriment throughout the course of their instruction.

Darcy's Study

During the time Georgiana was visiting with the Bennet sisters, Darcy had reviewed the paperwork from Bingley's solicitor, and the two gentlemen were nearly finished with their discussion. Knowing no conclusive decisions could be made without first seeing the properties, they tentatively set their trip for mid-September or shortly thereafter since Darcy had commitments during the month of August.

Towards the end of their meeting, Colonel Fitzwilliam arrived unannounced as was his usual wont.

"Ah, Richard, I thought I might see you here today. Are you not a little early for dinner?"

"Cousin, you know how fond I am of your cook. I would never pass up a good meal at your house and decided to get a head start beginning with some of your fine brandy."

"Why am I not surprised?" Darcy scowled while handing him a glass. "In anticipation, I have asked my housekeeper to set a permanent place for you at our table. I am sure Georgiana will be pleased. Bingley, you may as well join us too."

"Thank you, but I have plans for this evening."

"So, Bingley, what brings you here this afternoon?" the colonel asked while filling his glass. "From the looks of all that paper, I would say someone is in the midst of negotiations. Darcy, do not tell me Bingley is giving you trouble."

"Not particularly, even though my good friend is considering two country estates in *Hertfordshire,* of all places." He gave the colonel a knowing look. "It so happens one of the properties is but three miles from Longbourn, where the Bennet family resides."

The colonel dropped his jaw momentarily, shaking his head in amusement. "Bingley, I take it your interest in Miss Jane Bennet is growing."

"Not to the extent which you have implied. I am simply looking at a proposal for a country estate which has *nothing* whatsoever to do with Miss Bennet. On the contrary, Darcy seems to think if I consider an estate within such a close proximity to their home, it will be seen as though I am purposely singling her out."

"He may have the right of it if her mother is anything like the matchmaking mamas I have come in contact with. Frankly, I am hardly one to give advice on such matters since I have no estate of my own and am at the mercy of relatives until I secure a lady of means."

"As I have daily proof," Darcy mumbled under his breath.

"By the way, speaking of the Bennets ladies, I thought I heard singing when I came in. It sounded like one of the sisters could have been taking on German of all languages."

"Darcy?" questioned Bingley. "Am I to understand that Miss Bennet and Miss Elizabeth are here, and you have neglected to inform me?"

"Yes," he answered without enthusiasm. "It seems my house is besieged by women this afternoon. At first, Georgiana was to practice with her friend, Lady Lilyan, under the counsel of the Bennet sisters. Unfortunately, the original plan was altered earlier today when Lady Clarissa insisted on attending their rehearsal. And … since the Ashbourne sisters have *yet* to arrive, I suspect they will be here long after the Misses Bennet depart."

The two men broke into laughter while listening to Darcy's predicament. "No wonder you were so accommodating with regards to dinner," the colonel alleged. "You were seeking our protection. My, my… this could turn out to be a very entertaining afternoon, very entertaining indeed."

"Humph." Attempting to ignore their banter, Darcy began folding Bingley's papers and placed them back in the portfolio.

"Since we are no longer discussing my business affairs, I propose we all go to the music room and enjoy the company of some very lovely ladies. What say you, Colonel Fitzwilliam?"

"I shall be delighted! Are you coming, Darcy, or shall we make your excuses?"

"I shall do as you wish. At this point, I believe some music would be a welcome relief after listening to the two of you carry on."

A lively reel played in the background, and the three men could hear giggling and talk of dancing as they neared the music room. The colonel slapped both Darcy and Bingley on their backs saying, "My friends, it seems the Germans have left, and we are in for some fun!"

Entering the room, the gentlemen witnessed Elizabeth and Jane in the midst of leading Georgiana through an awkward turn. All at once, the music stopped, and the women lowered their heads in embarrassment while trying to suppress their laughter.

"What have we here?" Colonel Fitzwilliam teased.

"Brother, Richard, Mr. Bingley," Georgiana timidly replied. "I hope we were not disturbing you."

"On the contrary, my dear sister, I must inform you my companions have come here seeking amusement."

"Yes, Georgiana!" exclaimed the colonel. "It appears you are in need of a rescue. Being a true cavalry man, I would be remiss in my duty if I did not offer to partner you for the next set." He stepped forward, taking her hand, and kissed it as she gave him a demure smile and a slight curtsey.

Eager to join in the fun, Bingley followed suit and in turn placed a kiss upon Jane's hand saying, "Miss Bennet, I would be honoured."

It only remained for Darcy to do the same for Elizabeth. Yet, when the lady in question noticed his reluctance, she arched an eyebrow in his direction and quickly stepped over to the pianoforte where she offered to relieve Mrs. Annesley of her duties.

"Miss Elizabeth," he replied with embarrassment, "It would be my privilege to dance with you."

After curtseying, she playfully answered, "Mr. Darcy, you are all politeness. Yet, I am not inclined to dance. Mrs. Annesley has been playing for some time, and I would prefer to take her place and allow her to rest." She smiled sweetly and took a seat at the instrument.

"Miss Elizabeth, take no heed of Darcy," the colonel called out. "In general, he dislikes the activity and rarely dances. We shall change partners after the set and include you as well."

"Thank you, but for now, I am happy to play." With that, Elizabeth began a lively jig, inducing the two couples to dance with great enthusiasm.

Left feeling a bit foolish, Darcy walked over to the far side of the room and paused by the window, where he could look out and collect his thoughts. He had not intended to offend Elizabeth, but in his mind, his actions were just. Since she came from an inferior family, he reminded himself, her connections were nothing when compared to other members of the *ton*. How could he possibly justify the attraction? *I have responsibilities and obligations to which I must adhere. As it is, I have paid her far too much attention.*

After the Matlock dinner party, Darcy had resolved to distance himself from Elizabeth whenever he was in her company. Yet while listening to her music and laughter, he found his resolve failing. *Why am I always in an impossible situation when it comes to women?*

Today, Elizabeth Bennet was a guest in his home, and she had treated Georgiana with a sisterly affection which was so wanting in her life. Without looking in Elizabeth's direction, Darcy imagined her lovely face taking delight in watching the couples dance. Perhaps he could remain apart and simply observe their activity. Turning back from the window he attempted to do so, but with little success. Wherever Darcy looked, his gaze was repeatedly drawn back to Elizabeth and her sparkling eyes.

In truth, Darcy did wish to dance with her. Yet, in the end it mattered not since she had sensed his reticence and politely refused. If it were Lady Clarissa, she would have insisted he participate, making sure he partnered with her. That woman, however, held no real interest for him. Then again, neither did any other woman of the *ton*. Instead, a simple country miss from Hertfordshire had unknowingly caught his fancy.

Glancing at Georgiana, Darcy could not help but again feel gratitude towards the Bennet ladies. He had not seen his dear sister this happy in months. Little by little, Darcy began moving towards Elizabeth and stood where he could command a better view of her countenance without being easily observed.

Despite his subtle advances, Elizabeth was aware of Darcy's movement. As he stepped closer, she turned her head and teasingly asked, "Do you mean to frighten me by coming in this direction?" Darcy half smiled in anticipation of what she would say next.

"Sir, I shall not allow you to disturb me. There is a stubbornness about me which cannot be shaken at the will of others." Elizabeth slyly smiled. "I shall have you know my courage always rises with every attempt to intimidate me."

"Miss Elizabeth, surely you could not really believe me to entertain any design of alarming you. I have known you for several weeks now and have observed you often take delight in verbal repartee. Am I not correct?"

She smiled prettily saying, "Possibly. After all, one must have some tool at one's disposal while trying to make out another's character."

"Ah, more character analysis. Pray tell me what have you discovered in your more recent observations?"

"I regret to say I have made very little progress. For the most part, my current study is … puzzling, and it seems I shall have no choice but to continue on with my investigation."

Darcy chuckled, knowing full well she was referring to him. "So be it. I would by no means suspend your pleasure but will instead take pity on the *poor fellow* who happens to be the recipient of your current study." For a short time, the two of them continued on with their lively banter. When it appeared the dancers were beginning to tire, Elizabeth brought the dance to a close and ceased her playing.

"William," began Georgiana, a little out of breath. "I believe we should send for some refreshments. Could you please ring for a servant?"

"Yes, of course."

"Miss Elizabeth," exclaimed Georgiana. "I cannot remember when I have had such fun! Thank you so much for suggesting we practice today." She smiled while the colonel and Bingley gave a hearty second to her sentiments.

In a few minutes, the servants returned with some cool lemonade followed by a tray of fresh fruit and cheese. By the time they had finished eating, the Ashbourne sisters were announced, thus putting an end to their amusement. Lady Lilyan apologised for being late and eagerly greeted Georgiana and the Bennet sisters. Lady Clarissa, on the other hand, barely acknowledged Georgiana before singling out Darcy in conversation.

"You will never believe what a dreadful day I have had at the dressmakers. I was thoroughly humiliated by Madame Dupaix who had the audacity to have her *assistant* fit my gown for the Military Ball instead of doing it herself."

"How unfortunate," Darcy dryly answered, trying to conceal his displeasure.

"Furthermore, my dress looked nothing like the design which I initially selected. The sleeves were all wrong and the neckline was not centred properly, not to mention the fabric had more than one noticeable snag along the hemline. Why, in the end, I had no choice but to insist Madam Dupaix fire the seamstress who put such a hideous garment together and personally see to my order. I tell you, I have never been more inconvenienced."

"Undoubtedly." Darcy wondered how long he would have to listen to Lady Clarissa's mundane talk before she would allow Georgiana and Lady Lilyan to begin their rehearsal. Thankfully, Elizabeth had the presence of mind to redirect the conversation.

"Lady Clarissa, please forgive me for interrupting your conversation. I do not mean to be disrespectful, but may I suggest the girls begin their rehearsal? My uncle's carriage is due to return shortly, and Jane and I would dearly love to hear what Lady Lilyan and Miss Darcy have chosen to play before we take our leave."

Obviously displeased with the interruption, Lady Clarissa frowned as she ceased her discourse with Darcy and abruptly moved past Elizabeth to where the girls were standing. After speaking briefly with them, Lady Lilyan took her place in front of the pianoforte while Georgiana sat behind the piano keys. Lady Clarissa then took a seat where she could easily observe and make her comments.

Starting with the more technically difficult Mozart concerto, Georgiana appeared to be uncomfortable and made several unnecessary mistakes under the scrutiny of Lady Clarissa. Observing her uneasiness, Elizabeth quietly took a seat next to her friend so that she might turn pages while offering her support. Elizabeth's presence was calming, and her words of encouragement were enough to help Georgiana feel more at ease. From then on, her playing became effortless.

Fully aware of everything Elizabeth was doing to support his sister, Darcy could not help but gaze on her yet again. For the last hour, he had delighted in her company, and now, when Georgiana was in need, the object of his admiration came to her aid. *Heaven help me. At this moment, I am powerless in her presence.*

Not long after the girls had finished playing the first selection, the Gardiners' carriage arrived back at Darcy House. While Georgiana would have preferred the sisters stay longer, she graciously thanked them for a lovely afternoon and expressed her anticipation of seeing them again at the hospital concert.

With Jane and Elizabeth taking their leave, Bingley had little motivation for staying longer. Once the sisters and Bingley had departed, Darcy and the colonel retreated to the study for the remainder of the rehearsal.

As predicted, the ladies were invited by Georgiana to stay on for the evening meal. Even with Colonel Fitzwilliam in attendance and making light conversation throughout, Darcy was irritated by Lady Clarissa who insisted on dominating his attention. Despite his best efforts, by the time the sisters left his temples were throbbing and he was in want of nothing more than an ample glass of brandy and complete solitude.

CHAPTER SIX

THE CONCERT

Darcy House
Tuesday, 18 June 1811
The following week

he curtains fluttered back and forth as a cool, soothing breeze blew in through the open window. Darcy rolled over and reached for her soft, warm body, but she was not there. The mellow sound of her lovely voice humming a simple tune brought a smile to his lips.

Rubbing the sleep from his eyes, he asked, "Where are you, my love?"

"I am here," she answered from the balcony of their bedchamber.

Bathed in moonlight, he could see every curve of her silhouette beneath the thin sheath of her nightgown. Tempted by the sight, he stole out of bed and hurried to where she stood gazing at the stars.

"William, is it not beautiful?"

"Beautiful," he whispered although his eyes were fixed solely on her. Gently wrapping his arms around the one he loved, Darcy inhaled the scent of lavender as he burrowed his face in her long tresses. Then, ever so softly, he placed tender kisses on the side of her neck, continuing down to her exposed shoulder. She willingly turned in his arms and began sliding her hands up his chest until her fingers slipped into his hair, clasping him firmly

behind the neck. Her eyes were inviting, and his breath quickened as he lowered his head to claim her lips. In one swift motion, he picked her up and carried her to their bed.

"My darling, I love you."

"I am yours," she whispered.

To his dismay, a sudden gust of wind sent a shiver through his body, causing him to feel something was terribly wrong. Studying her face in the dim light, he wondered if the shadows were playing tricks on his vision. Pulling back in fear, he gasped when the woman in his arms leaned forward, allowing him to clearly see she was not his Elizabeth. She was....

"NO!" Darcy sat up in bed, drenched in perspiration. Struggling to be free of the sheets and regain his senses, he exclaimed, "Merciful Heaven, what is happening to me?"

Rising, he groaned while pushing the tangled mess aside and donning his robe. Immediately calling for a bath, he ordered his valet to have the water tepid for, at present, the heat radiating from his body was unbearable. Needing a few minutes, he walked over to a window, gripped the sashes, and breathed deeply. Every night since she was last in his home, he had dreamed of Elizabeth Bennet, and each and every night, the dream had become more vivid. "This has to stop. I shall *not* give in to this madness!"

Following his bath, Darcy left the house in need of a brisk walk. The quiet solitude of the early morning helped to calm his mind as he attempted to get it back under regulation. Upon returning, he heard the faint sound of Georgiana's music drifting through the halls. With her performance taking place later in the day, he chose to pay her a visit once he had pulled off his outer garments. Walking through the hallways to the music room, Darcy could hear his sister playing the same passage over and over again without success. Entering, he witnessed an audible sigh of frustration followed by the slamming of her fists on the keys.

"Georgiana, whatever is the matter?" He hurried to her side.

Immediately standing, she looked at him with embarrassment and answered, "Forgive me, Brother."

"Georgie, is there something wrong with this instrument? Does it require repair?"

"I am so sorry, William. It is Lady Clarissa." She dropped her head in shame.

"Lady Clarissa?" he questioned while lifting Georgiana's chin, forcing her to look at him.

"Yes."

"Go on."

"William, Lady Clarissa has changed the fingering on that particular passage three times now, and I find I can no longer play it without making mistakes. I had worked it out with Herr Schneider and had very little difficulty when Lady Lilyan and I first practiced, but...."

"Dearest, perhaps you should not worry about playing the new fingering. Since you are troubled, I suggest going back to whatever makes you feel most comfortable." Darcy gave her a hug and a look of reassurance.

"Thank you, I think I shall take your advice." She smiled reservedly.

Taking her by the hand, Darcy led Georgiana to the small sofa where they continued on in conversation. As of late, she had felt more comfortable in speaking with him and it was not uncommon for them to discuss her day to day activities as well as the progress she was making on her music. Today, however, Darcy was surprised when Georgiana chose to speak of a more serious topic. Her curiosity about the past inspired her to ask about their sister who had died in childbirth only two years prior to her own birth.

"William, do you ever wonder what Amelia would have been like if she had lived?"

Knowing Georgiana had been lonely and in want of female companionship, Darcy's heart could not help but ache for her as they spoke. "Let me think." He paused, wondering how he might answer her question without dwelling on their loss. "For one, I suspect she would have been very accomplished, much like you, and would no doubt have played the pianoforte divinely."

"Truly?" She blushed with his praise.

"Indeed. Then I wonder if she would have had dark hair like our mother's or lovely golden locks like yours or our cousin, Lady Jessica. If the latter were the case, I may have been driven to distraction trying to decide which sister was which.

Giggling, she replied, "Oh, William, the dark colour would suit me far better. I am afraid the lighter colour would remind me too much of Lady Clarissa."

Darcy rolled his eyes and shook his head in jest. "Please, please, dear sister, *not* Lady Clarissa."

"William, if Amelia *had* lived, I cannot help but wish our sister would have been much like Miss Elizabeth. She is so kind, and I am happy when she and I are together." Tears began to pool in Georgiana's eyes as she continued to speak. "Sometimes I think if I had a sister like her, I might have behaved better and would not have been such a disappointment to you."

Darcy clutched her to his chest and whispered, "My darling girl, I love you so very much. You are my dearest relation, and you *must* believe me when I tell you I am *not* disappointed. I only want for your happiness." Taking his offered handkerchief, Georgiana wiped her eyes and began to regain her composure.

"Georgie, it is still early. Have you broken your fast yet?"

"No, Brother, I have had little appetite today."

"Well, I for one am hungry and would like you to join me for at least a cup of tea. I think your practice will go much better if you take some nourishment." He smiled.

"I would like that."

"Very good. Let us go now."

~ ♫ ~

The London Hospital

Shortly before the appointed time, the Darcy party made their way to the lobby of the London Hospital where the Bennet sisters were awaiting their arrival. While everyone exchanged simple pleasantries,

Elizabeth wrapped her arm around Georgiana's and led her off to the side. "Miss Darcy, how are you feeling this afternoon?"

"I admit I am quite nervous and can barely keep my hands from shaking."

Elizabeth took both of Georgiana's trembling hands in her own and gently rubbed them. With a look of reassurance, she said, "Miss Darcy, these people will not judge you. What you do here is very healing for them. Dear one, you are sharing your gift with young men whose sacrifice cannot be measured. Remember, it is your privilege to help them in this way." Smiling, Elizabeth gave Georgiana a sisterly hug.

"Thank you, Miss Elizabeth. I shall remember."

The interaction between the two women did not go unnoticed by Darcy even with Lady Clarissa attempting to garner his attention in conversation. He was grateful for the understanding and support given by Elizabeth to his sister. Without question, he knew she was the kind of friend Georgiana needed in her life.

Walking into the dining area, his eyes continued to follow Elizabeth's every move. *I wonder if I could ever find a woman of her character among the ladies of the 'ton'. Georgiana would certainly benefit if I were able to make such a match. Being married to a woman like Elizabeth Bennet would definitely compliment my efforts in the management of Pemberley. Heavens, being married to such a woman would fulfil my every....*

Darcy momentarily pinched the bridge of his nose and shook his head in an effort to put an end to his musings regarding Elizabeth. Had he not already rejected those thoughts earlier in the day? Why must he continually be drawn in by her person? Could he not simply maintain a friendship with Elizabeth Bennet for Georgiana's sake without thinking of something more? Forcing himself to redirect his attention back to his companions and the concert, Darcy wished Georgiana well and took a seat.

Without delay, Elizabeth escorted the girls to the front of the hall and warmly introduced them to the attendees. For the battered soldiers and officers who had recently returned from the Continent, Georgiana and Lady Lilyan were visions of feminine elegance and beauty.

The lively first movement of the Mozart concerto was well received, and the audience appeared eager to hear more. Before beginning the second selection by Miss Paradis, Elizabeth spoke briefly of the remarkable blind woman who had become an accomplished musician despite her inability to see.

Moments later, Georgiana began the simple accompaniment to the beautiful *Sicilienne*. This selection was entirely different from the highly technical Mozart piece which the girls had just performed. It began with a sombre melody and quietly undulated back and forth before it was joined by the long-sustained tones of the flute. Meandering through the lower range then gently soaring to higher pitches, the listener became spellbound by both the music and the loveliness of the two young ladies who were performing it. When the selection was finished, the entire room erupted into enthusiastic applause. Both Georgiana and Lady Lilyan graciously acknowledged the audience before returning to their seats.

The entertainment continued with the reading of a narrative written by one of the wounded soldiers. Throughout his account, he managed to take the unspeakable reality of his former life in the field and alter the situations in such a way as to become entertaining. After much laughter and joviality, the presentation finally came to an end when Elizabeth announced she would conclude with a song written by Irish favourite, Thomas Moore. The poem was one which had become popular in England during the past several years, and Elizabeth encouraged the men to join her in the singing of the lovely ballad.

'Tis the last rose of summer
Left blooming alone;
All her lovely companions
Are faded and gone;

No flower of her kindred,
No rosebud is nigh,
To reflect back her blushes,
Or give sigh for sigh....

Thomas Moore - 1805

At the close, Georgiana and Lady Lilyan joined Elizabeth in order to personally greet the patients who were departing the dining area. After most of the attendees had left, Elizabeth stole a look at Mr. Darcy and smiled broadly when she received his positive nod of approval.

With casual conversations ensuing amongst those who were remaining, Georgiana quietly moved next to her brother and whispered a request. To her satisfaction, he responded with an affirmative gesture. Smiling, she returned to Elizabeth and Jane, who were still speaking with Lady Lilyan and Bingley.

"Miss Bennet, Miss Elizabeth, my brother has offered to take our party to Gunter's Tea Shop for a special treat this afternoon. If your time permits, may we invite you to join us as our guests?"

"Yes, you must both come!" exclaimed an enthusiastic Bingley. "My sisters always insist I take them to Gunter's whenever we are in Town."

For the next several minutes, Bingley continued to elaborate over the excellent variety of ices and creams. During that time, Elizabeth happened to take note of Lady Clarissa's more private conversation with Darcy. Throughout the exchange, his face had become stern and heightened with colour. Even though she could not make out all of what was being said, Elizabeth heard enough to know Lady Clarissa was decidedly making reference to herself and Jane.

"Mr. Darcy, did I hear you correctly? Did you just give your sister permission to invite those women to join us at Gunter's?"

"I did."

"Sir, you cannot possibly be serious," she hissed. "I shall be the laughingstock of all of my friends if we appear at a place of fashion with those two women. Why, they are nothing more than common workers for your aunt's charity. They are not women of our class, nor can they ever aspire to be."

"I do not care for this discussion. The Bennet sisters have been very kind to Georgiana, and I shall honour my sister's request."

"And just what have I been, Mr. Darcy? Did I not accompany my own sister to your home for each and every practice and offer my assistance? I am insulted, and I insist you recant your invitation."

In response, he glared back at the woman, silencing her entreaty with a flat, "Absolutely not."

Taking Georgiana's hand, Elizabeth refused to acknowledge the hateful looks which were being directed at her by Lady Clarissa. "Miss Darcy, it is most generous of you to want to include us in your party. Jane and I have never had the pleasure of visiting Gunter's, and our Aunt Gardiner has told us much of its reputation for creams and sweetmeats." She gave Jane a meaningful look hoping to convey an unspoken apology before continuing to address Georgiana.

"I am so sorry, but I regret to say we are unable to accept your kind offer this afternoon. Aunt Gardiner is besieged with paperwork for our committee today, and we have promised to assist. I suspect our uncle's coach will be arriving shortly, if it is not already here. Miss Darcy, once again, I am truly sorry." In reality, the sisters had not planned to look at the committee work until later in the evening and would have been free to accept Georgiana's offer. Perceiving Lady Clarissa's animosity towards herself and Jane, Elizabeth did not want to take the risk of embarrassing her friend in any possible way. Today was Georgiana's day, and so it would remain.

Having said their goodbyes, Mr. Bingley informed the others he would meet them at Gunter's after he escorted the Bennet ladies from the building and to their carriage. Before leaving the sisters, Bingley surprised Jane by producing a letter which had been written by Miss Bingley. "Miss Bennet, my sisters asked me to deliver this missive to you. It is my understanding they wish you to join them for a luncheon on Friday afternoon. Might you be available?"

Jane politely accepted the letter and after reading the invitation gave her answer. "Mr. Bingley, to my knowledge, my Aunt Gardiner has no need of me at that time. Would you be so kind as to inform Miss Bingley and Mrs. Hurst I shall send back my reply once I am able to confirm it with her?"

"I shall be delighted to do so." He nodded with approval, not taking his eyes off of Jane for a moment. "I, myself, shall not be home on Friday, but it would be my pleasure to make the arrangements for your transportation. I shall send word to your uncle once my sisters have received your confirmation."

"Thank you. You are most kind."

~ ♫ ~

Gardiners' Carriage

When the Gardiners' carriage pulled away from the hospital and Mr. Bingley could no longer be seen, the two Bennet sisters burst into enthusiastic chatter over Jane's invitation. Upon reaching home, their exuberance could not escape Mrs. Gardiner's notice when they entered the house.

"My, from the sound of your conversation, I take it the afternoon was very successful."

"Indeed, it was," affirmed Elizabeth. "Aunt, the concert was extraordinary! Miss Darcy and Lady Lilyan played superbly and were very well received. I am sure Lady Matlock will be pleased when she hears of the favourable reports."

"Very good," replied Mrs. Gardiner. She looked at both Jane and Elizabeth with curiosity and asked, "May I assume there is more?"

"Aunt," said Elizabeth. "Mr. Bingley's sisters have invited Jane to dine on Friday afternoon."

"I see." Mrs. Gardiner looked at Jane with interest.

"Before we left the hospital, Mr. Bingley presented me with a letter from Miss Bingley. Apparently, his sisters know very little of Hertfordshire even though they have passed through the county on their travels to the north. Since their brother is to look at properties close to where we live, they have invited me to visit so that I might speak of the neighbourhood. Mr. Bingley has also insisted on sending transportation for my convenience." She blushed. "Unless you have need of me, I would very much like to accept their kind invitation."

"Of course you may go, my dear. Elizabeth and I can manage without you for an afternoon." Mrs. Gardiner was pleased Jane would have the opportunity for a little society after putting forth so much effort into their committee work. Although she was not surprised to hear of Mr. Bingley's continued attentions, she felt it necessary to once again extend her words of caution.

"Girls, I do not mean to continually discourage you with my concerns, but I must remind you that any young man in Mr. Bingley's position might not always be able to do what his heart would dictate. It is true Mr. Bingley's fortune was made in trade. Nevertheless, he is now attempting to move in a much higher circle, and his attentions may turn out to be nothing more than a simple flirtation. Jane, I insist you be on your guard, and do not expect more than he may be able to give."

"Yes, Aunt Gardiner. I shall be careful." Thereafter, the discussion resumed with comments about the afternoon's performance.

~ ♫ ~

Later that evening, Elizabeth sat quietly in her room, reflecting upon the events of the day. She could not be more pleased with Georgiana's performance. Prior to the concert, the dear girl had been exceedingly nervous. Yet, she had managed to conquer her fears and performed beautifully. It would have been nice to have celebrated with her at Gunter's, but given the animosity displayed by Lady Clarissa, Elizabeth knew refusing the invitation was the right decision. Lastly, her thoughts could not help but turn to Mr. Darcy.

Before retiring, she and Jane had met for their usual night time conversation. After engaging in a lively discussion about the overpowering charms of Mr. Bingley, Jane surprised Elizabeth by turning the conversation to that of his friend.

"Lizzy, I hope you will not take offence at my presumption, but pray, do you think Mr. Darcy holds some partiality for you?"

Elizabeth swallowed, her eyes opening wide as she responded, "Jane, whatever made you ask such a thing?"

"Well, I am not entirely certain. While I spent much of my time attending to Mr. Bingley, I could not help but notice Mr. Darcy looking at you whenever I happened to glance in his direction. I know Aunt Gardiner has mentioned this before, but, Lizzy, today his gaze seemed in earnest. I suspect Mr. Darcy must feel some admiration where you are concerned."

Elizabeth could not control her giggles. "Admiration? I think not! Dear Jane, that look is nothing more than boredom, I assure you. As for anything else, I have been trying to make him out for weeks now and have failed miserably. In my opinion, I do believe he prefers to reside behind a thick suit of Medieval Armour, impervious to any weapon. Or, perhaps I should say, resistant to examination by an impertinent Bennet."

They both laughed. "Lizzy, you are too funny!"

"Jane, in all seriousness, he would surely put himself at great risk by forming an attachment to me. Can you imagine how furious Lady Matlock would be?"

"Yes, I can see she would not be happy, not in the least."

"Mr. Darcy was very kind when he assisted me in my plight with Lord Wolverton. Even then, I believe he only came to my aid because of the relationship we were forming with his sister. I admit we did have some conversation during our last visit to Darcy House, but in general he makes no effort to seek me out. I fear there is little more to say."

Closing her eyes, Elizabeth allowed her mind to drift back to her first encounter with Mr. Darcy at the bookshop. The thought made her shiver with delight. The smile he gave her, his touch, his scent, his masculine voice, and his protective nature were all so vivid in her memory. True, they had no understanding, but how could she not admit that theirs was an unusual connection? While they rarely spoke, she found herself being drawn to him. Whenever their eyes met, as so often they did, Elizabeth felt as though she were looking into the depths of his being, and he into hers. She had pretended to dismiss his attentions when speaking with Jane. Yet, Elizabeth would never forget Mr. Darcy had shown her a great kindness by assisting her in the face of one of the most infuriating men she had ever known. For that, she was grateful.

CHAPTER SEVEN

A SISTER'S HELPING HAND

Darcy House
Wednesday, 19 June 1811

*T*he day after the hospital concert, Georgiana awoke early, feeling refreshed and full of joy. What a change from yesterday when she had been plagued with uncertainty. At the time, she could not understand what had compelled her to volunteer for such an enormous task. Yet despite her fears, she was determined to honour her commitment and had succeeded in ways she did not anticipate.

When walking into the dining area, which served as the concert hall, Georgiana had quietly observed several of the recovering wounded in the audience. One man had lost a hand, another had his eyes bandaged, and a third no longer had feet to walk on. Disturbing as it was, she understood these men had given more for England than she could possibly comprehend. The young officers and soldiers, along with so many others who had come before them, had suffered their losses for people like her. This thought was humbling for Georgiana, and as she pondered her success, she was happy to have given something in return by sharing her love of music.

After dressing, Georgiana quickly descended the stairs in order to say goodbye to Mrs. Annesley, who would be departing shortly for Kent. With Georgiana lately feeling more confident, her companion had been granted a few weeks leave to visit her son's family and their new born child. Once the carriage left the house, Georgiana hurriedly broke her fast and retreated to the music room in search of more duets which she and Lady Lilyan might practice together. Pleased with the outcome of their first performance, both girls agreed they would like to participate again.

About mid-morning, Darcy interrupted Georgiana's practice informing her he needed to take a short trip to Pemberley. Having received an express from his steward, it seemed Mr. Clarke was in desperate need of his assistance. "Forgive me, I would not think of leaving you while Mrs. Annesley is away if it was not unavoidable. With tempers flaring amongst several tenants, it is best I begin travel as soon as I can get my affairs in order."

"I understand."

"Before I leave, I intend to send a note to our aunt. I could ask her to arrange a few outings with you during my absence. Would you like that?"

"If you think it best," she answered blandly. "Although, I wonder.... Might I also visit with the Ellingtons for a few days? Lady Lilyan has invited me on more than one occasion. I have selected several pieces of music which we could practice together, and I think my stay would be very enjoyable."

"I agree, but are you sure you will not mind Lady Clarissa overseeing your activities? I would not wish to see you frustrated by her machinations."

"I do not think she will concern herself with us since...." Georgiana lowered her head in embarrassment, not wishing to voice her thoughts.

"Georgiana, what is it you are trying to say?" He tilted his head to the side, trying to catch her look.

"Forgive me, William. During the course of our practice sessions, I

… I came to the conclusion Lady Clarissa's interest in offering her help was more for … for *your* benefit."

"I see." He cleared his throat and gave her a look which indicated he did not care to discuss Lady Clarissa's attentions to himself. "Well then, if it is your wish to visit Lady Lilyan, may I suggest you write her a short note? I shall be happy to include it along with one of my own to Lord Ellington, detailing my absence. In addition, I shall inform Aunt Eleanor. Even with her demanding ways, I know she means well. Perhaps you and Lady Lilyan would both enjoy an afternoon of shopping in her company. I shall also suggest dinner and an evening at the theatre if it would be to your liking."

"Yes, it would. Thank you, Brother."

"Very good, I shall see to it right away."

~ ♫ ~

Sunday
Three days later

Feeling more confident than she had in months, Georgiana was happy with the change in her routine. To begin with, Thursday brought forth a day of shopping where she and Lady Lilyan were accompanied by both Lady Matlock and Lady Ellington, who were good friends. On the next day, the two families joined for dinner and attended the theatre. Then on Saturday, Georgiana and her maid removed to Ellington House, where she planned to remain a guest for a few days. After enjoying a delightful afternoon of practice, she was treated to dinner and an evening of music at Covent Garden.

Following Sunday church services, Lord Ellington invited the girls to accompany him for an outing on horseback through the scenic lanes of St. James' Park. Georgiana had not been on a horse in months and was eager to ride if only in Town. While the day was overcast, it did not deter the Ellington party from setting out in mid-afternoon with the anticipation of a pleasant ride.

Unfortunately, they had not been out for more than an hour when the temperature dropped and a sudden shower ensued. The riders were forced to take temporary refuge in a small sheltered pavilion while they waited for one of the groomsmen to retrieve a carriage. By the time the little group arrived back at Ellington House, more than an hour had past.

Unknown to her hosts, Georgiana had felt a sore throat coming on earlier that morning. Even though she had promptly changed out of her wet clothes, she was unable to shake off the chill of the storm and eventually asked to be taken home to Darcy House. Following a hot bath, Georgiana took to her bed, hoping to feel better after a good night's rest.

~ ♫ ~

Monday, 24 June 1811

The following day, Georgiana awoke with a splitting headache, a stuffy nose, and a throat so raw that she could barely swallow. In some ways, she regretted telling her brother she would be fine in his absence for now she was feeling completely alone. Wishing for some companionship and remembering how kind Elizabeth had been, Georgiana impulsively penned a note and sent it to Gracechurch Street before the morning was out.

Dear Miss Elizabeth,

I find I am not feeling particularly well today, having caught a bit of a cold. My brother left for Pemberley last Wednesday on business and with Mrs. Annesley currently in Kent I believe I would enjoy some company. If it would not trouble you, I was wondering if you and Miss Bennet might be able to pay a short visit this afternoon or possibly sometime tomorrow. I know your presence would cheer me immeasurably. A maid will await your reply and accompany you back to my home should you be free to do so today.

Sincerely,
Georgiana Darcy

Gracechurch Street

"Excuse me, Mrs. Gardiner; a letter has come for Miss Elizabeth."

"Thank you, Daniels."

"Aunt, it is from Miss Darcy," noted Elizabeth with a look of surprise. "Oh dear, she is not feeling well and would like for me and Jane to call on her."

"I hope it is nothing serious."

"She says it is a little cold. If you remember Mrs. Annesley went to see her new grandchild and from what Miss Darcy says here, her brother is currently at Pemberley. Aunt, if you can spare us, I should like to go directly. Miss Darcy's maid is waiting for a response."

"Why, of course you may go. I can manage very well without either of you for the rest of the day. If you could wait but a few minutes, I shall prepare a small basket of herbs and oils which may help with her cold and include a poultice just in case she exhibits some congestion."

"Thank you, Aunt."

~ ♫ ~

Arriving at Darcy House an hour later, Elizabeth and Jane were shown into Georgiana's suite of rooms, where she was resting with her personal maid, Rebecca, in attendance. Though looking somewhat pale and listless, the girl managed to smile when the sisters were admitted. Hearing her cough, Elizabeth realised Georgiana was far worse than what her note had previously indicated. Taking some of the medicinal herbs from Mrs. Gardiner's basket, she asked Rebecca if a fresh pot of tea could be brewed for her mistress.

"Miss Darcy, we are truly sorry you have not been feeling well," said Elizabeth with concern.

"Miss Bennet, Miss Elizabeth," Georgiana laboured, not speaking above a whisper. "Thank you for coming. I hope I have not inconvenienced either of you. It seems my cold has gotten worse during the past few hours. Please forgive me for having sent my request."

"You have no need to apologise. We are glad you asked us to come, are we not, Jane?"

"Yes, indeed," she answered, stepping next to Georgiana's bed in order to plump up her pillows and make her feel a bit more comfortable. Touching the girl's forehead, Jane remarked that she felt quite warm and asked if she had a headache.

"A little," Georgiana replied, trying to suppress a cough. "Mrs. Troutman, our housekeeper, sent up some powders earlier, but the light continues to hurt my eyes, and my feet are a bit cold." Jane picked up a pair of bed socks and offered to help Georgiana put them on while Elizabeth pulled the curtains shut in order to dim the light.

"Lizzy, her feet are frozen, and her toes look positively blue. Miss Darcy, as soon as your maid returns, we should request some stones to be heated for your comfort."

"Thank you."

"May I ask if the apothecary has been sent for?" Elizabeth enquired.

"Yes, he was here earlier and left a draught on the side table next to the water pitcher."

"Good. I also think a cool compress might help with your headache and shall prepare one with some diluted lavender water." Elizabeth smiled, taking a small vial of the oil out of the basket.

"Our aunt has shown us how to use this oil. Her herb garden is quite large, and she is very particular about overseeing its care. My aunt's brother is an apothecary here in Town, and she grows several varieties of medicinal herbs which are essential for his business."

Jane wrapped a shawl around Georgiana's shoulders and continued, "Aunt Gardiner is also very knowledgeable of poultices and salves. After you have had some of her tea, if you like, we could try one of her remedies on your throat and chest while you rest." Georgiana weakly nodded her head in agreement, trying not to speak. In the meantime, Elizabeth prepared the compress and placed it on

Georgiana's forehead before adding another blanket to the bed coverings.

"Miss Darcy," spoke Elizabeth. "I would like to tell you how pleased everyone was with your performance of last Tuesday. Mrs. Madison says the wounded have spoken of little else for several days now." Georgiana shook her head in disbelief. "Do you doubt me?" Elizabeth raised an eyebrow. "I probably should not repeat this, but Mrs. Madison told us one of the officers made specific inquiries of you and Lady Lilyan and wrote a poem in your honour. He requested it be given to the two lovely young ladies who cheered his weary soul." All three women giggled. "Of course, Mrs. Madison told the young man it was *not* proper and confiscated his efforts. I regret to say the verses were later committed to the flame."

"Were you able to read them?" Georgiana managed to ask.

"I most certainly did," Elizabeth playfully answered. "Still, I am not sure if I should repeat what the young man wrote." She slyly looked from side to side, pretending to conceal a great secret. "If your brother knew what I am about to tell you, I might be banned from your company for imprudent behaviour." Georgiana squeezed Elizabeth's hand, silently imploring her to relate what she had read.

"Very well. To begin with, the poem was not entirely written by the gentleman's own merit. You see, even though some words were changed, I easily recognised the verses were written by Thomas Moore. Shall I?" Georgiana nodded, prompting Elizabeth to clear her thoughts and begin.

Farewell! But whenever you welcome the hour,
That wakens a song of mirth in your bower.
Then think of a soldier, who once welcomed it too,
I forgot my own grief on the day I saw you.
My grief may return, not a hope may remain,
Of few who have brightened my pathway of pain.
For I never shall forget the short vision that threw
Its enchantment around me, the day I saw you....

Thomas Moore 1788 (revised)

By the time Elizabeth finished, Georgiana struggled to hold back the tears which had welled up in her eyes. "Beautiful," she whispered.

Elizabeth patted her hand saying, "I agree. The young man was most sincere and paid both you and Lady Lilyan a great compliment."

About that time, Rebecca and a housemaid returned with a pot of tea and some of Cook's chicken soup, which she had made especially for her young mistress. Georgiana was propped up and with the sisters' coaxing, she was able to take a little of the soup and then some of the tea.

Whenever Jane had been ill, it was Elizabeth who had cared for her sister. Although Georgiana had a devoted brother, Elizabeth sensed her young friend longed for the same sisterly companionship which she and Jane shared.

"Miss Darcy," spoke Elizabeth after Georgiana settled back under her blankets. "I do not mean to impose myself upon you, but if I could be of service, I would be happy to remain here when Jane returns home this afternoon. If you like, I could help your maid care for you and keep you company until you are feeling better."

"Are you certain? You would do that for me?" Tears began to form in her eyes.

"Why, of course. I shall speak with your housekeeper at once and make the arrangements if you wish it. When Jane returns home in your carriage, she can pack a small trunk for me and have it sent back with your footman. Would you like that?"

"Yes, thank you. You are too kind."

"Then it is settled. Now, it would be best if you tried to get some rest. Jane will wait here while I go and settle everything with Mrs. Troutman. I shall return shortly."

With Georgiana's worsening condition, Elizabeth learned Mrs. Troutman had sent messages to the family physician, Lady Matlock and, by way of an express, to Mr. Darcy. The housekeeper had been worried about Georgiana and was more than happy to accommodate Elizabeth during her stay. Once the arrangements were completed,

Elizabeth returned to Georgiana's bedroom. Jane quietly gathered her belongings and took the carriage back to Gracechurch Street where she informed Mrs. Gardiner of what had transpired at Darcy House.

~ ♫ ~

During the rest of the afternoon, Elizabeth sat near Georgiana as she slept. Picking up a Bible from the side table, she read through several of her favourite passages and prayed for her young friend's recovery. *Dear sweet Georgiana. I cannot begin to imagine how much you have suffered, losing both of your parents at such a young age. As long as you will allow it, I shall treat you just as I would my own dear Jane.*

Putting the Bible back on the table, Elizabeth picked up a miniature of a young woman. Noticing the woman's lovely blue eyes were identical to that of both brother and sister, she assumed it was a picture of their mother, Lady Anne. Georgiana's hair colour was much lighter, but in every other aspect she looked remarkably like the woman.

I wonder if you would have approved of my friendship with your daughter. She gently fingered the edge of the frame, smiling back at the image. *I would like to believe you would not view me as so many in your circle have. Your face appears loving and kind. If only you were here for her.* Elizabeth continued to stare at Lady Anne's likeness. *He has your look, you know. I have seen it on occasion when he shows affection to Miss Darcy, and one other time when he happened to look my way.*

Carefully replacing the miniature, Elizabeth got up to change the compress on Georgiana's forehead and was grateful to find her fever had not increased. Later, when her charge awoke, she asked Rebecca to send for a little more of the chicken soup and told Georgiana everything had been settled with the housekeeper concerning her stay.

A short time later, Mrs. Troutman briefly entered bearing a message from Lady Matlock. With her nephew being at Pemberley, apparently it was Her Ladyship's intention to dismiss the Darcy family physician from Georgiana's case and replace him with someone of her own choosing. Since she fully intended to manage her niece's care, both Lady Matlock and her family physician, Mr. Purdy, would be attending Georgiana promptly at eleven o'clock on the following morning. In addition, Lady Matlock had also sent an express to Pemberley, informing Darcy of her intervention during his absence.

Distressed by this news, Georgiana's breathing became laboured and was followed by uncontrollable tears, and intermittent coughing. "Please, please, Miss Elizabeth.... You must stay with me when my aunt and Mr. Purdy come," she panicked. "My aunt's physician is very old, and his remedy for nearly every ill is ... is to bleed. He attended my mother before she died and William told me he used that procedure repeatedly. Because of what happened to our mother ... William is against the practice and would never allow it if he were here." Upon finishing, her coughing became so violent that she could not stop for a full five minutes.

Taking Georgiana in her arms and gently rubbing her back, Elizabeth held her until she became calmer. "Dearest, I promise you I shall do everything within my power to honour your wishes. I am so sorry about your aunt's insistence, but with your brother's absence, she is your nearest relation, and I believe Mrs. Troutman thought it best to inform her of your situation." Georgiana sniffed and nodded her understanding in response. After wiping her brow and offering her more of the warm broth, Georgiana was finally able to lie back against her pillows.

"Miss Darcy, I think it is time to try my aunt's poultice. It may smell a bit, but it should help you to breathe easier. If you can sleep for most of the night, I am sure you will feel far better in the morning, and your aunt's visit should not be so distressing."

Elizabeth's reassuring words prompted Georgiana to close her eyes and rest while the poultice was being prepared. Once it was finished and spread over her throat and upper chest, Elizabeth and Rebecca wrapped that area in a soft cloth and added another blanket. After administering the draught left by the apothecary, Elizabeth prayed Georgiana would sleep through the night. Alas, it was not to be as her night proved to be restless, often interrupted by coughing and strange dreams.

~ ♫ ~

Tuesday, 25 June 1811

The next morning commenced with preparations for the arrival of Lady Matlock and her physician. All in all, Georgiana had not slept more than five or six hours during the night and was feeling rather weak. After she had taken a little broth, Elizabeth suggested that Rebecca order a hot bath since their patient remained chilled. By the time Georgiana was made presentable, it was nearly eleven o'clock. Entering with Mr. Purdy, it was apparent Lady Matlock was not pleased.

"Georgiana, what has happened here? You were perfectly fine when I last saw you on Friday."

"I am sorry, Aunt," she whispered. "I had a sore throat and did not take precautions." Try as she might, Georgiana could no longer speak with ease and her words were interrupted with a series of violent coughs.

"Mr. Purdy, you will tend to my niece this instant. Miss Elizabeth, I shall speak with you in Georgiana's sitting room while the examination is being conducted."

Elizabeth could see the fear in her friend's eyes. Briefly squeezing her hand, she spoke reassuringly, "You will be fine, dearest. Your aunt and I shall only be gone but a few minutes."

~ ♫ ~

"Miss Elizabeth, I was astonished to learn from Mrs. Troutman that *you*, of all people, were here nursing my niece. I thank you for your thoughtfulness but would like to know how this has come about."

"My Lady, as you know, Miss Darcy and I have formed a friendship by your own insistence. I came here yesterday afternoon by her personal invitation. If you have no objection, I would prefer to continue on until Miss Darcy has made a significant recovery."

Lady Matlock looked at her with misgiving. "Miss Elizabeth, tell me, have you performed this type of service in the past?"

"Yes, I have, Your Ladyship. In my household, whenever someone was ill, it was I who attended them."

Carefully studying Elizabeth, her brow furrowed again. "Very well. Having known you for some months now, I shall accept the truth of your statement. For the moment, my only concern has to do with propriety."

"I beg your pardon?" Elizabeth could not believe her ears.

"Forgive me, I phrased my comment poorly. In my circle, a young woman of your status would not normally be permitted to nurse one of our own in this manner unless she was a close relative or a paid companion. Had I not known of your character because of our charity efforts, I might have suspected you to be a fortune hunter who was imposing herself upon this family." Elizabeth firmly set her mouth as Lady Matlock continued to speak.

"I mean no disrespect; nevertheless, I did notice your familiarity with Georgiana before leaving her room. True, I did request that you give my niece encouragement by drawing her into my charitable activities. Nevertheless, while she is ill, I would prefer it if you would keep any form of intimacy at a minimum. The preservation of class is something which I demand of all my committee members."

Astonished by her request, Elizabeth reservedly answered, "I understand your concerns, and I shall do my best." *Yes, I shall do my very best not to lose my temper and tell you just how hypocritical you and your ridiculous circle of friends truly are.* Elizabeth took a deep breath, smiled politely and said, "If there is nothing more, shall we return to Miss Darcy?"

Mr. Purdy had completed his examination and informed Lady Matlock it was not necessary to bleed her at this time. Since he was concerned about her inability to breathe with ease, he insisted on giving her both a draught for her congestion and some laudanum which would induce a much needed sleep. Should Georgiana's fever increase, he asked to be informed immediately. In such case, she would need to be purged and most likely bled. Lady Matlock was satisfied with her physician's recommendations and indicated she would post another letter to Darcy, apprising him of Mr. Purdy's evaluation. Assuming her niece's condition did not worsen, the two of them would return on Friday and reassess her progress at that time.

Once Lady Matlock and Mr. Purdy left her rooms, it did not take long before Georgiana burst into tears followed by an uncontrollable fit of coughing. Disregarding what the woman had said about propriety, she sat on the bed and held Georgiana in her arms.

"Please, Miss Darcy, please.... You must not let them upset you so for it will only make your recovery all the more difficult." Georgiana nodded as Elizabeth pushed the loose hair back from her eyes and kissed her on the forehead.

"In truth, it is a good thing your aunt intends to keep Mr. Darcy informed. When he learns of your illness, I am sure your brother will make every effort to return promptly and see to your care himself. In the meantime, let us have no more tears." Elizabeth wiped Georgiana's cheeks with her thumbs and gave her a fresh handkerchief.

"My Aunt Gardiner will be here in a few hours, and I know she will be a great comfort to us. Why do you not close your eyes, and I shall read aloud until you fall asleep." Georgiana managed a half-smile and did as she was bid.

Elizabeth retrieved the Bible and turned to Psalm ninety-one. Sitting next to Georgiana, she took her hand, saying, "This is a Psalm of protection, and its words are very comforting." By the time Elizabeth had finished all of the verses, Georgiana was sleeping peacefully.

~ ♫ ~

Later that afternoon

It was nearly five o' clock before Mrs. Gardiner arrived at Darcy

House. Relieved to see her, Elizabeth gave her aunt a hug and quickly took her to Georgiana's bedroom.

"Miss Darcy, I hear you have been feeling poorly."

Still experiencing some of the effects of the laudanum, it took a few moments for Georgiana to comprehend what was going on. Then between coughing and having difficulty breathing, her words barely came out. "Mrs. Gardiner, thank you for coming. I ... I am so sorry to be ... such a burden. Please forgive me."

"My dear, you must never think you are a burden. With your brother and Mrs. Annesley away, I am honoured you saw fit to send for Elizabeth. We shall help you in whatever way we can."

Mrs. Gardiner stepped closer to the bed in order to feel Georgiana's forehead. "Ah, there is yet some fever, Lizzy."

"I have tried both the lavender water and the willow bark tea. Even so, Miss Darcy has a bit of a headache and is nauseated. The draughts have not set well with her, and she can barely keep down the chicken broth."

"Miss Darcy, I believe Elizabeth told you my brother, Mr. Peter Williams, is an apothecary." Georgiana nodded. "I have just come from his shop, where I procured this special syrup for you to drink. It is made from ginger root and honey."

"Ginger root?" she questioned.

"Yes, a supplier from Jamaica provides my brother with the root. Traditionally, the root is ground into a fine powder which we use for baking. The root, more potent in its natural state, will ease your cough and help to settle your stomach. My brother has added a bit of honey which is also medicinal and improves the flavour. May I?" Mrs. Gardiner opened the bottle and, taking a spoon, aided Georgiana in swallowing the soothing elixir.

"Lizzy, I also brought some dried pieces of the root which may be steeped in hot water for tea. In addition, Peter gave me a few dried eucalyptus leaves which came from one of our British colonies by the way of an Italian supplier. The leaves need to be crushed and submerged in hot water. Inhaling the vapours will also temporarily help with Miss Darcy's congestion."

"Thank you, Aunt. Your advice is invaluable."

Mrs. Gardiner stayed on for another twenty minutes before taking her leave. Wanting to speak privately, Elizabeth escorted her aunt to the carriage.

"Lizzy, I hesitated to mention this in front of Miss Darcy, but it is imperative you do everything within your power to bolster the dear girl's spirits. If not, this illness could easily get the better of her, causing her health to decline even further."

"I had thought as much. If you remember, Mr. Darcy told me her emotions were fragile. Poor Miss Darcy became completely undone after she was attended by Lady Matlock and her physician. Mr. Purdy has a propensity to bleed."

"Oh dear, bleeding would only continue to weaken her."

"I agree. Aunt, I think there is something else not right here. It may have only been from the effects of the laudanum, but during her sleep, Miss Darcy frequently cried out in anguish. Though I have not put it all together, I am sure the source of her emotional distress is hidden in her dreams. She repeated her brother's name, over and over, and also the name of one other, George. If only she would confide in me, perhaps I could be of even greater help. I dare not push her, though, for fear of distressing her further."

Mrs. Gardiner took Elizabeth's hand saying, "I agree, Lizzy. It seems you must be patient. We shall keep the dear girl in our prayers. Meanwhile, I would like to be kept informed of her progress and if need be, I shall send Jane with more remedies." Acknowledging everything her aunt had said, Elizabeth embraced her, and Mrs. Gardiner boarded the carriage for Gracechurch Street.

CHAPTER EIGHT

A MOTHER'S TOUCH

Darcy House
Thursday, 27 June 1811

*T*wo days had passed, yet Georgiana's health had not improved. Even with all of the remedies left by Mr. Purdy and Mrs. Gardiner, her fever persisted and her relentless cough remained a constant source of discomfort. Elizabeth read to Georgiana and attempted to cheer her in various ways, but all in all, her efforts proved fruitless. About mid-afternoon, she decided to try something else and took out her sewing.

"Miss Darcy, might I ask if you have ever assisted with the tenant visits when residing at Pemberley?"

"Mrs. Reynolds, our housekeeper, has encouraged me to do so, but I admit I never have," she whispered.

"I am sure you would make an excellent ambassador for your family. Volunteering to perform for the hospital concert shows me you have a very generous heart." Georgiana smiled shyly at Elizabeth's praise.

"When I was your age, I began assisting my father with his tenant visits and found it enjoyable. This little baby gown is for Mrs. Dobbs, who is expecting her fifth child next month. If you were to look closer, you would see I am *not* the best with a needle." She chuckled. "Nevertheless, the goodwill created with such a small gesture cannot be measured.

"Aunt Gardiner says your mother was revered by all of Lambton for her kindness and generosity to the poor." Georgiana's eyes brightened on hearing mention of her mother. "I wonder if you have ever heard of my aunt's father, Mr. Fredrick Williams, who at one time was the apothecary in the village."

"I do not recall the name."

"When my aunt was but a young girl, she, along with her older brother, often helped their father in his shop. It was there she became privy to a very special charity project which was started by your mother. Apparently, your mother would call on various establishments in the village at the beginning of each month. It was during those visits Lady Anne became informed as to the needs and concerns of the community at large.

"After one such meeting, your mother proposed creating a charity which would facilitate the purchase of shoes for children of the poor. With the help of the Vicar, the shoes were distributed to those who were in need. According to my aunt, this service for the Lambton community continues to be funded by your family's estate. It is a lovely tribute to your mother's memory, is it not?"

"Thank you, it is. I know so little of my mother. If only she were here with me."

Taking Georgiana's hand, Elizabeth spoke kindly. "Miss Darcy, you may not realise it, but, in a way, your mother *is* here. Her goodness is present in your heart, and although I have not known you long, I truly believe you are very much like her. Now, I think you should rest." Georgiana nodded and eased down under her blankets, warmed by thoughts of her mother.

Friday

The next morning, Mrs. Troutman entered Georgiana's room with an express from Darcy. Elizabeth read it aloud while Rebecca continued to help Georgiana prepare for the dreaded visit of Lady Matlock and Mr. Purdy.

Dearest Georgiana,

I hope this letter finds you in better health than Aunt Eleanor gave me to believe in her notes. Needless to say, I was distressed to learn of your illness, and apologise for not being able to see to your care myself. Unfortunately, the situation between the tenants has been more complicated than I anticipated and resolving it has taken longer than I would have wished. That being said, an agreement was finally reached during today's discussions. By the time you receive this express, I shall have been on the road for some hours and hope to be back in Town no later than Sunday morning. My thoughts are with you, my darling sister.

Affectionately,
William

When Elizabeth finished reading the letter, Georgiana unexpectedly burst into tears. "I truly do not deserve him," she whimpered.

"Dear one, you must not disparage yourself in this way. You do yourself a great disservice. Your brother loves you very much."

Georgiana momentarily closed her eyes, opened them again, and looked sadly at Elizabeth. Trying to suppress another cough, she managed to say, "You have no idea. If you did, you would see I am right."

Taking her hand and speaking with sureness, Elizabeth responded, "Miss Darcy, it is true I am not aware of your private affairs, but I will *not* accept that you are not worthy of your brother's love and devotion. For now, let us think more positively. Your aunt will be here shortly, and it will not do for you to appear upset." Giving Georgiana a kiss on the forehead, Elizabeth continued to hold her hand while Rebecca finished plating her hair with a pretty ribbon.

Within the hour, Lady Matlock entered Georgiana's bedroom accompanied by Mr. Purdy. The grand lady walked over to the bed and felt her niece's forehead, frowning when she noticed the fever had not abated.

"What is this, Georgiana? Have you not taken all of Mr. Purdy's remedies?"

"Yes, Aunt, I did take them," she whispered, suppressing her coughs as best as she could.

"Miss Elizabeth, let us remove to Georgiana's sitting room while she is being examined." Anticipating her directive, Elizabeth smiled at Georgiana and followed Lady Matlock out of the room.

During the examination, Elizabeth attempted to divert Lady Matlock's attention by inquiring after the ongoing preparations for the Military Ball. Jane and Mrs. Madison had taken over many of her duties while she was nursing Georgiana, and Lady Matlock was pleased with what they had accomplished in her absence. Time passed quickly, and before long, Rebecca announced Mr. Purdy had completed his evaluation.

"Your Ladyship, I find Miss Darcy's health is yet in great peril. In addition to the slight fever which continues to persist, your niece has more congestion. I also regret to say several white pustules have formed in the back of her throat. Though she has taken the draughts, I fear it is difficult to proceed as I would wish since you say Mr. Darcy has insisted she not be bled. At this juncture, it appears our only recourse is to purge the girl."

With this new proclamation, Elizabeth gasped and rushed to Georgiana's side, taking her hand. "Surely you cannot mean it! Mr. Purdy, I beg you to please reconsider. Miss Darcy has not eaten well all week. With her poor appetite, she has barely consumed more than broth and tea. Can you not see she needs what little strength she has to fight this illness?"

The man's face reddened, and his demeanour became rigid. "Your Ladyship, this young woman's interference is insupportable. If you do not intervene, I regret to say I can no longer be of assistance here."

"Miss Bennet, your insolence is ill-advised, and I shall remind you that in my nephew's absence I have chosen to exercise authority over Georgiana's welfare. Notwithstanding your good intentions, I believe it is time for you to pack your things and return to your aunt's house before you do more harm."

"Aunt, please," Georgiana begged. "Please do not send Miss Elizabeth away. I need her. I shall submit if only you will allow her to stay."

"Dear Georgiana," Elizabeth spoke softly, ignoring Lady Matlock's displeasure.

"Very well, Georgiana, I will allow her to stay, provided she does as Mr. Purdy asks and that I hear no reports of her disregard." Elizabeth acknowledged in the affirmative. Satisfied, Lady Matlock took her leave, allowing the physician to complete his task.

Moments later, Rebecca began preparing Georgiana for the purging. A vial of thick, amber syrup which would be used to induce vomiting was set forth. Consisting primarily of ipecac, the smell of the elixir was putrid, and the initial taste alone was enough to induce a spasm in the poor girl who could barely drink the concoction without convulsing. Elizabeth steadied her friend as Rebecca held up the basin. Upon emptying her stomach, she continued to tremble, becoming faint. After the procedure was repeated, Georgiana collapsed onto the bed and curled up on her side, unable to hold back her tears. Minutes later, Elizabeth was shocked when she realised Mr. Purdy was now preparing a smoke enema.

"Mr. Purdy, I implore you. Will you not reconsider and postpone this treatment? Miss Darcy is much too weak to endure it. May we not see how she fares after the purging? Mr. Darcy will return here on Sunday, and I do not believe he would approve of this procedure in his absence." Elizabeth silently prayed the man would consider her pleas.

The physician nervously shifted his attention from Elizabeth to Georgiana and then back again. "Young lady, abandoning this treatment goes against my better judgement." He swallowed hard. "I am familiar with Mr. Darcy's reputation, not to mention his temper, once provoked." He pinched his brow as though remembering some unpleasant event.

"I would not wish the man affronted," he nervously muttered. Nodding, he finally said, "Yes ... yes, I believe I shall delay this procedure. In the meantime, I absolutely insist that you send for me should Miss Darcy's condition deteriorate any further before her brother's return. For now, I shall give her a dose of laudanum to induce sleep."

Eager to see Mr. Purdy take his leave, Elizabeth dared not protest any further. Once the physician packed his bag and departed, she and Rebecca helped Georgiana to change her gown and get back into bed. With the laudanum taking effect, sleep came quickly.

Incensed, Elizabeth could not believe the injustice Georgiana had suffered under the approval of her own aunt. Out of frustration, she was compelled to send another note to Mrs. Gardiner, informing her of what had taken place, and begging for her assistance should there be something more to offer.

Thankfully, Georgiana was able to sleep for a few hours, even though she was plagued with intermittent coughing. Later, when early evening began to set in and the laudanum began to wear off, Elizabeth and Rebecca encouraged their patient to drink a little of the broth. Unluckily, with Georgiana's stomach irritated from the purging, she was not able to keep the liquid down. While Elizabeth did her best to reassure the dear girl, it was not enough. Becoming confused, Georgiana continued to cry and begged for Elizabeth to help her find her mother.

Concerns for the girl only heightened when Georgiana began to greatly perspire, and her fever increased. The thought of recalling Mr. Purdy who would only inflict more of his horrifying procedures upon her dear friend prompted Elizabeth to send for ice. Instead, she and Rebecca took turns tending their patient's body with cool compresses in an effort to reduce her fever throughout the night. By the time the first signs of daylight emerged, both women were exhausted, and Georgiana had shown no signs of improvement.

~ ♫ ~

Saturday, 29 June 1811

About mid-morning, Jane arrived with two tinctures from Mrs. Gardiner: one to help settle Georgiana's stomach and another for her fever. Being shaken by the scene which greeted her, Jane quickly became uneasy and found the need to shorten her visit.

During the time which followed, there was little change and by late afternoon, Elizabeth had become weary. After refreshing herself, she took a short walk through the garden. Before returning, Elizabeth chose to go to the library. Each time she visited this room, she was in awe of the many volumes and collections held by the Darcy family. Her father's book room at Longbourn was meagre by comparison. Smelling the leather and wood, Elizabeth inhaled deeply. Her senses were calmed while enjoying the richness of this decidedly masculine room.

Walking slowly around the perimeter and touching the bindings of various volumes within the stacks, Elizabeth found herself wondering which ones were Mr. Darcy's favourites. Seeing a little book on one of the writing desks, she was curious to learn what he might have been reading. To her surprise, the book had been left open to the very poem she had sung at the Matlock's dinner party. After taking a ribbon of white lace from her pocket to mark the place, Elizabeth continued to leaf through the pages, noting the entire collection was devoted to the poetry of Thomas Moore. Looking at the inside cover, she also discovered it was signed by the author and addressed to none other than the object of her reverie, Fitzwilliam Darcy.

Wondering what else he might be reading, she came across a larger book which lay open on another table. Putting down the smaller one, her curiosity led her to find a favourite work of William Cowper. Picking up the volume, she sat down on one of the couches to read.

God moves in a mysterious way
His wonders to perform;

He plants his footsteps in the sea,
And rides upon the storm.
Deep in unfathomable mines
Of never-failing skill
He treasures up his bright designs,
And works his sovereign will.
Ye fearful saints, fresh courage take!
The clouds ye so much dread
Are big with mercy, and shall break
In blessings on your head.
Judge not the Lord by feeble sense,
But trust him for his grace;
Behind a frowning providence
He hides a smiling face.
His purposes will ripen fast,
Unfolding every hour;
The bud may have a bitter taste,
But sweet will be the flower,
Blind unbelief is sure to err,
And scan his work in vain;
God is his own interpreter,
And he will make it plain....

"Light shining out of Darkness," William Cowper 1779

This poem had much meaning for Elizabeth, and it appeared to be one which Darcy had also studied since various phrases had been underlined with personal notations written in the margins. On many occasions, she had referred to these verses when faced with a difficult challenge. Respectful of Cowper's message, Elizabeth was determined not to be taken in by the despair which threatened to engulf Georgiana and those who were concerned for her welfare. She would need to remain steadfast while supporting her friend during this illness. Closing the book and momentarily pressing it to her chest, Elizabeth was grateful for the reminders brought forth by the poem. She offered up a prayer for Georgiana's recovery and then with renewed energy, put the volume down and quickly left the Library.

Feeling refreshed, Elizabeth encouraged Rebecca to take an hour to see to her own needs. After changing the compresses on Georgiana's forehead and chest, Elizabeth sat on the edge of the bed and held her hand. Gently brushing some of the girl's long hair away from her moist face, Elizabeth began humming a lullaby in attempt to calm her restlessness.

After a few phrases, Georgiana opened her eyes and asked, "Has William returned? He knows where Mama is. Please, please send William to me."

"He will be home soon, I promise. You must not be frightened. I shall not let anything or anyone harm you." Georgiana closed her eyes and listened as Elizabeth quietly sang the simple tune which she had been humming.

"Sleep my child and peace attend thee, All through the night.
Guardian angels God will send thee, All through the night.
Soft the drowsy hours are creeping, Hill and vale through slumber
sleeping.
I my loving vigil keeping, All through the night...."

Musical Relicks of the Welsh Bards 1784

When Elizabeth's song faded back into a hum, Georgiana opened her glazed eyes and spoke again, "Mama, your song is beautiful. I have been searching for you for so long. I need your help." By this time, her tears were unrestrained.

Removing the compresses, Elizabeth climbed into the bed and cradled the girl in her arms. Taking out her handkerchief, she gently wiped the tears from Georgiana's face while shedding a few of her own. "I love you," she quietly said, caressing her forehead and cheek with her cool hand.

"Mama, I do not know what to do. I … I am so ashamed. He … he said he loved me, and that he wanted me to go with him. I was troubled; yet I told him I would go. George told me Father had always loved him, and if we went away and were married, William would be happy for us. Mama, I … I trusted Mr. Wickham." Georgiana's coughing increased with the strain of her sobbing.

"When William came, I was so happy to see him. I wanted to tell him about us, but … but something terrible happened. George … he … he did not love me after all. He … he lied. He … he only wanted my fortune and … and to hurt William. He *never* loved me," she sobbed, clinging to Elizabeth. "George and William quarrelled. William, I…." Again, her coughing increased. "Mama, please tell William how very sorry I am." She continued to cry, barely able to breathe.

Unhappily, this was the secret which had tormented Georgiana and had caused her to lose respect for herself. She had given her trusting heart to a cruel man who sought to make his fortune at her expense and shame. Elizabeth felt compelled to speak her mind but wondered if Georgiana would remember any of what she related in her fevered state.

"Georgiana," Elizabeth said taking hold of her shoulders. "Look at me, Georgiana. Please look at me." Elizabeth's commanding tone encouraged the girl to do her bidding. "My dear friend, you are not to blame yourself any longer. Your mistake was based on that man's deception. George Wickham is *not* worthy of you. You tried to love a selfish man who is not capable of loving anyone. You must stop punishing yourself by feeling guilty. Do you understand me?" Georgiana slowly nodded.

"Your brother loves you so very much. I love you. You *must* let go of these unpleasant thoughts, of George Wickham and of his lies. Promise me you will leave him behind. Do you think you can, dearest?"

"Mama, I shall try. I promise. I shall do it for you and for William."

"No, Georgiana," Elizabeth said with conviction. "You must do this for yourself."

Georgiana looked intently into Elizabeth's eyes and nodded. "Yes, Mama, I understand."

Elizabeth smiled tenderly and kissed the dear girl on the forehead,

then

drawing her back into an embrace. Georgiana closed her eyes. Within minutes, her breathing became calm, and she fell asleep. Touching her forehead, Elizabeth could tell the fever was finally beginning to abate. Feeling hopeful, she continued to hold Georgiana in her arms and closed her eyes.

Both women had slept for some hours and when the hall clock struck ten o'clock, Elizabeth began to stir. With Georgiana continuing to sleep peacefully and showing no further signs of fever, Elizabeth decided to return to her own room. If need be, Rebecca would awaken her should Georgiana's fever return.

Leaving the room, Elizabeth's mind was full. Poor Georgiana had been through so much with her illness, not to mention the confrontation with her aunt, and the remorse she had suffered over a man called George Wickham. After changing into her night clothes, Elizabeth draped a shawl across her shoulders and went to Georgiana's sitting room, where she found an extensive collection of romantic novels and poetry. Surely some light reading would settle her mind before retiring. Thinking of her younger sisters, Elizabeth chuckled to herself and began searching for one of Mrs. Radcliffe's more recent offerings. Finding one such book on the shelf, she proceeded to curl up in a large wing-back chair and began to peruse the text. With her mind beginning to calm and her eyelids becoming heavy, minutes later, Elizabeth drifted off into a peaceful sleep.

Darcy's Carriage

Nervously tapping the edge of his seat, Darcy grew more anxious the closer his carriage neared the dim lights of London. He would not be able to rest until he reached his home and discovered for himself how Georgiana was faring. It had not been quite two weeks since he left Town to deal with his estate problems. Even so, his body felt as though a month's worth of activity and travel had been forced into that short amount of time.

On returning to Pemberley, Darcy's steward quickly enlightened him about the precarious tenant quarrel. A drainage ditch, of all things, had nearly caused a revolt amongst the farmers on the south side of his property. Darcy shook his head in disgust recalling some of what transpired.

It had taken nearly two full days for the concerned parties to air their grievances and be physically investigated. Darcy was furious to learn that false pride and petty rivalry had led to a neglected drainage ditch and to the fouling of a shared well with arsenic. All of this was followed by another morning of discussion before Darcy could begin to implement his solutions. Needless to say, receiving Lady Matlock's express regarding Georgiana's health only added to the frustration the man was already feeling.

Having made his judgement in the case and having been assured by Mr. Clarke that he would carry out his directives, Darcy immediately set out for London. Since Lady Matlock had kept him informed of Georgiana's condition, his unease about her illness and what his aunt's physician might implement in his absence prompted him to return to Town as soon as it was humanly possible. Thankfully, much of his night travel was aided by a full moon. Combined with the carriage lanterns, he was able to return to Darcy House much earlier than he had originally anticipated.

Darcy House

Shortly after midnight, Elizabeth was awakened by the slamming of the large front door and the deep voice of the master loudly issuing orders to one of the footmen. A cold shiver came over her, and with a sense of panic, she knew without question she needed to return to her room. Quickly securing her shawl, Elizabeth put down the book and rose from her chair. Moments later she heard his heavy footsteps coming down the hallway and the door to the sitting suddenly room flew open.

"Georgiana, I have been so.... Miss Elizabeth Bennet!" Darcy exclaimed, abruptly stopping at the threshold.

"Mr. Darcy," she replied and bit her lower lip wondering what to do next. Clutching the shawl tightly about her shoulders, Elizabeth nervously swallowed and continued, "Sir, we did not expect you this evening." She awkwardly looked to the floor in embarrassment.

"Forgive my intrusion," he stammered. "I ... I saw the light and thought.... My aunt did not inform me that you were.... How is my sister?"

Elizabeth raised her eyes to look at him, giving a shy smile. "I think she is a little better, sir. It has been a difficult week. Thankfully, her fever broke earlier this evening, and it appears the worst is over." Darcy momentarily closed his eyes and gave a sigh of relief in response.

"Rebecca is in with her now and will remain so throughout the rest of the night."

"May I enquire how you happen to be here?" His eyes bore into hers causing her to blush as he spoke.

"I received a note from Miss Darcy on Monday stating she did not feel well. With both you and Mrs. Annesley gone, she asked if Jane and I would visit for a few hours. When we arrived, we were surprised to find her far worse than her note gave us to believe. Shortly after, it was agreed I should stay on and assist Rebecca. I am sorry if I have overstepped and invaded your family's privacy."

"Miss Elizabeth." Darcy started to move forward before checking himself. "You need not apologise. I am grateful you were able to come to my sister's aid. Thank you." His face softened, allowing a hint of a smile to emerge. "It seems you have sacrificed much to help Georgiana this week. Please know you are most welcome in my home and that I sincerely appreciate your kindness."

"Thank you."

The two of them continued to stare at each other for several moments without speaking. Elizabeth finally broke the silence by saying, "Mr. Darcy, I should inform you that your aunt's physician and I did not see eye to eye with regard to Miss Darcy's care.

"He did not bleed her, did he? I sent specific instructions that he *not* use the procedure."

"No, no, he did not."

"Thank God!"

"Regrettably, I could not prevent him from purging her. Lady Matlock was adamant and threatened to remove me from the house if I did not cooperate." Elizabeth heard Darcy curse under his breath as he raked his hand through his hair in exasperation.

"Sir, your sister was very brave."

Shaking his head in disapproval, he muttered to himself through clenched teeth, "My aunt will be hearing from me." Regaining his composure, he continued, "Forgive my outburst. It is late now, and you must be very tired. I would like to speak more of this in the morning." Darcy bowed and turned to leave. Before crossing the threshold, he looked back at Elizabeth. His face was more relaxed, and his eyes had softened. Accompanied by a half smile, he merely said, "Goodnight, Miss Elizabeth."

"Goodnight, Mr. Darcy." She smiled sweetly in return, and then he was gone.

CHAPTER NINE

A WALK IN THE PARK

Darcy House
Sunday, 30 June 1811
Early morning

*H*aving experienced a restless sleep after her late night encounter with Mr. Darcy, Elizabeth awoke feeling stiff and mentally unsettled. While she could not begin to erase the embarrassment of being found in her nightclothes, the lack of propriety had not been the only source of her discomfort. It was her overwhelming attraction to a man who had left her sensibilities in turmoil. Knowing she would have to get her feelings under better regulation, Elizabeth hoped to order her thoughts by taking an early morning walk.

Before leaving, she first stepped into Georgiana's room making sure all was well. To her relief, it appeared both Georgiana and her maid were sleeping peacefully. Quietly slipping back out of the room, she took the stairs and made her way to the rear entrance of the house. A cool, refreshing breeze blew against Elizabeth's face when she opened the door and walked out onto the pathway. The dampness of the morning fog had begun to lift allowing glimmering rays sunshine to filter through what was left of the dissipating clouds.

Anticipating her upcoming conversation with Mr. Darcy, Elizabeth was unsure of how much she should relate regarding Georgiana's disorientation and in particular, her references to George Wickham. It was a private matter and one her friend might not have shared under normal circumstances. Poor Georgiana was not quite sixteen years-of-age. Yet she had known such terrible heartache, first with the loss of her parents, and more recently, by the hand of someone she had trusted. In Elizabeth's estimation, Mr. Wickham was despicable, but she also knew she would need to speak with discretion when addressing Mr. Darcy about this delicate situation.

In reviewing her relationship with both Darcys, there was no doubt she and Georgiana had become close. They were much more like sisters than mere friends. On the other hand, her relationship with the brother was far more ambiguous.

"I wonder if Mr. Darcy would consider *me* a friend," she mused, allowing her mind to take a more playful turn. "I doubt if Lady Matlock would approve, knowing how she reacted to my time spent with Miss Darcy."

Noticing a small bird perched on the edge of a stone bath, she questioned, "Well, little one, what do you think?" The bird chirped as though responding in kind. "You are absolutely correct. She would *not* approve. And can you imagine what she would say if he were to consider me anything more?" Elizabeth could not help but giggle at the thought. "Why, Her Ladyship would probably launch into a tirade which could be heard from here to Cheapside. At any rate, it is not possible. A man like Mr. Darcy would never consider the daughter of a country squire in such a manner. Oh, *why* did I not listen to my aunt?" Elizabeth stamped her foot in frustration, scaring the little bird away. "I *never* should have let him into my heart!"

Elizabeth blushed recalling the way Darcy looked at her when he came upon her in Georgiana's sitting room. His intense gaze scarcely allowed her to keep her wits about her as they conversed. His mere presence alone stirred an unexpected longing in her heart and a physical sensation in her body which she had never before experienced.

"How shall I *ever* be able to face him today unless I put these impossible thoughts aside? I simply *must* do better!"

An old ballad which told the story of a young maiden who loved a Noble Lord came to mind. Although the Lord had returned the girls 's ? affections, he could not abandon his station for someone so far beneath him. Quietly humming the melancholy tune, Elizabeth knew its message could not be ignored. While her heart longed for Fitzwilliam Darcy, her head told her she could have no expectations whatsoever.

"I shall not allow myself to regret or wish for what can never be," she vowed. "I shall follow my own advice and think only of my experience with both brother and sister as it gives me pleasure."

~ ♫ ~

Like Elizabeth, Darcy awoke after sleeping only a few short hours. Even though he was exhausted from his trip, his concern over Georgiana's health and his attraction to Elizabeth had played havoc with his mind throughout the night. During his absence, Elizabeth had stayed at his home, taking care of his precious sister while she was ill. How surprised he had been when he found her in Georgiana's sitting room! The sight of Elizabeth standing before him in her thin night-gown and bared feet nearly left him speechless. At that very moment, Darcy had wanted nothing more than to take Elizabeth into his arms and touch his lips to hers. The thought of entangling his fingers in her long curls while caressing her neck with soft kisses was nearly his undoing. Never before had a woman moved him in such a way.

What Darcy needed at this very moment was a vigorous ride on his most spirited horse. *If only I were back at Pemberley!* While Andrews laid out his clothes, Darcy opened the window, seeking some fresh air. Listening for the early morning sounds, he heard the chirping of birds, the muffled clopping of horse's hooves on the cobblestones, and ever so faintly, he heard the sound of a woman's voice humming a plaintive melody. *Could it be she is also up and about at this hour?* Raking 5th ? his fingers through his hair in frustration, Darcy mentally debated as to whether or not he should seek her out. As the sound of Elizabeth's voice continued to taunt him, he quickly dressed and impulsively headed for the rear entrance to the garden, summoning a maid to follow in lieu of a chaperone.

Passing through the doorway, Darcy caught sight of Elizabeth leisurely strolling down a side path near the rose garden, periodically stopping to touch or smell one of the flowers. Minutes later, his footsteps were overheard on the gravel path, prompting her to turn and face him with an awkward smile.

"Miss Elizabeth," spoke Darcy, tipping his hat in salutation.

"Mr. Darcy." She curtseyed.

"I believe we are of one mind this morning. May I join you?"

"Please." She nodded in response.

"The garden here is lovely, but I thought I would prefer to take the lanes in Hyde Park today. Have you had the opportunity to visit the park during your stay in Town?"

"No, sir, I have not had the pleasure of walking its pathways although my aunt and uncle have promised to take us there before my sister and I return to Hertfordshire."

"I realise it is well before the *fashionable hour*, but might I persuade you to defy convention and accompany me there. The park is but a few blocks from here."

Gazing up into his blue eyes, Elizabeth found she could not refuse. Rewarding him with a warm smile, she answered, "Thank you, Mr. Darcy. I believe I shall." Darcy offered her his arm and the two left the garden followed by the maid.

"I confess I have truly missed the quiet and solitude of an early morning walk while being here in Town."

"I take it you are a great walker."

"Sir, you have discovered my secret." She arched a mischievous brow while tilting her head up in his direction. "I find I can walk for hours if the weather is pleasant and the scenery enticing."

"If that be the case, I know you would enjoy the prospect of Derbyshire. It is filled with lush, dark green woods, in addition to miles of rolling hills and streams set against the magnificent peaks.

Unlike London, the air is pure and refreshing; however, one would definitely need a mount to do it justice." After giving her a sideways look, he continued, "In truth, I actually prefer a vigorous ride to walking."

"Then it appears we are at odds, Mr. Darcy."

"So it would seem." He chuckled.

Upon entering the park, Elizabeth was in awe as she viewed an arbour of trees surrounded by rows of well-kept flower beds. Noting her delight, Darcy proceeded to give her his commentary, pointing out pertinent information about the vegetation as they walked along.

"Sir, I am surprised at your vast botanical knowledge and attention to detail," Elizabeth remarked. "Although you hale from the natural wonders of Derbyshire, I would not have suspected you to be a true naturalist," she teased.

"Ah, more character analysis."

"Perhaps I am just curious."

"With that in mind, I shall tell you my knowledge is not *all* of my own doing. My mother expressed a great interest in the study of botany, and as a child, I spent many hours under her tutelage. My education began with the exploration of the wilds of Pemberley and extended far beyond its boundaries. Some of the landscape in the north is extraordinary. When I am in the country, I often ride to one particular pass which is surrounded by a great many boulders. Near the top, one can almost see the source of the stream which makes its way down the mountainside, meandering onto the grounds of Pemberley, where it fills the lake and feeds the pond. The view is truly magnificent."

"I quite envy you, Mr. Darcy. My aunt tells me very little can best the natural wonders of Derbyshire. In Hertfordshire, we can only boast of Oakham Mount. While one cannot compare it to the grandeur of the Peaks, it is within walking distance of our house, and I often go there to escape the constant chatter which is generally brought on by my younger sisters."

As they progressed, their talk turned away from nature to that of literature. Having found what he assumed was Elizabeth's lace ribbon in his small volume of Thomas Moore before retiring, Darcy was curious to know which other books she favoured. He discovered their tastes were similar as to preference of authors, but her interpretation did not necessarily embrace his own. It was refreshing to learn she would not adopt his views simply to placate or impress him, as most women of the *ton* generally did. Elizabeth had a singular way of looking at things and did not hesitate in speaking her mind.

During the course of their conversation, Darcy felt it was his duty to broach the subject of Lord Wolverton. After reviewing the disturbing information his cousin had previously given him, he was still concerned for Elizabeth's safety when doing her uncle's bidding.

"Shall we sit, Miss Elizabeth?" He paused, motioning her to a nearby bench. "For some time, I have wanted to speak with you about the day we met at the bookshop."

"Oh?" She looked at him with curiosity.

"Do you remember the gentleman who was observing us?"

"Why yes, I do!" she responded with energy. "He was an older gentleman, rather short, with clipped whiskers, and he wore an unfashionable double-breasted black waistcoat with a cocked hat. His boots were not kept and were covered with dried mud, and he squinted through an odd rectangular eyepiece as he read his newspaper." Her attention to detail caused Darcy to smile.

"That is correct. You have described him admirably. After you left, I confronted the stranger."

"You did?!" Her eyes grew wide with surprise.

"Yes. The man claimed to have knowledge of me through his son, an old classmate from Cambridge. Since I had no recollection of this person, I asked Colonel Fitzwilliam to verify his story." Darcy frowned for a moment. "Miss Elizabeth, I do not mean to give you cause for alarm, but my cousin's sources believe our observing patron was following *you* on that particular day."

"Me?" she questioned, obviously startled by his revelation.

"Yes, I am afraid Lord Wolverton has many enemies who would not hesitate to obtain information from any of his acquaintances if they thought it to be profitable. My cousin mentioned that you and

Miss Bennet along with the Gardiners are often guests of His Lordship when he is in Town. At present, Colonel Fitzwilliam believes there is no cause for alarm. I, on the other hand, was compelled to make you aware of this information."

"Sir, please let me assure you I have done nothing to encourage His Lordship. In truth, I detest the man and cannot understand why any of his adversaries would be interested in me. Unless His Lordship presents himself at the Military Ball, I do not expect to see him in the foreseeable future. After that event, Jane and I shall be returning to Hertfordshire with my family. Even though we plan to be in Town for the Autumn Festival, it is unlikely we shall be here for the other events which are scheduled to take place during the heart of the season."

"I understand." He paused for a moment before continuing, "Miss Elizabeth, I hope you will not take offence, but I cannot help questioning your uncle's judgement by involving you in this type of business if only on occasion. In my opinion, espionage is no place for a gentlewoman."

"Mr. Darcy." Elizabeth spoke his name with authority. "I realise you are speaking out of concern, yet I must defend my uncle in saying he has been discreet and would never have used my assistance had it not been of the utmost necessity. Sir, I am not a spy, and I certainly do not know any of the particulars regarding the few messages which I have delivered on my uncle's behalf. For my part, you must recognise that it is difficult for me to refuse his request for assistance when I am living under his roof and protection."

"Forgive me. I did not mean to chasten your behaviour or purposely criticise your uncle. Because of what my cousin related, I have a genuine concern for your safety. In addition, my housekeeper tells me you have come to mean much to Georgiana during the past week. If something of a serious nature were to befall you, I know she would not take it well."

"Mr. Darcy, are you suggesting I should temper my friendship with Miss Darcy? Do you believe she could be in danger by associating with me?"

He half smiled. "You misunderstand me, Miss Elizabeth. I would never consider such recourse. I simply mean to put you on your guard, and if you do not object, I would like to speak with your uncle regarding Colonel Fitzwilliam's information."

"Mr. Darcy, surely you take too much upon yourself. You have already come to my aid on one other occasion where His Lordship was concerned, and I am embarrassed that I have not properly thanked you for your assistance."

"In my estimation, speaking with Mr. Gardiner is nothing out of the ordinary. As for the other, I need no thanks. I would do the same for any friend."

"Friend?" she questioned while studying his face in earnest.

"Yes, if you have no objection. With all that has passed between us since we first met, and now with your kindness to my sister, are we not more than mere acquaintances? Considering our conversation of the last hour, it would be difficult to think otherwise." He smiled unassumingly, causing her to do the same.

"You are correct." Elizabeth held out her hand and replied, "Mr. Darcy, I am pleased to call you my friend. Moreover, I shall humbly grant you permission to speak with my uncle if you will in turn accept my gratitude."

"It is as you wish." Taking Elizabeth's hand, he slowly lifted it to his mouth where he placed a tender kiss on her gloved fingertips. For several moments, he continued to gaze into her lovely eyes, nearly tempted to reveal what lay within his heart. "Miss Elizabeth, I...." With his next breath, Darcy suddenly recalled where he was and purposely cleared his throat while regaining his composure. Pulling back and sitting up straight, he continued to address her more formally.

"Miss Elizabeth, may I prevail on you a little longer? Although we have been in the park for some time now, I would like to hear an account of your time with my sister."

"Why, yes, of course."

"I spoke with Mrs. Troutman before retiring last night and was made fully aware of what transpired during the past week. My housekeeper expressed the highest praise for your assistance and assured me that you were *not* a force to be challenged when it came to my sister's care. Please accept my heartfelt appreciation for all you have done in my absence. I fear you have sacrificed much on her behalf."

"Mr. Darcy, your sister is very dear. How could I possibly do less?" Elizabeth spoke calmly, detailing what she had done to nurse his sister under the guidance of Mrs. Gardiner. So far, he approved. Unfortunately, when it came to the telling of what had transpired during the visits with Lady Matlock and Mr. Purdy, Darcy was incensed.

"My aunt had no business bringing that man into my home. He is incompetent! How could Georgiana possibly feel any relief under his care?"

Elizabeth gave no answer. Her look was solemn.

"Miss Elizabeth...." He studied her face for a moment. "Is there something more you have not told me?

"Sir." She swallowed. "After the purging, when Miss Darcy was most fevered, she was not quite herself and became unsure of her surroundings."

"Go on."

"In her distress she believed I was your mother."

"My mother?"

"Yes, Mr. Darcy." Elizabeth unconsciously reached for his hand. "While your sister was most fevered, she told me about … about Mr. Wickham."

Making a fist, he stiffened and closed his eyes. Upon opening them, he revealed an expression filled with rage, causing her to pull back in alarm. He seemed to look right through her as he spat, "Wickham!" Immediately rising and taking several paces, he quietly cursed the man while attempting to regain control over his emotions.

Elizabeth stood and moved to his side. Gently placing her hand on his forearm, she said, "Mr. Darcy, I am so sorry. I realise this is a very private matter, and I assure you I was the only person in the room when Miss Darcy spoke of her suffering. I shall pledge my secrecy, and no one will ever be privy to what was said. With her disorientation, it is possible your sister may not even remember what she revealed to me."

He nodded in acknowledgement. "Miss Elizabeth, other than you and Colonel Fitzwilliam, this incident has been shared with no one else. I trust you and have no doubt of your word. Please forgive my outburst."

"Under these circumstances, it was nothing, sir."

"George Wickham has been the bane of my family for more years than I care to say. He was the son of my late father's steward and grew up at Pemberley. We were childhood friends, and my father sponsored him at Cambridge, where we attended concurrently. At one time, Wickham was promised a generous living, which he later determined was not suitable. In lieu of the living, he chose a substantial monetary compensation. Unfortunately, his past actions have proved him to be selfish, dishonest and manipulative, and I can hardly bear to speak his name or think of him without abhorrence."

"Mr. Darcy," Elizabeth spoke softly. His eyes looked troubled when he finally met her gaze. "I need no further explanation. Sir, I love your sister as though she was one of my own, and I promise you I shall do everything within my power to support and protect her." Wrapping her arm through his, she offered, "Perhaps it is best if we return to the house." He nodded, quietly agreeing. The two of them left the park arm in arm and walked back to the house in silence.

CHAPTER TEN

TRANSITIONS

Darcy House
Sunday, 30 June 1811
The same day

To everyone's great relief, Georgiana's sleep was more peaceful than it had been in days. Once she awoke and was assisted with her toilette, she was able to break her fast with a simple meal. Following a short nap, she asked to be moved to her sitting room where she continued to rest in a chamber which was amply warmed by the late morning sunshine. There she lay comfortably on the reclining couch while Elizabeth read aloud.

Not long after, Darcy lightly tapped on the door intending to pay his sister a visit. To his surprise, her face was quite drawn and far paler than he had anticipated. Even so, as soon as she saw him, Georgiana's eyes brightened and she held out a hand as she welcomed him to her side with a sweet smile.

"William, I am so happy you are home." Her voice was hoarse and barely audible.

"Georgiana, I have missed you." He kissed her hand and pulled up a chair nearer to where she rested. "I thought you would like these roses from Mother's garden. The yellow is quite cheerful. Do you not agree?" He broke off one of the smaller flowers and handed it to Georgiana for her to smell.

"They are lovely and will look perfect with the lavender and daisies Miss Elizabeth brought earlier." Rebecca took the flowers and added them to the vase which sat on a low table in front of the chaise. Elizabeth quietly picked up her book and excused herself followed by Rebecca, allowing brother and sister their privacy.

"Dearest, after I received word of your illness, I hurried my business as best I could. I was very worried about you, Georgie." Again, he kissed her hand. "I trust you have been a good patient for Miss Elizabeth."

"Oh, William, I could not ask for a better nurse. Miss Elizabeth has been here since Monday afternoon and has taken such good care of me. She and Rebecca rarely left my side."

"So I have been told." He lovingly smiled.

"William, our aunt was very unkind to Miss Elizabeth." Georgiana closed her eyes for a moment while trying to suppress a few coughs and calm her thoughts. "Brother ... I fear I would have died had she had not been here to help me."

"Georgiana," he spoke with concern and squeezed her hand.

"When I was so very ill and terribly afraid, Miss Elizabeth comforted me and gave me encouragement. Not only did she see to my well-being, but she was my advocate in the presence of Aunt Eleanor and Mr. Purdy. I know our aunt would not approve, but I would very much like for Miss Elizabeth and I to use our Christian names. May I have your permission?"

Taking Georgiana in his arms, Darcy hugged her in response. "Why yes, of course. I would never deny you such a request." He could not believe his aunt had intimidated his sister to the point where she felt the need to ask for his approval where a dear friend was concerned.

"Georgie, our aunt was wrong in her treatment of Miss Elizabeth. I had a very informative discussion with Mrs. Troutman and know what transpired in this house during my absence. While it is true Miss

Elizabeth is not of our circle, she *is* a gentleman's daughter, and she should have been treated accordingly."

"Thank you, William. I shall speak to her when she returns. If only I knew of some way to repay her." She sighed. "I had thought about asking you to invite her to join us when we go to Brighton, but I do not think she is able to accept. Miss Elizabeth said she and Miss Bennet are expected to return home after the Military Ball. I shall miss her dearly."

"I understand. Perhaps the two of you can begin a correspondence when we are no longer in Town."

"I would like that. William," she paused looking hopefully into his eyes. "I was wondering…. Could you tell me something of our mother?"

Darcy smiled. "What would you like to know, sweet one?"

"I am not entirely sure. Please, just tell me anything you remember about her; what she liked or even something special the two of you did together."

"Well, I do remember she loved … flowers." He took another rose from the vase and, after breaking off the stem, carefully positioned the flower in Georgiana's hair. "Very pretty," he commented, causing her to smile.

"During the warmer months, Mama enjoyed seeing fresh flowers in many of the rooms at Pemberley and often did many of the arrangements herself. Then in the late summer and early autumn, she requested a variety of garden flowers be dried for her use when the weather turned colder.

"And since the conservatory was one of her favourite rooms, we often enjoyed afternoon tea or a light luncheon there. Afterwards, I would sit at her feet while she read stories." Darcy smiled in reflection. "When it was too cold to venture outside, she often said spending time in the conservatory warmed her heart and gave her a feeling of contentment."

"How lovely."

"Before you were born, I regularly accompanied Mama when she went out riding or took long walks about the grounds. Our mother loved nature and always carried a journal with her where she would sketch and make notes about her findings. As a young boy, Mama spent many hours making sure I learned as much as I could about the great variety of vegetation and animal life found about our grounds. When I was older, she also allowed me to collect insects and small creatures as well, and we spent hours studying them in the nature room."

"The nature room?" she questioned.

From Georgiana's bewildered look, Darcy knew his sister had no recollection of that special place. When she was but a small child, he often took her there and allowed her to touch the leaves of various plants while prompting her to say their names. She had favoured the delicate flowers which were in bloom, and it was not unusual for him to pluck one for her hair, just as he had done minutes ago.

"The nature room was a kind of greenhouse where Mama propagated her plants and where I kept my collection boxes. Sadly, Father insisted it be locked up after her death, and to this day, it has never been reopened." Darcy tried not to show his displeasure and continued by saying, "Then again, I do believe he stored all of her journals in the library at Pemberley. How would you like to look for them when we are again in residence?"

"I would like to very much."

"Perhaps we shall make a day of it. Now, where was I? Ah, if you remember her portraits, our mother was very elegant. She was tall and slim like you and wore the loveliest of gowns. A subtle scent of flowers hung about her, and I could always tell when she entered a room. Sometimes she wore lavender like Miss Elizabeth. At other times, she chose to wear rosewater or the gardenia scent from the bushes in the conservatory." He smiled again. "Green was one of Mama's favourite colours since it reminded her of the rich pine forest and represented new life for our lands."

Remembering a funny incident, Darcy let out a chuckle. "Once, when Father was gone from the house, Mama did something quite out of the ordinary."

"She did?" Georgiana eagerly listened, captivated by all he said.

"Are you a good secret-keeper, my little sister?" he teased.

"You know I am. William, please, *do* tell me," she pleaded like a small child.

"Very well. This particular adventure happened one day in early June when Father was away at Matlock. I was but ten at the time, the year before you were born. After our sister, Amelia, died, Mama suffered for many months, not only physically but emotionally. Yet, on this particular day, it seemed she no longer felt ill. She said it was to be *our special day* and that we would picnic down by the pond to celebrate.

"I remember she wore a simple muslin dress beneath a long white apron such as one the serving girls might wear. It was unusual for I had never seen her dressed in this type of attire. When we arrived at the pond, I saw the area had been prepared by the servants, and everything was in place for our picnic. There we spent much of the afternoon sketching and discussing some of the specimens which I found near the water's edge.

"We had almost finished for the day when Mama made an unusual request." Leaning closer to Georgiana and nearly whispering, he continued in all seriousness. "Georgie, Mama told me that she wished to learn how to *fish*, and she insisted *I* would be the one to teach her."

Georgiana burst into giggles at this revelation. "Did she really ask it of you?"

"She most certainly did, and I can still hear her laughter in my mind when she tried to bait the worm on the hook with very little success."

Shaking her head, Georgiana's hands flew to her mouth in an effort to suppress more giggles. "Oh, William! I do not think I could do it." She crinkled her nose and shook her head in protest.

"No? Though our Father would *not* approve, could it be I have neglected your education?"

"I think not, William. I would *never* care to touch a worm, though I do wish to know if Mama caught any fish."

"I hope you are not disappointed for I must tell you neither of us caught a single fish on that particular day. Fishing is a sport for the *very patient* as well as the *very quiet,* and I do believe the two of us scared nearly every fish away from our lines with all of our chatter." Darcy could not help but chuckle again when he finished his telling.

"Thank you, William. Your story was perfect. I wonder..... I wonder if I might tell you of ... of my dream."

"Your dream?"

"Yes, when I was most unwell, I dreamed of Mama."

Recalling what Elizabeth had told him, Darcy became sombre. "Please go ahead. I am honoured you wish to share your dream with me."

Georgiana spoke deliberately, attempting to relate all she remembered. "Brother, when I was fevered and felt the worst, I dreamed Mama was yet alive. She was with me in my room and sang the most beautiful song. Mama told me I was her precious child and that she loved me more than I could ever imagine." Watching the tears well up in her eyes, Darcy leaned closer and held her hand.

"William, she was so very lovely, and when she held me in her arms, I knew I was safe. I know Miss Elizabeth was in my room and perhaps I became confused, but at the time, it seemed as though Mama *was* there. And because of what happened, she remains with me ... here." Georgiana's free hand trembled as she lifted it and touched her breast. Managing to check his own emotions, Darcy took his handkerchief from his pocket and gently blotted the tears which had slipped down her cheeks.

"I am not quite sure how to say it, but after my dream, something in me has changed. While I have not completely thought it through, I find myself wanting to try harder. I *do* want to feel better, and I ... I think I can. Does this make any sense?" she asked.

"Georgiana, dearest, you make perfect sense. I love you so very much," he said embracing her.

"William, I have been considering something else." She pulled back to address him. "If you approve, I would like to assist with the tenant visits when we return to Pemberley. Miss Elizabeth told me she started making visits for her father when she was my age and feels sure my assistance would be welcomed."

To Darcy's amazement, here was yet another positive step in his sister's recovery which was inspired by Elizabeth. "If this is what you wish, I shall gladly support your efforts. You will bring much joy back into our estate by participating in an activity which our Mother loved so well. If you like, I shall ask Mrs. Reynolds to prepare a detailed list of our tenant families and their immediate needs for you to become familiar with while we are yet in Town."

Looking relieved, Georgiana smiled, "I would like that."

"Very good. Now, I understand Mrs. Gardiner offered her assistance to Miss Elizabeth during my absence and plans to visit you this afternoon. I think it would be best if you rested for a time. Shall I ring for your maid?"

"Yes, thank you. I am feeling a little tired."

Darcy kissed her on the forehead, rang for Rebecca, and departed the room. Heading down the hall and towards the study, he marvelled at the conversation he and Georgiana had just shared. Even though his sister had been ill, she had made such remarkable progress. *Elizabeth, how am I ever to repay your kindness? You came here, into my home, and found it within yourself to love and care for Georgiana while I was gone. I find you have not only touched her heart, but you have touched mine, and I shall be forever grateful.*

~ ♪ ~

Wednesday, 3 July 1811
Three days later

At Georgiana's request, it was agreed that Elizabeth would not be expected to return home until later in the week. With Mrs. Annesley currently in Kent, Mrs. Gardiner suggested that her personal maid, Sophia, be allowed to assist Elizabeth and serve as chaperone in her absence. Darcy readily agreed.

Each morning, Elizabeth would begin her day in Georgiana's room where the two women talked and broke their fasts together. From there, they moved into the sitting room and were joined by Rebecca and Sophia for several hours of sewing. Georgiana's newly-found enthusiasm for the tenant visits had prompted them to make items which would be taken back to Pemberley for that purpose.

Today, however, the activity included sewing of a different nature. Earlier, a parcel arrived from Mrs. Gardiner containing Elizabeth's new gown for the Military Ball. Her aunt had promised both Elizabeth and Jane new dresses in gratitude for all of the time they had devoted to the hospital charity. Once the fabric was selected from her husband's finest wares, Mrs. Gardiner sent the cloth on to her dressmaker, where Sophia's sister worked as a seamstress. There the women chose the patterns and the fabric was cut. After the dresses were basted together, they were sent back to the Gardiners' residence for Sophia to fit and finish stitching.

Intending to add a more personal touch to her gown, Elizabeth had begun to make small peach and creamy white flowers from silk ribbons. Wanting to help, Georgiana asked Elizabeth to show her how it was done. Once Sophia finished weaving a delicate green ribbon into the lace edges in the fabric of the lower skirt, she would begin applying the flowers to the dress.

As the women continued to work, Georgiana retrieved a dark green velvet pouch from the bottom of her sewing box. Carefully releasing the ribbons which held it shut, she smiled broadly while pouring some of the contents into her hand and holding it up for her friend to see.

"Elizabeth, do you not think these pearls would look lovely in the centre of the flowers and that the glass beads would add sparkle to the lower skirt? I can imagine your dress shimmering in the candlelight as you dance across the floor at the ball."

Gently fingering several of the tiny pearls and emerald beads, Elizabeth smiled. "Georgiana, these are exquisite. You are far too generous. I do not think I could accept them."

Ignoring Elizabeth's protest, Georgiana continued, "I have had them for many years and as you can see, they have yet to be used. Mrs. Reynolds took them from one of my mother's older gowns. When we add them to *your* gown, you will surely look like a princess."

"Oh, my," Elizabeth chuckled. "I do not need to look like a princess for the Military Ball. Why, with all your aunt is requiring of me, it is unlikely I shall even have time to dance."

"But you *must* dance! I shall tell William to ask you. Even though he is not particularly fond of dancing, I am sure he will take great pleasure once he sees you in this lovely dress." Her comments caused Elizabeth to blush.

"Why, it would be quite a shame to waste such an elegant gown on my aunt's errands. Please, please may I share these few treasures with you? You have been so kind to me, and I have done nothing in return."

"My dear friend, the only thing I shall ever need in return is to see you happy and well. Truly, it is enough." Georgiana looked at Elizabeth with such hope and expectation that there was little point in refusing her.

"Well, if you absolutely insist, I *may* be persuaded." She smiled, allowing Georgiana to have her way. Between the two friends and their maids, Elizabeth's dress received full attention and, over the next few days, turned out to be grander than what Elizabeth had first envisioned.

~ ♫ ~

Thursday, 4 July 1811
The next day

For the most part, Darcy did not attend the women during the morning hours, yet whenever he heard their laughter and chatter coming from Georgiana's rooms, he felt content. As the week progressed, his sister was growing stronger and more positive. She was happy and his heart warmed, knowing Elizabeth's companionship was exactly what his sister needed in her life.

Much to his own delight, after visiting each afternoon with his two favourite women, Elizabeth joined him for a walk in the garden while Georgiana napped. Often they would sit in the arbour and discuss a book, or they might simply speak of things which held their interest. On this particular afternoon, a sudden shower forced the couple to abandon their usual routine and seek amusement in the library.

Each time Elizabeth ventured into this room, she remained in awe of Darcy's collection. Today, she had been reading one of his books on farming techniques and surprised him by asking, "Mr. Darcy, with all of the responsibility and work your vast estate entails, I wonder ... are you happy being a landowner?"

Puzzled by her question, he replied, "Did you say happy?"

"Forgive me if my question was too personal." She fingered the edges of the book. "I was thinking of my father. As you know, we reside on a small estate in *Hertfordshire*." She arched a brow, reminiscent of their first meeting at the bookshop when they exchanged their watchwords.

"Yes, I remember." He smiled. "In general, I suppose I have never assigned the attribute of *happiness* to what I do. Of course, I do experience great satisfaction when I see that my tenants are making progress and their lands are thriving. Why do you ask?"

"Oh.... I guess I was just curious. I find this book reminds me a little of Papa. In truth, I do not think he enjoys being a country squire."

Not sure what to make of what Elizabeth had just said he approached her to see what book she was reading. "Miss Elizabeth, is this not one of my books on crop rotation?"

Elizabeth looked to Darcy with a teasing smile. "Yes, sir, it is." Then sitting taller, she continued, "Did I not tell you when assisting my father he has often regarded me as he would a son?"

Again he smiled. "I do distinctly recollect you giving me that *pertinent* bit of information. Miss Elizabeth, you will never cease to amaze me. I had no idea you had any knowledge of this type of farming procedure." Never had he imagined having this discussion with a young woman, let alone Elizabeth.

"While assisting my father, I have been privy to his various agricultural journals and have tried to encourage the implementation of innovative practices which might increase our modest yields. I simply cannot understand why he is resistant to change when he is so knowledgeable." She shrugged and returned the book to the table where she found it. "Perhaps it is because our property is entailed to my cousin Collins."

Puzzled by her statement, Darcy wondered how Mr. Bennet could not act responsibly. With the Bennet estate being entailed, it would have been prudent for Elizabeth's father to take every opportunity to improve his yields and provide more suitable dowries for his daughters.

Having observed a slight scowl on Darcy's face, Elizabeth decidedly changed the subject and reminded the gentleman of his promise to show her his collection of first edition Shakespearean works. Choosing one of the bard's comedies, for the next hour they took turns reading aloud while waiting for Georgiana to awaken from her nap.

~ ♫ ~

Later in the evening, Darcy sat behind the large mahogany desk in his study, attempting to look over several documents which needed his attention, including an update on the tenant dispute from Mr. Clarke. While he was pleased to know his judgements had proved sound, he found it difficult to give the letter his full attention. The earlier discussion he had with Elizabeth concerning her father proved troubling.

Mr. Bennet, I cannot understand why you did not make a greater effort to provide for your wife and daughters. It is not as though you were uneducated. Oxford is an excellent university and should have served you well. Surely you did not let the entailment discourage you, as Elizabeth implied.

Two days prior, Darcy had paid a visit to Mr. Gardiner at his residence in order to discuss his concerns over Elizabeth's safety when doing her uncle's bidding. While he knew of the man's reputation as a well-respected tradesman, he had approached their meeting with reservations. Unsure how Mr. Gardiner would view his interference when it came to Elizabeth, Darcy had hoped his apprehensions would not be dismissed, as they had been with Colonel Fitzwilliam and his uncle.

Much to his relief, Mr. Gardiner was receptive to his concerns and assured Darcy he would not take the information lightly. In speaking with the man, Darcy found Elizabeth's uncle had a keen mind. His manner was engaging and being one of the leading business persons in the trade community, Darcy was intrigued by the man's vast knowledge of investment. Quickly finding himself in deep discussion, he had stayed much longer than he had planned for their initial interview. Even so, upon reflection, Darcy wished he had taken a few minutes longer to enquire of Elizabeth's father. Although it was not his place to ask, he wondered if Mr. Gardiner's insight would have satisfied his curiosity about the man.

Pushing his papers aside, Darcy picked up his aunt's missive, which had arrived earlier in the day. Much to his displeasure, Lady Matlock intended to visit on the morrow. Knowing he could not let her behaviour towards Elizabeth or the abhorrent role played by Mr. Purdy in Georgiana's treatment be ignored, he was prepared for the inevitable. Crumpling the paper, he tossed it in the fireplace and proceeded to pour a glass of brandy.

Opening one of the side drawers to his desk, he reached for Elizabeth's ribbon of white lace. Wrapping it around his fingers, he whispered, "In less than two days, you will be gone. How shall I manage? You have cared for Georgiana and have brought so much joy into my life. I know in my heart that you belong with us. Yet how can this be without alienating my relations?" He sighed, tucking the lace into his breast pocket. He would have to be patient as he sought to find a solution to his dilemma. Darcy placed the glass on his desk and went up to bed.

CHAPTER ELEVEN

FAMILY TIES

Darcy House
Friday, 5 July 1811

*T*rue to her word, Lady Matlock arrived in the late morning with the intent of paying Georgiana a visit. Considering her niece's health had improved, she was surprised to find Elizabeth still in residence. Therefore, upon leaving Georgiana's suite, Her Ladyship went directly to Darcy's study with the intention of offering her unsolicited counsel.

"Fitzwilliam, it is a pleasure to see you." Lady Matlock held out her hand for her nephew to take. In doing so, he escorted her to a comfortable chair, though he remained standing.

"Thank you," he replied with reserve.

"I was pleased to see Georgiana doing so well. My niece was gravely ill the last time I saw her. I must say, had I not insisted on Mr. Purdy attending her, I am not sure how she would have fared."

"Aunt, I appreciate your attentiveness in my absence. Nevertheless, I would like to know why you dismissed my family physician and replaced him with your own. In the past, have I not made myself clear with regards to Mr. Purdy?" She stiffened in response.

"It was wrong of you to disregard my wishes. *You* may have confidence in his procedures, but I do *not* share your conviction." Darcy's displeasure only increased as he continued to speak. "I was present at my mother's bedside until the end and was privy to what went on when you and Father brought that man up from London. Aunt, I promise you, your Mr. Purdy will *never again* set foot in this house. I forbid it."

"Fitzwilliam, I do not appreciate your speaking to me in such a manner. Surely you must realise your mother's infirmity was nearly beyond hope by the time we brought Mr. Purdy to Pemberley."

"As I was well aware! I may not yet have been sixteen, but I was old enough to comprehend how my mother suffered needlessly at his hands during her final days."

"I beg to differ! Mr. Purdy was knowledgeable of the best procedures and medicines for her condition, and he did everything within his power to help my poor sister. In Georgiana's case, certainly you cannot deny she improved under his care?"

"Aunt." He momentarily closed his eyes and took a breath in an effort to control his temper. "In my opinion, my sister has improved under the care and devotion of Miss Elizabeth Bennet and none other. Having interviewed Mrs. Troutman, I know from every quarter what went on during my absence. Considering all she did for Georgiana, I find it deplorable that Miss Elizabeth was treated with condescension and disrespect by one of my nearest relations."

"Fitzwilliam, as much as I admire the young woman's abilities, Miss Elizabeth Bennet is neither related to our family nor is she employed by you. Considering such, I thought it was highly inappropriate for her to be attending Georgiana. Nephew, I hold nothing against Miss Elizabeth and have the greatest respect for her aunt. Yet, in all of my dealings with Mrs. Gardiner, neither of us has *ever* crossed the boundaries of propriety with regard to our prospective positions in life.

"Frankly, I am surprised you have allowed the woman to continue her stay. With your return and Mrs. Annesley elsewhere, there is not even a proper chaperone for the young lady. If you insist on keeping

Miss Bennet here for Georgiana's benefit, why do you not simply hire her on as a paid companion?"

"A paid companion!" he bellowed. "Aunt Eleanor, I realise Miss Elizabeth Bennet is not of our sphere, but she *is* a gentleman's daughter, and I would *never* dream of insulting her with such a request. She is currently a guest in my home, and as long as my sister wishes it, I shall not discourage their friendship. Moreover, the very day I returned, Mrs. Gardiner visited here and left her personal maid to wait on Miss Elizabeth and serve as a chaperone. Apparently, you failed to notice one additional person when you visited Georgiana this morning."

"Fitzwilliam, I would hardly call a lady's maid a proper chaperone."

"Enough! Aunt, your concern is noted, but at this juncture, I have found nothing objectionable about Miss Elizabeth's presence, and I shall be the one who decides what is appropriate or not in my own household. Georgiana has been my responsibility since the death of our father, and I shall continue to see to her welfare without this type of interference.

"Now, if you will excuse me, I have some pressing business to attend to. Please allow me to show you to your carriage." Darcy walked to the door and held it open for her convenience.

Quickly rising and smoothing her skirts in agitation, Lady Matlock angrily responded. "Very well, Nephew, I can tell when my words have fallen on deaf ears. You may think this conversation is over, but my concerns shall not be so easily dismissed. I fully intend to discuss this matter with His Lordship."

Haughtily passing through the door, she continued, "You need not show me out. When Georgiana is feeling better and your humour has improved, I shall expect to see the two of you for tea. Good day, Fitzwilliam."

~ ♫ ~

Darcy did not leave his study until it was time to join Elizabeth and Georgiana for fear of inflicting his foul mood on the women.

Even then, he was unusually quiet, choosing to listen rather than be an active participant in the conversation. Not until his afternoon walk with Elizabeth, was Darcy able to dispel the gloom left by his aunt's visit.

Later, both women were to join Darcy in the smaller dining room for a relaxing meal since this was the first day Georgiana felt strong enough to leave her chambers. Darcy asked his cook to prepare some of his sister's favourite dishes and insisted the room be decorated with fresh flowers to honour her. Shortly before joining the women, Darcy was greeted by Colonel Fitzwilliam, who walked into Darcy's study unannounced.

"Richard, I half expected you to come by. Having seen your mother earlier today, may I assume she has sent you on a fool's errand in the hope of talking some sense into me?"

"So it would seem," he chuckled. "In truth, when I learned Miss Elizabeth had been residing here for nearly two weeks, I was more interested in coming to satisfy my own curiosity."

"In that case, you will be disappointed for there is little to discover. You already know Georgiana was extremely ill and sent for Miss Elizabeth who was kind enough to attend her during my absence. Later, she agreed to stay on for a few more days while Georgie continued to recover. Much to your mother's objections, my sister has made remarkable improvement under Miss Elizabeth's care, and there is little more to offer. By the way, dinner is about to be served. May I assume you intend to join us this evening?"

He grinned. "You know me only too well, Cousin."

"Good. Georgiana will be pleased. Shall we?" He gestured to the door.

"Why, yes, thank you!"

~ ♫ ~

After greeting the women, Colonel Fitzwilliam was happy to give his undivided attention to his young cousin while they waited for dinner to be served. To his astonishment, she was eager to take up a conversation detailing her time with Elizabeth, and her plans to visit the tenants upon returning to Pemberley. Despite having been ill, he found Georgiana to be more amiable than she had been in months. Similarly affected was his normally reserved cousin.

Following dinner, the little party agreed to remove to the music room for a short time. Knowing Georgiana would not feel strong enough to play, Elizabeth graciously volunteered to take up the position at the pianoforte. Before the colonel could offer to be of assistance, Darcy quickly rose to the occasion and took a seat by her side offering to turn pages. Feeling playful, Elizabeth chose a lively song which had everyone chuckling throughout.

When love is kind, cheerful and free,
Love's sure to find welcome from me.
But when love brings heartache and pang,
Tears and such things, love may go hang....

Thomas Moore 1779-1852

Sitting next to Georgiana on the sofa, the colonel could not help but comment on his observation of Darcy. "Might I enquire what has happened to my taciturn cousin? I swear I have never known him to be so at ease when in the company of a beautiful woman."

Trying not to giggle, Georgiana replied, "Richard, William has been quite altered since he returned from Pemberley." She whispered, "I … I think it is Miss Elizabeth's doing. She has a way of drawing him out, and whenever she is with the two of us, we cannot help but enjoy ourselves."

"I see." The colonel nodded, permitting a broad smile to curl his lips.

After finishing, Elizabeth turned to Darcy and teasingly stated, "Now it is your turn. Will you not favour us with a song?"

"Forgive me, Miss Elizabeth." Obviously surprised by her mandate, he quickly rose and politely replied, "I do not sing."

Unwilling to accept his answer, she gave him a whimsical look and purposely drawled, "You *do not* sing or *will not* sing?"

"Do *not* sing." His answer was deliberate, causing her to look at him for a moment as though puzzled by something.

"Pray, Georgiana, do tell me. Does your brother have some defect which is preventing him from singing? Obviously, his speaking voice is deep and resonant, but could it be his singing voice is akin to one of the amphibious creatures which serenaded me from the garden pond this afternoon?" Georgiana covered her mouth in an effort to suppress her giggles while the colonel laughed so hard he had to wipe the tears from his eyes.

"Miss Bennet." Darcy arched a brow and looked at her with such intensity he caused her to blush. Clearing his throat, he proudly stated, "It appears I must preserve my reputation and prove I have *no defect* whatsoever." Taking on an air of superiority, he decidedly chose several pages from the top of the pianoforte and handed them to her without hesitation. "If you will be so kind as to make your selection from these sheets of music, I shall begin."

"As you wish, Mr. Darcy." She arched a brow in return. "All the same, if you have no objection, I shall reserve judgement until I have heard the song sung in its entirety." She smiled sweetly and proceeded to make her choice.

Following a simple introduction, Darcy began singing a traditional Scottish Ballad, *Barbara Allen.* Elizabeth had always found Darcy's speaking voice very pleasant, but in this instance, she was not prepared for the richness of his deep baritone as he sang through the first verse with much feeling. Before long, she joined him in harmony, and the two continued on together until the end of the song. Upon finishing, Elizabeth graciously conceded that Darcy did indeed exceed her expectations and thanked him for indulging her fancy.

In Scarlett Town, where I was born,
There was a fair maid dwellin'
Made every youth cry "Well-a-day!"
Her name was Barbara Allen....

Traditional Scottish Ballad

Afterwards, it became apparent Georgiana was beginning to tire. At Elizabeth's suggestion, the women thanked Darcy and the colonel for an enjoyable evening and said goodnight. Following their departure, Darcy and his cousin retreated to the study for a glass of port and a little more conversation.

Once the door was closed, the colonel could not resist questioning his cousin. "Darcy, if I may, I would like to know what the deuce is going on in this house. I swear I have never seen either you or Georgiana appear with such lack of restraint as I did tonight. Surely, this cannot be the work of *Miss Elizabeth Bennet?"* he prodded.

Darcy gave him a cold stare, saying, "I have no idea what you are talking about. Shall I pour?"

"Please. But if you do not mind, brandy would be more to my liking."

"As you wish."

"Cousin, I thank you for one of the most enjoyable evenings I have had in a long, long time. You know, Mother is quite rigid when it comes to status and connections, but frankly, she has missed the mark on this one. Miss Elizabeth has been an *excellent* influence on our dear girl."

"I agree. Her enthusiasm is infectious, and she has a way of drawing Georgiana out which I find engaging." He seemed to look past the colonel as he continued, "Elizabeth treats Georgie as though she was her own sister, and I doubt I shall ever be able to repay her for all of her kindness."

Hearing Darcy use Elizabeth's Christian name, the colonel nudged Darcy on the arm, breaking his reverie. "You know, I do believe Mother has missed something else here." Darcy frowned. "In her ranting, she merely spoke of Miss Elizabeth's relationship with Georgiana. I wonder how she failed to miss *your* interest in the woman."

"Richard, I have no *interest* in Miss Elizabeth. We have merely formed a friendship during her stay and nothing more."

The colonel could not help but laugh at his cousin's assertion. "Not from what I have observed." Darcy narrowed his brows and projected a most unwelcoming glare. "Why, if my mother had observed the looks which passed between the two of you when you were singing tonight, she would have moved heaven and earth to send your Miss Elizabeth back to Hertfordshire or wherever it is she came from."

"Richard, at this point, I care nothing for your mother's opinions. I am still furious with her for inflicting that medieval relic on Georgiana during my absence. Aunt Eleanor knew of my wishes regarding Mr. Purdy, yet she went ahead and exercised her own authority by insisting he tend my sister. Where Miss Elizabeth is concerned, I shall admit to nothing, and if you do not mind, I would prefer to end this discussion."

Throwing up his hands in surrender, the colonel shook his head. "Darcy, you are beyond hope. And to think, just a few weeks ago I heard you chiding poor Bingley for taking an interest in the elder sister." Darcy pretended to ignore him. "I must say, I *do* like Miss Elizabeth. She is positively refreshing. Why, after you refused to sing, I could not believe how easily she teased you into doing so." He chuckled.

Darcy cracked a smile, saying, "You have the right of it. Her teasing is merciless. I admit this house will be quite dull when she leaves tomorrow."

"I should most heartily agree. Listen, my friend, believe me when I say I am on your side. From what I saw tonight, Miss Elizabeth suits you. Heavens! *That* is a first if there ever *was* one. Of course, I may need to call in the militia in order to preserve the peace once you break the news to Mother."

"Richard!"

"Very well, I shall desist." He threw up his hands in surrender. "As it is, I was hoping to get your opinion on a little something I have been working on as of late. Nothing serious, mind you, but I thought a fresh perspective might give me some inspiration."

"I shall be happy to assist."

~ ♫ ~

Saturday, 6 July 1811

Elizabeth woke early with the intention of making her final preparations for the trip back to Gracechurch Street. She knew it would be
hard to leave. The last few days at Darcy House had been some of her
happiest. Here, she had been treated as though she were a part of the
family and not merely a guest. She had grown to love Georgiana as a
sister and Darcy.... Darcy had become much more to her than she had
ever dreamed possible.

"I cannot help but love you," she mused aloud, allowing her
thoughts to ramble. "I want nothing more than to spend the rest of my
days with you, Fitzwilliam Darcy: to cherish you, to see to your needs,
to be your wife in every sense of the word and to be the mother of
your children." She sighed. "But what of your society, and of all it
demands? What of your relations and their expectations for you? How
can I, in good conscience, ever expect you to return more than
friendship?"

Tears began to well in her eyes when she thought of her own
family. "I know it did not set well with you when I mentioned Papa's
indifference with regards to estate matters. What will you think when
you meet all of them at the ball?" She took a handkerchief and blotted
her eyes.

"Oh, Mama, if only you were not so outspoken. This society is far
different from what you are used to. These people will *not* understand.
There has to be a way to convince Papa that he must keep you and
Kitty and Lydia under better regulation. Lady Matlock will be furious
if something should happen at the ball."

Elizabeth splashed cold water on her face and pinched her cheeks.
For now, she would put those thoughts aside and make an effort to be
joyful during her final hours with the Darcys. With her trunk packed
and her bags secure, she quickly readied herself to join her friends in
Georgiana's sitting room where they were currently breaking
their fast.

~ ♪ ~

The day had proven to be sunny and pleasant. Still, upon entering the room, Elizabeth felt a slight shiver. There sat Darcy brooding over his coffee and newspaper while Georgiana wrung her handkerchief and bordered on tears.

Smiling with reassurance at both brother and sister, Elizabeth approached Georgiana and kissed her on the cheek. "Dearest, I am not going far. Even though I cannot remain here, it does not mean I shall forget you. I shall be thinking of you every single day as I forge through *endless* pages of your aunt's directives for the Military Ball." Georgiana could not help but smile.

"And if my time permits, I promise to come for a visit. In the meantime, I believe we should not wait to begin our correspondence until we have both departed Town. When I return to my aunt's home, I shall take the earliest opportunity of sending you the first letter. Would you like that?"

"I would, very much so."

"Then it is settled. We may write every day if you like."

"I would be more than happy to provide a footman to transport your letters back and forth," Darcy offered.

"Excellent!" said Elizabeth as she clasped her hands together. "Now, since it is such a fine day, I would like to suggest that your brother accompany you out to the garden after I leave. I am sure the fresh air and sunshine will make you feel infinitely better. Do you not think so, Mr. Darcy?" Her smile was encouraging.

"I certainly do."

"Very good." Elizabeth took a sip of her tea and began spreading jam over a slice of warm bread. "And if I may be so bold," she playfully continued, "I shall suggest that the two of you take the bench *furthest* from the pond. After all, I would not want your brother to be reminded of the unjust words which I spoke when I compared him to *nature* singing in all of its glory."

Her teasing remarks caused Georgiana to giggle, while Darcy simply shook his head and said, "Miss Elizabeth, you are incorrigible."

Their small party continued on in this manner until the Darcy carriage was loaded and ready for Elizabeth and Sophia to return to Gracechurch Street. When it was finally time for her departure, Georgiana stood bravely at the door, trying not to cry, while Darcy reluctantly escorted Elizabeth down the stairs to the carriage.

Before helping her inside, he momentarily held her hand and softly spoke her Christian name as though it were a tender caress. "Elizabeth, mere words will never begin to express my gratitude for all you have done. My sister has improved in ways I cannot measure. I am forever in your debt."

"Sir, the debt has been repaid by seeing Georgiana happy and by knowing she will continue to regain her health." She smiled warmly.

"You will be missed."

"Thank you."

Ever so slowly, Darcy raised her hand to his lips and kissed it, his eyes never leaving hers. An unspoken exchange occurred between the two, and words were not needed to say what was felt in their hearts. Their feelings had long transcended that of friendship for Fitzwilliam Darcy and Elizabeth Bennet were in love.

CHAPTER TWELVE

PATIENCE

Darcy House
Wednesday, 9 July 1811

The sound of floorboards creaking followed Darcy as he energetically paced back and forth across the length of his private domain. "Four days! Four very long days, and I have yet to see you, Elizabeth." Stopping to look at the delicate white lace ribbon which had seemingly become attached to his fingertips, he methodically twirled it over and over as he spoke with abandon. "My love, I know not how I shall endure it."

With Elizabeth no longer under his roof, Darcy wanted nothing more than to go directly to her uncle and make his wishes known. During her absence, it seemed as though his days were meaningless and his nights were endless. Feeling like a schoolboy who might dwell on any little trifle, the highlight of each day had become afternoon tea when his sister happily shared her most recent letter from her new correspondent. Checking his pocket watch, he could see it was nearly time to join her. Attempting to suppress his frustration, Darcy quickly straightened his jacket and went directly to Georgiana's sitting room.

"William," Georgiana cheerfully addressed him. "Please sit down. Shall I pour?"

"Yes, thank you."

"Cook has sent up some lovely biscuits, and Elizabeth's letter arrived not too long ago. Would you care for me to read it now?"

"By all means," he smiled.

"My dearest friend,

"I cannot begin to tell you how happy I am to learn of your continued improvement and look forward to seeing you once again. As it turns out, Jane and I shall not be able to call this week as we had originally planned. With the Military Ball so close at hand, the demands placed on our time have only increased with each passing day."

"Oh dear," Georgiana fretted. "I was hoping to show the sisters my new gown for the ball." Darcy could not help but frown. He, too, was hoping to see Elizabeth, if only to hear her laughter and to have her smile at him.

"Much to our disappointment, even next Tuesday's concert has been cancelled. Dear Georgiana, please believe me when I say I would much rather forgo a few of our committee meetings and enjoy an afternoon with you and your brother. Nevertheless, as my aunt has reminded us, our efforts have a higher purpose, and therefore, we must persevere. That being said, I am pleased to report the subscriptions for the ball have exceeded our expectations, and private donations continue to come forth.

"In truth, our preparations for the ball would be much simpler if we merely had but one ballroom to contend with. Alas, it is not to be. Lady Matlock has deemed the more affluent patrons, along with the landed gentry, military officers, and those who have given large donations, will have their own accommodations, while the remaining guests are to gather in another room.

"For the better part of the last two days I have been primarily occupied with overseeing the final preparations for the tea. In some respects, this has been quite pleasant, and I cannot help but compliment Lady Matlock with her own preparations. I was particularly impressed with the centrepiece she chose for the main dining area: an elaborate fountain with cherubs spouting forth plumes of water into a large receptacle where small goldfish are to swim. The workings of the fountain, concealed by potted plants and decorative vines, will be surrounded by several tables where the food is to be served."

Georgiana began to giggle with delight. "William, I cannot imagine a fountain with live fish being displayed inside of a building, let alone at a ball. Have you ever heard of such a thing?"

"I assure you, I have not. It sounds like something the Prince Regent would exhibit at one of his extravagant affairs."

"In addition, a smaller fountain spouting mulled sweet wine will be situated on the beverage table. Then, during the tea, French rolls and sweet breads will be served with a generous assortment of cold meats and smoked fish on large silver trays. Moreover, in the midst of all these trays, a variety of cheeses and roasted nuts will be displayed next to tiers of fresh pineapple, oranges, pomegranates, berries and cream."

"Oh, William, I love pineapple!"

"You do?" He puzzled at this comment.

"Yes, the Ellingtons have it growing in their orangery in Sussex. Lady Lilyan insisted I try it when I was lately their guest. I wonder if we might be able to grow it in our orangery at Pemberley."

"It is not a fruit I particularly care for, but since you have asked, I shall have Mr. Clarke make an inquiry as to its suitability."

"Thank you."

"Although I shall not attempt to describe the rest of the food in detail, I

would like to tell you Jane and I were allowed to sample several of the desserts yesterday afternoon. I admit I have never seen or tasted anything more delicious. I think you will particularly enjoy the pretty little sugar moulds which are crafted into delicate flowers and small animals. They are to be served in elegant porcelain cups filled with the most exquisite ices and creams from Gunter's. While there are many flavours to choose from, Jane and I were very pleased with the Pistachio and Barberry.

"As for the decorations and the musicians, I shall save that informa-tion for my next letter. Then again, if I give away too many of our secrets, you will no longer be surprised when you attend.

"For now, I shall bring this letter to a close. Please give my sincerest regards to your brother and tell him I have missed our conversations. I shall look forward to your next post, my dear friend.

"Lovingly,
Elizabeth Bennet"

Georgiana carefully folded the letter saying, "William, the final preparations for the ball sound lovely. But I do worry for Elizabeth and Miss Bennet. Our aunt is very demanding."

"She certainly is. I, too, am concerned." Knowing how his aunt had treated Elizabeth when she stayed at his home, he suspected her handling of both sisters was little better during the final days preceding the ball. *Dearest Elizabeth, if only I could see you. There is so much I wish to say. For now, I have no choice but to embrace patience.*

~ ♫ ~

Gracechurch Street

With her return to the Gardiner residence, Elizabeth found she had very little time to herself. In addition to preparing for the arrival of her own family, Lady Matlock insisted she manage nearly every aspect of the final arrangements for the ball. With the added stress, the memories of her time at Darcy House had become more precious than ever, giving her solace.

Elizabeth was pleased that she and Georgiana had been able to keep up their correspondence, and she looked forward to reading her missives upon returning home each day. On one day, her friend's letter was accompanied by a small book. Since Georgiana had made no mention of it, Elizabeth instinctively knew it was from Darcy. She giggled as she imagined him discreetly giving the book to the footman just before the carriage departed for Gracechurch Street. This particular book was the same collection of Thomas Moore's poetry which she had seen in the library at Darcy House.

Opening it, she ran her fingers across the bookplate displaying the Darcy crest. Noting he had signed his name in a very well-ordered hand, she read aloud, "Fitzwilliam Darcy." Smiling to herself, she clutched the precious book to her breast and murmured, "William." The little book soon became a secret treasure which fit nicely in her pocket and accompanied her wherever she went.

Girlish as it was, Elizabeth could not help but tuck the book safely beneath her pillow before she retired. And each night, when she did so, she remembered how he looked at her when they last parted. The sound of his voice as he lovingly said her name and told her she would be missed was forever imprinted in her mind. Could there be any doubt he loved her? No. Could he defy convention and act upon that love? She could not say.

~ ♫ ~

Monday, 15 July 1811
The following week

The Monday before the Military Ball brought the anticipated arrival of the Bennet, Philips and Lucas families to London. Since the Gardiners' house was not large enough to comfortably accommodate more guests than Jane and Elizabeth, it had been arranged for Kitty and Lydia to stay with their friend Maria Lucas and her family while Mr. and Mrs. Bennet and Mary would reside with a cousin of Mr. and Mrs. Philips. More than six months had passed since Elizabeth and Jane were last at Longbourn, and they were eager to see their friends and relations. Elizabeth hoped her fears regarding her family would not come to fruition and that being in Town would inspire them to use more discretion when it came to their behaviour.

With the arrival of the Bennet carriage, Elizabeth quickly realised her wishes were for naught. Lydia was the first to exit the carriage, and when she spoke, she arrogantly posed as though she expected the entire neighbourhood to take notice of her.

"Lizzy! Jane!" shouted Lydia. "It has been far too long!" The sisters briefly kissed her, not being allowed to say much more than a simple greeting while Lydia continued to chatter. "The trip was positively horrid! Was it not, Kitty?"

"Yes, we were all very...."

"It was *most* uncomfortable being confined in such a crowded space," Lydia interrupted. "The air was damp, and the drizzle was infuriating. Why, my curls have all but come undone and it will take forever to repair them once we go inside. But never mind about that. Lizzy, have I not grown taller since January?" She held her head high waiting for Elizabeth to acknowledge her declaration.

"Yes, I do believe you are a little taller."

"Jane, Mama says I shall be as tall as you by the end of the summer and that I shall have more beaux than either you or Lizzy did when you were my age." They all watched as Lydia twirled in place, boisterously laughing all the while. "AND though Mary is not interested, Mama says she will take *me and Kitty* to the dress makers while we are in Town. If you are not too busy with Lady ... what was her name again? Oh, never mind. If you are not too busy, you can both come with us. It will be such fun! With the militia being quartered in Meryton, Mama says Kitty and I shall have new gowns to wear to *all* of the Assemblies so that we might catch good husbands. Oh, if *only* I were Mary King."

"Mary King?" Elizabeth and Jane looked at her with curiosity.

"La, have you not heard? Why, Mary King has inherited TEN THOUSAND pounds. Can you believe it? I dare say I could buy every dress on Bond Street if I but had *her* money. She is such an unpleasant little thing and does *not* deserve any of it."

"Lydia, that is unkind," Jane chided.

"It is true, is it not, Kitty?"

"Yes, she…"

"Since Mary King has inherited, I dare say she hardly speaks with any of us now and is always walking around with her nose in the air." Lydia did a mocking imitation causing Kitty to laugh and Elizabeth and Jane to frown.

"I cannot believe her uncle is to bring her to the ball," continued Lydia. "Well, it is of no consequence. All of the officers should rather dance with me in any case. If *only* I could have come *here* to purchase my gown. As it was, I had to have it made in Meryton. Sometimes Papa is so mean. I tell you if he changes his mind and I do *not* get at least *one* new gown for the Assemblies, I shall surely die."

"As will I," echoed Kitty.

Jane and Lizzy looked at each other with dismay. "Perhaps Aunt Gardiner will be able to take you to one of Uncle's warehouses to choose fabric if she has the time," suggested Elizabeth.

"Whatever are you talking about!" exclaimed Mrs. Bennet who had overheard part of their conversation. "One of your uncle's warehouses indeed! I shall shop on Bond Street and no other. Your father has purposely tried to vex me on that point, but where the futures of my girls are at stake, I am determined to prevail." Jane and Elizabeth kissed their mother in greeting and then proceeded to welcome Mary and their father. Moments later, Mrs. Gardiner graciously invited everyone to come into the house.

"My dears, it is good to see you," said Mr. Bennet. Elizabeth and Jane each kissed their father on the cheek and then took one of his arms as the family ambled up the stairs and into the vestibule.

"The two of you were sorely missed," he remarked, handing his travelling coat to a servant. "I dare say, I have not had one moment of peace or heard one sensible thought spoken in our house or in the carriage for that matter since the day the two of you left Longbourn."

"Papa, we have missed you, too," said Elizabeth. "We shall have a nice visit once you have rested for a bit."

~ ♫ ~

After the family had refreshed themselves, they all assembled in the parlour for tea and biscuits. There they were to wait until dinner was ready to be served. Before the conversation had progressed beyond simple pleasantries, Mrs. Bennet began to speak in earnest.

"My dear sister, you have no idea what my poor nerves have suffered today. The journey here was tiresome, and we were all so very cramped in one carriage. I had insisted Mr. Bennet secure a larger vehicle for our trip, but he refused, as is often his wont. And with the roads being so poor, it is a wonder we did not break an axle or have something worse befall us. I tell you, sister, I am *thoroughly exhausted.*"

"I am sorry to hear it," spoke Mrs. Gardiner. "Would you care to rest upstairs for a time?"

"Thank you, I shall rest a little later. First, I must speak with Jane." Mrs. Bennet waved her handkerchief for Jane to come closer.

"My *dearest* girl, it is most urgent we speak of Mr. Bingley before another minute has passed." Her voice became high pitched with excitement. "A man who is in possession of FIVE THOUSAND a year must *not* be overlooked! I always did say that you could not be so beautiful for nothing! I predict he will give you a very large allowance once you are married. Just think of the pin money and jewels you will have and the carriages…. Oh my, I shall go completely distracted."

"Mama," interrupted Lizzy, attempting to relieve Jane's discomfiture. "How can you talk on about Mr. Bingley in this manner? Jane has had little opportunity to be in his company. He has never called on her, and he certainly has not made a declaration."

"Oh, never you mind, Miss Lizzy. It makes no difference. The fact is Mr. Bingley's own sisters invited our dear Jane to their home for the purpose of getting to know her and learn more of our neighbourhood. Is that not sufficient encouragement?" Jane was obviously embarrassed by her mother's continued effusions for the colour rose in her cheeks, and she did not utter a single word.

"Mama, we are in London which is very different from Hertfordshire," Elizabeth pressed. "Mr. Bingley is making his way in this society, and we are *not* a part of it. Since being in Town, I have seen the workings of the *ton*, and we cannot assume Mr. Bingley has singled out Jane in the manner of which you speak."

With this statement, Mrs. Bennet turned on her daughter. "Elizabeth Bennet, you are vexing me! My poor nerves cannot take your impertinence. I would prefer you leave well enough alone. When the opportunity presents itself, *I* shall attend to Jane and Mr. Bingley myself.

"Jane dear, let us sit over here so we may discuss this matter more privately and *without* your sister's interference."

"Yes, Mama." Jane dutifully obeyed.

"Papa," Elizabeth whispered. "I beg of you to intervene with Mama as well as with Lydia and Kitty. The more affluent people whom I have met while working on Lady Matlock's committee are so different from all of our acquaintances in Meryton. They are ruthless when it comes to connections and decorum. Mr. Bingley is now making his way into that sphere, and if he *does* show an interest in Jane, any interference from Mama could discourage the man."

Mr. Bennet took Elizabeth's hand and chuckled. "Now, Lizzy, you must not worry yourself over your mother's enthusiasm or even that of your younger sisters. The London elite have much better things to do than to take note of three rather silly women from Hertfordshire. Any person who cannot see past their deficiencies is not worthy of your notice. I say let them have their fun. You and Jane are gracious and have always held yourselves in good stead."

"But, Papa, surely you can see they will be...."

"Come now, Lizzy." He frowned. "Let us have no more of this talk. It has been a long day, and I would prefer to enjoy my tea in peace."

"Yes, Papa," she said, knowing the topic would need to be revisited well before the ball. Instead, father and daughter talked about what had taken place in their neighbourhood since Elizabeth's absence. To her satisfaction, Mr. Bennet also enquired about her charity work and seemed to show a particular curiosity as to what happened with Mr. Blakemore, the patient who had experienced the memory loss.

"From what we have recently heard, Mr. Blakemore is doing remarkably well although he has yet to fully regain his memory."

"I am pleased to hear it, my dear. War can be a nasty business. With my cousin Collins coming to Town, I could not help but be reminded of the poor soldier and how he assisted you in finding the man's family."

"Mr. Collins is coming here? When do you expect him? I would like to make his acquaintance and thank the man personally for all of his assistance."

"His letter states he plans to be here in two days' time and will attend the Military Ball."

"How very odd. Being a member of the clergy, it seems strange he would come to Town merely to attend a ball."

"Yes, well, there is a bit more to tell." He chuckled for a moment. "You see, his noble patroness, *the honourable Lady Catherine de Bourgh,* has deemed *Mr. Collins* should extend the olive branch to our *unfortunate* family in an attempt to make amends for the entailment on the estate. Apparently, he will be in Town seeking a new wife from amongst the women in *our* family." Peeking over the rim of his glasses, his eyes began to twinkle as he gauged her reaction.

"Papa!" Elizabeth gasped. "What are you trying to say?"

"Perhaps you would care to read his letter, my dear. It is quite lengthy, let me assure you." He took the letter from his coat pocket. "Mr. Collins should arrive in Town on Wednesday and will be returning with us to Longbourn for a fortnight."

Elizabeth eagerly took the letter and read the detailed description of his position in society and his intentions towards her family. "Oh, Papa, can he be truly serious?"

"So it would seem. And with Mr. Bingley having taken some notice of Jane, your mother is quite determined to see that Mr. Collins bestows his olive branch upon *you*." He chuckled, obviously taking delight in the absurdity of the situation.

"Oh, Papa, please do not allow her to go on so."

"Why, Lizzy, do not tell me you are going to be affronted and not partake in the fun?"

"Papa, by all indications given in this letter, Mr. Collins is in earnest. Having previously read his correspondence and now this letter, I know I could never marry such a man, and I refuse to lead him on."

He raised an eyebrow while looking in his wife's direction. "*You* may think that way, Lizzy, but your mother will *never* accept your unwillingness to do your part." Again he chuckled, causing Elizabeth to stiffen. "Come now, give me back the letter. Do not distress yourself, my dear. I am sure it will all prove to be quite a delightful diversion in the end. Cheer up." He patted her hand. "I shall not force you to marry Mr. Collins."

"Yes, Papa," she sighed, shaking her head.

"Now, let us go to dinner and enjoy the rest of the evening. Shall we?" Taking his arm, Elizabeth was unable to rally her spirits as they walked into the dining room.

CHAPTER THIRTEEN

TACTICS OF A DIFFERENT KIND

*M*r. William Collins, a young man of five and twenty, considered himself a person of distinction and good prospects. Having graduated from St. John's College at Oxford University and being recently ordained, Mr. Collins became qualified for the position of Rector with one of the most illustrious patrons in all of Kent, Lady Catherine de Bourgh of Rosings Park.

The Hunsford Parish had been without a permanent cleric for more than three months, and her Ladyship was determined to employ a Rector who could be moulded into the type of God's servant who would suit her needs. When Mr. Collins was introduced to her by a member of the ministerial board from St. John's, she knew he would be such a man.

Now, fairly established in his new position and having benefited from the many privileges of which few others could boast, Mr. Collins had become a very proud man. He was not only provided with a sound and well-maintained rectory, but he was also given a land glebe of nearly 100 acres which he could farm himself or let out for additional income. With the tithe provided by Her Ladyship's parishioners and his own economic stability, Mr. Collins was confident in his ability to please and secure a bride from amongst his Bennet cousins.

Gracechurch Street
Thursday, 18 July 1811
A few days after the arrival of the Bennet family

"Elizabeth Bennet!" Her mother's shrill voice was filled with agitation and displeasure. Mrs. Bennet had taken great pains to arrive at the Gardiner residence much earlier than was her usual wont with the intention of speaking to her second eldest. Elizabeth had been largely unavailable since her arrival, and on this particular morning, Mrs. Bennet was determined to have her say.

"You are trying my nerves. Will you not sit down and allow me to speak to you in a more civilised fashion?"

"Mama, I am so sorry, but Jane and I are about to leave."

"Lizzy, I have been in Town since Monday afternoon, and you have given me very little time to make my wishes known with regard to your future husband. This is not to be borne. Mr. Collins arrived yesterday, and you were *not* there to greet him, *nor* were you able to dine with us at dinner. How can I possibly keep your cousin interested when he has yet to meet you? Lizzy … Lizzy, are you even listening to me?" Elizabeth had been organizing her notes while Mrs. Bennet continued to talk.

Closing her satchel, she kissed her mother on the cheek and answered, "Yes, Mama, I did hear you. Again, I *am* sorry. Jane and I must leave now or we shall be late for our committee meeting. It is the last one before the Military Ball, and there is yet much to accomplish today."

"Lizzy, I forbid you to go. Her Ladyship has taken far too much of your time. Surely, she will understand my predicament. It is not easy having five unmarried daughters."

"Mama, I promise we shall return well before Sir William's dinner party. I shall meet him then. It is impossible for me to remain here and speak further when the ball is tomorrow evening."

"Very well, Lizzy, I shall expect to see you later today, and when you *do* meet Mr. Collins, it is imperative you pay him every civility. I do not know what shall become of us once your poor father meets his demise. If you do not secure Mr. Collins, I fear we shall all starve in the hedgerows. I am sure of it." Tears had begun to well in her eyes as she spoke.

"Oh, Mama, it will do you no good to become upset." Elizabeth lovingly squeezed her mother's hand. "Papa is alive and well. You should endeavour to enjoy your time in Town and not worry so. I am sorry, but Jane and I *must* take our leave now." Both girls kissed their mother and quickly departed in the coach which had been waiting for the last quarter of an hour.

In truth, Elizabeth was relieved that she was not able to stay and talk with her mother. Oh, why had she been singled out as the one daughter who was most suited for Mr. Collins's attentions? In reality, she had no intention of encouraging the man, no matter how much her mother insisted. Closing her eyes and taking a deep breath, she was startled when Jane reached over and took her hand.

"Lizzy, I am sure all will be well. Please do not allow Mama to upset you."

"Jane, you are too good. What would I do without your steady support and reassurance? You heard her. She has set her mind on Mr. Collins, and it will not be easy making my wishes known on the matter. I am grateful for the assistance our cousin gave us with Mr. Blakemore. Yet, while I have never met the man, from what little I have learned through letters, I am certain we would never suit one another."

"Surely Papa would never force you to marry him."

"No, he has told me as much. Yet, I fear he will do little to discourage Mama in the process. Please, Jane, let us speak no more of it for the present. I wish to review a few things with you before we arrive at our meeting."

The past two days had proven to be very demanding for Elizabeth as she attended to every last detail put forth by Lady Matlock. Thankfully, there was only one more day until the grand event would come to fruition. Once the Military Ball was over, it would be a pleasure to take her leave of London for a few weeks and return to Longbourn for some much needed rest. Since the majority of the preparations for the Autumn Festival were currently in place, her assistance would not be required until the beginning of September.

~ 🎵 ~

Sir William's Lodgings
Later that evening

In an attempt to bring family and a few friends together before the Military Ball, Sir William Lucas had decided to host a dinner party at his lodgings. Having been appraised by Mrs. Bennet of Mr. Bingley's presence in Town, Sir William felt it was his civic duty to invite Bingley and his sisters to his gathering. Considering the gentleman would be visiting the Meryton neighbourhood in search of a country estate, this would be the perfect opportunity to make his acquaintance. In addition, the invitation was also extended to Colonel Forster, his wife, and a few of the officers who would be in Town for the ball.

Because Elizabeth had seen little of her family and friends since their arrival in Town, she had been looking forward to spending the evening at Sir William's party. Upon greeting her dear friend Charlotte Lucas, the two women clasped hands and eagerly renewed their acquaintance.

"Charlotte, it is good to see you. I have missed our time together."

"And I have missed you." They embraced.

"Eliza, you must tell me all. In your absence, it seems both you and Jane have become a rather frequent topic of conversation in Meryton. I understand your status in society has been elevated while assisting Lady Matlock. According to your mother, at least one of you will return home with the promise of a wealthy husband."

"Oh, Charlotte...." Elizabeth chuckled. "Do not think for one minute we have accomplished anything in *that* respect. For the most part, Jane and I are treated little better than hired servants by the more affluent."

"I am surprised to hear it."

"My dear friend...." She playfully arched a brow. "You have no idea what it means to be reminded of your place in society by some of London's *finest* or subtly propositioned by their depraved husbands when those same wives are looking for their *own* amusement."

"I am heartily sorry to hear you have had to endure such treatment by those who might have been more appreciative of your efforts. It is good you can make light of your misfortunes under the circumstances." Charlotte glanced in Jane's direction and continued, "I will say, however, it appears all is not lost where Jane is concerned. Mr. Bingley gives the impression of being a very pleasant fellow and pays her a great compliment."

"Yes, I think she is quite happy with his attentions. Much to Miss Bingley's and Mrs. Hurst's chagrin, their brother seems to be taken with Jane."

"His sisters?" questioned Charlotte, wanting to know more.

"They are among some of the haughty who blatantly look down and criticise people of lesser consequence. In *their* case, I can see no justification since Uncle Gardiner has told us Mr. Bingley's fortune was made in the trade profession."

"I see. I wonder if anything will come of his notice. Jane seems rather reserved in his company. Perhaps she should do more to encourage him. It will be a great disappointment to your mother if they do not at least enter into a courtship. It seems she has been telling her closest friends an engagement between the two of them is eminent."

"Please tell me you are exaggerating! While he is clearly smitten, they have only been in each other's company but a few times, and they certainly have not formed an understanding."

"I wish I could say otherwise, and if I am not mistaken, it looks like your mother is currently forwarding her intent."

Taking note of her mother whose manner appeared to be overbearing, Elizabeth was mortified as she watched her conversing with

Mr. Bingley. "Mama," Elizabeth uttered in dismay. "Thank goodness the Darcys are not here."

"Did you say the Darcys?"

"Yes. Please excuse me for a few minutes. I shall try to dissuade Mama from her scheming before she embarrasses us all." Walking to her mother's side, Elizabeth could see the displeasure on the faces of Mr. Bingley's sisters as Mrs. Bennet vociferously conversed with their brother.

"Mr. Bingley, I understand you will be visiting Meryton in the early autumn."

"Yes, Madam, you are correct. While my plans are not set, my solicitor *is* currently making arrangements for me to view two properties in the area, possibly one more. You see, my late father fervently wished for me to take a country estate."

"What a pleasant prospect for our neighbourhood! I would like to give you a bit of my advice on that end. Let me assure you, I am quite familiar with *all* of the properties which are currently available." Bingley attempted to respond, but was interrupted by Mrs. Bennet who continued to talk.

"First, there is Purvis Lodge although I regret to say the estate is quite small and would never do for a man of *your* means. Then there is Haye-Park, which will become vacant just after Michaelmas. The house and grounds are infinitely superior to those of Purvis Lodge, and the coveys are excellent for hunting. Lastly, we have Netherfield Park, which is even more promising and is but *three miles* from Longbourn and the Bennet estate. Let me assure you, it will not disappoint, and we would be *delighted* to have you as our neighbour. Oh, do promise me you will take dinner with our family when you come to make your inquiries."

"Thank you, Mrs. Bennet. It would be my great pleasure to do so."

"Your visit in September will be very timely since my sweet Jane will be back in residence." She pointedly smiled at Jane, ignoring her uneasiness. "While there is still much to be accomplished with Lady Matlock's charity, I find I have been without my dear Jane for far too long.

166

I dare say you would not wish to miss her when you are in the neighbourhood."

"Indeed, Madam, I would not."

"As you can see, Jane is by far the prettiest of all of my daughters and has the loveliest disposition. Do you not agree, Mr. Bingley?" Bingley and Jane both blushed at Mrs. Bennet's assertions.

"Of course you do, but who would not? Sir, it was very kind of your sisters to invite Jane to dine with them so they might come to know her and enquire about the neighbourhood. With so many preparations for the ball, it is a shame she has not had the opportunity to return the favour." Mrs. Bennet took a moment to acknowledge the women with a nod of her head.

Throughout the woman's discourse, Elizabeth's hope of redirecting the conversation had been met with little success. Her mother paid her no heed and did not stop talking until she took note of the arrival of Colonel Forster and a few of his officers.

"Please forgive me, Mr. Bingley, but I must greet Colonel Forster and his party. Mrs. Forster is quite fond of my Lydia, you know, and has become her particular friend. I do hope we shall have the chance to continue our discussion later."

"Certainly, it would be my pleasure."

Elizabeth was aghast at what had just taken place. Not only had her mother succeeded in embarrassing herself and Jane, but also Mr. Bingley and his sisters. Once Mrs. Bennet excused herself, the Bingley sisters gave each other a knowing look and quickly retreated to the refreshment table where Elizabeth could not help but hear their unguarded laughter. Even though Jane continued to smile, her face had become pale and she seemed to be having some difficulty breathing. Noticing her discomfort, Bingley suggested she take a seat near a window where there was a cool breeze. Despite what had just taken place, Bingley remained constant, graciously attending to Jane's needs.

"Eliza, I see your intervention was to no avail. It took a group of red coats to divert your mother's attention away from Jane and Mr. Bingley."

"Please, do not say another word. My mother is insupportable, and my greatest fear is that I shall not be able to keep her and my younger sisters under good regulation when my family attends the Military Ball. I shall have many duties to contend with tomorrow night, and it will be impossible for me to monitor their every move."

"Will your father not help?"

"Charlotte, as much as I love Papa, I am sure he will simply stand back and savour every absurdity which comes his way. If only he would listen to reason. This event is far more elegant and refined than any assembly or private ball we have ever been to in Meryton or any other part of Hertfordshire, for that matter. Her Ladyship has invited several dignitaries and many persons of great wealth and consequence, and I pray my family will not embarrass me while they are in her presence."

"If there is any way I can help, I shall do my best to assist."

"Thank you, my dear friend. For now, please let us talk no more on this subject. I had hoped to enjoy myself this evening."

"Of course."

Taking note of the young officers who were now speaking with Kitty and Lydia, Elizabeth remarked, "Perhaps you can enlighten me on some of the more recent changes which have taken place in my absence. I imagine Meryton is hardly the same with the Militia Regiment being quartered there. Do you happen to know the two officers who are speaking with my sisters?"

"The officer with Kitty is Captain Robert Denny, and the taller one with Lydia is Lieutenant George Wickham. Mr. Wickham has recently purchased his commission and is fairly new to the neighbourhood."

"Did you say Lieutenant *George Wickham?*" Elizabeth stiffened in alarm and could not help but stare at the man, remembering all of the heartache he had caused Georgiana.

"Why, yes. Mr. Wickham has become a particular favourite among the ladies in Meryton since joining the Militia Regiment. I must admit his charming manners and refinements are rather pleasant."

"Charlotte, those are *not* words I should use to describe that man. I have heard a most alarming report of Mr. Wickham, and believe me when I say it was not favourable." Elizabeth tried not to frown as she continued to stare at him in the company of her sisters.

"Whatever do you mean, Eliza?"

"Although I am not at liberty to divulge the specifics of what I know, I can say with certainty that Mr. Wickham is *not at all* what he appears to be."

"I see. Then … if what you say is reliable, I cannot help but wonder if the tale he related concerning his reduced circumstances is accurate."

"What tale might that be?"

"According to the Lieutenant, he grew up on the Pemberley estate in Derbyshire where he had been a favourite of the old master. He implied there was some jealousy on the part of the son, Mr. Fitzwilliam Darcy, if I am not mistaken, and a living was denied. Consequently, he has been reduced to his current level of poverty and was forced to take a commission as an officer."

"Charlotte." Elizabeth fought to control her anger. "Mr. Fitzwilliam Darcy happens to be the nephew of Lady Matlock. While serving on her committee, I have had the pleasure of meeting both him and his sister. From what I have heard of Mr. Wickham, the story the man tells is a complete falsehood, and he has slandered the Darcy name in spreading such rumours. I tell you, the Lieutenant is dishonest in every sense of the word and is *not* to be trusted."

"This information is surprising and certainly puts Mr. Wickham in an unfavourable light. Eliza, are you certain?"

"Yes, I am."

"Well then, may I ask what you intend to do?"

"I am not sure, but I promise you, I shall find a way to take care of this matter and make Mr. Wickham's true character known. Please, let us take a short walk in the garden. At this moment, I cannot bear to look at him for another minute. Some fresh air would be most welcome."

The women retreated to the garden and did not return to the house until shortly before dinner was to be served. Earlier, Wickham had taken note of Elizabeth and was curious to meet the woman who was so intent on watching him. When he again noticed her with Charlotte, he petitioned Lydia to make the introductions. Annoyed that she was no longer in command of his attentions, Lydia childishly grabbed Wickham by the arm and pulled him to where the two friends were standing.

"Lizzy," snapped Lydia. "This gentleman wishes to make your acquaintance. Miss Elizabeth Bennet, may I present Mr. Wickham. Mr. Wickham, my sister. I believe you already know our neighbour, Miss Lucas." Lydia turned in a huff leaving Wickham to converse with the women.

Wickham, acting as though nothing was amiss, smiled charmingly and bowed. "How pleasant it is to see you again, Miss Lucas. Miss Elizabeth, I have heard much of you from your lovely sisters and have looked forward to making your acquaintance."

Elizabeth returned his greeting with reserve. "Thank you, Mr. Wickham. I trust you have enjoyed your stay in Meryton."

"Yes, I have. The neighbourhood is very agreeable and I suspect our unit will be there for some duration. I understand you have been in Town since January."

"You are correct, sir. My elder sister and I have been assisting our Aunt Gardiner and the Countess of Matlock with her charity preparations to raise funds for the new hospital wing. May I assume you are in Town to attend the Military Ball?"

"At present, Mr. Denny and I are here functioning as aides to Colonel Forster for the next several days. Although we shall be on assignment tomorrow, once we have finished our business, it is our intention to attend the ball a little later in the evening."

"I see." Elizabeth tried to remain attentive but could not help thinking she must alert Mr. Darcy of Wickham's plans for Georgiana's sake.

"Miss Elizabeth, you mentioned Lady Matlock. I wonder if you have ever happened to see her nephew, Mr. Fitzwilliam Darcy, or his sister, Miss Georgiana Darcy, while you were in Town."

"Mr. Wickham, you misunderstand my relationship with Her

Ladyship. Although the Darcys are relatives of Lady Matlock, I am merely a member of her committee and nothing more."

"Ah, I see. I simply enquired as it has been some time since I have seen them. You may not know it, but I grew up on the Pemberley estate where my father was the steward. At the time, I was a great favourite of old Mr. Darcy and was promised a generous living. I regret to say it did not take place due to a judgement put forth by the son."

"I beg your pardon, sir, but we have only just now met. I hardly think this is the type of conversation you should use to recommend yourself."

"Miss Elizabeth, you are absolutely correct. Forgive me. I should not have spoken of the matter. I was curious about the Darcys and nothing more. You see when Miss Darcy was a child, she was quite fond of me and I was hoping I might make her acquaintance again if only at the ball."

Elizabeth could hardly suppress her anger as he dared to speak of Georgiana. Forcing herself to appear calm, she answered, "I am sorry that I cannot provide you with any pertinent information on either of the Darcys. While I am assisting Lady Matlock with this event, you must understand we travel in very different circles."

"Yes, of course." Wickham smiled. "Perhaps both of you ladies will honour me with a dance tomorrow evening." While Charlotte responded favourably to his inquiry, Elizabeth informed him she would be overseeing her committee's efforts during the course of the event and could not commit to dancing at present. Before the conversation went any further, their group was approached by Mr. Collins, who had earlier asked Elizabeth to be his partner at dinner.

"Cousin Elizabeth, I have been looking for you. Ah, Miss Lucas. May I once again compliment you on the honour which has been extended to me this evening by your estimable father? It was exceedingly generous of him to include me in his invitation, and I might add that I am enjoying myself prodigiously."

"Thank you, Mr. Collins. You are most welcome. May I enquire if you have been introduced to Mr. Wickham yet this evening?"

"No, Miss Lucas, I am sorry to say I have not had the pleasure of meeting one of His Majesty's finest."

"Mr. Collins, this is Lieutenant George Wickham. Mr. Wickham, Mr. Collins."

"Mr. Wickham. Please accept my sincere appreciation for the honour which you have bestowed upon me," Collins said with adulation. "I cannot help but commend every one of our brave officers for the dedication and sacrifice they have given in service to our great country. Had I chosen to become a military chaplain, my own service would have been insignificant by comparison."

"Mr. Collins. You are too kind."

"As my esteemed patroness, Lady Catherine de Bourgh, would say, *'We can never underestimate the value of a good military man.'* Why, her own nephew, Colonel Richard Fitzwilliam, is a decorated member of the Cavalry. I wonder if you have ever happened to come across him in your tour of duty."

At the mention of Colonel Fitzwilliam, Wickham momentarily furrowed his brow and cleared his throat before responding. Elizabeth was sure Wickham's uneasiness had sprung from the fact that the colonel was one of Georgiana's guardians.

"I do know of Colonel Fitzwilliam, but I regret to say I have not seen him in many years." Wickham quickly glanced about the room before continuing, "Pray, excuse me. I see Colonel Forester is speaking with some of my fellow officers and I believe I should find out if I am needed before going into dinner."

"By all means, I would not wish to keep you," the cleric offered.

"Mr. Collins, Miss Lucas, Miss Elizabeth." With a slight nod of the head, Wickham smiled charmingly and walked away.

"Now, Miss Elizabeth, if you recall, I am to escort you into dinner. Perhaps Miss Lucas would allow me to do her the honour as well." The women thanked him, each taking an offered arm. For the next two hours, Mr. Collins was in a state of rapture, since he had not only one, but two women at his side.

In an effort to impress the ladies, Mr. Collins took every opportunity to expound on the endless affability and superior manners of his esteemed patroness, as well as the grandeur of Rosings Park. Elizabeth was grateful Charlotte occupied much of the exchange throughout dinner for it gave her time to further observe Mr. Wickham. Without question, she would do everything within her power to see that he was kept from entering the Ball and from bringing further harm to Georgiana.

CHAPTER FOURTEEN

THE MILITARY BALL

London
Friday, 19 July 1811
The following day

*L*ondon was bustling with activity since patrons from many localities travelled into Town with the promise of attending the acclaimed Military Ball. The amount of public notice and enthusiasm generated by this event had by far exceeded the expectations of Lady Matlock and her committee. Having spent the better part of their day attending to the final preparations, Elizabeth and Jane had little time to return home and ready themselves for the evening. While Jane's assistance would not be needed at the event itself, Lady Matlock had insisted Elizabeth return well before the guests arrived in order to personally see that everything was as it should be.

On entering the main ballroom, Elizabeth was very pleased with the final transformation of all she surveyed. The room itself shimmered with luminous lanterns and rows of candelabra and was ornamented with elaborate floral arrangements and arbours. The musicians had finished tuning their instruments and had begun to play soothing background music in anticipation of the guests who would be arriving shortly.

For now, it appeared Elizabeth need only check on several items with the head of the service and convey Her Ladyship's final instructions. By the time she completed her task, the ballroom had begun to fill with guests, many of whom were passing through the receiving line where the grand lady and her party stood.

Weighing heavily on Elizabeth's mind was her encounter with George Wickham. In observing him, she could easily see how poor Georgiana had been taken in by his charm and lies. It was imperative she find a way to alert Mr. Darcy of Wickham's presence in Town and of his intentions. At the moment, he was facing away from her and engaged in conversation. *If only he would turn this way.*

Just off to her right, Elizabeth noticed Colonel Fitzwilliam, who was in the process of obtaining a drink from one of the serving footmen. She would have preferred to speak privately with Darcy, but since he was currently occupied, the colonel proved to be her next best option.

"Miss Elizabeth Bennet, how pleasant it is to see you again."

"Colonel Fitzwilliam."

"Please allow me to extend my compliments. My mother's praise of your work is hardly sufficient for all I have seen here this evening."

"Sir, you are too kind. Lady Matlock has assembled an extraordinary group of people who are members of her committee for this event, and it has been my privilege to assist both your mother and my aunt during all of the preparations."

"May I offer you a glass of punch?"

"No thank you. If you do not mind, though, I would like to take a few minutes of your time, as there is something I wish to speak of."

"Of course." Seeing the serious expression on her face, the colonel replaced his drink on the tray and followed Elizabeth through one of the service entrances and into an area which was relatively unoccupied.

"Miss Elizabeth, whatever is the matter?"

"Sir," Elizabeth spoke in a hushed voice. "I must inform you that *Mr. Wickham* is in Town aiding his commanding officer, and it is his intention to attend the ball later this evening."

"Wickham," he spat. "And how did you happen to come by this information?" His expression was grave.

"Mr. Wickham is part of Colonel Forster's regiment lately quartered in Meryton. Last night, Sir William Lucas, one of our friends from Hertfordshire, hosted a small dinner party for our families and a few other guests. Mr. Wickham happened to be one of the officers in attendance. Having heard of my committee work with Lady Matlock, he enquired after Mr. Darcy and more specifically of *Miss Darcy*."

"Darcy told you of her misfortunes?" He frowned.

"Only in part, sir. It was Miss Darcy who first related the incident when she was most fevered, though I doubt she remembers. Please rest assured, I have only spoken of her grief to Mr. Darcy and none other. I apologise for my rashness, but at the present, I could think of no other way of informing Mr. Darcy of Mr. Wickham's intentions. I am concerned for Miss Darcy's well-being."

"You did right to tell me, Miss Elizabeth, and I appreciate your assistance. I shall speak with my cousin at once and see to the matter myself. You need not worry. Wickham will *never* gain admittance here." He bowed and quickly left the service area.

Appearing as though nothing was amiss, Elizabeth returned to the ballroom and stood next to the wall. From there, she watched Colonel Fitzwilliam take Darcy aside and briefly explain the situation. Within minutes, the colonel took his leave and Darcy began looking about the room until he saw her. With a mere nod of his head, Elizabeth knew that all would be well. She smiled, and for a few brief seconds the intimacy created by their unspoken exchange caused the colour to rise in her cheeks. Moments later, he was at her side.

"Miss Elizabeth, I have never seen you looking lovelier."

Trying not to show her discomposure when Darcy bowed over her hand and kissed it, she smiled and simply said, "Thank you."

"I believe it is *I* who should be thanking you. Once again, you have come to Georgiana's aid. It seems I am forever in your debt." She could not help but further blush at his compliment.

"Dearest Elizabeth," he spoke softly. "Thirteen days have been far too long." The look in his eyes caused her heart to quicken and her knees to become weak.

"Thirteen days," she murmured, captivated by the man who stood before her. Had they been alone, she was sure he would have defied propriety and kissed her.

Recalling where they were, he proceeded, "I realise your time is not entirely your own this evening. Still, I wonder if I may request your hand for a set later on if you happen to be free."

"I would like that." She smiled, causing him to do the same. "I shall have some time following the tea. My mother has arranged for me to dance the first set with my cousin, Mr. Collins, but perhaps the second would be to your liking."

"Very much so. And if you can spare a few minutes now, may we go and greet my sister? I know she is most eager to see you."

"Thank you. I have been looking forward to seeing Georgiana this evening."

"At present, she is speaking with my cousin, Anne. The taller woman on her left is my Aunt, Lady Catherine." He offered his arm and the two of them walked to where his relations were conversing.

"Aunt Catherine, Cousin Anne," spoke Darcy. "If I may, please allow me to introduce Miss Elizabeth Bennet of Hertfordshire. Miss Jane Bennet, her older sister, and her aunt, Mrs. Gardiner, have all been assisting Aunt Eleanor's committee these past six months." Lady Catherine nodded her approval.

"Miss Elizabeth, my aunt, Lady Catherine de Bourgh and my cousin Miss Anne de Bourgh."

"Miss Elizabeth Bennet," Lady Catherine acknowledged, carefully examining the young woman who stood before her.

"Lady Catherine, Miss de Bourgh, it is a pleasure to make your acquaintance." She curtseyed. "Miss Darcy." Again she curtseyed in acknowledgement of her dear friend.

"Miss Bennet," spoke Lady Catherine, "I have heard much of you from my rector, Mr. Collins. I understand that you are one of five sisters with no male heir for your father's estate. What an inconvenience it must be to have one's home entailed away from the female line. Thankfully, that was never the case with my late husband, Sir Lewis de Bourgh. My daughter is the sole heiress of my estate in Kent." Somewhat embarrassed by the inappropriate mention of her family's predicament, Elizabeth tried to appear unaffected during Lady Catherine's discourse.

"Mr. Collins, as you know, is here at my insistence. Under my counsel, he means to make amends to your family with an offer of marriage to either you or one of your other sisters. Despite the entailment, your mother may be comforted to know all is not lost." Elizabeth's eyes opened wide with surprise at Lady Catherine's officious comment.

"Your Ladyship, please believe me when I say Mr. Collins is in no way obligated to...." Before Elizabeth could finish, Miss de Bourgh began to cough, prompting Lady Catherine to interrupt her response.

"Mrs. Jenkinson, there must be a draft coming through the door in this part of the room. I insist you take Anne away from here at once and have her seated where she will be warmer."

"Yes, Your Ladyship."

"Miss Elizabeth, my daughter has a very delicate constitution as you may have surmised." She paused for a moment, taking note of another party paying their respects to Lady Matlock. "Fitzwilliam, is that not Lady Ellington and her family?"

"Yes, Aunt," he replied. His voice was terse and his demeanour rigid after hearing what Lady Catherine had said with reference to Elizabeth and Mr. Collins.

"I do not believe I have seen Her Ladyship since before the death of Sir Lewis." She abruptly turned and moved to greet her old friend, who did the same upon seeing her.

Noticing how upset Georgiana was by Lady Catherine's remarks, Elizabeth reached for her hand and quietly said, "I know your aunt means well, as does my mother. Please, let me assure you I have *no* intention of marrying Mr. Collins."

"I am glad of it." Georgiana's voice quivered in response.

"Come. Let us try to ignore what was said. Would it not be better to put on a cheerful face and join me in greeting Lady Lilyan and her sister?"

"Yes." She forced a smile.

While Darcy was fully aware of his sister's distress, he was confident Elizabeth would be able to calm her. Seeing the Ashbourne sisters moving in their direction, Darcy purposely stepped forward to greet them, allowing Georgiana a few moments of privacy with Elizabeth.

"Lady Clarissa, Lady Lilyan, good evening." Darcy bowed in acknowledgement and continued by offering up a few of the accustomed civilities. Even so, the exchange between Elizabeth and Georgiana did not go unnoticed by Lady Clarissa, who momentarily frowned at the familiarity between the two women.

Possessively latching on to Darcy's arm, she insisted on him escorting her to where the women were standing. "Miss Darcy, it is good to see you have recovered from your recent illness." Georgiana thanked her and nodded with a slight curtsey.

"And Miss Elizabeth," she said with a note of sarcasm in her voice. "I certainly did not expect to find you socializing this evening. It was my understanding that Lady Matlock had asked you to oversee the workings of this event."

"Yes, indeed, my duties as a committee member are many. I do anticipate, however, having a bit more time later in the evening." Elizabeth responded without appearing to be affronted. "For the present, you must allow me to take my leave. I trust all of you will enjoy your evening." She politely curtseyed and bid them adieu.

~ ♫ ~

From the instant the musicians began to play the opening refrains of the first tune, the dance floor quickly filled with lavishly dressed patrons who moved effortlessly throughout the candlelit room. Lady

Matlock was highly complimented on her success, and the members of her committee could not have been more pleased.

To Elizabeth's great relief, certain persons in her family had remained relatively inconspicuous during the opening hours of the ball. Yet, as the time drew nearer to the serving of the tea, this was no longer the case. In truth, she had expected her mother to carry on over Mr. Bingley and Jane. Unhappily, Mrs. Bennet's boisterous manner was nothing when compared with Lydia's folly.

The first incident involved the senseless girl slipping a few pieces of ice down the inside of Captain Denny's collar and causing a commotion amongst his peers. Even though the captain tried to remain discreet, Lydia drew unwanted attention to the poor man's discomfort with her high-pitched laughter and unladylike behaviour. Not long after, her mischievous nature tricked her friends to assist with yet another scheme.

"La, Denny, is that not Mary King sitting with her uncle? I cannot imagine why she is not dancing." Lydia laughed with abandon. "I admit I do feel sorry for the little mouse. Denny, I *insist* you dance with her. After all, you are an officer, and it is your gentlemanly duty to make sure young ladies are paid their due when there is a shortage of male partners."

"If you wish it, Miss Lydia, I shall be happy to oblige."

"Wait here with Sanderson. I shall not be long. Come, Kitty."

"Lydia, what are you going to do?" Kitty whispered with apprehension.

"You will see. Once we reach Mary, I shall need you to carry on with most of the conversation while I take care of things."

"Lydia, you do not even like her. What are you about?"

"Just do as I say. It will be such a good joke."

After the two sisters approached Mary King and exchanged a few greetings, Lydia turned away pretending to wave at someone who had caught her attention. With the other two women now seated and continuing on in conversation, Lydia stepped behind Mary where she guardedly tied the dangling ribbon sashes of the girl's dress to the back of her chair. Once the deed was done, Lydia excused herself, leaving Kitty to finish the exchange. Captain Denny was not aware of what had taken place and readily obliged Lydia, who sent him off to fulfil her purpose in asking Mary to dance.

Thus far, Elizabeth had been ignorant of what Lydia had done. Still, after seeing her sister whisper in the captain's ear while gesturing to Mary King, she feared something was amiss. As Denny moved towards Mary it became obvious he would ask her to dance. When the girl made an effort to stand, she lost her balance, crying out in alarm and spilling a cup of punch down the front of her gown. Seeing Mary's sashes knotted to the back of her chair, Elizabeth immediately rushed to the girl's aid and began to untie them. In doing so, she could not help but notice Lydia doubling over with laughter at Mary's misfortune. Insisting on Kitty's help, the two sisters quickly took Mary to the women's necessary room where they attempted to repair the damage.

Leaving Kitty with Mary, Elizabeth returned to the ballroom with the intention of confronting Lydia. She was relieved to see the mess left by the accident had been cleaned, but to her dismay, Lydia was not to be found. Noticing her father, she went directly to his side.

"Papa, where is Lydia? Did you see what happened? She has created such a scene, and Miss King's dress is ruined. You must find her at once and address what she has done. Lydia's behaviour is inexcusable."

"Do not fret, my dear. I have sent your sister to the other ballroom where she will be less noticed by your more *prestigious* associates." He chuckled to himself. "Captain Denny and Lieutenant Sanderson are to keep an eye on her there, and hopefully she will not get herself into any more trouble."

Elizabeth closed her eyes for a moment, trying to remain calm. "Papa, this is nothing to make sport of. I am so embarrassed. Lydia cannot be allowed to continue on in this manner. Her behaviour *must* be checked. *Please,* will you not speak with her again?"

"Very well, Lizzy." He patted her hand. "Your concern is noted. I shall seek her out and insist she remain where she is if it will ease your mind. My dear, with so many dancing, I sincerely doubt if Lydia's foolishness was even noticed."

Elizabeth could not believe how easily her father dismissed what had taken place. Glancing over his shoulder she happened to catch the look of Lady Matlock who was staring at her with disdain. Nervously gripping his arm she said, "But, Papa, someone very important *did* notice. It was Her Ladyship."

Her father quickly sobered upon looking in the direction of the grand lady. "Ah, so I see."

"Please do *not* allow Lydia to come back in here under *any* circumstance. I shall send Kitty to you once she is finished helping Miss King. First, I must go and apologise to Lady Matlock."

Walking towards Her Ladyship, Elizabeth's unease continued to grow. Thankfully, Mr. Darcy was not in sight. She silently prayed he had not been witness to her sister's shameless behaviour. Before she was able to offer up an apology, Lady Matlock sharply spoke.

"Miss Elizabeth Bennet. I cannot begin to tell you of my displeasure. I shall say this only once. If your younger sister is so foolish as to set foot in this room again, I shall have your entire family removed. Is that understood?"

"Yes, Your Ladyship. I beg your leave to apologise on behalf of my family for my sister's unpardonable actions. My father has assured me she will not be returning."

"Very well, see that it is so."

With her face in flames, Elizabeth squared her shoulders and promptly returned to Kitty and Mary King. Mary's dress was stained beyond repair and there was no choice but for her to leave the ball with her uncle. Once things were settled and Kitty had been escorted by her father out of the ballroom, it was time for the tea to begin. At this very moment, Elizabeth desperately wished she could relegate her duties to someone else and quietly disappear. *Oh why, just this once, could they have not misbehaved?*

Unknown to Elizabeth, Darcy had observed the entire incident. With his mind in turmoil, his unease grew to the point where he could no longer carry on a conversation with anyone who would require more than a one syllable answer. By the time Colonel Fitzwilliam returned with confirmation that Wickham had been taken care of, Darcy's anxiety had increased to the point where he found it difficult to breathe. Since Georgiana was currently occupied with Lady Lilyan and no longer in danger from Wickham, he excused himself and left the ballroom in great need of fresh air. Compelled to walk, he could not help but think aloud as he moved away from the building.

"Elizabeth, if these people are your family, then I must be living in a nightmare. How can your youngest sister possibly be related to you? Her behaviour is unconscionable. I cannot believe your father has allowed her to appear *here,* of all places, exhibiting such a blatant lack of decorum. Combined with your mother's incessant talk of Bingley and your elder sister, it is not to be borne. Can your father do nothing to check either of them? Dear God in Heaven, what am I to do?" The man continued on like this for some time and did not return to the ballroom until the tea was finished and the dancing was about to begin again.

~ ♫ ~

Elizabeth was well aware Darcy had left the Ballroom and did not return for the tea. How she longed to speak with him. Yet, what could she possibly say in defence of her family? Nothing! After what had happened, it would be an embarrassment to both him and Georgiana if he were to acknowledge her, let alone claim their dance.

Despite all of this, Elizabeth knew she would still have to stand up with Mr. Collins once the dancing recommenced. If she could only have a few minutes to herself before having to endure the next humiliation she might be able to collect her thoughts. Alas, it was not to be for within minutes Mrs. Bennet was at her side instructing her how she was to behave around her *intended.*

"Mama, might Mr. Collins and I simply forego the dance and sit off to the side where we can engage in conversation. I find I have a headache and dancing will only make it worse."

"Absolutely not! Mr. Collins has been very patient and I expect you to show him every civility by dancing. You have done nothing but try my nerves since we arrived in Town and I shall hear no more of your excuses. Here he comes now."

As Mr. Collins approached the women, Elizabeth could not help but notice Mr. Darcy had finally returned to the ballroom and was currently standing next to Georgiana. Grouped with his relations and several members of the Ellington party, he barely acknowledged them. For the most part, his demeanour appeared solemn and he was not inclined to speak.

"Ah, Cousin Elizabeth! I see you are free from your duties for the present, and I have come to claim your hand for the next set."

She nodded without saying a word. Mr. Collins paid his compliments to her mother, then held out his arm and escorted Elizabeth to the dance floor where many of the guests were beginning to assemble.

"I would like to congratulate you on your part in this evening's delightful festivities," he simpered. "The tea itself was beyond anything I could have imagined. Such artistry, such lavishness.... Why even Lady Catherine remarked on the superior quality of the displays."

"Thank you, Mr. Collins. Under the direction of Lady Matlock, it was many weeks in the making."

"I must confess, in my profession it is a rare thing for a humble clergyman such as me to have the privilege of participating in an event where so many persons of rank and distinction are in attendance." He continued to speak in a louder voice, "Then again, perhaps it is not quite so unusual, considering how much notice I have received from my esteemed patroness, *Lady Catherine de Bourgh.* And if I am not mistaken, I believe *you*, my dear cousin, are in a fair way to being noticed by her as well." To Elizabeth's horror, Mr. Collins leaned in a little closer and smiled as though he were attempting to flirt.

Embarrassed by his behaviour, she purposely took a step back and quietly replied, "You are a most fortunate man."

"Thank you. I am happy to know your sensibilities do you credit and that you do not underestimate my importance to Her Ladyship."

Arrogantly raising his head and looking about to see who might be taking note of him, Mr. Collins held out his arm and directed Elizabeth to the line which was now forming. Standing opposite of her, he donned a satisfied look and began the dance with an awkward bow.

Elizabeth, in turn, politely curtseyed and wondered how she would endure being in such close proximity with the man for an entire set. Not only was she revolted by his presumptuous conversation, but also by a musty odour which emanated from his clothing. Combined with the scent of an unappealing fragrance, Elizabeth's sense of smell was assaulted to the point where her headache became far worse.

During the course of the dance Mr. Collins nearly tiptoed through the patterns in an effort not to misstep. His figure was not much more than average build and height, but since he did not carry himself well, he appeared to be an oddity on the dancefloor. By the time the dance was well underway, more than a hint of perspiration had begun to trickle down the side of his face. Consequently, the man was forced to take out his handkerchief and blot his forehead after nearly every turn, thus distracting himself from the patterns.

Throughout the entire display, Darcy became more irritated by what he saw and wondered how Elizabeth's own mother could insist that she stand up with such a ridiculous man. Moreover, Mr. Collins' peculiar performance was beginning to attract notice from several people who had been standing close at hand, resulting in an undercurrent of laughter. And if this was not enough, Mrs. Bennet had now made her way to where Lady Catherine was standing with the intention of taking up a conversation.

"Your Ladyship," Elizabeth's mother nervously began. "Do they not make a handsome couple?"

"Yes, Mrs. Bennet, you were correct. I do believe she will do quite nicely for Mr. Collins."

"Please allow me to thank you again for your assistance. You have no idea what a worry it is for a mother to have so many unmarried daughters."

Overhearing his aunt speaking with Mrs. Bennet in this familiar way, Darcy could hardly suppress his anger. Georgiana, who was equally distressed, tightly gripped her brother's arm while trying to check her tears. Then, without warning, a disturbance took place on the dance floor when Mr. Collins, who no longer had command of the order of steps, turned the wrong way and injured a lady's foot. He immediately apologised to the woman, but not before accidently backing into another gentleman and causing him to lose his balance. Angered, the offended man threatened to expel Collins from the dance floor and would have done so had not Elizabeth taken her partner's arm and directed him back into the line. Although their group continued to dance, Elizabeth's distress could not be concealed.

"Brother, please, is there nothing you can do?" Georgiana pleaded.

Bracing himself for what was about to come, Darcy gave her hand a gentle squeeze and directly strode to where Elizabeth and Mr. Collins were dancing. With Mr. Collins attempting to turn Elizabeth but moving in the wrong direction, Darcy quickly stepped forward and claimed her hand. Collins, recognizing Darcy as Lady Catherine's nephew, reddened and abruptly left the dance floor in search of his patroness.

This sudden change in partners did not go unnoticed by those who were ready to further their gossip, nor by Lady Clarissa, who had been taking great pleasure in watching Elizabeth's predicament from where she was dancing. Upon witnessing Darcy's actions, she became incensed. Leaving her own partner during the middle of the set, she intended to voice her displeasure to Lady Ellington."

"Mother, did you see what he did?" she hissed.

"Who, my dear?" Lady Ellington looked around but was unaware of what had taken place.

"Mr. Darcy," she spat. "He has humiliated me in front of all of my friends. For the entire evening, he has refused to dance, and *now*, without any warning, he chose to replace that fool, Collins, and is standing up with Miss Elizabeth Bennet. She may be a member of Lady Matlock's committee, but from what I have seen here this evening, the woman is little better than one of Her Ladyship's hired attendants. I tell you, Mama, I have been meanly insulted, and I insist you speak with Father at once."

"Lady Ellington, is something amiss?" Lady Matlock enquired, catching part of the conversation. "What is it you are saying of my nephew?"

"Your nephew, indeed! My daughter has been slighted."

"Slighted?" Lady Ellington waved her hand in the direction of the dance floor where it was easy enough for Lady Matlock to surmise what had taken place. Her face suddenly grew taut when she spied her nephew dancing with Elizabeth. Considering Mr. Collins, who had begun the set, was now speaking in earnest with Lady Catherine, she could easily surmise what had taken place.

Elizabeth had been on the verge of yielding to her emotions when Darcy stepped forward and took her hand. Gazing at her new partner and comprehending what had taken place, a lone tear escaped from the corner of her eye. Despite great peril to his standing, she knew Darcy had risked much by coming to her aid, and for that, she was grateful. Each time he took her hand and gazed into her eyes, her despair seemed to vanish. For those few precious moments, Elizabeth felt as though she was loved and protected.

Once the set was over, Darcy spotted the Gardiners and took the liberty of leading her to where they stood. After briefly greeting her aunt and uncle, he bowed to Elizabeth, kissed her hand and returned to Georgiana's side. Seconds later, all of the ugliness of the situation returned with a vengeance.

"Fitzwilliam Darcy, what have you done?" bellowed Lady Catherine. Refusing to acknowledge his aunt, Darcy turned the other way and proceeded to escort Georgiana from the ballroom and into the hallway which led out of the building.

"Darcy, this is not to be borne! I insist you come back here at once. We are *not* finished."

Seeing Lady Matlock's look of disapproval, Elizabeth's face began to flush. She could not help but hold onto Mrs. Gardiner's arm for support. "Aunt, I think I shall be sick."

"Lizzy, let us sit down over here." She motioned to some vacant chairs. "Edward, I believe Lizzy is in need of a glass of wine if you would be so kind."

After sitting for a few moments Mrs. Gardiner asked, "Are you feeling any better?"

"A little."

"Lizzy, I do not mean to pry, but tell me honestly, do you and Mr. Darcy have an understanding?"

"No, Aunt, we do not. But...." She began to tremble. "I do believe he cares for me, as I do for him."

Mrs. Gardiner placed her arm around Elizabeth when she began to cry. "I fear this will not turn out well, my dear," she whispered, giving Elizabeth her handkerchief. "I am so sorry."

"Forgive me, Aunt. I did not mean to cause such a spectacle. Please, could we not go home?"

"Yes, I shall ask Edward to make the arrangements. He is coming now with your drink."

"Thank you."

"Here you are, Lizzy. This should help calm you."

With shaky hands, Elizabeth held on to the glass and took a sip of the wine. Mrs. Gardiner informed her husband they would need to leave and asked him to appraise Jane and Mr. Bennet of what had happened. He would also need to alert Mrs. Madison so that she might assume Elizabeth's duties for the remainder of the evening.

Trying to calm her nerves, Elizabeth continued to sip her wine and prayed that she would be left alone. Unhappily, it was not to be. Taking notice of her mother and Mr. Collins coming in her direction, she put down her glass and attempted to prepare herself for what was to come.

"Elizabeth Bennet! I am very displeased with your behaviour. Just what do you mean by slighting our Mr. Collins and dancing with *Mr. Darcy* of all people? I do *not* care if he *is* the nephew of Lady Catherine *or* Lady Matlock. It is Mr. Collins who was to be your partner, and you will make an apology to him this instant." The man appeared to be very satisfied with Mrs. Bennet's reprimand and waited for Elizabeth's apology donning a look of smugness upon his face.

Attempting to keep her mother calm and avoid further embarrassment, Elizabeth complied. "Mr. Collins, I humbly apologise if I have in any way offended you. While I cannot vouch for Mr. Darcy, I do not believe he meant to slight you. There must have been some misunderstanding. After all, he is well aware of your position in Hunsford and certainly would not wish to insult you or his aunt."

Flattered with Elizabeth's apology, Mr. Collins responded with triumph, "I thank you, Cousin Elizabeth. Perhaps it is as you say. After all, Mr. Darcy is a favourite of my esteemed patroness and her own daughter, Miss de Bourgh." The man proceeded to bestow a lengthy kiss to her hand. Even though Elizabeth's face flushed with humiliation, she refrained from expressing how upset she truly was.

While this exchange appeased Mrs. Bennet's nerves for the moment, she felt it was necessary to put further strictures on her daughter. Looking sharply at Elizabeth, she chided, "Lizzy, I forbid you to continue on with any of your duties. You will be escorted by Mr. Collins for the remainder of the evening. If necessary, I shall speak with Lady Matlock myself and insist she engage someone else to take your place."

"Mama, I am not feeling well. Uncle Gardiner has already gone to inform Papa that we shall be leaving."

"Leaving? What do you mean?" she said with a raised voice.

"I have a headache, and I am in desperate need of some fresh air. Please, please do not make me stay."

"I most certainly shall. Elizabeth Bennet, if you cannot dance, you will sit right here and converse with Mr. Collins until I say otherwise."

"Fanny," interrupted Mrs. Gardiner. "The ball will soon be over. May we not put this off until tomorrow where we can continue the discussion in the privacy of our home? We are expecting all of you for dinner, and I am sure Lizzy will be feeling better at that time."

"I suppose you are right," Mrs. Bennet huffed. "But, Sister, I have been ill used this evening, and I blame it all on Elizabeth."

Mrs. Gardiner gently took her niece by the arm saying, "Come, Lizzy, we should go. Mr. Gardiner will be waiting." The two women quickly left the ballroom, followed by Mrs. Bennet, who continued to rant. Mr. Collins returned to his esteemed patroness eager to relate what had transpired and to offer his condolences over the unpleasantness of the entire situation.

Boarding the carriage, Elizabeth was thankful she would not have to endure the presence of her mother on the ride back to Gracechurch Street. Even though the Gardiners and Jane had been very kind, as soon as they all arrived, Elizabeth wanted nothing more than to be left alone. *If only things had turned out differently.*

CHAPTER FIFTEEN

DISTURBING PROSPECTS

Darcy's Study
Sunday, 20 July 1811
Two days later

"*D*arcy! Darcy! Open up, man!" Colonel Fitzwilliam continued to knock, unrelenting in his purpose.

"Richard, stop that incessant pounding," a gruff voice called from the other side of the door. "Go away, and leave me alone."

"Mrs. Troutman, may I have the key? Thank you. Please tell Andrews to prepare a bath for the master then join me here. And if you would be so kind, bring us a pot of your strongest coffee? I fear we shall need it."

"Yes, sir. Right away."

Opening the door, the colonel was greeted with the stench of foul air. "Darcy, what the deuce is going on? It smells like a stinking latrine in here."

"Not so loud. My head...." Darcy lay sprawled out on the couch with one arm covering his eyes. A moment later, he groaned even louder when the colonel drew back the curtains and opened the window to let in some light and fresh air.

"Cousin, you need a bath. I have been with drunken foot soldiers who smell better than you. Up you go."

Struggling with a wave of nausea, Darcy put his head in his hands and leaned forward on his knees. "Richard, I am going to be sick."

The colonel quickly came forth with a half full wastepaper basket, hoping it would be enough to accommodate his cousin. Once his stomach was purged, Darcy leaned back and closed his eyes. "Richard, I appreciate your concern, but will you please leave? I need to work this out on my own."

Darcy's housekeeper quietly entered with a tray conveying the pot of coffee. After filling one of the cups, she immediately left the study.

With shaky hands, Darcy took the cup and began to drink. "Richard, it is no wonder you are an officer. I suspect you *never* take no for an answer."

He chuckled. "You have the right of that! Now drink up before I pour the rest of this cup down your sorry throat." Over the next quarter of an hour, the colonel continued to replenish Darcy's cup until he could drink no more.

"So.... Are you going to tell me what the deuce is going on here?"

"No, I am not."

"According to Mother, it seems I missed the scandal of the season at the Military Ball while I was off conversing with a very lovely lady out on the terrace. May I assume your pathetic state has something to do with Miss Bennet?"

"Elizabeth," he said, shaking his head wearily. "Why could I not have fallen in love with one of those insipid women of the *ton?* It would have been far simpler."

"Nothing in life is simple, Cousin. You, of all people, should know that. If we did not have these *trials* to work through, how would we grow in character and appreciate the things which are truly important in life?"

"Spare me your philosophy."

Noticing the miniature of James Darcy laying on the floor, the colonel picked it up and put it on the table. "Let me guess. May I assume you were trying to sort this out with your father?"

"What is there to sort out? His response is always the same. 'Fitzwilliam, the choice of a wife is not to be taken lightly. Your first duty is to preserve our family's name and the longevity of this estate. The next mistress of Pemberley must be one who is worthy of the position and should come from a family who will match you in rank and wealth. Of course, I would not deny you love; nevertheless, I charge you to choose wisely.'"

"Remarkable. If I did not see you sitting right here in front of me, I would swear it was Uncle James speaking. Listen, you know this has been the way of our family and others like us for generations. It is rare that people in *either* of our positions marry for love."

"Richard, I shall *not* give her up! I cannot do it."

"I understand, and I am confident you will manage to work it out." Just then, the door opened and Darcy's valet entered. "Good! Andrews is here. Let us have no more serious talk for the present and get you to your chambers."

Andrews proceeded to assist the colonel in getting Darcy to his feet. The three men slowly walked out of the study and up the stairs to Darcy's rooms where a hot bath was waiting.

"Well, Cousin, since you are now in the capable hands of your valet, I shall leave you to his care. I believe your sister is in much need of my counsel, and unlike you, she will be far more appreciative." He scoffed.

"Georgiana." Darcy winced. "Have you seen her?"

"Yes, it was *she* who sent for me. You gave her quite a scare by locking yourself away for the whole of yesterday and yet this morning. Our dear sweet girl broke into tears the minute she saw me."

"She does not deserve any of this."

"I heartily agree. If you have no objection, I shall return later for dinner and insist that you make it up to her." He turned to go.

"Richard.... Thank you."

The bath proved to be exactly what Darcy needed. It was refreshing after closeting himself in the study since returning from the ball. With his head beginning to clear, he knew it was time to address what had happened. The question was how.

Prior to the ball, Darcy had planned to ask Elizabeth if he could call on her at Gracechurch Street with the intention of proposing. Once she had given her consent, he would have gone to her father and asked for his permission. Yet, the behaviour of the Bennet family in a public setting had left Darcy stunned and unsure of how to proceed. From the outset, he knew that Elizabeth's relations were far beneath his own, but he never dreamed they would act in such a shocking manner. *Dearest Elizabeth, how shall we get past this? I pray to God I can come up with a solution.*

~ ♫ ~

Monday, 22 July 1811
The next day

Upon awaking, Elizabeth was pleased to see the sky beginning to clear after two full days of rain. Sadly, it was not enough to lift her sorely diminished spirits following the disastrous Military Ball. Elizabeth had endured the humiliation with as much dignity as she could summon. To her dismay, she knew nothing could ease the shock or discomfort which her dearest friends must have suffered by the hand of her own family. Sweet Georgiana was like a sister to her and she could not deny Mr. Darcy had become the one man who held her heart. The thought that she might no longer have either of them in her life left a feeling of emptiness which was impossible to shake.

Since the ball, Elizabeth had yet to face her mother or Mr. Collins. Between the inclement weather and having suffered a bad case of nerves because of her *second eldest,* Mrs. Bennet had insisted the family dinner be put off until Tuesday. *If only Papa had intervened.*

Elizabeth could not help but wonder if her father might have felt some remorse over what had happened to her, for on the previous day, Mr. Bennet had been summoned to Gracechurch Street by Mr. Gardiner where the two of them had spent the majority of the afternoon closeted in her Uncle's study.

At first there had been an argument, most of which Elizabeth could not make out with the exception of her own name being loudly spoken by both men. In the end, Mr. Bennet emerged from the study and left the house without acknowledging anyone. Mr. Gardiner had told the women that they were not to worry. Although he gave no information about what had been discussed, he and Mr. Bennet would convene again. Following Tuesday's dinner, Mr. Bennet would address the entire family.

~ ♫ ~

After breaking her fast, Elizabeth sat in the parlour with her sister and aunt where they tended to their various tasks. About mid-morning, Mrs. Gardiner was interrupted by Daniels who handed her a post.

"Girls, this letter is from Lady Matlock. Would you care if I read it aloud? I suspect it concerns all of us." Elizabeth and Jane agreed. The inevitable could not be put off.

"Mrs. Gardiner,

"I trust my letter finds you well. To begin with, I wish to thank you and your nieces for the effort which was put forth during our most recent charity event. All things considered, the Military Ball was a great success, and I look forward to more notice and support from the community as the committee proceeds with the rest of our scheduled events.

"That being said, I must now address a situation of a far less pleasant nature. As you well know, there were several embarrassing incidents which took place during the course of the evening. I do not mean to find fault with you, my dear friend; still, the improper behaviour exhibited by some of your relations cannot be overlooked. Since it has reflected poorly upon our efforts, I regret to say I have no choice but to terminate our relationship."

"Oh, dear, I was afraid of something like this." Mrs. Gardiner's frustration was apparent when she momentarily paused in her reading of the letter.

"In light of one particular occurrence involving Mr. Darcy, Miss Eliz-abeth and Mr. Collins, I must also insist your nieces have no further contact with either my niece or nephew. This is not simply my wish, but it is also the fervent desire of my sister, Lady Catherine de Bourgh. True, it was I who initially promoted the connection for the sake of my niece. In light of what has taken place, I realise I was mistaken to do so. Miss Darcy is awaiting her first season, and further association with either of your nieces will only bring her censure and lessen her ability to make a good match.

"In the case of my nephew, the apparent attraction between him and Miss Elizabeth did not go unnoticed and has since placed Mr. Darcy in a rather precarious situation. Because of his higher station in soci-ety, there can never be an alliance between my nephew and your niece. Such a union would not only degrade Mr. Darcy but would adversely affect our entire family. I trust you are sympathetic to my position and will take the liberty of informing Miss Elizabeth of our wishes. If I have offended you in any way, I sincerely apologise, though it could not be helped under the circumstances.

"Lady Eleanor Fitzwilliam, Countess of Matlock"

Mrs. Gardiner let out a huff. "To be dismissed and insulted in such an unfeeling way.... My dears, if you will excuse me, I wish to send Her Ladyship a reply while all of this is fresh in my mind."

"Aunt, I...."

"No, Lizzy, I will not allow you to accept any of the blame for what has happened. I was witness to what took place at the ball, and you are not to be faulted. Regarding Mr. Darcy, it is unfortunate he did not use better judgement instead of risking both of your reputations. It will be *his* lot to sort it out with his relations despite what this letter says." She threw it down on the table in disgust.

"Lizzy, Jane, I am exceedingly proud of the two of you, and I shall not accept Lady Matlock's criticism and dismissal without first having my say on the matter. Admittedly, the *ton* takes pride when it comes to proper decorum and preserving their place in society. Even so, for the sake of our poor soldiers, it is a pity some part of it could not have been overlooked." Having voiced her opinion, Mrs. Gardiner rose from the table and left the room.

"Lizzy, I wish to lie down for a time. I find I have developed a headache and shall not be good company."

"I am truly sorry, Jane." Elizabeth squeezed her sister's hand. "I will come up a little later." No longer interested in finishing her sewing, Elizabeth put her basket to the side. Picking up Lady Matlock's letter, she slipped it into her pocket and went outside for some fresh air.

~ ♫ ~

Later that afternoon
The garden

Continuing to feel quite restless, Elizabeth chose to be useful in Mrs. Gardiner's herb garden by taking on the task of snipping a basket of fresh lavender. Following the heavy rains, many of the tiny flowers were fully opened and in need of cutting before they fell from the stems. Trimming back the dead branches and filling her basket with those she wished to harvest for her aunt's oil, Elizabeth enjoyed the calming fragrance as well as the solitude.

Not long after she had begun, Elizabeth was startled by the sound of heavy footsteps walking on the gravel path. Turning in that direction, she was astonished to see none other than Mr. Darcy coming towards her. Quickly putting the basket on the ground, she removed her garden gloves and smoothed her dress in the hopes of looking somewhat presentable. The closer he got, the more her heart quickened.

"You came." She shyly smiled.

"Yes." He bestowed a half smile in return while unnerving her with the intensity of his gaze.

"I thought I should never see you again," she quietly said.

He smiled reassuringly. "Elizabeth, I could no more stay away from you than I could cease to breathe." He lifted his hand to her face where he lovingly caressed her cheek with his fingertips. "May we sit and talk for a while?"

"Yes, thank you. There is a bench just over here."

Once they were seated, Darcy reached for Elizabeth's hand and kissed it before speaking. "I have missed you. Forgive me for not coming sooner. These last days have been … difficult."

Like her, the dark circles which lay beneath his eyes betrayed that he, too, had not slept much since she last saw him. "Mr. Darcy, are you well?"

"I am well enough though I have been struggling with a solution to my quandary. I only pray my decision will be sufficient to overcome the obstacles in our path."

Continuing to hold her hand, Darcy looked off into the distance as he searched for the words. Moments later, his face sobered and his voice became more deliberate. "Elizabeth, it is your family. Why did you not caution me about them?"

She stiffened, prompting him to release her hand. "Forgive me," she replied. "It is never easy to speak of one's family, particularly with regard to their failings."

"I understand. Yet, in this case you should have made them known to me since their behaviour cannot be ignored." Darcy rose and began pacing. While he did not want to cause her pain, he could no longer refrain from voicing the concerns which had been a source of torment to his sensibilities.

"Elizabeth, I do not wish to insult you, but I cannot help but lay the blame of what took place at your father's door. While he is not of my sphere, he *is* an educated man. As such, he should have exerted better regulation over your mother and your younger sisters at the ball. How am I to call such a man *father* when my own father was the model of everything proper?

"For the sake of our marriage, I was willing to overlook the fact that we are not equal in standing and wealth. Then again, how can I, in good conscience, be expected to overlook the blatant lack of propriety which is exhibited by so many in your family? I have a responsibility to Georgiana and to my own family, to our future children, and to my estate."

Elizabeth could not feign ignorance as to the root of Darcy's concerns. Still, she would not cower beneath his accusations and assumptions. "Mr. Darcy, what is it you are trying to say?" Her tone was no longer soothing but had become agitated in response to his offensive attempt at a declaration.

"Elizabeth, I realise this may be painful for you, but if I am to save face with my family and certain members of my society, it is imperative we break with all of your relations once we marry. I can find no other solution. Even then, I fear it may not be enough."

Elizabeth's head was spinning. As much as he was in the right, could he possibly expect her to deny her family? Taking a deep breath, she questioned, "Mr. Darcy, are you not getting ahead of yourself?"

He immediately stopped pacing and faced her. Elizabeth had risen from the bench. Her face was flushed, her mouth was set and her eyes flared as though they were on fire.

"Before you continue to demean my relations and take me for your bride, may I remind you that you have *not* made me a proper offer of marriage? Neither have I chosen to accept said offer, *nor* have I approved of or even been consulted in your carefully thought out ultimatum?"

"I beg your pardon. Perhaps I did get ahead of myself, but surely you are toying with me. What madness would cause you to spurn my hand and remain with your relations after all that has taken place?"

Attempting to rein in her temper, she replied, "What madness indeed! Mr. Darcy, in essence, you have just informed me your family name and standing in society would be tainted were we to wed. If I understand you correctly, *sir*, you are offering *me* the opportunity to throw off *all* of my *disgraceful relations* in exchange for a life in a society which I have come to dislike, a society which has never shown me any consideration, a society which considers me and my family wholly unacceptable."

Darcy's complexion suddenly became pale and then reddened with anger. He was struggling for composure and began to clench his fist. "Elizabeth, you cannot seriously mean to side with your family after the humiliation which they have caused you?"

"Sir, you leave me little choice. The Bennets may be *vulgar,* but they are still my family, and I love them. Furthermore, when you speak of breaking with *all* of my relations, may I assume my dearest sister, Jane, and my beloved aunt and uncle are to be included in this censure? They, *too,* are my relations, are they not?" Darcy's silence served to confirm her assertion. "I am sorry, Mr. Darcy, but what you ask is unreasonable. I cannot forsake my family to suit *your* purpose, and I could *never* be happy under those conditions."

"Then … then you are refusing me?"

"I am."

"Do you not understand I cannot abandon the wishes of my own family and that of my late father? What choice do I have?"

Willing her eyes to remain locked with his, she assertively answered, "Mr. Darcy, you may simply choose *not* to marry me."

"Elizabeth, what are you saying? Do you not love me?" His eyes blazed with emotion.

Unable to endure the pain which she saw on his face, Elizabeth turned her back on him and spoke resignedly. "What purpose would it serve to answer that question? Can you not see an alliance between us is impossible?"

"No, I do not!" Darcy declared, forcibly turning her back to face him.

"Mr. Darcy, I am *not* a woman of the *ton.* Since coming to Town, I have been reminded on a daily basis that I do *not* belong in your society. If you need further affirmation, perhaps you would care to read the letter which your aunt so *graciously* sent to mine earlier today." She took the letter from her pocket and thrust it into his hand. "Lady Matlock has made her wishes very clear, sir, and has expressed herself without reservation."

Incensed, Darcy took the missive and nearly crumpled it as Elizabeth continued to speak. "While helping my Aunt Gardiner, I have been subjected to gross arrogance and pride from many members of *your* society and have been scrutinised and judged unfairly because of my *lack* of wealth and connections. I have done everything within my power to assist your aunt with her charity and have expected nothing but courtesy and respect in return."

Elizabeth paused for a moment. Her voice became soft as she continued, "Throughout our many discussions and the kindness you have shown me, I had come to believe *you* were different. Mr. Darcy ... William, I do not wish to cause you pain, but today your words have wounded me. Please forgive me, but I *cannot* marry you."

Darcy felt as though he would explode. This is not what he had expected. He could not understand how his proposal had gone so awry. "And this is your final answer? You will *not* marry me?"

Squaring her shoulders and mustering every ounce of courage she had to repress the tears which were forming in her eyes, she answered with conviction, "No, sir, I shall not."

Darcy took a step back. His demeanour became rigid and his face void of any former semblance of love. "If this is your final answer, then there is little left for me to say. I shall leave you. Please accept my best wishes for your health and happiness." Making a slight bow, he quickly turned and left the garden.

Watching him go, Elizabeth could no longer hold back her tears. Minutes later, she ran down the path and into the house, refusing to answer her aunt's inquiry about what had taken place. From there, she went straight to her room and locked the door. With trembling hands, she removed his little book from her pocket. Clutching it to her breast, she collapsed on the bed and cried in earnest. She cared not that her sobs of anguish could be heard throughout the house. At this moment, her heart was breaking for Elizabeth Bennet knew she would never see Mr. Fitzwilliam Darcy again.

CHAPTER SIXTEEN

THE AFTERMATH

The same day

*D*arcy silently cursed as he strode to where his carriage was waiting. *Blast it all! Who does she think she is to refuse me, a Darcy? I can name any number of women who would gladly accept my hand in marriage. Has she no idea what I represent? I am my family and the bearer of the Darcy name and all it entails. Incredible!* Motioning the footman aside, he climbed into the carriage and slammed the door shut. Tapping on the roof with the end of his walking stick, the driver immediately left Cheapside for Grosvenor Square.

Darcy clenched his fist and pounded it without mercy into the padded cushion. *Dear Lord, why must I be tested at every turn? What more do you want of me?*

He searched his mind hoping to find an answer, but there was none to be had. "Elizabeth," he finally choked out, then slumped against the back cushion and closed his eyes until the vehicle arrived at his townhouse.

Giving orders not to be disturbed, Darcy went directly to the study. Having shed his coat, he loosened his cravat and opened the liquor cabinet. Still feeling the after effects of his recent bout with brandy, he merely poured himself a shallow glass of port and took a sip.

Unfolding his aunt's letter, Darcy read the insults directed towards Mrs. Gardiner and her nieces, not to mention the reference to his own person. "Aunt Eleanor, if you think I shall let this slide, you are sorely mistaken. I SHALL speak my mind in this matter." Disgusted, he threw the letter on his desk and took out his writing materials. After penning a note to Lady Matlock requesting a meeting with her and Lady Catherine at their earliest convenience, Darcy left the study and made arrangements to go to his club. It was the first day of a long-awaited billiard tournament, and he knew there would be much activity. Surely, he could lose himself in that place for a few hours and escape the reality of what had taken place between him and Elizabeth.

The Club

Walking up the stairs to White's, Darcy could sense the excitement and anticipation of the tournament which seemed to permeate the air. Handing his hat and gloves to an attending footman, he heard talk of wagers and speculation over who would finish at the top of the slate by the end of the day's matches.

Not intending to mingle with his peers, Darcy went directly to the club library where he picked up one of the more popular war journals. Trying to immerse himself in military rhetoric and strategies, he found the distraction was not enough to keep him from thinking of the one person who invaded his every thought. *Elizabeth, it is hopeless. I love you beyond all reason. What am I to do?* He leaned back in his chair and closed his eyes.

~ ♫ ~

An hour later

"Cousin, wake up! It is me, Richard."

Rubbing his eyes and trying to suppress a yawn, he answered, "What are you doing here?"

"Frankly speaking, I am once again doing the bidding of my sweet cousin."

"Georgiana?" He lifted his brows in question. "What has happened?"

Tossing Lady Matlock's letter into Darcy's lap, the colonel frowned, "You should have known better than to leave this hateful thing lying about." Darcy groaned upon recognizing the offending missive.

"After overhearing Mother and Aunt Catherine discussing your request for a meeting, I decided to pay you a visit. It was then I found our dear girl in tears. It seems after you left this afternoon, Georgie sent a footman with a note for Miss Elizabeth. Not having heard from her since the ball, she was worried. Mrs. Gardiner sent a reply indicating her niece was indisposed but would see that she was given the letter. Concerned for Miss Elizabeth and wanting to speak with you, Georgiana wandered into your study and...."

"Merciful heaven! Is there no end to this madness?"

"Apparently not today. Come on, Cousin. Let us leave. I have a carriage waiting."

As soon as they left the club and entered the vehicle, Colonel Fitzwilliam began his interrogation. "So, are you going to tell me what happened between you and Miss Elizabeth? I assume it was *she* who gave you my mother's letter."

Shutting his eyes, Darcy reached up and pinched the bridge of his nose in an effort to stave off a slight headache. Looking back at the colonel, he simply said, "She refused me. What more is there to say?"

"*Refused you?* Are you serious, man?" His eyes narrowed in puzzlement. "Because of the letter?"

"Richard, I would rather not discuss this."

"Just *what* did you say to her? Please, do not tell me you recounted certain events which took place at the ball and disparaged her family during the course of your addresses."

"Worse."

"Worse?!"

"I essentially told her once we were married we would have to make a complete break with her relations if I was to preserve my standing in society."

The colonel shook his head in disbelief. "Good God, you certainly know how to deliver a proposal. Knowing the outcome, I am sure Mother and Aunt Catherine would have been pleased."

"Richard, stop!"

"Why, I can hardly take it in. First, she had to endure what happened at the Military Ball, and at the hands of her own family, no less. Next, she was affronted by Mother's letter, and finally, *you* chose to deliver your less than *praiseworthy* proposal. It is a wonder Georgiana even received a response at all."

"Must you go on?"

"Yes, I must, for Georgiana's sake. I need to know if you intend to allow her to continue on with the connection, assuming Miss Elizabeth would even be agreeable after what she has suffered."

Darcy ran his hand over his face and rubbed his chin before dropping it back to his thigh. "I should never insist that Georgiana give up their friendship."

"And what of that damning letter? What do you intend to do about it?"

"Yes, the letter," he nearly spat. "Your mother and Aunt Catherine will definitely be hearing my opinion on their interference from that quarter. May I assume your father is in agreement with them?"

"As far as I know, Father is unaware of the letter. With the tournament, he has been at the club all day. If you like, I shall do a bit of reconnaissance on your behalf and promote your position. I would be glad to support you at this alleged *meeting* which you have requested. Not to mention, I would like to be present when you give your set down," he chuckled.

"Richard, I see no humour in this situation. You may do as you wish. For my part, I want nothing more than to be finished with this insanity."

Within minutes, the two men arrived at Darcy House. Standing faithfully by the window, Georgiana had been watching for their return and anxiously greeted them at the door as they ascended the stairs.

"William...."

To his dismay, Darcy could see the stains of tears on her face. "Let us go inside, dear one."

No sooner had Darcy shut the door to the study than Georgiana began her seemingly endless stream of questions. "Did you see her, Brother? Was it Elizabeth who gave you our aunt's horrible letter? Was she upset? Do you think she will ever want to see me again? What shall we do? I am so worried for her. How could our aunt be so cruel?"

"Georgiana, dearest, please.... Here, let us sit."

"I am sorry, William."

Looking into her waiting eyes, Darcy sat next to his sister and held her hand. "To answer some of your questions, yes, I ... I did see Miss Elizabeth. It was she who gave me the letter, and yes, she was very upset."

"Oh, William, what did you say to her? Did you assure her we should never turn her away?"

His expression was unreadable. "My dear, it is ... it is complicated, and I do not care to relate all of what was said." Georgiana frowned a little at his response. "I shall tell you; however, I have requested a meeting with our aunts, and I fully intend to address what was put forth in the letter. At this juncture, I cannot vouch for Miss Elizabeth, but I shall not prevent you from remaining friends if it is what the two of you desire."

Bursting into tears, Georgiana fell into her brother's embrace. "Oh, thank you, William," she sobbed. "I love Elizabeth so very much and I cannot bear the thought of never seeing her again."

"I know," he said, closing his eyes and feeling her pain as acutely as his own.

"William, please may I write to her and tell her myself how sorry we are about the letter? And please, if she is willing, may we call on her before we leave Town?"

Not wanting to disappoint Georgiana or reveal his own discomfiture, he ordered his face and calmly replied, "Yes, I think a letter would be appropriate. As for the visit, my ... my time is limited this week. If Miss Elizabeth responds favourably to your request, I shall arrange a proper escort for you and Mrs. Annesley to the Gardiner residence. Perhaps it would be best to see her later in the week. Allow her a few days to ... recover. Did you not tell me you and Mrs. Annesley planned to volunteer at the hospital with the *Correspondence Hours* on Friday?"

"Yes, I did. Might we be allowed to call on her afterwards?"

"If it is of no inconvenience to Miss Elizabeth, and she agrees, you may go."

"Thank you, Brother. I shall write to her at once and send a footman with my letter in the morning." Georgiana kissed his cheek, and hurried off to her room.

"That was well done. Although I must express my astonishment at your willingness to allow her to visit Miss Elizabeth at the home of her *relations,* considering what you previously demanded."

Darcy just shook his head and covered his eyes as he sat in the chair and leaned forward on his desk. "I found ... I could not deny her in this," he murmured.

"Well then, since my little cousin is in far better spirits than when I first saw her today, I shall take my leave. Should you require my counsel, you know I am always at your disposal. Do take care of yourself." He gave Darcy's shoulder a brotherly squeeze and left without saying another word.

~ ♫ ~

Gracechurch Street
Tuesday, 23 July 1811
The next day

Curled up in the window seat, Elizabeth leaned her head against the damp glass and sighed. The memory of what had transpired only yesterday remained raw in her mind. Following her argument with Darcy, Elizabeth had closeted herself in her room and refused admittance to both Jane and Mrs. Gardiner until much later in the evening. Finally seeing them, she could not help but cry anew, and it was some time before she could fully explain what had happened. Sadly, neither woman could offer up words of consolation which could begin to erase the grim reality of what had transpired or ease the heartache she continued to feel.

An early morning shower was now coming to an end, and Elizabeth knew she would need to steel herself if she was to face her mother and Mr. Collins later in the afternoon. Slipping Darcy's little book back into her pocket, she quickly straightened her dress and left her room to join Jane and Mrs. Gardiner who were already breaking their fast.

"Good morning, Lizzy, I hope you are feeling better."

"Thank you, Aunt. I am."

"My dear, another letter has come for you from Miss Darcy. I was about to send it up to your room. Her footman is waiting for a reply."

Elizabeth hesitated, then took the missive and sat down to read it.

Dearest Elizabeth,

I hope this letter finds you in better health today. You have been in my prayers ever since the Military Ball. After receiving Mrs. Gardiner's note stating you were indisposed, I have been even more concerned for your well-being.

Please forgive me, but I must tell you I am aware of the distasteful letter which my Aunt Eleanor sent to Mrs. Gardiner. I found it quite by accident in William's study and was most distressed by its implications. William assured me he would not ask me to abandon our friendship, should you be willing to continue on.

I beg you to accept my humblest apology for the unfeeling manner in which you, Mrs. Gardiner, and Miss Bennet have been treated.

Thankfully, my brother has told me he intends to address what was said in the letter with our aunts.

If it is not too much to ask, I would dearly love to see you before William and I leave for Brighton on Monday. You may recall that Mrs. Annesley and I plan to volunteer for the Correspondence Hours at the hospital on Friday. Perhaps we could call on you before returning to Darcy House if it is convenient. William is very busy this week and will not be able to escort us. Even so, he has given his permission and will make the arrangements for us, should you be amenable.

Again, I truly apologise for any discomfort you have experienced. I shall look forward to hearing from you.

Lovingly,
Georgiana Darcy

Tears trickled down Elizabeth's cheeks as she finished reading through Georgiana's letter and handed it to Mrs. Gardiner. "Dear, sweet Georgiana," she whispered to herself while drying her eyes. "Aunt, I can scarcely believe Mr. Darcy would allow his sister to retain a friendship with me, let alone allow her to call here with Mrs. Annesley after what passed between us. And to think he would speak with his aunts about Lady Matlock's letter is nearly beyond my comprehension. If you do not mind, may I accept her request?"

"Why, of course you may."

Elizabeth hurried to the desk and quickly took out a sheet of paper. With trembling hands she was barely able to prepare her pen. *What can this mean? After my refusal, I thought he would want nothing more to do with me, yet he did not deny Georgiana.* Minutes later, Elizabeth finished her note and gave it to the footman.

Georgiana, my dearest friend,

Please forgive me for not having answered your earlier letter. I regret causing you undue distress over my situation. I, too, should dearly love to see you and humbly accept your request to visit on Friday afternoon. Your brother has been very kind. Please extend him my gratitude. I shall look forward to seeing you then.

Sincerely,
Elizabeth Bennet

~ ♫ ~

Early afternoon

A soft knock on the door was followed by Jane quietly entering Elizabeth's room. "Lizzy, I am sorry to disturb you, but our family and Mr. Collins have just now arrived. Papa has gone into Uncle's study, and Mama is insisting you come down at once. She would speak with you privately in the garden."

"Oh, dear." Elizabeth's face paled and Jane looked at her with concern. "Do not worry, I shall be fine. Please tell her I shall come directly."

It was not a particularly warm day, but in an effort to control her nerves, Mrs. Bennet persisted in fanning herself while she awaited Elizabeth. This was to be the day she would most certainly be saved from the hedgerows. Nevertheless, in the back of her mind there was yet an element of doubt, as her least favourite daughter could be very headstrong if given the opportunity.

"Mama, Jane said you wished to speak to me."

"Lizzy, I shall come straight to the point. I was exceedingly vexed with your behaviour towards Mr. Collins at the ball. You have no idea what flutters and palpitations I have suffered because of your behaviour. Why, it is a wonder I am even here today. To think you might have cost us our dear home is nearly more than I can endure. Fortunately, Mr. Collins is willing to give you another chance. It is the express wish of Lady Catherine de Bourgh that he chooses a wife from one of my daughters, and I shall not be disappointed."

"Mama, please, I beg of you. Do not put me in the position where I shall have to refuse him."

"Refuse him? Whatever are you talking about, you foolish girl? How can you be so selfish? You have no choice in the matter. Just who do you think you are, Miss Lizzy? You may have been living here in Town for the past seven months and may have kept company with Lady Matlock and her rich friends, but it does not mean you are any better than the rest of us. You do *not* have the luxury of refusing any man. Not that any other man would even have you with your impertinent ways. No, for once you will do what I ask. These are my final words."

"Mama...."

"Lizzy, I am warning you. If you defy me on this, your sufferings *reword* will be nothing compared to what you experienced at the ball. Now wait here and I shall send Mr. Collins out to speak with you."

~ ♫ ~

Not able to quell her frustration, Elizabeth began to pace the length of the pathway. *Mama, even though you may wish to disown me, I cannot possibly consent to your demands. Papa, please, please, you must be true to your word and not force me to marry that man.*

"Cousin Elizabeth." Mr. Collins gave her a little wave and proceeded to walk down the gravel path to where she stood. Seeing his head cocked to one side and a silly grin on his face, Elizabeth wanted nothing more than to turn and run from the garden. Squaring her shoulders and forcing herself to remain in place, she stood and replied somewhat coolly, "Mr. Collins."

"My dear, dear cousin, I must tell you how well you are looking this afternoon."

"Thank you."

Stepping closer, he took her hand and kissed it. Elizabeth could see her mother watching from the window and involuntarily shivered as his mouth touched her bare skin. Pulling it free, she inadvertently wiped her hand on the side of her dress and took a step back.

Not to be discouraged by her disinclination, he continued in earnest. "I dare say, shyness becomes you and it is particularly welcome after that embarrassing display of late. My fair cousin, as you may surmise, I have requested this private audience with the permission of your respected mother." Elizabeth stared at him in all seriousness, but made no reply.

Taking out his handkerchief, Mr. Collins wiped his brow and cleared his throat before beginning his well-rehearsed speech. "First, I should remind you it is the wish of my esteemed patroness, Lady Catherine de Bourgh, that a man such as I become an example, nay, a beacon of light unto the parish in which I have the greatest fortune to be an ambassador of our creator. Consequently, I find I am now in the position to take a wife and thus fulfil those additional expectations which my post requires. For years, it has pained me to know our families were not able to reconcile their differences over the entailment of your home. As I stated to your honoured mother, I am prepared to offer up an olive branch in your favour, allowing *you* to take your place by my side as Mrs. Collins." Looking pleased, he paused to allow for Elizabeth's response.

Scarcely able to maintain her composure, Elizabeth declared without hesitation, "Mr. Collins, I am sensible of the obligations and honour you have bestowed, but I simply cannot accept your proposal of marriage. While I respect your position, I do not love you, and my heart forbids me to accept your declaration."

Mr. Collins stared at Elizabeth for a few moments, unable to determine if she was in earnest. "My dear cousin, perhaps you are not aware of the advantageous position which you would be placed in when becoming Mrs. Collins." He frowned for a moment before continuing, "In this instance, I do believe that love is insignificant. Let me elaborate. In becoming Mrs. Collins, you will be noticed by all persons connected to Rosings Park and the house of Lady Catherine de Bourgh. You will be sought out and given as much due as your position will allow. Her Ladyship has provided me with a very generous living, which includes recent improvements to the parsonage.

"Since Lady Catherine will see to it herself that we economise, I deem we shall be very comfortable in our humble situation. Furthermore, at such time as your father leaves this earth, I shall become Master of Longbourn and *you* will become its Mistress. I am not insensible to the plight of your mother and sisters. As Master, I shall see they are looked after and cared for."

"Mr. Collins, I appreciate your kindness and your offer is more than generous. Yet, I firmly believe we are ill suited to one another and neither of us would be happy in this marriage which you suggest. Forgive me, but I must decline."

Mr. Collins narrowed his brows and momentarily studied her before responding. "Under normal circumstances, I would think this resistance was nothing more than a flirtation often put forth by young ladies who are about to become engaged. Yet, in this instance, I do believe your reticence comes from something greater." Astounded by his criticism, Elizabeth looked at him in wonder.

"Cousin Elizabeth," he continued in a haughty manner. "I know what I saw at the Military Ball, and if you are under the misconception that the nephew of my patroness will make you an offer, you are mistaken. I have heard it from her Ladyship's own mouth Mr. Fitzwilliam Darcy is engaged to her daughter, Miss Anne de Bourgh. Surely you must realise a man in Mr. Darcy's position would never offer for someone of your status. His only interest in you would be to take a mistress, and let me assure you Lady Catherine would never allow it."

Elizabeth was incensed and raised her hand as if to strike him. "How *dare* you insinuate such a slander?" Watching him cower under her ire, she threw up both of her hands in disgust. "Oh, what am I thinking? You are not worth my disdain. Nothing you have said will *ever* entice me to reconsider your offer. Mr. Collins, my answer is no, a thousand times, no!" Elizabeth turned and walked brusquely past the man and towards the house.

Mrs. Bennet, who had been watching from the window, was

beside herself with what she had witnessed. Rushing to block her daughter from entering she nearly yelled, "Elizabeth Bennet, what have you done?"

"Mama, please, let me pass."

"You thankless girl," Mrs. Bennet continued as Elizabeth stepped around her and hurried to her room. "Very well, I shall see to Mr. Collins myself, and if he is no longer willing to have you, let it be known from this day forth, you are no longer my daughter!"

Hastening down the garden path, Mrs. Bennet called out in her high-pitched voice, "Mr. Collins, Mr. Collins. You must pay no heed to Elizabeth's foolish ways. Sometimes I simply do not understand my own daughter. Please forgive her impertinence. I shall have Mr. Bennet make her see reason."

Despite all of her effusions, Mr. Collins returned her supplications with disdain. "Mrs. Bennet," he spoke coolly. "It seems I have erred in judgement. Miss Elizabeth has refused me, as you see. This final incident has allowed me the opportunity to review her character. It now appears to me your daughter would make a poor mistress for my home in Hunsford, not to mention an inadequate wife to a clergyman of my standing. If you will excuse me, I believe I should rethink my position with your family."

"Mr. Collins," her voice trembled. "I assure you Elizabeth does not know her own mind in this matter."

"It may be as you say, Mrs. Bennet. Then again, I *do* know mine, and at this juncture, I have decided to withdraw my interest."

"But, Mr. Collins," she pleaded. "I have other daughters. There is Mary, whose knowledge of doctrinal issues might be quite useful. And then there is Kitty. While she is younger, I can assure you she would behave far better than Lizzy. Mr. Collins, will you not reconsider?"

"Possibly, but certainly not before I have spoken with my patroness. It is imperative I send her a message asking for an interview. Excuse me."

Mrs. Bennet followed him into the house, talking all the while. Ignoring her, Mr. Collins asked a servant to take him to a more private area of the house where he could compose his letter in silence.

Frustrated, Mrs. Bennet immediately removed her petition to the study where Mr. Bennet was conversing with Mr. Gardiner.

Without knocking, the lady rushed through the door. Appearing distraught, she placed her hand over her heart and said, "Mr. Bennet, Mr. Bennet. We are all lost!" She gasped for air before collapsing into the nearest chair. "Whatever shall we do? Lizzy has refused Mr. Collins, and now he says he will not have her. You must go and speak with Mr. Collins at once. Husband, he is your heir!"

"Edward, let us continue this discussion later."

"Take your time, Thomas. Fanny, I shall ask Madeleine to attend you." Mr. Gardiner promptly took his leave, allowing his relations to converse in private.

"Oh, Mr. Bennet, we have raised a most ungrateful daughter." Tears poured forth from her eyes as she called out, "Thomas, please. I need my smelling salts."

"Fanny, calm down. Here, drink this." He handed her a glass of wine which he had just poured for himself.

"I shall have nothing more to do with Lizzy!" she shrieked. "We are ruined, and it is all because of her headstrong ways. I must insist she stay here in Town with my brother and sister when we return to Longbourn. If there is any possibility of Mr. Collins wishing to pay court to one of our other daughters, we cannot further insult him with her presence. Oh, my head is spinning and I can hardly take a breath."

Mr. Bennet dampened his handkerchief with water from the pitcher and handed it to his wife so she might blot her flushed face. "Mrs. Bennet." He scowled. "Did I, or did I *not* specifically ask you to give up your design in matching Lizzy with Mr. Collins?"

"But, Mr. Bennet, what was I to do? When have you *ever* taken an interest in the welfare of our unmarried daughters or made an effort to secure their futures? It has always been left to me."

For once Mr. Bennet could not dispute his wife's complaint. Taking her hand, he replied, "It is true. I *have* neglected my duty, and for that I am heartily sorry, my dear. Nevertheless, I shall no longer continue on in such a manner. To that end, Edward and I have been in much discussion over these past few days, and we have worked out a plan. It will require many changes once we return to Longbourn. Mrs. Bennet, from this day forward, I *shall* take a more active role in securing the future for our daughters."

"Mr. Bennet, explain yourself, I do not understand," she whimpered. Before he could answer, Mrs. Gardiner entered the room. Upon seeing her, Mrs. Bennet burst into a new bout of tears. "Oh, Sister, you have no idea what I suffer," she wailed.

"Madeleine, please come in. If you would be so kind as to look after Fanny while I speak with Mr. Collins, I shall return shortly."

CHAPTER SEVENTEEN

A LITTLE RAY OF HOPE

Gracechurch Street
Tuesday, 23 July 1811
The same day

*H*aving left Mr. Collins and her mother, Elizabeth chose to remain in her room until it was time to join the family for dinner. No matter how hard she tried, it was impossible to block out the remembrance of so many wearisome events. "Oh, to be away from all of this madness," she fretted.

Stopping in front of the mirror, she placed her hands on her hips and declared, "Nothing can erase the follies of my family; not to mention that *you*, Miss Elizabeth Bennet, have now refused *two* offers of marriage!" Elizabeth momentarily covered her eyes, no longer able to look upon herself. *It is of little use. In this instance, it is nearly impossible to follow my own philosophy and think only of the past as it gives me pleasure.*

Walking to the window, Elizabeth observed the darkening sky and suspected it would likely rain before the afternoon was over. If it continued into the evening, there would be yet another vexation for her mother.

"Oh, Mama, why must you always be set against me? I truly *do* understand your concerns. More than you know."

Gently touching her pocket, Elizabeth took out Darcy's little book and held it reverently in her hands. Once again, she tenderly caressed the place where he had written his name. "William...." A single tear slid down her cheek. Wiping it with the palm of her hand, she closed the book and slipped it back into her pocket. Moving to the bed, Elizabeth quietly curled up on the soft covering and closed her eyes.

~ ♫ ~

"Lizzy.... Lizzy," Jane spoke softly while gently touching Elizabeth's arm. "I am so sorry to disturb you, but you need to wake up. Papa would like to see you in Uncle Gardiner's study. He said it is of some importance."

"I was sleeping so soundly. Is it very late?" Elizabeth yawned and stretched a bit before sitting up.

"We have yet another hour before dinner."

"Thank you. Please tell Papa I shall be down in a few minutes." Elizabeth tidied her hair as best she could and straightened her dress before descending the stairs to speak with her father.

~ ♫ ~

"Papa, Jane said you wished to see me."

"Yes, daughter, come in and shut the door." She entered and took a seat close to where he sat.

"Lizzy, as you know, your uncle and I have been in conference for several days now. Consequently, there are several new arrangements which will greatly affect our family. I thought it best to inform you before making my announcement later this evening."

"Papa?" she questioned with uncertainty.

"Never fear, my dear. My word to you is good. You will not be required to marry Mr. Collins. I would not wish that particular fate on any of my daughters though it might indeed save your mama from the *hedgerows.*" He purposely cleared his throat.

"Based on your uncle's recommendation, I have hired an older couple who will be residing with us for some months. Mr. Henry Holyoak has tutored many young people throughout his career, and I shall be employing him to oversee lessons for your younger sisters. In addition, his wife shall instruct them in the fundamentals of proper etiquette. As much as I hate to admit it, your uncle had the right of it. I have done both you and Jane, nay, all of my family, a disservice by condoning behaviour which … I no longer find amusing. I am sorry, Lizzy, but much of what you have suffered of late is a result of my own doing, and … I owe you an apology."

"Papa, please. You are not responsible for the decisions made by my sisters or even Mama. After all, there is some personal choice to be made in every situation."

"Yes, but in *this* instance, I *am* to blame. No, Lizzy, I shall not allow you to make me feel better with your kind words. I shall not rally until I have begun to implement the plans which your uncle and I have worked out *and* have seen some positive results." He could not help but furrow his brow while formulating his next thought.

"What is it, Papa?"

"While it is no fault of your own, I regret to say I cannot allow you to return with us to Longbourn."

"Papa…."

"Do not be alarmed, my dear. This is not meant to punish you by any means. I am doing this for your benefit. After you retreated to your room, Mr. Collins wrote a lengthy letter to his patroness explaining his current distress. Rather than wait for her reply, he chose to deliver it in person. I have since received word from my *heir*, as he so purposely reminded me. Apparently, Lady Catherine has advised him to abide by his original plan and accompany us back to Longbourn when we leave Town on Saturday. In light of your refusal, he has requested that he be allowed to complete his visit *without* your presence. That being said, he will not be dining with us this evening— a small consolation."

"I see."

"Although his request on its own would not be enough to influence my decision, there *is* the problem of your mother and younger sisters to consider. Once we return to Longbourn, I predict the changes I plan to implement will create quite a disturbance in our house. Until your mother is able to adjust, both your uncle and I agree she will be difficult and we do not care for you to suffer any further by her hand. When I see that she and your sisters have made sufficient progress, I shall send for you."

"Papa, I am so sorry. I did not mean for any of this to happen."

"Lizzy, as I said, you are not to blame. In time, we shall all weather through what is to come and hopefully be the better for it.

"Now, if you will indulge me for a few minutes, I wish to acquaint you with something else. Since you have assisted me so faithfully with estate matters in the past, I would like for you to take a look at these documents."

Elizabeth could not help but be amazed when she perused her father's papers. "It says here you are planning to make improvements on two vacant cottages, repair the fences in that area and put in a new well. These efforts will undoubtedly help to secure new tenants, but how can we afford to do so much? All of this will be a great undertaking. Then here it says you are also considering the implementation of some form of crop rotation with the spring plantings. Papa, how will you manage?"

"I am still working out the details with your uncle. Fortunately, Edward has not only found Mr. and Mrs. Holyoak, but he has introduced me to a man who will make several visits to Longbourn in order to assist me with the tenant and farming matters. Your uncle and I are currently in the process of securing the funds for these projects. Even though our estate is entailed to Mr. Collins, I assure you that I intend to stay around for some time." He chuckled. "It may take a bit, but I am hoping to make our estate more profitable and eventually increase your dowries."

"Oh, Papa, I really do not know what to say."

"Yes, well, I am sure your mama and sisters will have a great deal to say once I explain matters and inform them they will not have as much pin money at their disposal."

Elizabeth eagerly gave her father a warm hug. "Papa, if you persevere on this course, I know you will be successful. I only wish I could return sooner and be of some immediate assistance. Are you sure I must stay in Town? Could I not come home after Mr. Collins leaves? I will gladly endure Mama's censure if I can be of help."

"Lizzy, that is all very good, but for now it is best we abide by my current decision. There will be time enough for you to assist me during the coming months. Your mama will not make our lives easy, and though you say you will be able to weather her *poor nerves*, I assure you, there is only so much of *that* one man can endure." He raised one eyebrow and shrugged off the thought. "My plans are fixed."

"Yes, Papa, I understand."

Taking her hand, he continued, "If you do not mind, I wish to have a few moments of solitude before I face your mother and sisters. Run along now." Happier than she had been in days, Elizabeth kissed her father and left the study in search of Jane.

what about Jane?

~ ♫ ~

Darcy's Study
Wednesday, 24 July 1811
The next day

Colonel Fitzwilliam paused in the doorway before greeting his cousin. He wondered how long Darcy had been staring out of the window for his knuckles looked positively white where he tightly gripped the sashing. "Are you ready?" he asked. Startled by the sound of his cousin's voice, Darcy turned and looked at him with a scowl.

"What's wrong? I hardly think that face will make a favourable impression on my mother and Aunt Catherine," he chuckled.

Darcy rolled his eyes in disgust. "It is a pity you were not here thirty minutes ago. Perhaps your humour would have appeased some of *Lord Ellington's* disdain."

"Ellington was here?"

"Yes," he answered tersely.

"I suppose he came by merely to demand an apology for slighting his *charming* daughter."

Darcy let out a sardonic laugh taking the colonel by surprise. "Precisely! And I suspect he was sent by his officious wife to do the deed. Had it not been for Georgiana's friendship with Lady Lilyan, I would have sent the arse packing. Can you believe it? He had the nerve to tell me that because of my *ungentlemanly behaviour* at the ball, I am no longer considered a *viable candidate* for the hand of his lovely daughter."

"Well, it seems as though some good came from the discussion. You were never interested in her forty thousand pounds to begin with."

"Richard!" Darcy glared.

"Come on, let us leave. What I have to say should rid you of your dour mood. Father has decided to attend your little gathering with the intention of supporting you in the discussion."

"Are you in earnest?"

"Cheer up, man! It will all be settled before long, and afterwards we should be able to head over to the club and watch the last rounds of the tournament before they proceed to the finals." Darcy gave his cousin a wry smile, and the two of them left for Matlock House.

~ ♪ ~

Matlock House

Entering the house, the gentlemen heard the loud voice of Lady Catherine echoing throughout the hallways. She was obviously upset and her tirade only served to cause Darcy more anxiety as he and Colonel Fitzwilliam approached the parlour.

"When Mr. Collins came here yesterday seeking my advice, I knew at once her sights were set on our nephew. I do not understand with what arts and allurements she has drawn him in, but it will not be borne. I tell you, Fitzwilliam is promised to Anne. My sister and I planned it since before they were born. I swear to you I shall find a way to destroy her before I allow that obstinate, headstrong girl to set one foot into our family."

Not being able to stand for any more of her verbal abuse, Darcy practically burst through the closed door and demanded, "Of whom can you be speaking, Aunt Catherine?"

"Fitzwilliam, Richard, we did not hear you come in," stated Lady Matlock, motioning her sister to desist her ranting with the wave of her hand. The lady refused to be swayed.

"Do *not* toy with *me*, nephew. You know perfectly well of whom I speak. I am speaking of *Miss Elizabeth Bennet*! As it is, I was shocked to witness her unseemly behaviour and your besotted attentions at the ball. I only pray that you have not compromised her. If you think we shall allow an alliance with such a family, you are mistaken!"

"Unseemly behaviour! Compromise! How dare you slander Miss Elizabeth in this manner?!"

"Catherine," insisted Lady Matlock. "This is not the way to proceed. Fitzwilliam, Richard, please be seated. You are both making me nervous." The colonel took a seat next to his father, who had stoically come into the room during Lady Catherine's outburst. Darcy chose to remain standing.

"Fitzwilliam," this time Lady Matlock spoke directly to her nephew. "I do not personally hold anything against the young lady. Indeed, for being little more than twenty years-of-age, I find Miss Elizabeth to be one of the most capable and engaging young women I have ever met. Nevertheless, after what we witnessed at the ball, it is imperative both you and Georgiana sever any connection you may have with the young lady and her relations." Darcy clenched his jaw, trying not to interrupt. "We cannot be associated with people whose lack of decorum and want of propriety is so wanting."

Giving his aunt an icy stare, Darcy responded in a biting tone of voice. "Yes, you could not have made yourself more perfectly clear on *that* matter."

Lady Matlock returned his look, refusing to back down.

"Fitzwilliam, I do not believe I understand your full meaning here. What is it you are trying to say?"

"I am saying that without regard to *my* sentiments or feelings, you have implemented a mandate concerning Georgiana and myself of which I did not approve. Furthermore, you have insulted three women who have gone far beyond what was required of them in assisting you and your committee. I have read your letter, Aunt, and let me tell you I do NOT appreciate your interference in my affairs. It is wholly unacceptable."

"Unacceptable, indeed!" shouted Lady Catherine. "You see, Eleanor, we are already too late. He has made her an offer. I tell you, I shall never allow it to stand. Nephew, you are to marry Anne."

Ignoring her sister, Lady Matlock questioned, "You have read my letter? I wonder how you came by that missive. Are you truly on such intimate terms with Miss Elizabeth Bennet?"

"We have been … friends." He stared at her, curtailing his answer.

"Fitzwilliam, I am sorry to have offended Mrs. Gardiner and her nieces, but I could see no other way around this problem. In truth, it saddens me that Madeleine Gardiner will no longer be assisting me with my charity endeavours. With her superior connections to the trade community, it is a great loss, I assure you.

"Even so, I shall stand by what I said in my letter. What I did was for the best. We have our family's name to uphold, and it now appears we must take over and protect your name as well. Like Catherine, I am of the mind that there exists more between you and Miss Elizabeth than I was formerly aware of. The thought of that young woman replacing your dear mother as Mistress of Pemberley is insupportable. Nephew, please tell us that the two of you are not engaged."

Darcy coldly answered, "We are not."

"Thank heaven!" Lady Catherine exclaimed.

"Catherine, please! Fitzwilliam, for my own peace of mind, may I have your assurance that you will never enter into such an alliance?"

Glaring, he responded with anger. "I shall promise no such thing. I am my own man and shall not be intimidated by you or anyone." He held his hands up in an effort to stifle their protests.

"Aunt Eleanor, Aunt Catherine, you may be my closest relations, but you do *not* have the right to decide what is best for me and that includes choosing who I shall or shall not be associated with. I have been Master of Pemberley since my father died nearly six years ago. During that time, I have done everything within my power to successfully run my estate, as well as take responsibility for Georgiana. I am nearly eight and twenty, yet the two of you have undermined my position and have chosen to insult my integrity. With regards to Anne, let it be known I shall never marry her. When I do make my choice for the next mistress of Pemberley, it will be just that: *my* choice.

"As for Miss Elizabeth Bennet, while I cannot condone the actions of certain members in her family, I shall *not* sever Georgiana's friendship with her based on your demands. The kindness which she bestowed upon my sister during her recent illness can never be repaid. These are my final words." With no further acknowledgement, Darcy turned to leave.

"Not so hasty, if you please. We are by no means finished here, Fitzwilliam!" shouted Lady Catherine. "If you persist, I shall take legal action to have Georgiana removed from your guardianship."

With her threat, Darcy halted and faced his aunt. "What did you say?" he bellowed. "I shall break with you this instant if you insist in pursuing such treachery!"

"Catherine, Eleanor, I have heard enough! You will both be silent!" Lord Matlock rose from his seat and walked towards the door, where Darcy stood.

"Fitzwilliam, one moment please." Turning back to his wife and sister, Lord Matlock proclaimed, "*I* am the head of our family, and as such, I am putting an end to this nonsense. There will be no more disparaging words against our nephew, and neither of you will discredit him by challenging his guardianship of Georgiana.

"For years I have stood by and watched the two of you attempt to control the lives of our young people, and for what benefit? Catherine, under your parentage, your own daughter has become a shell of a woman. When has she ever been allowed to be her own person or make her wishes known? It is no wonder she is always sickly. I should have insisted Anne come to live with us long ago if only to give her a respite from your demanding ways."

"Gregory, you have no right!"

"Yes, I do, Catherine. I am your elder brother and I *can* exercise that right. Anne is of age, and if she were properly advised, you would now be in the dowager's house, and she would be mistress of Rosings Park."

"How can you say such a thing? Anne is *nothing* compared to me."

"And whose fault is it, Catherine? You have done everything within your power to hide her away and suppress her true nature. If I did not already have the problem of Reginald to address, I would be taking up her cause this very day."

"Gregory, of what are you speaking?" his wife asked.

"Eleanor, as you are aware, the current life of our heir is nothing more than one of debauchery and dissipation. I suspect he has always had these tendencies, but over the years we have done little to help him. We certainly did not do him a service when you insisted we arrange his marriage to Lady Barbara. In retrospect, I am heartily ashamed an alliance was made without regard to the wishes of either person. Reginald came to us with his objections, yet we went ahead and forced his marriage. What good has ever come of their union? She was of the finest circles, as was he. Even so, both of their reputations are now tainted, and they have yet to produce an heir.

"As you may recall, several years ago I entrusted our son with two of our smaller properties, so he might gain experience as a proper landowner before assuming his rightful place at Matlock. I have recently had confirmation from my solicitor that both of those estates have been turned over due to gaming debts."

"Gregory, when did this happen? Why have I heard nothing of this matter until now?" his wife interrupted.

"Eleanor, please allow me to continue. At present, I have the opportunity to purchase one of the properties back, but the second is irretrievable. Reginald still retains his house here in Town, but if his ways are not regulated, the solvency of that property may also come into dispute.

"Where Fitzwilliam is concerned, I shall not stand by and allow either of you to dictate to our nephew when it comes to marriage. Fitzwilliam has proven himself since the day he assumed his rightful place as heir of Pemberley, and I shall trust his judgement and support his decision to make his own choice when he is ready to take a wife.

"As for the Bennet family, I have heard both of your objections with regard to status and fortune. In the past, I might have agreed with your judgements; however, at this point in time, I have little to comment on where they are concerned. My dealings thus far have been with Mr. Edward Gardiner, whom I hold in very high regard. Unknown to you, Eleanor, I along with several other friends entered into a business arrangement with the man some five years ago. Since then, our investments have proved financially sound. Considering the monetary drain which our eldest son puts on our estate, I have been grateful for Gardiner's assistance. At this juncture, I shall do *nothing* to disparage our friendship or our business connection by censoring his relations."

"You cannot be serious!" Lady Matlock protested. "These people are an embarrassment to our way of life. And pray, why was I never informed about these business dealings with Madeleine Gardiner's husband?"

"Frankly, Eleanor, it has been some time since you have shown any interest in the running of our estate. I do not fault you since you have devoted your time and efforts to your charities and do an admirable job with the running of our household. At present, these are issues which I do not care to discuss any further. You will simply have to accept my discernment."

When Lord Matlock had finished his discourse, both women chose to speak at once in an effort to make their own sentiments known. Throwing up his hands to silence them, he spoke again, "I shall hear no more. Believe me when I say this conversation is at an end!

"Richard, Fitzwilliam, if you will both join me in my study, I have something further that I wish to discuss with the two of you in private." The three gentlemen quietly left the sitting room where the two women remained stunned at what they had just heard.

~ ♫ ~

The study

Lord Matlock went directly to the cupboard and took out the decanters. "Which would you prefer, brandy or port?" All three chose brandy, quickly downing their drinks and opting for another.

"Father, I must commend you. What I have heard today restores my faith in the potential of our manhood. I never expected to leave a room where Mother or Aunt Catherine did not have the final say," the colonel chuckled.

"Yes, well, it was long overdue."

"Uncle, although I do appreciate your support, I must apologise for having put you in this position. I did not intend to be a source of conflict."

"Fitzwilliam, there are things which I have failed to address in the past, and much of today's discord could have been avoided had I not played along with the supercilious attitude which is so typical of most men in my position. I was sincere when I said I trust your judgement and that I would support your decisions."

"Thank you. Your confidence means much to me."

"Father, you indicated you have something else you wish to discuss with us. May I assume you are referring to my elder brother?"

"Yes, son, it does. Since coming of age, I have given Reginald responsibilities which he has not taken to heart. As I previously mentioned, I chose to give him the management of Oakridge Head and Winfield Manor. From these two small estates, he had the opportunity to increase his income while gaining some practical experience. Unfortunately, he has abused the privilege. Needless to say, I have since frozen all of Reginald's accounts, and he is henceforth on a strict allowance until such time as I see fit to give him an increase. Hopefully, I shall not reach my demise before I am able to set him straight. I only pray he is not beyond rehabilitation."

"Unbelievable," the colonel shook his head. "My brother has been given so much, yet he consistently abuses his privilege. Father, is there some way I may be of assistance?"

"There is something. I have the opportunity to buy back Winfield Manor before the debt is sold to another."

"I cannot believe you intend to buy back your own property."

"I do. It is Lord Wolverton who currently owns Reginald's debt. I have already asked my solicitor to put in motion the sale of Braidisel Castle in Scotland in order to recover Winfield and to clear several other *pressing debts* which your brother has accrued. If you recall, Winfield Manor comprises a fair amount of acreage adjacent to our northern property, and rather than diminish our family holdings in that area any further, I decided it would be judicious to purchase the debt and deed the land to you, son."

"To me? Father, what are you saying?"

"I am saying that I am giving you the opportunity to become a landed gentleman with the stipulation that you attempt to make Winfield a viable estate once again.

The colonel, shocked by his father's generosity, was nearly rendered speechless. "Thank you. I ... I never expected such a gift. Why ... I can barely comprehend it."

"Richard, you have been a loyal son and have risked much over the years in service for our country. In my mind, you are deserving of far more. Now, from what my solicitor tells me, Winfield Manor is in some disrepair and barely clears fifteen hundred a year. Yet, if the estate is looked after, I am convinced the income can more than double in due time. While I know you cannot assume the full responsibility with your current commitment to the Crown, I shall make arrangements for my land steward to view the property and begin making recommendations once everything is settled with Lord Wolverton. I would see to it myself, but I have several obligations which will require me to be in Town well after Parliament adjourns for the season. Not to mention, there is this business with your brother. At any rate, I suspect it will be some months before I am able to return to Matlock."

"Uncle, if you like, I shall be happy to lend my assistance in your absence. After Georgiana's birthday, I plan to return to Pemberley for a short time and would be happy to look at the property while I am there."

"Thank you, Fitzwilliam. I would appreciate your help."

"It is nothing, Uncle. Richard, perhaps you might join me at some point and we could make a day of it. What say you? "

"I shall do my best to arrange it." He grinned, slapping his cousin on the back. "Just be sure to have my new wine cellars fully stocked with your finest before I arrive." All three men chuckled. During the next hour, the preliminary paperwork which was left by Lord Matlock's solicitor concerning the sale of the castle and the purchase of the manor was reviewed and suggestions were made. Shortly after, Darcy took his leave so that father and son would have some privacy while determining how they might further help the viscount.

CHAPTER EIGHTEEN

SISTERS

Gracechurch Street
Friday, 26 July 1811

For more than a half an hour, Mrs. Gardiner had been distracted by her niece who continued to pace back and forth in front of the parlour windows. Needless to say, her embroidery had suffered, and she now found it necessary to remove the last of her fine stitches. "Lizzy, please, will you not sit down for a bit? Your fretting will not bring Miss Darcy here any sooner than she is able."

"I am sorry, Aunt. Forgive me. If I do not move, I think I shall burst. At the moment, there are so many uncertainties to consider. While I do not believe Mr. Darcy would have told Georgiana of his proposal or of my refusal, she must have had many questions concerning Lady Matlock's letter. I have no idea what explanation he gave her and certainly no knowledge whether or not Mr. Darcy actually discussed the letter with his aunts. Obviously, he was true to his word in supporting our friendship or she would not be coming here today. It is all so unsettling."

Pausing for a moment, Elizabeth slipped her hand in her pocket and touched the little book which rarely left her side. Then, looking even more distraught, she asked, "Dare I enquire about Mr. Darcy? I know we parted badly, but still, I am concerned for his well-being." Quickly turning back to the window, she exclaimed in exasperation, "Oh, what is taking so long? Do you think they could be having difficulty with the roads after this morning's rain? I know Gracechurch Street is well-maintained, but it looks as though there are several uneven places in the road which have yet to be repaired."

Mrs. Gardiner came forward and warmly placed her arm around her niece's shoulder. "My dear, all will be well. Come, this basket of flowers needs some attention. I am sure you can make the arrangement more pleasing with very little effort. Meanwhile, I shall ask one of the servants to stand porter and watch for Miss Darcy's carriage."

Doing her aunt's bidding, Elizabeth busied herself with the flowers in an attempt to distract her thoughts. Seeing the sprigs of lavender, she picked one up, closed her eyes, and took a deep breath. The smell was calming. Time passed quickly as she worked on the basket, and before long, the women were informed of a stately carriage bearing the Darcy Crest entering the busy street. Prompted to return to the window, she watched the vehicle slowly traverse the rutted road with anticipation. Fifteen minutes later, Georgiana, Mrs. Annesley, and Rebecca finally arrived with an escort of three footmen in addition to the driver. Elizabeth could not help but smile, thinking of the very protective brother who carefully planned every detail of her friend's visit.

~ ♫ ~

"Georgiana!"

"Elizabeth!" The two women immediately took each other's hands.

"My dearest friend, I have missed you so very much." Elizabeth smiled broadly.

"I feared I would never see you again." Tears threatened to spill from Georgiana's eyes.

"I know, but now we are together." Elizabeth squeezed her hand. "I am delighted to see all of you. Please, do come in. The parlour is this way. My cousins are anxious to make your acquaintance—the girls in particular."

The women walked into the parlour where Mrs. Gardiner and her four children awaited their arrival. The boys, Edward and Matthew, politely bowed and tried not to fidget as they stood by their nurse during the introductions. Shortly thereafter, the boys were excused, leaving their older sisters who were invited to remain. Respectfully exhibiting their best behaviour, Margaret and Grace sat in quiet awe of the beautifully dressed young lady while the women conversed.

"Miss Darcy, may we enquire of your time with the *Correspondence Hours?*" Mrs. Gardiner asked. "Elizabeth and I are both eager to find out how you and Mrs. Annesley fared this afternoon."

"We enjoyed ourselves very much. Once again, I cannot begin to thank you enough for suggesting we volunteer for the activity. The officer whom I assisted was a young lieutenant by the name of Mr. Horne. He had lost some vision and had a minor hand injury which prevented him from writing. Having received letters from his wife and sister, he was most grateful for my assistance in answering them since they have not been able to visit."

"My dear," spoke Mrs. Gardiner. "You have no idea how pleased I am to hear of your success. The wounded are very deserving of our compassion."

"Thank you. It was our privilege to help in this way." Smiling, Georgiana continued, "If our time permits, we shall try to volunteer again when we return from Brighton. My cousins, Lord and Lady Helmsley, are to host a house party for the month of August."

"So I have heard. Lizzy mentioned you would be leaving in a few days' time," remarked Mrs. Gardiner. "It is my understanding Brighton is quite active at this time of year with the Prince Regent in residence at his summer palace. May I ask if you have ever visited that locality?"

"I regret to say I have not. Until recently, the Helmsleys were out of the country and have not resided at their home in Sussex for many years. After my mother died, Father did not care to leave Pemberley unless it was absolutely necessary. On occasion, I have travelled with

William to visit our Aunt Catherine and cousin in Kent but never to the seaside."

"Then I imagine your time will be quite lovely."

"I hope so. Lady Jessica has been looking forward to our stay. Just yesterday, William received a letter from her saying she would like to take me shopping and is planning for all of us to attend several musical concerts at the palace. Then for my birthday, my cousin has arranged for her guest, Miss Paradis, to spend an afternoon with me so that I may have a private lesson and learn from her musical expertise." She smiled with delight.

"Georgiana, this is wonderful news!" Elizabeth responded with enthusiasm. "I am so happy for you. Have you decided what you are going to play yet?"

"I have, but I shall need to practice very much in order to feel confident. Thus far, I have chosen a movement from a Mozart concerto and one other from a Beethoven sonata. It is possible Lady Lilyan and I may have the opportunity to play our duets at one of my cousin's gatherings since her family has also been invited to the house party. Lord Ellington's country estate is not far from my cousin's home."

"What good fortune! Miss Paradis will no doubt be very pleased. Why, I do not believe I have ever heard anything lovelier than her composition when you performed it at the hospital concert. The two of you play with such artistry and grace."

"Thank you." She blushed.

"Georgiana, it sounds as though Lady Helmsley cares for you a great deal. Did you not mention that your mother and cousin were childhood friends?"

"Yes, Lady Jessica's mother was my Grandfather Darcy's sister. Our cousin's family spent many summers at Pemberley, which is not far from Matlock where my mother's family lived. Since they were all such good friends, Mama was often invited to stay at Pemberley as Lady Jessica's particular guest whenever her family was in residence."

"I wonder ... is it possible your trip to Brighton might provide an opportunity for you to learn more of your mother from your cousin?

Surely, she will have many remembrances of their time together. Why, you could begin a journal and record whatever information Lady Jessica is able to recollect. You might even continue on by interviewing other relatives or some of the older servants who reside at Pemberley, such as Mrs. Reynolds. With your housekeeper being in residence for so long, I suspect she will be able to tell you much of your dear mother."

"Thank you. I love your suggestion. Since my illness, William and I have often talked of our mother, and I could also record his stories along with whatever else my cousin has to say. William recently gave me a new journal which would be perfect for my narrative."

"I am pleased to hear it. Before long, you will have a very special book filled with many treasured memories."

Following a little more conversation, tea was served. During the course of their visit, Mrs. Gardiner happened to ask, "Miss Darcy, have you made any more progress with your plans to begin making tenant visits when you return to Pemberley?"

"Yes. I recently heard from Mrs. Reynolds, and she assures me she will have everything in place for me to begin when William and I return home. During the interim, she has sent me a list with information about several families who have small children. Rebecca and I have since begun sewing items we can include in our baskets."

Mrs. Gardiner glanced in the direction of her daughters. "When I mentioned to my girls that Elizabeth had encouraged you to take on the activity, the two of them offered to make a small contribution." Georgiana looked at the sisters with curiosity. Throughout the entire visit, both Margaret and Grace had remained very polite, quietly drinking their tea as they listened to the women converse. Now, however, being a little nervous with the attention they were receiving, they could not refrain from giggling.

"Sophia, could you please bring forth the small trunk and open it? Girls, you may show Miss Darcy what you have made."

"Miss Darcy," Margaret spoke with enthusiasm. "My sister and I have been making cloth dolls for nearly two years. Cousin Lizzy gives some of them to Uncle Bennet's tenants, and Mama also leaves some of the dolls at the church for the children of the poor."

"Oh my," Georgiana exclaimed when Margaret handed her one of the dolls. "I cannot believe you made this. The stitches on her face are perfection, and her little dress is charming."

"Papa gave us the cloth from his warehouse, and Miss Sophia showed us how to stitch the dolls and embroider their faces," Grace offered as she brought forth another doll for Georgiana to look at.

Having remarked on the doll as well as the remainder of those in the trunk, Georgiana kindly reached for each of the girls' hands. "Miss Gardiner, Miss Grace, I cannot begin to say how impressed I am with your work. Your generosity will be greatly appreciated when I tell our tenants about the two young ladies from Town who made these special gifts for their children."

"Thank you, Miss Darcy," they echoed in reply. Afterwards, the girls were excused to join their brothers in the nursery. Following their departure, Mrs. Gardiner invited Mrs. Annesley to join her in the garden, allowing Elizabeth and Georgiana some privacy. Sophia and Rebecca were also given leave to enjoy each other's company and withdrew to another part of the house.

~ ♫ ~

"I am sorry Jane is not able to be with us. Since my family is returning to Longbourn tomorrow, my mother was in need of her assistance this afternoon."

"Please tell Miss Bennet how much we enjoyed volunteering today and that I hope to see her again the next time we are all in Town."

"I shall be sure to tell her."

"You must be looking forward to returning to your home. It has been far too long since I was last at Pemberley, nearly a year now."

Trying not to alarm her friend, Elizabeth endeavoured to speak with care. "Georgiana, I shall not be returning to Longbourn. My father and uncle have decided it would be best for me to remain in Town."

"Has something happened to prevent your return?" she asked with concern.

"Please do not distress yourself on my account. I shall tell you, but first, I would like to apologise to you for the poor behaviour exhibited by some of my family members at the Military Ball. I am so sorry to have put you and your brother in such an embarrassing position by being associated with me."

"Elizabeth, there is no need...."

"Oh, yes, dear one, there is." She reached for Georgiana's hand. "Moreover, I am grieved with the knowledge you have read Lady Matlock's letter and that it has caused you pain. Still, despite everything which took place at the Military Ball, I wish to tell you some good has come of it."

"Indeed?"

"Yes. With the help of my Uncle Gardiner, Papa has enlisted the services of an elderly couple who will be joining our family at Longbourn and will remain there throughout the end of the year or possibly longer. Mrs. Holyoak will instruct my younger sisters in the ways of society while her husband will be tutoring them in subjects which are designed to enrich their minds. You see, we did not have a governess when we were younger."

"I cannot imagine such freedom. I have never been without a governess or a companion. Forgive me," she said looking a bit puzzled. "But why, may I ask, should this prevent you from returning with your family to Longbourn?"

"Well, my mother and younger sisters have not taken kindly to the changes imposed by my father and would like to cast the blame on me because of what happened at the ball." Elizabeth could not help but notice her friend's expression turn from curiosity to one of displeasure. Taking a calming breath, she continued. "Mama is also very upset with me because I have refused to accept the hand of ... Mr. Collins."

"No!" Georgiana's hand flew to her mouth in horror.

"Although I knew my mother favoured the match, I did not realise there was an agreement made between her and Mr. Collins which was thoroughly sanctioned by Lady Catherine. If you recall, Mr. Collins is my father's heir. Had I accepted him, my family would have been protected in the event Papa became ill or died.

"Since Mr. Collins will be a guest at our home and prefers to visit *without* the reminder of my refusal, I am to stay here. It may only be for two or three months or at the very latest until my aunt and uncle travel to visit my family in late December."

"I am grieved to hear it."

"Please, do not distress yourself. I promise I shall be fine. Furthermore, I shall be spared Mr. Collins' pointed sermonettes and his lofty references to his noble patroness." Both women giggled with Elizabeth attempting to make light of what had happened.

"Is there nothing I can do to help you?" Georgiana implored. "Could you not possibly reconsider and come with us to Brighton? It is not far and I am sure my cousins would not mind in the least if I brought you as my particular friend."

"Oh dear, I … I could not possibly…. I mean … although your brother is in support of our friendship, I … I believe it would not be prudent for all of us to be seen together in society for some time." Her face became heated at the thought of being in Mr. Darcy's company.

"My sweet friend, you have no idea how much I would enjoy going to the seaside. But if I were to accompany you, I know there would be some talk of what transpired at the ball, and I simply could not bear to have either you or your brother censured on my account. For the time being, it is better for me to remain here with my aunt and uncle."

"I understand." Georgiana knitted her brows while reviewing what her friend had told her. "Elizabeth, I do have another thought. My cousin's house party will only last through the end of August at which time I shall return with her to Town and reside at Ferversham House. William will be gone for much of September, and it would give me great pleasure to host you as my guest."

"I am not sure." She hesitated. "My staying as your guest might still be a bit awkward. I would not wish to impose upon any of your family, considering my current disgrace."

"Elizabeth," Georgiana spoke softly. "Yesterday, William talked with Aunt Eleanor and Aunt Catherine about the letter."

"He did?"

"Yes. I suspect their conversation was not pleasant since he did not tell me specifically what was said. Even so, William did say that Lord Matlock has chosen to support his decision with regard to our friendship."

"I am astonished!"

"Perhaps it will not be so bad after all. William told me both of our uncles have had business dealings with one another, and because of their relationship, my uncle will hear no more slander of you or your family from my aunts."

"Georgiana ... I.... I hardly know what to say. Lord Matlock is most generous." Elizabeth paused to consider all she had heard. "Very well, in light of what you have just told me, I shall discuss your offer with my aunt and *possibly* reconsider. But only if your brother believes the invitation is sensible and if your cousin has no objection after being told of my predicament."

"Thank you. I shall do my very best to persuade them." She smiled. "Now, before we part, I wish to give you a gift." Reaching for her reticule, she took out a small box and handed it to Elizabeth.

"Georgiana, what is this?" Elizabeth gasped when she opened the box and discovered a beautiful bracelet. The delicate adornment was crafted with small clusters of diamonds and emeralds shaped like tiny flowers. In awe of the lovely gift, she quietly confessed, "I have never seen anything quite like this. It is so simple, yet so very elegant. My sweet friend, I am sorry, but I cannot possibly accept such a gift. It is far too much."

Ignoring her protest, Georgiana held out her own wrist saying, "After my illness, I asked William to have identical bracelets made for both of us. Please allow me to help you with yours."

Elizabeth marvelled at Georgiana's persistence. Her friend was certainly becoming more assertive. Still, she extended her hand with reluctance. Once the bracelet was fastened about her wrist, she marvelled at how the tiny jewels sparkled and shimmered when she turned her hand in the light. "You are far too generous. I hesitate to keep this."

"The bracelet is very special, and it is something I would have shared with my sister, Amelia, had she lived."

"Amelia? Oh, dear. Forgive me, I did not know."

"My sister would have been two years older than me. Mama carried her to the end of her confinement, but the babe was stillborn."

Taking Georgiana's hand, Elizabeth offered, "Dearest Georgiana, I am so very sorry."

"Our bracelets were made from a broken necklace which belonged to my mother."

"I cannot believe you wish to share this treasure with me, and I thank you with all of my heart." She embraced Georgiana and smiled lovingly.

"I, too, have a gift for you." Picking up a book from the small side table, Elizabeth opened it and handed Georgiana a bookmark. "This is rather insignificant when compared to your gift, but even so, I think you will like it since I made it especially for you."

"How lovely!" she exclaimed carefully touching the delicate lace around the edge of the fine linen.

"The lace is from France."

"From France?"

"Yes. Uncle Gardiner has not been able to import French lace for some time, but this piece is taken from a card which he gave my aunt before the embargo."

Continuing to touch the tiny hearts and daisies surrounding the fine emerald lettering on the pale linen cloth, she read aloud, "*A heart which freely gives is never lonely.* What a beautiful thought, and it is something I have only begun to learn. Thank you."

"You are most welcome." She hesitated for a moment before continuing. "If I may, might I enquire of your brother? With everything that took place at the ball, and now this business with your aunts, I worry for his well-being."

"I do admit he has kept to himself for the past several days, but it is not uncommon, since we are preparing to leave Town."

"Yes, of course. Yet, knowing Mr. Darcy, I suspect the events of the past week may be weighing heavily on him even though he may not show it. During my short acquaintance with your brother, I have come to understand he is one who would shoulder the burden as well as the responsibility of strife within your family while giving the impression nothing is amiss. In light of what has happened, it is possible he may be in need of your support."

"*My* support?"

"Yes. Since you are one of his dearest relations, it is within your power to help him."

"I am embarrassed to say I have never considered the possibility of William needing me in such a way. He is always so steady. What would you suggest I do to help him?"

"Well, I cannot answer to specifics, but I would suggest you be observant and try to cheer him in small ways. If he sees you are happy, I believe it will help to put his mind at ease when he is dealing with so many difficulties."

"I understand, and I shall be happy to do as you suggest."

"I know you will, and I also know you will be a great comfort to him. Now, may I propose we go out to the garden? Aunt Gardiner has prepared some cuttings of her favourite herbs along with a small notebook of recipes and natural remedies for Mrs. Troutman."

"Please. I would love to see her garden." The two women happily walked outside to where Mrs. Gardiner and Mrs. Annesley were looking at an unusual plant. Fascinated by the conversation, Georgiana expressed a strong interest in learning more about some of the remedies which were written in the notebook. All in all, their visit had passed more quickly than anyone would have wished, and soon it was time for the ladies to take their leave and return to Darcy House.

Before they boarded the carriage, Elizabeth took a moment to speak privately with Georgiana. "My dear friend, you have no idea how much your visit has meant to me this afternoon. Your presence here has warmed my heart. Please take care of yourself and do look after your brother."

"I promise, and I shall write to you most faithfully." With tears in their eyes, the two women embraced one another and said goodbye.

"I shall miss you, my little sister."

"And I, you."

Georgiana was assisted into the carriage and waved as the vehicle pulled away. Elizabeth continued to watch until it could no longer be seen and then returned to the house, feeling quite alone.

CHAPTER NINETEEN

MAKING AMENDS

Darcy House
Friday, 26 July 1811
Late afternoon

$\mathcal{U}$pon returning home, Georgiana removed her outer garments and went directly to Darcy's study. Being bid to enter as soon as she knocked, she opened the door and greeted him with a cheerful smile before rushing to his side.

"I gather you have had an enjoyable afternoon."

"Oh yes, William, the *Correspondence Hours* proved far more beneficial than I anticipated, and my time with Elizabeth and Mrs. Gardiner was perfect. I only wish you could have come with us."

"It is just as well I did not join you since I prefer not to be the only man in a room full of chattering women." Georgiana giggled.

"Come, let us sit and you can tell me all about it." He took her hand and gestured to the small sofa.

"Brother, the officer I helped was a lieutenant from Somerset. He was very grateful for my assistance. Thankfully, his injuries were not as severe as some of the others, and I think he will be able to return home soon.

"Sadly, the patient Mrs. Annesley assisted was far worse. The officer had lost most of his right arm and it will not be easy for him to work once he recovers. Mrs. Annesley learned his family were tenants on an estate in Kent, not too far from where her son lives."

"War is a difficult thing. Loss of life is to be expected, but in these instances when we actually see the atrocities of battle for ourselves, we cannot help but take pause." He squeezed her hand. "My dear sister, I am pleased you and Mrs. Annesley were able to help in this way and I am very proud of your efforts."

"Thank you," she modestly answered. "I told Mrs. Madison we shall contact her when we are available to volunteer again."

"Very good. Now," he said with more reserve. "Might I hear of your time with Miss Elizabeth?"

"Oh, William!" She beamed. "It was so good to see Elizabeth and her family. Mrs. Gardiner has a lovely house. She served tea, and we ate the most delicious lemon tarts. Her young daughters, Margaret and Grace, were allowed to join us. Having heard of my planned tenant visits from Elizabeth, the girls presented me with a small trunk of cloth dolls which they made for me to give to some of the children who live on our estate. Brother, their generosity was touching."

"I am sure their efforts will be well received."

"Mrs. Gardiner also took us on a tour of her herb garden and gave me a variety of cuttings for Mrs. Troutman to have planted here if you have no objection."

"Of course not."

"She also prepared a notebook with recipes and suggestions of how to use the herbs. I would like to make a copy for myself so I can share it with Mrs. Reynolds when we return to Pemberley."

"I think our housekeeper would welcome such an offering." Darcy smiled, trying to hide the guilt which he was concealing while listening to his sister talk of Mrs. Gardiner's thoughtfulness. At this moment, he was not proud of what he had demanded of Elizabeth during his failed proposal, nor could he block the memory of her refusal from his mind. Disturbing as it was, he needed to hear more.

"Tell me, did Miss Elizabeth accept your gift?"

"She did. At first she was hesitant, just as you said she would be, but when I told her of Amelia, she relented."

"Georgiana Darcy!" he chided. "It sounds to me like you took advantage of Miss Elizabeth's kind heart."

"Forgive me, William, I did. I know I should not have, but Elizabeth is like a sister to me and I wanted her to have the bracelet. After her apology and all she told me, I feared she would not take it."

"What apology?" He frowned.

"Brother, Elizabeth apologised for her family's conduct at the ball and for the discord which occurred between you and our aunts." Not proud of what his own behaviour had been when he last saw Elizabeth, Darcy did not respond but merely shook his head in disbelief.

"She also expressed concern for *your* well-being."

"*My* well-being?"

"Yes, Elizabeth said with all of our family troubles of late, she thought you might be in need of ... of *my* support."

Noticing the loving expression which radiated from his sister's face, Darcy could not help himself and embraced her in an attempt to hold back his emotions. "Yes, Georgiana, it is hard to admit, but at times I do need you. Miss Elizabeth is very wise."

"There is more," she stated when he released her.

"More?"

"William, Elizabeth is not returning to Hertfordshire with her family. Both her father and uncle have determined it would be best for her to remain in Town for several months."

"Why for several months? I cannot believe she has done anything that warrants such a separation from her own family."

"She did not tell me all of it, but after what happened at the ball, Mr. Bennet has decided to implement some changes when his family returns home. For one, Elizabeth says her father has hired a married couple for the sole purpose of tutoring the younger girls and instructing them in the ways of proper decorum."

Darcy furrowed his brows. *If only he had taken them to task years ago, perhaps....* Clearing his throat, he noted, "I suppose that is hopeful, but why should this prevent Miss Elizabeth from returning to her home?"

"Brother, it is the worst. Not only is Mrs. Bennet unhappy with Elizabeth because of Mr. Bennet's mandates, but she is very cross with her for refusing Mr. Collins' offer of marriage."

"Good God!" Darcy immediately rose, needing to move. "I cannot believe it. Was she very much upset?"

"I think so, but she kept it well hidden. Her greater concern was for the censure you and I might experience in allowing our friendship to continue. I did try to offer her solace and asked her to reconsider my offer and come with us to Brighton, but she refused."

"Naturally," he bitterly said out of frustration. Then regaining his composure and trying not to upset Georgiana, he sat down again and asked her to continue.

"With what happened at the ball, Elizabeth says it would be better for her to remain with her aunt and uncle, away from society for the present." She paused for a moment. "William, I did present her with one other possibility, and I would like your help if you think it is wise."

"Go on."

"I asked Elizabeth to consider staying with me once I return to Town in September. I thought she would enjoy being my guest at Ferversham House while you are away." He raised a brow and unconsciously held his breath, half hoping Elizabeth had accepted.

"She was still reluctant, but when I mentioned the outcome of your meeting with our aunts and Uncle Gregory, Elizabeth said she would consider my offer. Her final answer would depend on your opinion of the matter and whether our cousin had any objection to the plan after learning of her current situation."

"By all means, I shall help you. Miss Elizabeth is…. She is your friend, and I shall speak with Lady Jessica on your behalf at the earliest opportunity."

"Thank you, William." She clasped his hand. "I knew you would help me."

He squeezed her hand in acknowledgement. "In the meantime, you should continue on with your correspondence and cheer Miss Elizabeth with your letters."

"I shall be more than happy to do so. Oh, I nearly forgot. I wanted to show you what Elizabeth gave me." Georgiana opened her reticule and took out the bookmark, handing it to her brother. "Is it not lovely? Elizabeth embroidered it with one of her favourite sayings."

Taking the precious gift in his hand, Darcy reverently touched the tiny hearts and flowers as he softly read the words aloud, "A heart which freely gives is never lonely."

Reading those simple words caused Darcy to undergo an onset of emotion which threatened to shake his entire being. *A heart which freely gives....Is this the lesson I am to learn? Can I even begin to make such a claim for myself? Certainly, I would do anything for Georgiana, but can I say that of my dealings with others?* Darcy groaned inwardly while his sister continued to talk. *Dear Lord, what have I done? If I was a man who freely gave, I would have put aside my objections and would have treated Elizabeth with the respect she deserved.*

Trying not to show his pain, he gave the bookmark back to Georgiana and admitted, "Yes, it is a lovely thought, and one I believe we should both strive to embrace. Georgie, you have had a long afternoon. May I suggest you take some time for yourself while I finish here? I still have much to accomplish if we are to leave for Brighton as planned."

"Yes, William. Shall I join you later for dinner?"

"Please do. Richard plans to be here as well, and I am sure he will enjoy hearing about your afternoon." After kissing her on the forehead, she quickly hugged him and left the room.

~ ♫ ~

Darcy told Georgiana he would continue on with his work, but at this moment, that task was the furthest thing from his mind. Not able to sit, he began pacing the length of the room with vigour. "How could I have been so selfish? I never even honoured her with a proper proposal. Everything I said was about *me, my* stupid pride, *my* family, and *my* obligations." He hung his head in shame. *Dear Lord, forgive me. I have unjustly hurt the one woman who has given me so much.*

Taking out the strand of white lace from his breast pocket, Darcy looked intently at the treasure which lay in his hand. For many weeks, it had remained his constant companion, a reminder of her. Its simplicity and purity symbolised Elizabeth's gracious heart and he refused to part with it, now more than ever.

"When I was distressed, your kind words gave me comfort and hope. Dearest Elizabeth, I am so sorry. How can you ever forgive me? I did not deserve your love." Stepping to the window, he peered out into the garden. Trying to extend his gaze beyond what was physically there, he whispered in a hoarse tone. "Elizabeth, I swear by my love for you, I shall take this lesson to heart, and I *shall* be a better man for it."

~ ♫ ~

Cheapside
Monday, 29 July 1811
Early morning, several days later

Darcy took out his pocket watch and checked the time yet again. His appointment with Edward Gardiner was less than thirty minutes now, and his carriage had been at a standstill for nearly fifteen. One of his footmen had informed him that an overturned wagon was stopping the flow of traffic up ahead, hence the delay. The street could not bear such an obstruction, at least not with the disproportionate number of carts and wagons which regularly filled the thoroughfare in this section of Town. Determined not to be late, Darcy chose to leave his vehicle and proceed on foot after giving instructions to his driver to meet him at the appointed address once he was able to do so.

While Darcy was not averse to walking, it was not an easy task making his way through the crowded market area towards the buildings which were owned by Edward Gardiner. It seemed like every available space on this street had been taken over by vendor carts and filled with local residents who were eager to barter for the best prices.

Passing cart after cart, an odd sensation came over him as he began to observe the day-to-day lives of the people who made their livelihood here. In the past, Darcy had abhorred the material conditions in this part of Town. Today was different. Moving amongst these people, he could not help but embrace compassion for those whose lot in life was so different from his own.

After turning the corner leading to the warehouse district, the road finally opened up, and the stench of fish and garbage which had permeated much of the market place began to dissipate. All in all, there was still a fair amount of activity in the neighbourhood, but not enough to hinder Darcy's progress. Walking at a quick pace, he managed to arrive at his destination with a few minutes to spare.

~ ♫ ~

Gardiner's Warehouse

"Lawd above! *Bad* morning, governor. Biddle at yer service, sir."

Darcy could not help but smile as he looked at the kindly old man and handed him his card. "Good morning, Biddle. I believe Mr. Gardiner is expecting me."

"Blimey! Yes, 'e said what I should brin' ye in as soon as ye arrived. *Isle ov Wight* dis way, Mr. Darcy, sir. Nuff said, yeah?"

"Thank you." Darcy nodded and followed the ageing man who limped his way down the long corridor to Mr. Gardiner's office. This particular building, teaming with activity, was Gardiner's main centre for shipping and receiving from the docks.

Knocking on the door, Biddle announced, "Mr. Darcy is 'ere, sir."

"Very good," Gardiner spoke from behind the desk. "Johnny, see that these invoices are given to Mr. Burke at once."

"Yes, sir." The young boy took the folder and quickly exited while Mr. Gardiner rose and extended his hand to Darcy.

"Mr. Darcy, please be seated. May I get you something to drink?"

"No, thank you." Darcy nervously took a seat and began to speak. "I appreciate your kindness in allowing me to call this morning. My sister and I are due to begin our travel today, but I found I could not leave Town in good conscience without first coming to apologise."

"I understand." Mr. Gardiner nodded but said nothing more.

"To begin with, I wish to address Lady Matlock's deplorable treatment of Mrs. Gardiner, Miss Bennet, and Miss Elizabeth. I am embarrassed to say I read the disgraceful letter which was sent to your wife from my aunt, and I am sorry that it was ever written. Since then, I have spoken to both of my aunts, and with Lord Matlock's support, they will no longer be allowed to disparage your family. Mr. Gardiner, I beg you to extend my apologies to the ladies."

"I shall see to it." Again he nodded.

Not able to sit any longer, Darcy rose and took a couple of steps then turned and stated, "Mr. Gardiner, I am sure you are well aware your niece and I had words earlier last week and that we did not part well."

"Yes, my wife informed me of Elizabeth's distress."

Darcy momentarily closed his eyes, imagining the worst. "Sir, I cannot begin to think of the manner in which I addressed your niece without abhorrence. At the time, I was only concerned with my own affairs and thought nothing of the unreasonable demand I was placing upon her when … when I offered her my hand. At the time, I was desperate to find a solution which might have allowed me to continue on with my obligations to society as I saw fit. Regrettably, I gave little regard to Miss Elizabeth's desires or needs. In that respect, I am as culpable as my aunt. Through my own foolish pride, I have offended and hurt the one woman I hold most dear, and I deeply regret it."

"Mr. Darcy, our situation is difficult. You and I come from very different circles. Perhaps it was too much to expect that we could forsake those traditions which have been ingrained in our upbringing."

Darcy shook his head. "Sir, you are too kind. While my family is steeped in tradition, *I* should have known better. I realise the damage which I inflicted can hardly be undone, but I do, nevertheless, offer you and your family my humble apology on that account."

"Thank you, Mr. Darcy. I shall convey your sentiments."

"Mr. Gardiner," he hesitated. "Forgive me, if I may, there is one more matter I would like to mention. From my sister, I have learned Miss Elizabeth was not allowed to return with her family to Longbourn."

"Yes, that is so."

"Georgiana cares deeply for your niece. She will be returning to Town at the beginning of September and will reside with our cousin, Lady Helmsley, at Ferversham House for the remainder of the month. As I am sure you are well aware, Georgiana invited Miss Elizabeth to be her guest during that time. My sister knows nothing of my recent interactions with your niece. Even though there is potential for some awkward moments, please tell Miss Elizabeth I shall not impose upon her with my presence during her stay without her approval. I assure you I would not seek her out unless it was her wish.

"I pray you would encourage Miss Elizabeth to accept my sister's offer. Lady Helmsley does not adhere to the unspoken rules of the *ton*. I can assure you my cousin will welcome your niece based on her relationship with my sister and upon my recommendation, not on gossip or unwarranted accusations."

"Thank you, Mr. Darcy. I appreciate your candour and shall be happy to speak with my wife and Elizabeth on Miss Darcy's behalf."

"That is all I ask." Darcy rose and extended his hand. "I appreciate your kindness."

Mr. Gardiner smiled taking his hand. "Son, it took a good deal of resolve for you to come and see me today. That says much for your character." The gentlemen said their goodbyes and Darcy left the building in search of his carriage.

~ ♫ ~

Gracechurch Street
That same day

Elizabeth sat quietly in the front parlour attempting to finish the embroidery on her handkerchief. The flowers were daisies and sweet

Williams. It was one she had begun before the military ball, but had not been able to pick up after her quarrel with Mr. Darcy. Seeing Georgiana had eased her mind where *he* was concerned.

"Excuse me, Miss Elizabeth. Miss Darcy's footman is at the door and has come with a letter. He insists on giving it to you himself. Shall I show him in?"

"Thank you, Daniels. Please do." Elizabeth knew the Darcys were due to leave Town today and did not expect to hear from Georgiana. Wondering if something was amiss, she quickly rose and waited for the footman to enter. Upon taking the letter, she noticed her name was not written in the hand of her friend, but in that of Mr. Darcy. The servant bowed and immediately took his leave, not waiting for her reply as was his wont whenever Georgiana wrote. Putting the letter in her pocket, she quickly grabbed her shawl and went out to the garden where she would not be disturbed. Considering the impropriety in receiving his letter, she was grateful her aunt had not been present at the time it was delivered.

Sitting nervously on the same bench where she and Mr. Darcy had last sat together, Elizabeth's heart pounded mercilessly, and her face flushed in anticipation of what he might possibly have to say. Tears threatened to leave the corners of her eyes as she carefully opened the missive and began reading.

Dearest Elizabeth,

Forgive me for addressing you as such, but I find I can think of you in no other way. Despite what was said between us, you shall be forever dear to my heart. Thus, I find I could not leave Town without first offering you my sincerest apology.

Since last we met, I have had much to reflect upon. In all honesty, I find I do not care for the man who addressed you on that shameful day. Georgiana showed me the bookmark which you gave her, and I wanted you to know how profoundly your words have affected me. "To freely give," as you so simply put it, is something I believe you

*have done for your entire life. It is a part of your good nature and
something I have long forgotten.*

*As a young child, I had the most excellent model of a woman who
freely gave to others. She was my very own mother. With her actions,
she tried to teach me what was important in life. For her, it was not
wealth, position, or status she valued. It was integrity and the doing of
good works.*

*After my mother died, little by little, I forgot or perhaps I even chose
to ignore what was important to her. I strove to be more like my
father in order to gain his notice. He was a good man who was
revered as a generous landlord, yet he was very rigid in his beliefs.
Driven by dignity, duty and honour, I regret to say my father did not
freely give of himself in the same way my mother did. He merely did
what was required of him while staying true to the unspoken rules of
our society.*

*In reviewing my own behaviour, I realised I have been selfish in
regard to you. Had I been otherwise, I would never have proposed to
you in a manner which was so beneath your dignity. I thought only of
my wants, needs, and responsibilities. While I have never truly cared
for the conventions of the 'ton,' in this instance, I gave priority to their
dictates rather than the needs of the one person in this world whom I
cherish above all others. I could not see past my own discomfort long
enough to realise I was causing you pain of the acutest kind with my
demands. In retrospect, I realise your reproofs were much deserved.*

*At this juncture, I do not believe I have earned the right to ask for
your forgiveness as I do not yet deserve it. Instead, I wish to humbly
apologise for the pain I have caused you. I shall only add, God Bless
you, dearest Elizabeth.*

Fitzwilliam Darcy

CHAPTER TWENTY

DEEP IN MY HEART

Gracechurch Street
Monday, 12 August 1811
Two weeks later

*S*itting at the dressing table, Elizabeth could not help but frown at her reflection in the looking glass. It had been two weeks since she received Darcy's letter, and still her eyes bore the evidence of restless sleep and teary eyes. Each night his presence invaded her dreams and each day the thought of him never left her for a moment. In her mind, she was not formed for melancholy; yet where *he* was concerned, her heart continued to ache. Reaching for her treasured book of Thomas Moore verses which now contained his letter, she gave it a reverent kiss and tucked it safely away in her pocket before starting her day's activities.

Knowing that precious missive word for word, Elizabeth allowed a hint of a smile to grace her lips. Darcy said he did not deserve her forgiveness, yet she had forgiven him upon reading his heartfelt words. To her surprise, he had further humbled himself by going to her uncle's warehouse and formally offering his apology before leaving Town. It mattered not they had parted badly. For Elizabeth

Bennet, Fitzwilliam Darcy was the best of men, and he owned her heart. "William, I love you dearly," she whispered, "now more than ever."

~ ♫ ~

Mrs. Gardiner had been sorting through some old correspondences when Elizabeth entered the parlour. At the recommendation of the parish rector, the two women were asked to assist with another charity. Today, they would begin sending out requests to several acquaintances who might show an interest in forming a committee for this endeavour. While the new project was not nearly as grand as the building of a military wing for the London Hospital, Elizabeth believed it was every bit as worthy. Mr. Thomas Cranfield was in need of funds to support his Sunday afternoon schools for the poor. The schools not only taught children and adults to read, but they distributed food, clothing and shoes to those who were enrolled in the school.

"Lizzy, an express came from Miss Darcy a few minutes ago and there is also a letter from Jane which arrived in the morning post. My dear, it seems you are quite popular today."

"Thank you, Aunt." She eagerly picked up her letters looking at the direction on each.

"Please take your time. I have sent Miss Darcy's footman to the kitchen after his long journey from Brighton. As usual, the young man says he will be staying the night at Darcy House and will return for your reply in the morning. I can leave you to your solitude if you like."

"Thank you, but no. I would prefer you to stay. I shall be happy to share the news when I am finished."

Elizabeth took a seat and opened her friend's letter first. As she suspected, it was a final confirmation of her invitation to be a guest at Ferversham House in September. "Georgiana says that all is settled, and her cousin plans to arrange several outings for us during my stay. In addition to shopping, which Georgiana dearly loves, Lady Helmsley wishes to take us to a new exhibit at the Royal Museum as well as one or two evenings at the theatre. She also mentions something about a large dinner party which will be given in honour of Lady Helmsley's friend, Miss Paradis, who is due to return to the continent. Apparently, there will be quite a bit of musical entertainment on that particular evening, and Georgiana has been asked to perform. Aunt, I can hardly believe it. Imagine! *I* am to be a guest of a viscount and his wife!" Elizabeth giggled.

"I am very pleased for you, Lizzy."

"If Mama only knew, she would insist Papa send money for new clothes and would no doubt post the letter herself before rushing off to tell Aunt Philips. Who knows? When I next write to Jane and tell her of my news, Mama might possibly begin to forgive me for refusing Mr. Collins. After all, my visit with Miss Darcy is sure *to put me in the path of many rich men.*" She playfully laughed.

"Lizzy, it is good you can make light of your situation, though I dare say you *will* be in need of at least two or three new gowns for the occasion. If you have no objection, I think tomorrow should be the perfect day for us to visit the dressmaker and choose some patterns. And since your uncle has mentioned he has a new shipment of silks at his warehouse, I know we will have some of the finest fabrics to choose from."

"Thank you, Aunt. You are too kind."

"Think nothing of it my dear. Of course, you do realise it is possible you may see Mr. Darcy while you are at Ferversham house. Even though he told Edward he would not impose upon you during your stay, it would be very strange for him not to call upon his sister when he returns to Town."

"Yes, I know." Elizabeth became quiet.

"Do you not care to see him again?"

"I *do* want to see him, very much so. But if you recall, when Mr. Darcy last spoke with Uncle, he said he would not seek me out unless it was *my* wish. How am I to make my sentiments known? I have asked Georgiana to extend my regards to him when we correspond, but that is hardly the same thing as telling him what I truly desire."

"It seems you will have to wait until you are in residence as Miss

Darcy's guest. Until then, all we can do is to trust that everything will eventually work out for the best."

"I only pray you are right."

"Now, tell me what news do you have from Longbourn?"

Elizabeth picked up her second letter and gasped aloud as she began to peruse the lines. "Aunt, you will not believe it. Jane says Mr. Collins has proposed to *Charlotte Lucas* and she has accepted."

"Mr. Collins! I am astonished. Why, the man is not very constant, is he?"

"No, he is not! I can imagine Mama has been keeping to her rooms ever since she heard the news. Poor Jane will be expected to tend her throughout her misery. Oh dear, she also says Mr. Collins insists on marrying as soon as the banns have been read. Evidently, he cannot be away from his post in Hunsford for too long. This surely did not set well with Mama."

"I should think not."

"After this report, I doubt if my invitation to stay at Ferversham House will be enough to ease Mama's vexation with me. I do hope that Mrs. Holyoak will be able to help Jane console her. If you do not mind, I would like to answer both of these letters before I take up our correspondence for the charity."

"Go right ahead, my dear."

~ ♫ ~

After nearly two hours of writing letters, both Elizabeth and Mrs. Gardiner decided to stop for the day and enjoy a cup of tea. About that time, there was a knock at the front door and a servant entered the parlour bearing a gentleman's card.

"Elizabeth," said Mrs. Gardiner with pleasure. "It is Mr. Bishop. Daniels, please ask Mr. Bishop to come in and join us."

"Aunt, I never expected Mr. Bishop to visit here," Elizabeth whispered. "I do hope there is nothing amiss with any of the musical events for the hospital charity."

"Those, too, are my sentiments."

"Mrs. Gardiner, Miss Elizabeth Bennet. How lovely it is to see both of you this fine afternoon." The gentleman energetically bowed and graciously accepted Mrs. Gardiner's invitation to sit down and enjoy a cup of tea.

"Mr. Bishop, it is such a pleasure to see you again. I trust you have been well."

"Why, yes, never better." Elizabeth served him while he continued to talk. "Forgive me for having called without any notice. I happen to be on a rather *peculiar* errand this afternoon." Both women looked at each other with curiosity and then back again at Mr. Bishop.

"I shall get straight to the point. Several weeks ago, I received a commission to compose a song for *you*, Miss Elizabeth."

"For me?" Her face flushed.

"Though the commission has been paid, I regret to say your bene-factor remains anonymous."

"Mr. Bishop," Elizabeth cautiously spoke. "Surely you must realise that it is highly improper for me to accept such a gift."

"I thought you would say as much, but the two hundred pounds which I was paid was incentive enough for me to complete the composition and bring it here."

"Two hundred pounds!" exclaimed both Elizabeth and Mrs. Gardiner.

"Yes, yes, that is correct." Mr. Bishop chuckled taking the manuscript from his satchel and handed it to Elizabeth. "Tell me, are you not in the least bit curious to hear it or perhaps even sing the song yourself?"

Looking at the title page, Elizabeth's eyes grew wide as soon as she recognised her name written in the dedication. Calming herself, she read aloud, *"Deep in my Heart."* Then turning the page, she smiled and noted, "I see it is a ballad."

"How could it be otherwise? Having heard you sing several ballads at one of Her Ladyship's committee gatherings, I was particularly inspired. Miss Elizabeth, when you sing, you present a depth of feeling for the words which few others possess. Believe me when I say it took very little effort on my part to compose this song for you."

"Mr. Bishop, you are too kind." She blushed. "Truly, I do not deserve such praise. Aunt, while I do not intend to keep the song, I admit I do wish to hear it."

"As do I, my dear. Mr. Bishop, if you would be so kind, the clavichord is just over here. I apologise that we do not have a better instrument for you to play on."

"Think nothing of it, Mrs. Gardiner. Shall we try it together, Miss Elizabeth?" he asked while taking a seat.

"If you insist, I will do my best."

"Very good, let us begin." The song, a simple ballad of love, was perfectly suited to Elizabeth's voice. Even though the melody was new to her, it flowed effortlessly as she began to sing the poetry of the first verse.

Not the soft sighs of a cooing dove,
Nor those frail words that speak of love;
Not till thou say'st "I love thee truly,"
Will I believe thee mine,
Till thou say'st "I love thee", thou say'st I love thee;
Till thou say'st "I love thee truly, truly, truly",
Will I give my heart to thee....

Henry Bishop 1786-1855

By the time Elizabeth and Mr. Bishop were finished, Mrs. Gardiner was in tears. "Please, please forgive me." She took out her handkerchief to dry her eyes. "Elizabeth, that was simply beautiful and, Mr. Bishop, there can hardly be enough words to describe your talent. The melody captured the essence of the words and I was moved, very much so. Thank you, sir."

"Mrs. Gardiner, I am humbled." He smiled at Elizabeth, "Your singing was exquisite, my dear. Tis a pity I cannot hire you to become a part of my opera company."

Again she blushed before asking, "What will you do with the song?"

Bursting forth into a broad grin, Mr. Bishop rose from his chair and stated, "Miss Elizabeth, as far as I am concerned, my obligation is fulfilled. I have composed the song and have presented it to you. What *you* do with it is entirely up to *your* discretion. Yet, should you choose to give it *back* to me, I would be honoured if you would permit me to feature it in the ballad opera which I am currently writing. I assure you there will never be any reference to your name or to the circumstances surrounding the composition of this song. Furthermore, should your benefactor choose to contact me at some future date, I will simply inform him that you refused to accept the song."

Elizabeth looked to her aunt who smiled and nodded. "Lizzy, it would be a terrible loss not to allow others to hear Mr. Bishop's composition. Of course, it is up to you."

Elizabeth clasped her hands together and looked down for a moment in thought before answering. "Yes, Mr. Bishop." She beamed. "I freely give the song back to you, and you may use it in whatever way you see fit, providing my name is not associated with it."

Bowing, Mr. Bishop exclaimed, "Thank you, Miss Elizabeth! You will not regret your decision. Mrs. Gardiner, once my opera is complete, it would be my great pleasure to host you and your husband along with Miss Elizabeth at one of our opening performances."

"We should be delighted," replied Mrs. Gardiner.

"Very well then, I will keep you informed of our progress." Mr. Bishop bowed after placing the song back in his satchel. "Now if you will excuse me, it would be best if I took my leave." The women thanked him for his visit, and he departed.

Brighton
August, 1811

In this part of England, nothing could compare to the splendours of Brighton. Here the salty air was fresh, and the view of the coast where the land met the sea seemed to have no end. For those who

260

would seek its pleasures, Brighton's offerings were abundant. By day, one could take a leisurely stroll down the ocean side promenade or be seen in one of the more prestigious tea rooms. Then for those who were more adventurous, the delights of sea bathing or boating might be explored.

Once the evening hours approached, there were concerts to attend, followed by balls or card assemblies lasting into the wee hours of the night and early morning. It was here the Prince Regent spent much of the summer, residing in his lavish Marine Pavilion. Because of his presence and influence, Brighton was seen as a town of fashion, art, music, and culture, as well as a place where one could be constantly amused.

Both Darcy and Georgiana were pleased to see their cousins who had been living on the continent for so many years while the viscount served as an ambassador for England. The Helmsleys had long been family favourites of the Darcys, and learning that their cousins would be remaining in England brought brother and sister great joy.

True to his word, Darcy spoke with Lady Jessica about Elizabeth's situation shortly after his arrival. The viscountess was not unfamiliar with what had taken place at the ball since Lord Ellington had previously spoken with her husband about Darcy's slight of his eldest daughter. Much to Ellington's surprise, Lord Helmsley would not tolerate any unfavourable discussion of his cousin, nor would he allow the spread of rumours at his wife's house party. While there did exist some unspoken tension between Ellington and Darcy, nothing ever came of it. Lady Clarissa was much admired by Lady Helmsley's guests, and once her attention had been taken by one Lord Edmund Tilbury, a young earl who had recently inherited, Darcy was all but forgotten.

~ ♫ ~

Saturday, 17 August 1811
Early morning

261

Having reached the top of a large bluff on the eastern side of his cousin's property, Darcy looked out over the horizon and breathed in deeply. From this picturesque spot, he could easily view the bay leading towards the English Channel as well as the magnificent chalk cliffs which lined the coastal area. Though the air was damp, the cool breeze blowing against his face was refreshing. When visiting his cousins as a youth, this particular view had been a favourite since he had often come here to draw with his mother. How he longed for her loving words and advice. If only she was yet alive.

The time had passed slowly for Darcy since coming to Brighton. Without Elizabeth by his side, he felt empty. There had not been a day when he did not long to return to London with the intent of seeking her out. Knowing he needed to resolve what he had learned about himself since their parting, Darcy resisted those desires and remained where he was.

Today, however, Darcy would make a greater effort to suppress his feelings where Elizabeth was concerned and he would try to enjoy himself for Georgiana's sake. It was her sixteenth birthday, and Lady Jessica had many activities planned. He could not help but smile when remembering how confident and happy she had been of late.

It had not been easy for Georgiana as a child, growing up without their mother. She was barely four years-of-age at the time of their mother's passing. Following Lady Anne's death, their father had become withdrawn, often giving her little notice. With their father's passing some six years later, his dear sister had experienced even greater loneliness and heartache. As much as he tried, he knew he could never replace the absence of their parents in her life and to a great extent this saddened him.

Walking along the bluff, Darcy's mind wandered back to the time of Georgiana's birth. Lady Anne had suffered for months during her pregnancy and her loved ones feared she might not even survive her confinement. Thankfully, Lady Jessica had been at her side during much of that time. His cousin not only supported and encouraged his mother, but she had shown him great kindness when he was most distressed.

For nearly two days, Lady Anne had been bedridden. Men and especially children were not permitted to enter the birthing area, and it angered eleven-year-old Fitzwilliam when he heard her cries and could not offer her comfort. The boy had been waiting in the hallway close to her rooms when his cousin Lady Jessica came upon him.

"Please, please, may I not see her? I have to tell Mama that I love her." His voice faltered. "Can ... can you not take me in for just a few minutes?

"My dear boy, you must be brave," Lady Jessica responded. "This day is a very challenging day for your dear mama. It is not possible for you to see her, but I shall gladly give her your message." She kissed his cheek.

"Fitzwilliam, will you do something for me?"

"Yes," he nodded looking at her with anticipation.

"Very good. I want you to go back to your room and say a prayer for your mama and the babe. Then I would like for you to go down to the kitchens and ask cook to feed you and to prepare a picnic basket. In the meantime, I shall send for Mr. Reynolds. It is a very fine day for fishing and I expect the two of you to spend your time at the pond until I send for you. It will make your mama very happy when I tell her that you will be at her most favourite spot in all of Pemberley. Do you not agree?"

He nodded. "Yes. Do you think the babe will come today?"

"I do, so we must be strong for both of them."

Fitzwilliam squared his shoulders. "I will do as you ask."

"You are a good boy. After you return and you are able to see your mama and the new babe, you may tell her about your day."

Forcing himself back to the present, Darcy inhaled deeply. His mother was no longer with him, but she had left him a precious gift, his sister. Since meeting Elizabeth, she had become more confident and had chosen to embrace life. Georgiana was blossoming into a lovely young woman whom his mother would have been very proud of. *rewrite*

In two days, he would be off to Pemberley. Darcy had much to accomplish in a few short weeks before returning to Town in mid-September. There was the autumn harvest, which was about to begin, an old dam in need of reconstruction, and then of course a short trip to Winfield Manor on behalf of Colonel Fitzwilliam and his uncle.

Having spent so many months away from his estate, the thought of doing physical work and riding about his land was restorative. Once he returned to Pemberley, Darcy knew he would be able to think clearly in regard to himself and Elizabeth. There was something about his home which was calming, a balm to his soul. At Pemberley, he would feel renewed, and when he returned to Town, he would know exactly how to proceed.

Closing his eyes for a few moments, Darcy spoke aloud, beckoning the wind to carry his words to Elizabeth. "My love, though we parted badly, I swear I shall do everything within my power to make amends. I know I do not deserve you, but I love you with all of my heart and I shall never give you up." Opening his eyes, he turned and slowly walked back to the house.

CHAPTER TWENTY-ONE

ANTICIPATION

Thursday, 29 August 1811
Gracechurch Street

"*M*iss, I think this dress is my favourite. There is just a little more to pin on the hem, and then you may take it off."

"Sophia, the dress is exquisite!" exclaimed Elizabeth. "You and your sister have created a work of art from the cloth we selected, and I look forward to wearing it at Lady Helmsley's party."

"Thank you, miss."

"I love how the tiny flecks of gold thread shimmer in the silk overlay. And the flowers your sister sent over for the lower skirt add the perfect compliment. Do you not think so?"

"Yes, I do. Earlier, I asked Mrs. Gardiner if we might have some of the jasmine flowers from her bushes for your hair and she agreed. They should be in bloom for some weeks and will complement the flowers in your dress."

"They would be lovely indeed! The smell is heavenly and I have long wished for such plants at Longbourn. Once the dress is finished, all I will need is a matching pair of silk slippers and my lace gloves.

Sophia, I am so very happy my aunt has given you leave to attend me during my stay at Ferversham House. Whatever would I do without your help?"

"Tis nothing, miss. I shall enjoy waiting on you and seeing Rebecca again."

In truth, words alone could not begin to describe the happiness Elizabeth was feeling on this particular day. While she was pleased with her dress, a brief conversation with her uncle was all it actually took to lift her spirits. For the first time in weeks, Elizabeth's heart felt light. She would see Darcy and in her mind, all would be well.

"Lizzy, I have received a letter from Mr. Darcy. As you know, the gentleman assured me he would not impose upon you with his presence during your stay at Ferversham House without your consent. Yet, today, he is asking permission to call on you when he returns from Pemberley. Mr. Darcy hopes to be back in Town the day before Lady Helmsley's dinner party for her Viennese guest. He says, however, if you are set against him, he will abide by your decision and entreat you no further. How shall I respond?"

Nearly overcome with emotion, Elizabeth answered, "Uncle, please tell him I do wish to see him and that I shall look forward to his visit with great pleasure."

Sophia was finishing the last of the stitches on the hem when Elizabeth heard the sound of running feet hurrying through the hallway and stopping just outside of her door. Following three short knocks, the door was swung open with energy.

"Cousin Lizzy!" exclaimed little Grace stopping abruptly at the threshold of Elizabeth's room, her face filled with awe. "You look like a princess!" The little girl slowly walked into the room and circled around Elizabeth while taking in every detail of her new gown.

"Why, Grace, you sound just like Miss Darcy. She said the same thing to me when she saw Miss Sophia preparing my dress for the Military Ball. There are a few extra pieces of lace on the table which we did not use. Would you like one for your dolly?"

The child's face lit up with delight. "Yes, I would, thank you. When I add it to her dress, I know it will be as lovely as yours." Elizabeth watched as Grace picked up the lace and twirled in place with her doll. Afterwards, she curtseyed and pulled out a folded letter from her pocket.

"Mama asked me to give you this. May I be excused now?"

"Yes, you may. Thank you."

Elizabeth took the letter and chuckled to herself when she recognised the writing. This was the third letter her mother had sent in less than a week's time. After removing the gown and changing back into her day dress, Elizabeth took the opportunity to sit by the window and read what her mother had written.

Lizzy,

You know not how I suffer with my poor nerves. I have cried and pleaded with your father to allow me to travel to Town in order to advise you on the last of your clothes for your stay at Ferversham House. The man is positively obstinate and will not yield on the point no matter how much I beg him. Nor will he send more money for laces and ribbons. Your father simply has no understanding of what it takes to secure a husband. He says we must sacrifice and make do as he has already invested his money in a new tenant roof for the Bensons, and there are no more funds to be had for frivolous necessities.

I never thought I would rue the day when my own husband would put a tenant's roof above one of his daughter's wellbeing, yet it has come to pass. Mrs. Holyoak says we must endure it as best we can, but I tell you, Lizzy, I am sorely vexed. I only pray your Aunt Gardiner has taken you in hand and that you will be presentable in company when you join Miss Darcy. Do not forget you will be staying with very influential, wealthy people, and I expect you to put your best foot forward and not run on in your usual manner. Please write as soon as you are able and put my poor mind at ease.

As always,
Mama

Elizabeth folded the letter and put it aside. Knowing she would need to appease her mother's nerves with descriptions of her new gowns, she had saved samples of cloth, ribbons and laces specifically for that purpose. Her mother would surely take delight when receiving her next letter. Mrs. Bennet had long been dismayed over her daughter's refusal of Mr. Collins, but as of late, an unspoken truce was reached between the two women. With Elizabeth being invited to Feversham House and Mr. Bingley's anticipated visit to Hertfordshire rapidly approaching, Mrs. Bennet was hopeful that one, if not both of her daughters, would make a very good match.

According to Jane, the Bennet family had taken some weeks to adjust to their new way of life. At first, it had been difficult for Kitty and Lydia, in particular, who did not take kindly to the lessons. More recently, Elizabeth was happy to learn that her younger sisters were finally applying themselves. If they continued to progress, her father had promised to consider allowing them to attend one of the local assemblies as a reward.

With regards to estate matters, there was no question that Mr. Bennet was taking a more active role as Master. Where he had once held little interest in the running of his property, he was now diligent in visiting his tenants and listening to their concerns. As for the family, Mr. Bennet made it a point to spend a full hour discussing the activities of the day with the women in his household before retreating to his book room in the evenings. During such times, he reviewed their progress and encouraged his wife and daughters to persevere in their endeavours.

In retrospect, Elizabeth wished her father had chosen to amend his ways long ago for it would have saved all of them much heartache. Had it not been for her Uncle Gardiner's intervention, she doubted her father would have taken the initiative to begin such an arduous task. Elizabeth was grateful for all of the progress which was now being made and dearly hoped she would be allowed to return home once her time at Feversham House had come to an end.

~ ♫ ~

Ferversham House
10 September 1811
Tuesday morning, nearly two weeks later

For two solid hours, Georgiana had diligently practiced the Beethoven piano sonata which was a gift from Lady Jessica. When the Helmsleys resided in Vienna, they had the opportunity to hear Herr Beethoven perform on several occasions and greatly favoured the composer's music.

To Georgiana's delight, her cousin's guest, Miss Paradis, had taken a personal interest in her musical training while in Brighton. The blind musician often supervised Georgiana's practice, and as of late, had encouraged a vigorous study of whatever Beethoven piano literature was available for her use.

In the meantime, Elizabeth sat quietly tying off the last stitches of her embroidery. The fine cloth handkerchief adorned with Sweet Williams and hearts, would inhabit a cherished place within her pocket alongside her treasured book. *In four days' time, William will be here. In just four days, I shall see him.*

Throughout her stay, Elizabeth delighted in hearing much about a younger Fitzwilliam from Lady Jessica who often related stories of Lady Anne for Georgiana's benefit. From her many narratives, it was quite obvious mother and son were very close. On occasion, references had been made to the old pond and to the nature room, two places at Pemberley where Lady Anne and her son had spent many hours in each other's company.

"Even as a young girl, your mama loved the pond," remarked Lady Jessica. *"Surprisingly, it was there where your father first became interested in my dear friend. Although James found the study of nature to be unusual for a woman of the 'ton,' he came to appreciate Lady Anne's passion for the land and what it had to offer. I shall never forget when your mama told me that James had commissioned the conservatory to be built for her as a wedding present. She could not have received a better gift. A year later, he ordered the construction of a nature room so that she might have a place to store her equipage and further her studies. Then later, when Fitzwilliam*

came along, your mama's passion only increased with her determination to teach your brother everything she knew about the land and what it had to offer."

Smiling, Elizabeth remembered the miniature Lady Jessica had shown her and Georgiana of Darcy when he was but ten years-of-age. Having enjoyed the gentleman's narrative when they walked through Hyde Park together, she could easily imagine him engaged in his studies alongside his mother. A lone tear slipped from the corner of her eye. How she wished Lady Anne was yet alive for both of her children. Not wanting to dwell on the sadness, she quickly brushed the moisture from her cheek and rose to take a turn about the room.

Noticing Elizabeth's movement, Georgiana stopped her practice and asked, "Would you not care to join me in a song? This particular passage has been difficult to master and I find the need to play something simpler, if only to clear my mind and rest my fingers for a bit."

"I would be delighted. What do you suggest? Perhaps you would enjoy an English ballad."

"That would be nice, but I was thinking of going back to the love song which my cousin gave us earlier this week."

"You wish to relax by playing more Beethoven?" Elizabeth teased.

"Yes, I do." She smiled. "It is such a lovely melody." Georgiana began to hum the tune while looking through several sheets of music. "Ah, here it is. *Zärtliche Liebe*, Tender Love."

"My dear friend, you are a true romantic. Tis a pity my German is so poor for the beauty of this song will be wasted as I struggle with *ich und auch*."

"Elizabeth, we have worked tirelessly on your pronunciation of those sounds and your German is fine. Shall we begin?"

"As you wish."

Ich liebe dich, so wie du mich.... (translated)
I love you, as you love me,
In the evening as on the morrow.
Not a day has passed that we have not loved,
That we have not shared our sorrow...

May God's blessing be upon you, my life's joy....

L. van Beethoven 1795 published in 1803

"Elizabeth, that was beautiful. May I persuade you to perform it with me on Saturday?"

"Oh, dear," Elizabeth sighed. "I am not sure." Her hesitancy was not because of her German or even because she would be putting herself forth in front of Lady Jessica's friends. It was because Darcy would be there. How could she sing a song of love and not sing it for him? His latest letter to Georgiana indicated he would not be back in Town until Saturday. And if he did not have time to call on her before the party, she certainly did not wish to cause him any embarrassment by singing the song.

Unknown to the girls, Lady Jessica happened to enter the room while they were practicing. Although Elizabeth had only been in residence for two short weeks, she had become very fond of her guest. Consequently, Her Ladyship had undertaken the unspoken task of restoring Elizabeth's reputation within her circle of friends. Dear Georgiana loved Elizabeth like a sister, and from the tender way Darcy had spoken of her at Brighton, she suspected their attachment to be far more than friendship.

"Forgive me for interrupting your practice. I heard your lovely music from the hallway and found myself compelled to join the two of you. Miss Elizabeth, I hope you are not troubled over the German. Let me assure you your pronunciation is quite good and I would be pleased if you sang the Beethoven song on Saturday."

Unable to refuse her hostess, Elizabeth responded, "If you wish it, I shall be happy to do so."

"Thank you. And if you do not mind, I think we should all go to the ballroom now. I understand the tuning of the new pianoforte is complete and I would like to hear how the instrument sounds in that particular room."

Georgiana clapped her hands together with enthusiasm. "Oh, yes! Do let us go. The ballroom ceilings are rather high and I think our music will sound divine in that room. Do you not agree, Elizabeth?"

"Yes, I am sure it will be very grand."

"Girls, I also wanted to tell you I received confirmation from Mr. Bishop that he and his musicians will be here tomorrow afternoon. After assembling a small platform stage for their part of the entertainment, he has extended an invitation to observe his rehearsal."

"Elizabeth," Georgiana spoke with enthusiasm. "I can hardly wait to see their presentation. It will be such fun."

"I agree. Mr. Bishop's music is exceptional, and I look forward to hearing the selections from his newest ballad opera."

The three women continued talking as they went to inspect the changes which had been made in the ballroom for Lady Helmsley's party. Silently, Elizabeth could not help but wonder if the song Mr. Bishop had composed for her might be part of his presentation.

~ ♫ ~

The Ballroom
The next day

"Ah, Your Ladyship! I hope our presence here today does not pose any inconvenience. Please accept my gratitude in allowing us to come in preparation for Saturday's performance." To Elizabeth's amusement, Mr. Bishop behaved much as he had done when working with the committee, finishing with an exaggerated bow before kissing Lady Helmsley's hand.

"You are most welcome, Mr. Bishop. I trust the accommodations are to your liking."

"Everything is simply perfection, My Lady."

She nodded in acceptance. "Sir, I would like to introduce you to my niece. Miss Georgiana Darcy, please allow me to present Mr. Henry Bishop."

"I am pleased to make your acquaintance, Miss Darcy." He bowed with enthusiasm while Georgiana shyly curtseyed and thanked him.

"I understand you already know Miss Elizabeth Bennet," Lady Jessica remarked.

"Indeed! Miss Bennet was a great help to me when Lady Matlock called upon my assistance with the hospital charity. Miss Bennet, once again we meet."

"Thank you, sir. It is a great pleasure to see you here. I must say, we are all eager to hear selections from your new opera this afternoon."

"Ah, yes, I am sure you will find my music quite delightful!" he boasted. "The plot is a comedic satire about a wealthy young woman who is under the guardianship of her aging uncle. Because her marriage portion is very large, her suitors are many. In an effort to eliminate the less desirable gentlemen, her uncle has devised a difficult test. Any eligible man of consequence must pass the test before he may compete for her hand. An absurd concept, is it not?" Mr. Bishop chuckled at his own remark, causing the women to smile. Moments later, Mr. Bishop asked the women to be seated while he finished speaking with his musicians.

The hour proved to be entertaining as the three women watched the composer and his performers rehearse and make adjustments to their scenes. The comic characters were lively and the music which Mr. Bishop had thus far presented was masterful to say the least. There was no doubt in Elizabeth's mind that his presentation would be well received.

A short intermission was called in order to make some changes for the final scene. By the time the props and furniture were in place, Elizabeth wondered what could be amiss since Mr. Bishop appeared to be agitated. Running his hands through his hair in exasperation, the man suddenly turned and looked directly at her. A sinking feeling came over Elizabeth when he walked to where she sat and spoke with all seriousness.

"Miss Bennet, I wonder if I might impose upon you to assist. Miss Feron, our soprano, has not been feeling well and insisted on leaving the rehearsal before we perform the final scene. For the sake of conti-

273

nuity, would you be able to step in and sing her ballad, or do I ask too much?"

"Mr. Bishop, I am flattered, but since I am not familiar with the music, I dare say I might not be of much help to you."

"Ah, but that is the beauty of it, Miss Elizabeth. The ballad is the same song which I recently played for you and Mrs. Gardiner when we last visited. If you recall, I mentioned I had planned to include the song as a part of my latest opera. Do you not remember it?"

Elizabeth could sense the colour rising in her cheeks. "Yes, I do. The song is lovely, indeed."

"Oh, please, Elizabeth," Georgiana begged. "I would dearly love to hear you sing Mr. Bishop's song."

Elizabeth smiled and looked to Lady Jessica who nodded in approval. "Very well then, may I have a copy of the music?"

The composer beamed as he offered Elizabeth his arm and gestured towards the performing area. "Thank you. It will only take me a moment to retrieve the music sheets, and then we may begin."

After Elizabeth was given some instruction about the scene, she took a position where she would say a few lines and then sing the ballad. Even though Elizabeth would never voice her sentiments, she was thrilled to be singing a song which was written especially for her. When she finished, all those who were present broke into applause and congratulated Elizabeth on her performance.

Georgiana could not contain herself and rushed over to her friend with tears in her eyes. "Elizabeth, your singing was so beautiful! Why, it was as though Mr. Bishop's song had been written solely for you and none other."

"Those are my sentiments entirely," added Mr. Bishop with a twinkle in his eyes. "Miss Elizabeth, if I may, I would like to present you with this copy of my song. Your performance was superb. I must not say this too loud, for fear of offending my prima donna, but even *she* has never sung my music with such heartfelt emotion."

Elizabeth was touched by the composer's compliments and found herself compelled to accept the music. "Thank you, Mr. Bishop. You are too kind." With that, he kissed her hand in gratitude and returned to his musicians in order to give them some final instruction. Shortly after, Lady Jessica took her leave of Elizabeth and Georgiana who planned to adjourn to the music room and continue their practice in preparation for Saturday's performance.

~ ♫ ~

Darcy's Carriage
Thursday, 12 September 1811

The wheels of the carriage rumbled down the drive and onto the dark road which marked the start of Darcy's long journey back to Town. The trip from Pemberley to London had never been to his liking. This time, in particular, it would be difficult to embrace forbearance when he desperately longed to see Elizabeth. He knew without question that he would never be whole until he had made amends and won back her heart.

Once he had returned home, it had not taken much for Darcy to put things into perspective where she was concerned. Pemberley and all it stood for had been restorative to his weary soul. Without hesitation, he had written and petitioned Mr. Gardiner to ask his niece if she would agree to see him when he returned to Town. Having received a positive response from her uncle, he felt encouraged. As soon as he was able, Darcy planned to call on Elizabeth with the intention of asking her forgiveness and renewing his addresses in a proper manner. When he next returned home, it was his fondest wish that Elizabeth be by his side. In his mind, she belonged at Pemberley and he vowed to spend a lifetime loving and caring for her if she would but allow it.

Touching his breast pocket, Darcy removed a small velvet pouch containing his mother's ring. It had been given to Lady Anne by James Darcy when he first proposed. The centre stone, a flawless emerald surrounded by smaller diamonds and pearls, was set in a simple gold band. Holding it up to the carriage window, Darcy enjoyed watching the early morning light catch the inherent sparkle of the gems. Smiling, he remembered how his mother had loved this ring. The emerald was her favourite stone for it reminded her of nature, of new life, and of Pemberley. For Darcy, this ring symbolised the hope of a future with Elizabeth. After carefully returning it to his pocket, he found the light had improved enough to begin reading.

Several books lay on the carriage seat, but none had piqued his curiosity more than the one which he hastily took from a locked cabinet before leaving the manor house. It was one of his mother's journals and he had decided to surprise Georgiana by bringing it back for her on his return trip. Like the Nature Room, Lady Anne's journals had been locked away by James Darcy after her death with instructions they not be disturbed. How wrong to have kept them hidden all of these years when they might have given comfort to his sister. During his youth, Darcy had spent countless days at his mother's side, and he regretted not sharing more of his memories with Georgiana until recently.

Rubbing his fingers over the soft leather cover of the journal, he reverently touched his mother's embossed initials in the lower right hand corner before taking it in hand. On opening the book, he discovered two sealed letters within the first pages, one addressed to himself and the other to Georgiana. The ink was faded where their names had been written by an unsteady hand. At first glance, he instinctively knew these letters were written by his mother during her final days.

The accompanying instructions indicated his letter was to be opened on his twenty-first birthday while Georgiana's was to be opened on her sixteenth. Darcy wondered why his father had never made him aware of their existence. It would have meant so much to both him and his sister to have had her words on the days which they were meant to be read.

Ironically, today, September twelfth, was his birthday. He was no longer a young man of one and twenty for he had passed that age by seven years. The date on his letter indicated his mother had written her message just two weeks before her death. Knowing how much pain she had endured and how weak she had been during that time, he marvelled at the treasure which he now held in his hand. His mother may have been gone for twelve years, but holding her precious letter brought her so very close. It was as though she was sitting beside him in the carriage, sharing her thoughts.

23 July, 1799

Fitzwilliam,

My son, my first born, when you read this, I shall no longer be with you on this earth. Words alone can never describe the joy and happiness I have known as your mother. Throughout your life, not a day has passed when I have not thanked our Father in heaven for sending you to me.

By the time you read this letter, you will have graduated university. You will have reached manhood. I know these next years will be challenging as you accept the enormous responsibility of helping your father and eventually becoming master of our grand estate. As you begin to take on this task, I pray you will remember what I have tried to teach you during the time we were yet together.

Fitzwilliam, while you have been given much, all of your wealth will have little meaning if you do not treat those who have been entrusted to your care with integrity and respect. As a member of the landed gentry, you are a fortunate young man. You have it within your power to make a difference in the lives of so many. I have always looked on this charge, not as a duty, but as a privilege. If you see your role in this way, your duties will not become burdensome to you, and you may execute your tasks with joy.

One day, you will take a wife. I pray she will be someone whom you can love and cherish and one who will help you bear the responsibility of the estate. Your father will not hesitate to advise you of your duty to your station in making a good marriage. Though I do not wish to contradict him, I also wanted you to know it is my desire that you marry for love.

Years ago, had I not fallen in love with your father, I would have refused to marry him, despite the expectations of our families. Thankfully, my elder brother respected my wishes and would not have forced the match had I not wanted it. That being said, I find the necessity of cautioning you where my sister Catherine is concerned. I know she has a plan for you and your cousin Anne to marry and will not easily be swayed to change her mind. Although I dearly love my niece, this has never been my desire. I wish you to follow your own heart in this matter and not be swayed by the pressures of our family or position. Finally, I charge you with the care of your beloved sister Georgiana. She has been a blessing to our family. When both your father and I are gone, the two of you will yet have each other, and for that, I am grateful.

My son, I pray your life will be filled with happiness and love. While we shall no longer see each other in the physical form, when you remember me, I shall be with you, in your heart, as you are now in mine.

Your loving mother,
Anne Amelia Fitzwilliam Darcy

With tears misting in his eyes, Darcy quietly folded the letter, placing it in his breast pocket next to Lady Anne's ring. On today, of all days, he could never have dreamed of receiving such a gift. His mother's words, written so long ago, gave him comfort. It mattered not that he had already decided upon his course. The burden of guilt with respect to his father's demands had been lifted. *I love you, Mama. Thank you.*

CHAPTER TWENTY-TWO

REUNION

Ferversham House
Early Evening
Saturday, 14 September 1811

"Sophia, again I must thank you for all of your help. The dress is absolute perfection, and I cannot imagine wearing anything lovelier." Elizabeth squeezed her maid's hand with affection.

"You are very beautiful, miss." She blushed in return. "If you please, I would like to adjust the flowers and curls on this side of your hair. The pins seem a little loose." She deftly rearranged them and then said, "There now, I believe we are finished."

"Oh, yes, they look much better. Thank you. You have no idea how nervous I am about tonight's dinner party. If only Mr. Bishop had not requested I perform with his musicians."

"Is it certain Miss Feron will not be able to sing?"

"Yes. Her cold has not improved and I understand she has some difficulty speaking, let alone being able to sing. I am fortunate Miss Darcy took such a liking to Mr. Bishop's song." Elizabeth smiled thinking of her friend's enthusiasm. "Having gone through it so many times, I had no difficulty recalling the words when I practiced earlier with Mr. Bishop."

In truth, Elizabeth's apprehension was not so much about the evening's performance. Rather, it was the thought of seeing Darcy which unnerved her. Earlier, Lady Jessica had received an express stating his travel had been delayed and he would not arrive until much later in the evening. *How can I sing two intimate love songs in his presence when we have not yet spoken to each other since that horrible day? Will he know I am singing them for him and that I love him dearly? I simply must be patient.*

~ ♫ ~

Lady Jessica's Party

"Elizabeth," Georgiana whispered. "I know my cousins have invited nearly a hundred people for their dinner party, but seeing so many all at once leaves me feeling a bit uneasy." Her body looked stiff, and she obviously could not resist the urge to wring her hands in an effort to calm her nerves. "I only hope I do not falter while playing the Beethoven."

"Dearest, you will be fine. You played beautifully during our rehearsal this afternoon. As for your cousin's guests, most of them are merely close friends whom the Helmsleys have not seen in many years. Remember, you are honouring Lady Jessica and Miss Paradis with your participation, and I am sure your music will be greatly appreciated."

"Thank you. Oh dear, I see my aunt and uncle have arrived." Georgiana dropped her hands to her sides and tried to remain poised. Lady Matlock acknowledged her niece with a nod and beckoned her to come forth with a wave of her hand. "I do hope Aunt Eleanor will be pleased with my performance. At times, she can be rather critical. Pray excuse me."

Elizabeth could not help but wonder how she and her aunt might be treated by the grand lady should there be an opportunity to converse. For the moment, it appeared those thoughts would have to wait since her attention was unexpectedly taken by none other than Lord Wolverton. His Lordship had recently arrived, and it appeared as though he was deciding where he might best make his entrance. Noticing her, the man quickly made his way through the many guests who were waiting in line to greet their hosts and did not stop until he stood next to Elizabeth.

"My dear, you are truly bewitching this evening," the man droned, speaking in such a way that only she could hear. Elizabeth continued to smile, refusing to acknowledge his remarks. Smelling strong drink on his breath, she purposely stepped away from him.

"This is no way to treat me, not after all I have done for you." Again he moved closer.

"*You*, sir, have done nothing but humiliate me," Elizabeth quietly hissed, still refusing to look at him.

"Did you not receive my song?"

"*Your song?*" she asked facing him and glaring with disgust. "For *your* information, I refused to accept that particular song, and the music was promptly returned to Mr. Bishop. As far as I am concerned, there is nothing more to be said."

"I think not," he overstated, perusing her body with lust. "I am used to having my own way, and I believe we *shall* continue this discussion before the night is over—in private, I might add." His smile was unnerving. Following a prolonged kiss to her hand, Lord Wolverton walked away, leaving Elizabeth shaken by his words.

Moments later, Georgiana returned to her side accompanied by Colonel Fitzwilliam who seemed very much aware of her discomfort. Relieved he did not verbally address what he had witnessed in front of Georgiana, she strove to regain her composure.

"Miss Elizabeth, It is a great pleasure to see you once again." He nodded with a slight bow.

"Colonel Fitzwilliam." Elizabeth curtseyed, still somewhat unsettled by her encounter with Lord Wolverton.

"Georgiana tells me we shall have the pleasure of hearing you sing with Mr. Bishop's musicians tonight."

"Yes, Mr. Bishop has honoured me with his request and I sincerely hope my performance will not disappoint."

"Miss Elizabeth, you are too modest. I have heard you sing on more than one occasion and look forward to your presentation."

"Sir, you are too kind."

"Richard, I was present at her rehearsal today and Elizabeth was magnificent! Why, I distinctly heard Mr. Bishop proclaim Miss Feron could not have sung his composition more beautifully."

"Georgiana!" She blushed.

"Miss Elizabeth, I have great faith in my little cousin's musical discernment and have no doubt we shall all be delighted."

"Thank you."

"Now, if you lovely ladies will please excuse me, I find I must speak with a certain gentleman who is in great need of my point of view." He graciously bowed and proceeded to join Lord Wolverton and a few other others who were conversing. Elizabeth wondered if the colonel intended to speak with him on her behalf. If so, she hoped his intervention would be enough to discourage His Lordship from bothering her any further.

~ ♫ ~

Mercifully, the next forty-five minutes proceeded without incident. Ever since Colonel Fitzwilliam had spoken to Lord Wolverton, it appeared the offending gentleman would keep his distance. Still, Elizabeth felt the need to acquaint Mrs. Gardiner with what had happened and sought out her aunt as soon as the opportunity presented itself.

"Elizabeth, your dress is stunning and you look lovely this evening."

"Thank you. I do not know what I would have done without Sophia's assistance. I am pleased to say both she and Rebecca have been given permission by Lady Jessica to attend our performance later on."

"Your hostess is most accommodating. My dear, may I ask how

you are faring with all of the excitement this evening? I noticed you in conversation with Lady Matlock earlier and trust she did not cause you undue distress."

"No, not in the least. Indeed, Her Ladyship was cordial and there was not the slightest hint of disfavour. I frankly did not expect to be acknowledged after what was said in her letter. Apparently, Mr. Darcy's intervention on our behalf was more successful than we anticipated. To my astonishment, Her Ladyship enquired about our charity work with Mr. Cranfield. It seems she heard about it from one of her friends and wishes to speak with you during the course of the evening. I am under the impression she would like to make a donation."

"How unexpected! Of course I shall be happy to give her the necessary information. Speaking of Mr. Darcy, I see he has not yet arrived. May I ask if something is amiss?"

"Lady Jessica received an express from him this afternoon. Apparently, his travel is taking longer than he expected due to a poor stretch of road. Considering the amount of rain we have had during the past two days, it is not surprising. I cannot deny my nerves are not what they should be where the gentleman is concerned. I desperately wish to see him, yet at the same time I am fearful. It makes no sense whatsoever."

Mrs. Gardiner took her niece's hand. "My dear, if it is of any comfort, I venture to say Mr. Darcy's feelings may be of a similar nature, considering what has passed between the two of you."

Elizabeth blushed at her remark. "I suppose it is true." She paused to make sure no one was listening. "Aunt, Lord Wolverton is here." Mrs. Gardiner momentarily frowned looking about the room until she saw him.

"He greeted me earlier and was very imposing. I do not trust him."

"I am so sorry and shall inform your uncle directly."

"I think Colonel Fitzwilliam may have already had words with him on my behalf."

"Colonel Fitzwilliam?"

"Yes. He happened to witness my distress when Lord Wolverton insisted on making himself disagreeable. Not long after, I observed the two of them speaking to one another. Their demeanour suggested the conversation was not of a pleasant nature."

"I see."

"There *is* one more thing. It was Lord Wolverton who commissioned the song. Fortunately, he has no knowledge I am singing it tonight."

"Elizabeth, you are not to worry. You refused to accept the gift, and I am sure Mr. Bishop will abide by your agreement should Lord Wolverton happen to disclose his patronage. I shall also keep watch, and if I see you being affronted in any way by His Lordship, I shall insist your uncle intervenes."

"Thank you."

~ ♪ ~

At the appointed time, Lady Helmsley and her husband invited everyone to join them in the large dining room for dinner. To her great relief, Elizabeth was pleased to see Lord Wolverton placed some distance away from her. Happily seated between Mrs. Gardiner and Georgiana, she finally found herself more at ease.

Shortly before the third course, Georgiana was handed a note by one of the footmen. "Elizabeth, it is from William," she spoke softly. "He has arrived at Darcy House and plans to be here in time for the entertainment."

Without warning, Elizabeth's stomach began to flutter and her face flushed. She was not able to calm herself until Mrs. Gardiner took her hand and whispered. "Lizzy, breathe deeply and relax your shoulders. You will be fine."

"Forgive me, Aunt. It is too much. Mr. Darcy, Lord Wolverton, so many important people, my performance...."

"Elizabeth, you can do this. I suggest you face each event as it presents itself and not dwell on everything all at once. At present, His Lordship is occupied. You were introduced by Lady Jessica to her friends and have been treated well. Mr. Darcy will be here in due time. Now, I suggest you concentrate on your performance since unnecessary worry will only increase your anxiety and affect your singing. Do you not agree?"

"Yes, thank you, Aunt."

~ ♫ ~

Following dinner, the gentlemen separated to the library for port and cigars. Upon their return, the guests were invited to assemble in the ballroom for the evening's entertainment. The room had been fully decorated with an elaborate display of flowers and candelabra and Lady Jessica's beautiful pianoforte was positioned in the front of the room for all to admire as they entered and took their seats.

About that time, Mr. Bishop eagerly sought out Elizabeth with some final instructions. While listening to him, a peculiar sensation came over her and she could not help but smile. *He is here. I know it!* Continuing to nod in response to Mr. Bishop, Elizabeth could not resist slyly looking about the room. Through the din of the crowd, she could easily make out his low baritone voice whenever he spoke. At last, she saw him conversing with Georgiana and Lady Jessica.

One look, please.... One look is all I need. To her relief, Darcy responded to Elizabeth's silent petition. Lifting his head and gazing in her direction, he noticed her. *William.* Her smile, warm and inviting prompted him to do the same. His eyes never left her for a moment and Elizabeth could do nothing to calm her racing heart. His look was all she needed to restore her confidence. Without exchanging a single word, she knew all would be well between them.

~ ♫ ~

While awaiting the start of the entertainment, Elizabeth and Georgiana found themselves seated close to Lady Jessica who would be introducing the evening's musical offerings. Since speaking with Mr. Bishop, there had not been an opportunity where she and Darcy might exchange even the briefest of civilities. At the moment, both he and Colonel Fitzwilliam had separated themselves from the group and appeared to be speaking to one another in earnest. Elizabeth could not help but wonder if her encounter with Lord Wolverton might be the topic of their discussion. Thankfully, His Lordship continued to be occupied by Lord Matlock and a group of gentlemen who were still congregated in the back of the room.

"Elizabeth, I am grateful you have agreed to sing first. It will be much easier to warm my hands on your song before playing the Beethoven Sonata."

"I, too, am a bit nervous," she confided. "As for the Beethoven, I have no doubt you will perform beautifully."

Following their introduction by Lady Jessica, Elizabeth began with the German love song. Her voice flowed effortlessly and lilted throughout the hall as she sang the simple Beethoven melody. She did not have to look in Darcy's direction to know his eyes never left her for a moment. Fearing her own feelings might be revealed in front of so many of Lady Jessica's guests, Elizabeth dared not visibly return his regard though her heart was full. Upon finishing, she politely acknowledged the audience and resumed her seat.

Before Georgiana began to play, Lady Jessica spoke briefly of what her young cousin had accomplished during the past month under the tutelage of Miss Paradis. Georgiana had always been a favourite of Lady Jessica who did not hesitate to acknowledge how pleased she was to be presenting her on this special evening.

Graciously taking her seat at the pianoforte, Georgiana played the three movements of the Beethoven sonata with great energy, leaving no evidence of the nervousness Elizabeth had been privy to. Not only did Georgiana perform the music with technical perfection, but she also played with a maturity and passion which Elizabeth had never before witnessed. Greeted by resounding applause and countless bravos at the close, Lady Jessica stepped forward to claim her cousin's hand and share in her success. Afterwards, it was announced there would be a brief intermission for the purpose of accommodating Mr. Bishop and his musicians.

"I am so proud of you, my dear friend," Elizabeth whispered, squeezing her hands. "I have never heard you play with such feeling."

"Thank you. I am still shaking."

"Then it is fortunate you do not have to stand up with Mr. Bishop and his musicians for the next presentation. Please forgive me. I believe I must join them now."

Turning to go, Elizabeth had not taken more than three of four steps before seeing Lady Matlock followed by Mr. Darcy, coming to congratulate Georgiana. As their eyes met, she paused, no longer able to move. Again her heart quickened, and her cheeks warmed. He was so close. Yet, when Mr. Bishop suddenly appeared in front of her and motioned for her to join his fellow musicians, she knew there would be no possibility of speaking with him until much later.

~ ♫ ~

Lady Jessica graciously welcomed her guests to the next segment of the entertainment by first introducing Mr. Bishop. Speaking with enthusiasm, the composer began to enlighten the audience about what would be taking place during his part of the musical presentation.

"I thank you, Lady Helmsley and esteemed guests. This evening it is my great pleasure to present two delightful scenes from my newly composed Ballad Opera, *The Suitors*. This extraordinary work will be performed in its entirety during the upcoming season as a part of Lady Matlock's continued efforts to raise money for the London Hospital. Before we proceed, however, I would like to make a brief announcement. Perhaps some of you may have heard my leading soprano took ill earlier this week. A few days ago, it became apparent Miss Feron would not be able to sing this evening, and I found myself imposing upon one of Lady Helmsley's guests for assistance. Happily, Miss Elizabeth Bennet has graciously agreed to perform with us and will be playing the part of Lady Chloe in tonight's offering.

"In my comical farce, *"The Suitors,* we find three eligible bachelors who are all vying for the hand of our lovely heiress, Lady Chloe. Lord Thaddeus Ardingley, her aged uncle, has set in place a test of wits in order to evaluate any potential suitor wishing to compete for her hand. In the first excerpt, we shall be introduced to three noble lords who have come together for that purpose. As you may well imagine, our gentlemen are somewhat flawed and do not hesitate to exhibit their *deficiencies* within a comedic dialogue and lively trio.

"To complicate matters, the lovely Lady Chloe happens to be in love with a gentleman who has yet to come forth and present himself as a competitor. In the second scene, Lord Ardingley chooses to question his niece about the young man who has engaged her affections, wishing to know the truth of the matter. In response, Lady Chloe will sing *Deep in My Heart,* a song I believe you will find to be one of the most beautiful ballads ever set to music by my own hand. Now, without further ado, let us begin!"

Mr. Bishop quickly positioned himself at the pianoforte. Giving the downbeat for the string quartet to begin with a sprightly overture, the mood was set for what was to come. The first scene proved to be very entertaining, giving those in the audience many occasions to chuckle at the absurdity of the situation. At the completion, Mr. Bishop played some transitional music allowing Elizabeth time to get up from her seat and take her place on the stage. Moments later, the next scene began.

"My dear, if this man cares for you, why has he not made himself known to me as a potential suitor? What manner of man is he who will not come forth and present himself for my competition?"

"Uncle, I assure you he is a good and honourable gentleman and will make himself known in due time."

"Chloe, you must tell me. Do you have an understanding with this particular man?"

"No, Uncle, I do not. Yet, he has touched my heart, and I would accept his hand should he return and declare himself."

"My dear niece, I was afraid of something like this." Her uncle shook his head in dismay as Elizabeth walked to the centre of the stage and began to sing.

Deep in my heart thou art my treasure rare, thou hast my love,

288

None with thee can compare. But till thou say'st "I love thee truly,"
I'll not believe thee mine; Oh say, "I love thee truly, truly, truly,
Give thy heart to me.... (2nd verse)

Henry Bishop 1786-1855

Darcy watched with fascination as Elizabeth acted out her part and sang through the tender words of Mr. Bishop's ballad. He was not only taken by the beauty of the song, but by the beauty of his one true love. He knew without question she was singing for him and none other. Elizabeth Bennet had become *his melody* for she owned his heart. She was the one woman who completed him and the one woman whom he would spend the rest of his life cherishing and loving to the best of his ability.

At the close, not a sound could be heard until Elizabeth bowed her head, thus ending the scene. As with Georgiana's performance, cries of bravo and spontaneous clapping resounded throughout the ballroom. Mr. Bishop came forth and took Elizabeth by the hand, encouraging the rest of the musicians and actors to join them in greeting Lady Jessica's guests. There would be some minutes for everyone to converse while the pianoforte was being moved for Miss Paradis.

Elizabeth was immediately besieged by guests who wished to extend their praise for such an extraordinary performance. With so many demanding her attention, it was not surprising Darcy chose to remain apart for the time being. Elizabeth did not mind since she preferred to speak with him in private. Looking briefly in his direction, her heart was warmed when he smiled at her with great affection. *Soon, soon I shall be with him.*

After the pianoforte had been repositioned and the flowers and candelabra were moved in place, the guests were encouraged to resume their seats. Miss Paradis was introduced by Lady Jessica who began by making mention of the woman's life as a composer and performer in Vienna. The talented pianist was then guided to the instrument where she began by playing one of her own compositions.

Rather than taking a seat, Elizabeth made her way to the refreshment table situated near the French doors on the far side of the room. Although the room was not particularly warm, with so many people about her, she felt flushed and could not seem to get a proper breath. Had Elizabeth eaten more throughout the day and not picked at her food during dinner, she might have felt better.

Fresh air, I must have fresh air. With Miss Paradis beginning to play, Elizabeth put down her drink and quietly slipped through the doors and out onto the porch. The garden was well lit with lanterns and the glow of a full moon. Breathing deeply, Elizabeth was refreshed by the cool air and continued down the stairs and onto the pathway. *There, I am better. Now, if I can only be patient a little longer.* Her thoughts were interrupted by the sound of footsteps hurrying down the path. Turning, Elizabeth smiled seeing it was none other than her maid.

"Sophia, did my aunt send you?"

"Yes, miss. Mrs. Gardiner asked me to find you and make sure you were not feeling poorly. May I get anything for your comfort?"

"Thank you for asking. I was feeling a bit faint just a few minutes ago, but let me assure you, I am perfectly well now. It seems a little fresh air was all I needed to clear my head. Forgive me for taking you from the concert. Please let us return to the house. I think we can enter without being noticed."

"Yes, miss."

Unfortunaely, their intentions were thwarted by Lord Wolverton who startled them with his sudden appearance. Roughly pushing aside the maid who had purposely stepped in front of her mistress, Wolverton forcibly grabbed Elizabeth's hand and pulled it to his lips for a lengthy kiss. Seeing the panic on Elizabeth's face, Sophia quickly ran back to the house, knowing she would need to get immediate help without calling any unwanted attention to Elizabeth's predicament.

"Elizabeth, how pleasant it is to finally have you to myself."

"Your Lordship!" Elizabeth glowered, attempting to pull her hand free. "I have told you repeatedly, it is *Miss* Elizabeth, and I insist you address me as such. Now let go of my hand before I scream for assistance."

Laughing, he released her hand and continued on in jest, "Come,

come, my dear, by now we are good friends, are we not?" His gaze roamed the length of her body, implying he had something of an untoward nature on his mind. As he did so, he continued to step closer, prompting Elizabeth to back further down the path. "Tell me, Elizabeth, why did you not sing *my* song tonight? I certainly paid Bishop well enough for it. Was it not to your liking?" Again he laughed.

"YOUR song!" she exclaimed pushing his hand away from her face. "I told you, that song was given back to Mr. Bishop, and it no longer belongs to either of us."

Placing both of his large hands on her shoulders, Wolverton hissed, "*That* song, my dear, was a declaration! You had no right to give it back."

"A declaration!" She nearly screamed, struggling to escape his grip. "Explain yourself, sir." Elizabeth's heart pounded so hard she thought her chest might burst. She had to get away from this madman before he tried to compromise her any further.

"My dearest Elizabeth," he drawled out. "I heard about your *unfortunate* exile from Hertfordshire and simply wanted to make you a better offer."

"A better offer? YOU, sir, are inebriated, and I am going to take my leave."

As she boldly pushed her hands against his chest in an effort to escape his hold, Wolverton grabbed her left hand by the wrist, twisting her arm and holding it tight enough to cause her pain. "Not so fast. Would you not like to hear my proposal? I find I have tired of my current paramours and would prefer to take you in their stead." His smirk was sickening.

Elizabeth promptly slapped him across the face with her free hand and shouted, "Leave me be! My maid has gone to get my uncle, and you will be hearing from him before this night is over!"

"Good! Let him come. I shall need a witness to your compromise if I am to get what I want." Moving his face closer to hers, the man's eyes became enflamed with a lustful need.

Terrified, Elizabeth tried again to pull herself free. Her writhing caused him to laugh all the more as he persisted in bending and twisting her fingers to the point she cried out in anguish. "Please, you are hurting me. I beg of you, stop!"

Despite her struggles, Lord Wolverton managed to place his free hand firmly around Elizabeth's waist and pulled her closer with the intent of kissing her. Before he succeeded, however, she was released with a violent jolt. The sudden crack of a man's fist connecting with Wolverton's face sent him reeling to the ground.

"Get up, you worthless excuse for a man," Darcy bellowed. Elizabeth watched Darcy grab Wolverton by his arms and forcibly pull him back to his feet. Gripping the lapels of his jacket, Darcy spat through gritted teeth, "How dare you touch her? From this moment it would behove you to NEVER seek the company of Miss Elizabeth Bennet again. You have insulted a gentle lady, and I shall not stand for it! If I *ever* hear of you coming near her, you will have the Devil to pay, and I swear I shall personally see to it. Do you understand me, *Your Lordship?*"

Wolverton moaned in the affirmative. With a sound punch to the stomach, Darcy sent him back to the ground in agony. Seeing Colonel Fitzwilliam running down the pathway, Darcy spoke with loathing, "Richard, His Lordship is in need of your assistance. See to it I never see his sorry face again."

"Cousin, it would be wise to get Miss Elizabeth to the study. I have already intercepted her maid and instructed her to ask Mr. and Mrs. Gardiner to wait for you there." The colonel then pulled at Wolverton, who was doubled over, and half dragged him to the waiting carriages.

Elizabeth could no longer contain her emotions and began to weep in earnest. Her hand was throbbing with pain, and she could not keep her body from shaking. Taking Elizabeth into his arms, Darcy held her, gently caressing her back. "My darling, I should have been here sooner. Forgive me. As soon as I saw Wolverton follow you into the garden I....Oh, my love, I swear that man will never come near you again."

"William, I am so sorry," she sobbed. "I did not mean to...."

"Shh, you did nothing wrong." His voice was calming. "We must do as Richard says and get you to the study before someone else comes this way." Looking at Elizabeth with concern, he took out his handkerchief and began to dry her eyes. "Did he hurt you?"

"My, my hand.... I cannot move my thumb."

"Here, let me see." Darcy carefully removed the lace glove from Elizabeth's small hand, causing her to momentarily whimper in pain. Her wrist had begun to swell, and several fingers were now bruised and red. Seeing what Wolverton had done to Elizabeth, Darcy cursed under his breath. Not able to tell if her thumb was broken, he declared, "I believe this needs immediate attention. Do you think you can walk?"

"Yes, I.... Please, if you would assist me."

Placing one arm about her waist and firmly holding her uninjured arm for support they began to walk slowly. "We can enter the house through the side door over there and go directly to the study. I shall send for.... Elizabeth?" Her previously rosy cheeks had paled. Seeing her eyes begin to glaze, Darcy quickly lifted her up into his arms and strode with determination towards the house. "Elizabeth, try to breathe deeply, my love. It would be better if you did not faint."

"I shall try."

Elizabeth willingly wrapped her free arm around Darcy's neck and rested her head against his chest. The sound of his deep voice whispering words of reassurance was calming. Darcy's long strides quickly carried her to the side entrance where he kicked open the door and made his way to the study. The Gardiners and Elizabeth's maid were waiting in the room and the women came to her aid as soon as he placed her on a reclining couch.

"Sophia, Miss Elizabeth's hand has been badly injured. Please go to the kitchen and bring back some ice and a wrap for your mistress. Mrs. Gardiner, I shall find the housekeeper and make sure no one else is admitted to this room. After sending a footman for my personal physician, I shall inform Lady Helmsley of what has happened and return."

"Darcy, what is going on here?!" accused Mr. Gardiner.

Glaring in anger, Darcy snapped, "Later!"

~ ♫ ~

Georgiana had returned with Darcy and was now seated at Elizabeth's side, nearly in tears. Waiting for the physician to arrive, Mrs. Gardiner quietly did what she could to ease her niece's pain with the assistance of Sophia. In the meantime, not a word was spoken between Darcy and Mr. Gardiner. As soon as Mr. Mitchell was admitted, the two men went directly to an adjoining room for a private conversation.

"Darcy, what the deuce has happened? It is obvious my niece has been compromised. I would like some answers, and I want to know what *you* intend to do about it."

"Gardiner, you are a little ahead of yourself. Miss Elizabeth's injury was inflicted by Lord Wolverton."

"Good God!" Mr. Gardiner's face took on an ashen hue. "I had words with him earlier this evening regarding Elizabeth, but I never dreamed.... Forgive me, this is entirely my fault."

"Yes! It is! After all I told you of Wolverton's desires, could you not have done more to protect her? Had I not followed His Lordship out to the garden, there is no telling what might have happened." Darcy raked his hands through his hair in frustration, leaving Mr. Gardiner mortified with the thought.

"To the best of my knowledge, my cousin's servants are discreet, but all it would take is for one person to make known what has happened and Miss Elizabeth would be utterly ruined. She is blameless, and I shall not stand for it. I only pray we may be able to pass off her injury as an accident." Darcy paused and looked at Mr. Gardiner in earnest. "For some time, it has been my intention to renew my offer of marriage to your niece. If she should choose to accept my hand, I wish her to do so because it is *her* choice and not because of what has taken place here tonight." The strain existing between the two men did not abate until Mrs. Gardiner knocked on the door and interrupted them with her presence.

"Edward, Mr. Darcy, Mr. Mitchell has finished examining Lizzy. Apparently one of her fingers was badly sprained and he also had to manoeuvre her thumb which was dislocated. He is wrapping her hand now and will call again in two days' time. Thankfully, nothing was broken. Miss Darcy and Sophia are preparing to take Lizzy to her room, but perhaps the two of you would care to see her first. Do not be long."

Before leaving, Mrs. Gardiner gave Darcy a reassuring smile, knowing full well what had transpired between him and her husband. Seeing the pain on his face, she gently touched his arm and offered, "Mr. Darcy, all will be well. We are grateful for your caring and assistance."

Letting out a sigh of relief, he responded, "Thank you." Her simple words, *all will be well,* were exactly what he needed to hear at that very moment.

Mrs. Gardiner left the room, prompting Darcy to turn back and address her husband. "Gardiner, forgive me for my harsh words. I should not have spoken so. It seems part of the fury I wished to aim at Lord Wolverton was instead levied at you. Please accept my apologies."

Mr. Gardiner nodded. "I understand, son. Nevertheless, I believe your words were justified. My brother, Bennet, left Elizabeth under my protection, and I have failed. Despite your warning, there is now no question I have been far too lenient where His Lordship is concerned. Forgive me." Darcy nodded his acknowledgement, and the two men shook hands before returning to the study.

Wanting a more detailed account of Elizabeth's injury, Darcy asked Mr. Mitchell to remain after Elizabeth was taken to her room. Both gentlemen conferred with the physician while they waited for Mrs. Gardiner to finish speaking with Sophia and Georgiana regarding Elizabeth's care. Upon her return, Darcy was pleased to hear Elizabeth had fallen asleep following a mild dose of laudanum given for her pain. He then accompanied the Gardiners back to the ballroom so they might all pay their respects to the Helmsleys before leaving. By the time Darcy returned to his own home, it was nearly dawn, and he was exhausted.

CHAPTER TWENTY-THREE

LOVE RENEWED

Darcy's Study
Tuesday, 17 September 1811
Late morning

"*R*ichard, come in. I have been waiting for you."

"Sorry I am late, Cousin. I needed to look in on Lord Wolverton before coming here. Father was concerned since none of his messages have been returned following the *mishap*. During my visit, I found the man has no recollection, whatsoever, of accosting Miss Elizabeth. Nevertheless, he did remember the sting of your wrath and was quite put out by the black eye he is now sporting, not to mention a loose tooth. Needless to say, His Lordship was in a foul mood. Despite his resistance, I did manage to secure a letter of apology for his offences and will see it in Gardiner's hands before the day is over."

"Wolverton is a disgrace to his title."

"*That* is an understatement. The reprobate has cancelled all of his immediate obligations and plans to do nothing more than frequent the lesser known gaming rooms until his pretty face recovers. As a precaution, I have assigned a man to follow him and make sure he stays out of trouble."

Darcy shook his head and raked his hand through his hair in frustration. "Richard, if I ever come face to face with that sorry excuse for a man, I swear.... What he did to Elizabeth was unconscionable."

"May I ask how she is faring?"

A sardonic laugh escaped Darcy's mouth. "Funny you would ask. My dear sister has appointed herself not only nurse, but protector and has thus far refused me access to her patient."

"Our little Georgie?" The colonel broke into laughter.

"I admit it was perfectly understandable on Sunday, given Elizabeth was asleep most of the day. But … when I attempted to visit on Monday morning, my physician was attending her, and *naturally* Georgiana insisted Elizabeth rest after his visit was concluded. I tried again in the afternoon and was still denied since Mrs. Gardiner was administering a poultice to help with the swelling. Even though I stayed on for dinner, I was thwarted yet another time by my *devoted sister* who insisted she and Elizabeth would take dinner in her patient's room."

"It sounds like you could use my help. Shall I come along and distract our little nurse?"

"No thank you." Darcy raised an eyebrow while sporting a sly grin. "I am determined to manage on my own today. With the family escorting Miss Paradis and her servants to the docks, I believe I shall finally have something going in my favour. Fortunately, our Georgie determined the outing would be too much excitement for her patient, and to my benefit, Elizabeth is at Ferversham House *without* her jailor, as we speak."

"Well then, I shall be brief. If you will give me the paperwork detailing your recommendations for Winfield Manor, I shall be on my way and leave you to your destiny." He smiled and patted Darcy on the shoulder.

"The documents are right here. I think you and Uncle will be pleased with my findings. The property your father is giving you has been sorely neglected since coming under your brother's management. Even so, I suspect you can begin to turn a profit once a few changes have been implemented. My steward and I made a thorough survey while I was in Derbyshire. Per your approval, I would be happy to assist you with some of my suggestions yet this autumn. We discussed my findings with your father's land steward, and I have included his recommendations as well. I cannot begin to say how much I am looking forward to the day when you are able to give up your dangerous exploits and become my permanent neighbour."

"Thank you, Cousin. I wish I could say it would be sooner rather than later." He sighed. "Wellington has already requested I be recalled to active duty by the first of the year."

Darcy frowned. "I doubt the Prince Regent *or* your father will want to let you go back to the front at this point in time. You are far too valuable to the Crown as an agent for the *Secret Guard*."

"We shall see. It is difficult with talk of the French invading Russia, not to mention the tension between our country and the United States. In truth, I think I can be of greater service with my current assignment, but then it is not up to me to make the decision."

"I trust your superiors will see your worth and keep you here."

"One can only hope." The two men conversed for a few more minutes before going their separate ways.

~ ♪ ~

Ferversham House

"Sophia, I am so nervous. How do I look? Are there any loose pins in my hair? I wonder if I should have worn the other dress. No ... No, this one is definitely more cheerful although gloves will never do with this bandage. Perhaps I might wear the shawl."

"Truly, miss. You are lovely. I believe the gentleman will be pleased."

"Thank you. Forgive me. I must sound as foolish as a schoolgirl. I do think, however, we should remove the sling. I cannot have Mr. Darcy finding me wearing this offending thing when he comes to call.

As it is, I suspect he will be distressed enough seeing the bandage and discolouration on my fingers." Sophia carefully untied the knots and removed the cloth so as not to hurt her mistress.

"Oh, that feels much better," Elizabeth remarked as she slowly moved her arm and tried to wiggle her fingers. "Of course, Miss Darcy will not be pleased since I have disobeyed Mr. Mitchell's orders, but it cannot be helped. If you would assist me with the shawl, I think shall be able to hide my hand somewhat. But do leave off the bonnet. It is such a lovely day to be out in the garden, and I prefer not to be bothered with it. Thank you. Now, please tell me again. I need to hear everything. What did Mr. Darcy say yesterday before leaving the house?"

"While you were resting, miss, I was informed Mr. Darcy wished to speak with me. After he gave me the roses for your room, he asked if you had been sleeping well and if you had experienced much pain. He insisted on knowing the exact wording used by Mr. Mitchell during your examination and wanted a detailed account of every procedure administered to your hand. Then he quietly said, 'Please inform Miss Elizabeth I shall be calling promptly at two o'clock on the morrow.' Tis all, miss."

Elizabeth could not help but smile knowing her William would not be satisfied until he knew all. In her mind, he was every bit the protective nurse that Georgiana had been. "Thank you, Sophia," she replied. "I know Mr. Darcy appreciated your assistance. Let us go to the garden now and wait for him there. If you like, you may bring along your hand work to occupy the time while Mr. Darcy and I visit."

Elizabeth leisurely walked down the garden path being careful not to jostle her injured hand. While it was not particularly cool, the early signs of autumn were everywhere. Many of the flowers had ceased to bloom and several of the trees were beginning to lose their colourful leaves. The gardeners were busy cultivating the ground plants near the house, and other workers were making preparations to shut down the beautiful fountain for maintenance and cleaning. If Elizabeth were at Longbourn, she and her sisters might be preparing dried flowers and herbs for making fragrant perfumes and nosegays on a day such as this.

Being able to delight in the sounds of nature and inhale the fresh air was calming. It felt good to be away from all of the fuss which had accompanied her injury. Still, the anticipation of seeing Darcy was somewhat unsettling. Elizabeth could no more suppress the memory of his strong arms and his masculine scent than she could stop breathing. The reassuring sound of his calm and steady voice as he carried her into the house played over and over in her mind. He was the one man whom she loved with all of her heart, and the thought of seeing him caused her to shiver with delight.

Pausing to inhale the sweet smell of a single rose still bearing all of its petals, Elizabeth's thoughts were interrupted by the sound of someone coming down the gravel path. *William.* Turning to face him, she could see his gaze clearly fixed on her. A broad smile graced the corners of his mouth, bringing his ever-so-charming dimples into play. Seeing him carry the most beautiful bouquet of white flowers, Elizabeth gifted him with an equally radiant smile. Her heart quickened as the man's long stride quickly closed the distance to where she stood. Improper as it was, Elizabeth wanted nothing more than to rush to his side with the hope of being engulfed by his warm embrace.

"Elizabeth," he intimately said while taking her right hand and bestowing a tender kiss upon it. "How are you feeling? Does your injury give you much pain?"

"My hand is a bit sore, but in truth, I am far better today. You need not worry."

Looking at her partially concealed hand, a noticeable frown crossed his brow. Returning his gaze to her face, he offered, "I thought you would enjoy these flowers. The gardenia was favoured by my mother and was prized above all others.

Smiling, Elizabeth acted as though she had not seen his momentary displeasure. Touching one of the woody stems, she lightly ran her fingers across the bark and over one of its smooth, shiny leaves before leaning forward to inhale the rich fragrance emanating from the delicate flowers.

"The smell is exquisite. I do not recall seeing these flowers in your garden or inside of the solarium when I stayed at Darcy House. Pray, wherever did you find them?"

He smiled shyly, "They are from Pemberley. I happened to bring back three of the potted bushes on my return trip. I would be honoured to offer one of the plants to your aunt if you think she would enjoy it. My father purchased several bushes for the conservatory at Pemberley and over the years, they have been maintained and propagated. The bushes will be in bloom for several more weeks."

Elizabeth felt a few tears prickle in her eyes, touched by the care Darcy had taken in bringing her this treasure. "Thank you. I love them," she answered, closing her eyes and inhaling once more. "I am sure Aunt Gardiner will greatly appreciate your gift."

Pleased, Darcy motioned for Sophia to come and take the bouquet but not before he had broken off one small flower and handed it to Elizabeth. "Shall we walk for a bit? If I recall, there is a bench at the end of this path where we can sit and talk."

"Thank you. After being confined to my room for the past two days, I am quite happy to be out of doors. I never dreamed my shy young friend would be such an *attentive* nurse." She chuckled.

"Ah, yes, dear Georgiana. Like you, I have had to abide by her directives." He offered his arm and the two of them began a leisurely stroll. They chatted about Elizabeth's stay at Ferversham House and of his trip to Pemberley until they reached a bench located beneath a shaded arbour. Sophia thoughtfully took a seat further back on the path where she would attend to her needlework, allowing the couple to speak privately.

In this serene spot, the sounds of the gardeners had faded into the distance and were replaced by the intermittent sounds of nature. "It is so peaceful here," Elizabeth commented. "One might almost believe we were in the country. It has been many months now since I have taken the paths to Oakham Mount in *Hertfordshire.* She arched a brow in his direction while emphasising her shire watchword. "I must confess I do miss it."

Smiling at her playfulness, he returned, "I understand. Though I was in *Derbyshire* but a few days ago, I find I also miss my home when I am here in Town." Gesturing towards the flower, he asked, "May I?"

Handing the Gardenia back to Darcy, Elizabeth silently watched him hold it up for his inspection. Breaking off a little more of the woody stem and discarding a few of the lower leaves, he carefully placed the flower in her hair. Elizabeth could not help but think how very handsome he looked as he studied and repositioned his offering. Attempting to hide her nerves at such an intimate gesture, she chose to tease him a little.

"Mr. Darcy, you seem quite adept at this task. Pray, may I enquire about your training?"

"You give me far too much credit," he chuckled, causing her to smile. Being in such close proximity, Elizabeth could feel herself flush while looking into his eyes. Seconds later, he lifted his hand and tenderly stroked the side of her face with the back of his bare fingers, teasing loose one of her curls in the process. Although his touch was warm, it sent shivers through her entire body. She continued to watch as his gaze lowered to her injured hand. Carefully pushing aside the edge of the shawl, he gently took her hand and lightly placed a kiss on each of her bruised fingertips.

"It grieves me to bear witness to what you have suffered. I should have done more to protect you from that beast." His face filled with anguish. "To think what might have happened had I not followed him."

"Please, do not dwell on those thoughts. You came to my rescue and nothing else matters."

"Elizabeth." His face sobered. "When I remember what I said to you last July, I … I am ashamed. My behaviour at the time was unconscionable. You are more precious to me than life itself, yet I persisted in insulting you with my demands. Despite what transpired at the Military Ball, it was wrong of me to disparage your family. You did not deserve that kind of censure from me, and I humbly beg you to forgive my arrogance and prideful judgement. I was entirely wrong."

"William, rest assured, I bear no ill will. As much as I love my family, there can *never* be an excuse for such poor behaviour. I, too, am sorry for the unkind words spoken between us." Elizabeth looked down at their joined hands and then back again into his eyes.

"I was so very happy when you allowed Georgiana to call at Gracechurch Street. Then later, after reading your letter, all was forgiven."

Observing a single tear slip from the corner of her eye, Darcy softly wiped it away with his thumb. Still holding her hand, he raised it to his chest and spoke in earnest, "Elizabeth, words alone can never express the depth of my love for you or what is here within my heart. You are a part of me, and I shall love you until my dying day. Though I am not worthy, I humbly implore you to accept my hand in marriage and consent to be my wife."

"William," she spoke softly. "I am yours, now and evermore. Yes, I shall marry you."

With heart overflowing, Darcy gently lifted her chin wishing to seal their pledge with a kiss. "My love, you have made me the happiest of men." Unable to resist any longer, he leaned in and claimed her mouth. The taste of her warm, sweet lips was nearly his undoing. Elizabeth Bennet was finally his, and from this moment, he believed he would never want for anything.

Breaking their kiss, Darcy opened his eyes and was moved by what he saw. She was so beautiful, so tempting. Without reservation, he pulled her back into his embrace and held her close, all the while whispering endearments. He wanted her to know that she was safe and protected. She would be his wife, the mother of his children, and he would spend his days giving her love and comfort.

"My darling, I have something to show you," he finally said. Releasing his hold, Darcy lightly kissed her forehead and then put his hand into his breast pocket and retrieved the velvet pouch. He could not help but smile at her delight as he carefully loosened the ties and took out Lady Anne's treasured ring. The brilliant jewels sparkled in the sunlight as he held it in his palm for her to see. "If it pleases you, I would be honoured to have you wear my mother's ring as a symbol of our love."

"William, oh my," she gasped, taking the ring in her hand. "It is exquisite. I ... I am touched."

Next Darcy presented Elizabeth with a simple gold chain. "I thought perhaps you could wear the ring around your neck until your hand heals and I am able to place it on your finger."

"It is lovely," she answered, barely able to check her emotions.

Darcy threaded the ring onto the chain and carefully fastened it around her neck. Seeing the tears flow from her eyes, he quickly handed her his handkerchief. "Elizabeth," he said with concern.

"Forgive me. I did not mean to cry. While I never met your mother, I have learned so much about her from Lady Jessica's stories and from reading her journal with Georgiana. Lady Anne has become very dear to me, and now with her ring, she will forever hold a cherished place within my heart."

Darcy embraced her again, attempting to regulate his own emotions. "My mother would have loved you. Quite by accident, I recently found a letter she wrote shortly before she died. Elizabeth, it was my mother's fondest wish that I marry for love."

Elizabeth could see his eyes were now filled just as hers were. "William...."

Without hesitation, Darcy instantly crushed her into his strong embrace, claiming her lips with a passion she did not expect. "My dearest love," he whispered, barely breaking their kiss. "Please tell me I shall not have to wait long before claiming you as my own. I swear I would marry you this very day if it were possible. Elizabeth, I do not wish to deprive you of the courtship you so rightly deserve, but would it be too much to hope we might marry within a month's time?"

"William," she spoke, her voice was soothing. "I can assure you my feelings are the same." The muscles in his face and body visibly relaxed causing her to smile. "I have never wanted an elaborate affair. All I have ever desired was a simple wedding and to be married for love, to live my life with a man I truly respect, and to raise our children in a happy, loving home."

"Elizabeth, I promise you I shall always strive to be that man."

"I know." She lovingly smiled. "I must warn you, however, my mother will probably insist on a longer engagement in order to make her preparations, and Papa is not likely to give his consent without some resistance."

"Your mother I can understand, but your father.... Surely your father would wish to see you well settled."

"Indeed. Still, Papa has sorely missed me these nine months, and now, just as I was about to return to Longbourn, he will have to part with me yet again." She bit her lip, trying to stifle a giggle. "It is possible he will enjoy provoking you in his own subtle way and make you earn his favour before giving his permission."

"I see." Having never engaged the man in conversation, Darcy was unsure what to make of her remarks.

"William, you are not to worry. I freely give you my permission to pay him back in kind, as Papa will love the challenge."

He chuckled in amusement. "Perhaps my trip to Hertfordshire with Bingley will not be so tedious after all."

"I suspect not. Even so," she paused, becoming more serious. "I do hope you can appreciate the changes Papa is trying to make within our family. His efforts are sincere."

"Georgiana told me something of the matter before we left for Brighton, but for the most part, I am ignorant. If it pleases you, I would like to hear more." He continued to hold her hand, offering his reassurance.

"Yes, of course, although it is somewhat awkward to explain. For reasons I do not fully comprehend, up until now I fear Papa never fully accepted the responsibilities which came with being a husband, father, and landowner."

"I see. Please continue."

"Not until after the Military Ball did my father admit to some of his own shortcomings. Sadly, had it not been for Uncle Gardiner, it is entirely possible things would have remained as they have always been. Since then, however, Papa has embarked on a very different path. Before leaving Town in July, he hired an elderly couple, who are serving as tutors for my younger sisters. Jane says at first there was much resistance, but as of late, they have made significant progress."

"I am glad to hear it."

"Uncle Gardiner also arranged for a land steward to consult with Papa on a monthly basis. At his suggestion, Papa has begun to take some measures which he hopes will improve the estate and our family's financial stability." She demurely smiled. "While in the past Papa would rarely leave his book room, Jane says he now rides out to meet with our tenants on a regular basis. I know he could have taken these measures years ago, but the fact remains he is now making an effort."

"Elizabeth, I respect your father for having taken on this new course. Embracing change is not easy even though it may be for the best." Continuing to hold her hand with affection he added, "If I may, there is something more I wish to speak of."

"Yes, William."

"It concerns what transpired the day I confronted my aunts about the distasteful letter which was sent to Mrs. Gardiner."

"Oh...."

"I shall not burden you with all that was said between us, but I did want to apprise you of the good which came forth because of Lord Matlock's intervention. In addition to silencing my aunts on the disapproval of you and your family, my uncle assured me he would support my decision when it came time for me to choose a bride. Once I have secured your father's consent, I plan to make our engagement known to His Lordship and remind him of his pledge. I promise you, Elizabeth, no one will ever disparage you or your family within my presence without consequences."

"Thank you, William. You are too good."

"No, my love, I am not. But for you, I shall strive to be a better man each and every day."

For the next hour or so, Darcy and Elizabeth continued on in quiet conversation and stolen kisses. Before leaving Town with Bingley on Friday, Darcy planned to make arrangements for the settlement papers, apply for a special licence, and attend to some necessary estate business. In the meantime, Elizabeth would speak to her aunt, Georgiana, and Lady Jessica about assisting with her wedding clothes. She would also send a letter to her father informing him of her engagement to Darcy and of his intention to secure his permission when he called.

With Elizabeth's hand injury and Darcy's scheduled departure to Hertfordshire, there would be little time for outings over the next few days. Darcy planned to come by the house each afternoon to visit with Elizabeth and stay on for dinner so they could be in each other's company as much as possible. Before long, a footman entered the secluded path, pausing for a brief conversation with Sophia. The Helmsley carriage had been spotted on the avenue, and the family would be arriving soon.

"My love, I fear our time alone has been far too short. After so many weeks apart, I can hardly bear to share you with the others."

"Why, Mr. Darcy," she teased. "If we do not return promptly to the house and appear as though nothing out of the ordinary has taken place, we may find ourselves subject to the disapproval of Georgiana."

Darcy feigned a scowl. "Yes, Miss Elizabeth, I fear you have the right of it. Under *your* tutelage, I do believe my shy sister has become a creature whom I can no longer recognise." They both chuckled.

"In all seriousness, William, do you think she will suspect anything of our engagement when she sees us together? Since my injury, Georgiana has become very observant and notices everything."

"I do not doubt it, and I know nothing would please her more than to learn you will soon be her sister. May I suggest we wait for her in the house and tell her now?"

"Please." Darcy held out his arm for Elizabeth, and the two began their walk back to the house, elated to share their news with Georgiana and the Helmsleys.

CHAPTER TWENTY-FOUR

NEW LOVE

Ferversham House
Wednesday, 18 September 1811
The next day, early morning

*L*azily snuggling beneath the counterpane, Elizabeth smiled to herself with great delight. "William." A girlish giggle escaped her lips as she closed her eyes and recalled with pleasure the all-consuming power of his sweet kiss. "Oh, tell me I am not dreaming. Am I truly going to be Mrs. Fitzwilliam Darcy?" Another giggle burst forth, and she quickly covered her mouth thinking she might awaken someone with her mirth. Sitting up, Elizabeth reached for her treasured book and gingerly opened the pages to where she had already placed a few petals from one of Darcy's beautiful roses.

"I wonder if I shall have any trouble pressing the gardenia since I have little knowledge of the flower," she murmured, pushing back the bed covers. Elizabeth slipped her legs over the side of the bed and quickly went to the sewing box to retrieve her scissors. The sweet fragrance of the gardenias filled the room and Elizabeth hoped she might have enough of them to make a small amount of perfume with her aunt's help. Gently touching one of the larger blooms, she marvelled at the silky texture. Clumsily taking the branch in her injured hand, she frowned before proceeding. "*You* are going to have to do much better if I am to remove these petals without damaging them," she chided.

The cloth which bound her wrist and fingers was tight, and the knot would not budge no matter how hard she tried to loosen it. Taking the scissors in hand, Elizabeth began cutting at the base of the knot and did not stop until she was able to pull off the wrapping. Her swollen fingers were no longer a deep purple colour, but instead a much lighter shade of red and muddy yellow. The most offensive colours still remained around her thumb, but at least she could move it without initiating too much pain. Determined to ease some of the stiffness, Elizabeth rubbed all of her injured fingers in the manner which Mrs. Gardiner had done.

Afterwards, Elizabeth held up the ring which remained on the chain about her neck and compared it to her finger. "I doubt William will be able to slip this on before leaving for Hertfordshire. Well, it is of no matter. I will gladly wear it next to my heart while he is away." She kissed the ring and dropped it down the front of her nightgown. Though the metal felt cool against her bare skin, the mere thought of Darcy once holding it in his hand caused her to feel suddenly warm. Elizabeth would never forget the look in his eyes after he fastened the chain around her neck and proceeded to kiss her with more passion than she ever imagined possible.

"Oh, my!" A sudden need to cool her face prompted her to moisten a cloth which lay next to the basin. "There, that is much better. I had best focus on the task at hand." Calming herself, she was able to return to preparing the gardenia petals and securing them between the pages of a large book which lay on her nightstand.

Satisfied, she next removed some coloured threads, a sharp needle and her thimble from the sewing basket. It was Elizabeth's intention to add her new initials to the handkerchief where she had previously embroidered the corners with Sweet Williams. Since the early morning rain had ceased and the sun was now filtering through the window, this proved an excellent time to resume her sewing. Hoping she could manage with her thumb, Elizabeth took a seat and began to separate the threads. Having completed her sketch of the design before retiring, she was eager to begin. Elizabeth worked with the utmost care and precision, embroidering each tiny stitch of love for her dear William.

Initially, Darcy was not expected to visit Ferversham House until later in the day. Knowing Elizabeth was an early riser, however, he decided to alter his plans and break his fast with her before setting about his business. With this in mind, Elizabeth put aside her work after an hour or so of diligent sewing and waited for Sophia to attend her. Hearing a light knock on the door, she smiled and answered, "Come."

To her surprise, it was not Sophia but Georgiana who opened the door. Dressed in her night gown and robe, Georgiana tiptoed into the room and quietly shut the door.

"Am I disturbing you?"

"Not at all, please join me. It appears I am not the only one who is fully awake on this lovely morning." Elizabeth smiled, motioning her to the small sofa, and the two women took a seat.

"Elizabeth, I simply could not stay in bed any longer. My mind is too full. I am so happy William has asked you to marry him. I could never ask for a better present than to have *you* as my very own sister. It has been my fondest wish ever since you first stayed at Darcy House. Please, tell me I am not dreaming."

Seeing the tears glistening in Georgiana's eyes, Elizabeth held open her arms and embraced the dear girl with emotion of her own. "Sweet one, you are not dreaming. It is true—William and I are to marry, and all three of us shall be a family."

"I am glad of it." She shyly smiled continuing to hold back her tears.

"Georgiana, you are as precious to me as any one of my sisters, but do not forget you will have four more of us who will be equally delighted to claim you as their own." Again she smiled reaching for her hand. "I only hope you will be able to withstand all of the attention my two youngest sisters will shower upon you once they begin to admire your beautiful gowns and accessories. Be forewarned, Kitty and Lydia never tire of ribbons or laces and will insist on hearing about the latest fashions. And Mary, who practices the pianoforte most diligently but has never had the advantage of a master, will no doubt be eager to glean some of your musical expertise. I wonder.... How will you manage with so many of us?" she teased. Expecting to cheer the girl out of her sentimentality, she was surprised when Georgiana did not rally but quickly hid her face behind her hands and began to cry.

"Dearest, what is it?"

"Forgive me." She sniffled, searching for a handkerchief. "I did not mean to lose my composure. Even though William and I are close, there are ... there are things which I would rather say to another woman. And ... and now that I have you, Elizabeth, I fear you will think poorly of me once I speak of what has tormented me for so long."

Certain of what Georgiana was alluding to, Elizabeth took her hands and said, "Dear one, I could never think poorly of you. May I ask if this distress has to do with Mr. Wickham?"

Georgiana's face became ashen as she whispered, "Did William tell you?"

"No, he did not. During my stay at Darcy House, *you* actually spoke of him when you were most fevered. From what you told me, I surmised enough of the story to understand Mr. Wickham was unprincipled and imposed himself upon you for his own personal gain. Out of concern, I *did* mention your distress to William when he first returned from Pemberley. At the time, he merely confirmed what I suspected. Be not alarmed, for not even Jane knows of your troubles."

"Then ... you do not think ill of me?"

"Why, of course not. Georgiana, I love you so very much. No matter what has happened, all I see is your goodness. You do *not* disappoint me, and I could *never* think ill of you."

"Truly?"

"Truly."

The two of them hugged, and Georgiana quietly began to speak of what had been preying upon her heart. She began by telling Elizabeth how lonely she had been growing up without her mother or any children her age. It had also been difficult for her when she was away at school since she did not easily make friends. As for Ramsgate, that situation left the girl feeling even more isolated and alone. She and her brother had grown very close after the death of their father, and she missed him terribly.

When Mr. Wickham attended her, he often spoke of Darcy and her father with great affection. He reminded Georgiana of childhood events and of the happiness which they all had shared. In her vulnerable state of mind, she allowed Wickham to take advantage of her insecurities, filling her loneliness with attention and a promise of love.

"Georgiana, you were only fifteen at the time, and if I am not mistaken, is not Mr. Wickham nearly twice your age?"

"Yes, he is."

"Dearest, Mr. Wickham is not an honourable man, and you were the victim of a deceitful plan. I actually met him at a gathering here in Town just before the Military Ball, and he did not impress me in the least. I am sorry to say I found him to be vain and very impolitic when we spoke, as he was not above spreading falsehoods. At the time, my sisters had informed me he was a part of the militia which was quartered in Meryton. More recently I learned the man is rumoured to be a deserter because of his mounting debts. I fear many have been deceived."

"Elizabeth, I was so foolish."

Seeing more tears well up in Georgiana's eyes, Elizabeth could not help but embrace her dear friend again. "I am so sorry. While it is best to know the truth, I did not intend to bring you further anguish by speaking of Mr. Wickham in this manner. My sweet friend, it is true you erred in judgement, but given the lies the man was perpetrating and having a better understanding of his true nature, can you not forgive yourself and be at peace over this matter?"

"I want to, but...."

"Georgiana, I do believe you have learned from your mistakes. Yet, unless you let go of the past, you will not truly benefit from what has happened. I have always thought it better to think of the past only as it gives us pleasure. Would it not be wise to adopt some of my philosophy in this instance?"

Nodding, Georgiana answered, "I know you are right, and I do want to be free of this burden. I shall try."

"I believe you can. Like your brother, you possess a great strength of character."

"Do you honestly think so?"

"Why yes, I do. I first saw it when you chose to perform for the wounded at the hospital concert. And now, during these past few days, I could not have asked for anyone more devoted to my care than you. Dear Georgiana, although William and I have yet to say our vows, in my heart, we are sisters."

"Sisters."

Elizabeth smiled and lovingly kissed her. "If at any time, you should need to speak of this again, or of any other troubling matter, please know you will always have my support."

"I am glad of it."

"Now, having sufficiently covered that topic, I propose we speak of something less serious. Shall we?"

"Please."

"Very good. How would you like to return with me to Longbourn and spend some time with all of your new sisters and family before the wedding?" Georgiana's eyes lit up. "I have already spoken to William, and he approves. At present, our house has many occupants. With both you and Rebecca joining us, we shall be a rather close group, if you do not mind."

"Oh, Elizabeth, any accommodations your family can make for me will be perfectly fine, and I promise I shall try to be the very best of sisters during my stay." She beamed with enthusiasm.

"Then it is settled. I only need to finish my letter to Papa informing him of my plans to bring home yet *another* daughter." She chuckled. "I can imagine poor Papa with seven women in his family. Why, he may have to revert back to spending an inordinate amount of time in his book room if only to escape all of the excessive chatter. Let us hope that gaining a son in your brother will help to ease his suffering." Elizabeth's playfulness caused Georgiana to giggle.

For the next hour, Elizabeth talked more about her sisters and parents and what else Georgiana might expect during her stay at Longbourn. As soon as Elizabeth's hand improved enough for her to leave the house, they planned to shop for gifts which they could give to her family. Considering her injury, Elizabeth was grateful Lady Jessica had taken it upon herself to make arrangements for the dressmaker to take her measurements and begin the selection of patterns and fabrics for her wedding clothes at Feversham House. Mrs. Gardiner was to arrive mid-morning to lend her assistance. Between the ministrations of the two women and Georgiana, Elizabeth hoped her mother would not feel the need to make a fuss over her apparel when she returned home.

~ ♫ ~

The Library
Friday, 20 September 1811
Two days later, early morning

"Sophia, it seems we have traversed the stairs without waking the household. Thankfully, a candelabrum has been lit for our use. Did you see to it?"

"Yes, miss, I spoke with a footman earlier."

"Very good."

Elizabeth moved to the window and pulled back the curtains, peering into the darkness which was barely lit by the first rays of light. "Thank you again for helping me at this early hour."

"Tis nothing." Sophia straightened the back of Elizabeth's dress and then adjusted the ribbon which held her long hair in place. "As always, you look lovely, miss."

Turning, Elizabeth clasped Sophia's hands and said in earnest, "I am so happy you will be remaining on as my personal maid once I have married Mr. Darcy. We have shared so much together since coming here."

"Mrs. Gardiner was kind to make me the offer and I am very happy to continue serving you."

"Have you ever journeyed to the north?"

"No, miss, I have not. My family has always lived in Town, and I must confess I look forward to seeing the country."

"Well then, we shall venture there together. Sophia, I hope you will not miss your sister too much. Rest assured, Mr. Darcy and I shall periodically return to Town, and I hope the two of you will be able to see each other at those times."

"Thank you. My sister shares in my good fortune, and we plan to correspond regularly while I am away."

"I am glad to hear it. Now, I wonder where we should put my box." Elizabeth slowly looked about the room taking in all of the flat surfaces on the various tables. "Ah, I see the perfect place. Do put it over there on the small table by the sofa."

Sophia did as she was told and then took her leave. This one time Elizabeth was determined to see her William without a chaperone. Darcy had broken his fast with her each morning and returned every afternoon, but with all of the activity in the house, there had been little time for private conversation since his proposal.

Taking her newly finished handkerchief out of her pocket, Elizabeth gave it a kiss before placing it on the table next to her box. Then feeling a little impetuous, she removed the ribbon which held her hair. Folding it neatly and placing it on the table, she hoped Darcy would not think her a complete wanton in appearance when he saw her unbound tresses. After carefully repositioning everything on the table two or three times, she smoothed the front of her dress and stood facing the door in anticipation of seeing him. Not long after, Darcy's carriage arrived at Ferversham house, and the sound of his heavy footsteps could be heard in the hallway.

Opening the door, Darcy quickly walked into the room placing his hat and gloves on a side table. Taking in the full view of his beloved, a beguiling smile came over his face. There stood Elizabeth with her dark, silky curls hanging loose about her shoulders, tempting him, and reminding him of the night when he had come upon her in Georgiana's sitting room. Her sparkling eyes beckoned him to join her, and he barely whispered her name before striding with determination to where she stood and embracing her.

His kiss was passionate, and Darcy could not help but run his fingers through her hair as he held her close. "Elizabeth, I may sound like a schoolboy, but I have often dreamed of touching your hair in this manner while stealing sweet kisses. How is it I am so blessed this morning?"

She pulled back slightly saying, "William, forgive my forwardness, but I wished to give you something very personal to remember me by on your journey."

"And what could possibly be better than the remembrance of your tempting kisses, my love?"

William's mischievous grin and masculine dimples were nearly her undoing. Attempting to control her own desires, Elizabeth arched an eyebrow in playful defiance. "William, although I do not object to kissing you, I wish to give you something more tangible."

"Oh?"

"I thought to give you a lock of my hair, but if you persist in holding me in this manner, you will have great difficulty in cutting it."

"Elizabeth." His mien became serious. "You would let me cut a lock of your beautiful hair?" Darcy could not believe what she had offered.

"Yes." She smiled with affection. "There in my box you will find a pair of scissors to do the deed. Then all we shall need is to bind the cut ends with thread and tie it with a piece of the ribbon."

Caressing her face with his fingertips, Darcy lifted her chin and tenderly kissed her lips. "My love, I never expected to receive such a precious gift."

Slowly releasing Elizabeth from his embrace, Darcy proceeded to open the box and placed the scissors on the table. Taking Elizabeth's hand, he kissed it and then turned her around so he might choose which lock to cut. Before taking the scissors in hand, however, he was determined to examine all of her long curls, committing to memory every detail of this special moment. Not able to resist the temptation, he twirled some of her curls around his fingers. With others, he simply held them to his face and inhaled the scent of lavender. His ministrations, interspersed with teasing featherlike kisses to the back of her head and neck, continued on for several minutes.

"William, what are you doing?" Elizabeth finally asked, feeling a little giddy from the touch of his caresses.

"Indulge me for a bit longer, my sweet. I am making a very important study. It would not do for me to take a cutting which is either too long or too short. Then, I must take care to cut it from a place where the shorter strands may be well hidden by your maid when she assists with your hair."

"William." She began to giggle. "Sophia will be returning shortly and if you do not cut my hair very soon, I shall have to ask her to do it in your stead."

"You must have patience, my love. Our week apart will be quite arduous, and I am resolved to savour every pleasure this task will afford."

Not able to resist his playfulness, Elizabeth quickly turned in his arms and found herself enveloped in a kiss which left her breathless. "William, please," she nearly begged.

"So be it, my darling." He heaved a great sigh. "I shall concede to your wishes."

"Thank you." She giggled and faced away from him.

After cutting the lock of hair and indulging in another heated kiss, the two of them worked together to bind the cut ends with the thread.

"William, how is it you are so adept at binding my hair with such a fine piece of thread? "

"My dear, you must never underestimate the abilities of a true angler." He appeared serious. "In the past, I have used the very finest

317

of threads when preparing my own flies for fishing and therefore, I believe I shall be quite competent in completing this task."

"Mr. Darcy, do you mean to tell me you are comparing the binding of my hair to something you would make to catch a fish?"

Darcy chuckled at her teasing rebuke. "No, my love, I would never be so callous."

"I certainly hope not!" She arched an eyebrow in defiance.

He returned her look with a kiss on the nose, causing her to smile. As soon as they finished binding the ends, Elizabeth declared, "It appears all we have left to do is wrap the binding with a piece of this ribbon." For a moment, Darcy hesitated and looked sheepishly at Elizabeth as though he were a little boy being caught doing wrong.

"William.... What is it you are not telling me?"

His voice grew soft. "I was wondering if you care to use *my* ribbon."

"*Your* ribbon?" He nodded and then produced the ribbon of white lace which he had found left by Elizabeth in his library so many weeks ago. She gasped and took it in her hand, giving him a knowing look. "I was wondering what happened to this. *Your* ribbon, indeed!" They both broke into laughter.

A moment later, Darcy carefully held the cut hair while Elizabeth tied the white lace around the bound ends. Before Darcy could place the lock in his pocket for safe keeping, Elizabeth reached for her handkerchief and handed it to him.

"I thought you might like to wrap it in this." She smiled prettily waiting for his reaction.

"Elizabeth...." He gave her a questioning look upon recognizing the Sweet Williams and her new initials in the corner. "My dearest, with your injured hand, however were you able to manage?"

"In truth, I finished the flowers some time ago." She gave him a shy smile. "After we became engaged, I knew it would not be complete until it displayed my new initials."

Darcy fingered the lettering as he spoke. "*E ... A ... D....* May I ask what the A stands for? I fear I do not know your middle name."

"It is … Anne." She beamed. "William, your mother and I share the same name."

In one motion, Darcy crushed Elizabeth to his chest and whispered, "Oh, my dearest love, you have no idea how precious you are to me at this very moment." Filled with emotion, he held her tightly until he could regain his composure. Then without breaking his gaze, Darcy reached into his pocket and took out a velvet pouch, very similar to the one which had held his mother's ring.

"I, too, have a gift for you, my love." Opening the pouch, he took out several decorative hair pins and placed them in her hands. Fashioned like flowers, some of the pins formed from the finest gold and silver were simply adorned with diamonds, rubies, and sapphires, while the others were enhanced with delicate seed pearls.

"William, I do not know what to say. They are so very lovely." She lightly kissed him on the lips. "Thank you."

"May I?" he asked. Elizabeth nodded, and Darcy took one of the pins and lovingly placed it in her hair.

"I have never worn anything so beautiful. Each time I wear them, I shall think of nothing but your sweet caresses." The two of them shared a lingering kiss, knowing Darcy must soon depart.

"My darling, I shall miss you so very much," he reluctantly said.

"And I, you." They silently held each other for a few moments.

"Once I secure your father's permission, I shall send an express back here to the house with confirmation. Since I have already applied to the Archbishop for the special licence, it should not take long to complete the necessary arrangements and publicly announce our engagement. I have spoken with Bingley, and he understands I shall be returning to Town next Friday and shall remain until I am able to escort both you and Georgiana to Hertfordshire."

"William, I never dreamed I could be so very happy." Following one final kiss, Darcy took his leave. With unshed tears brimming in her eyes, Elizabeth quickly stepped to the window and watched him board the carriage. Turning back to bid her farewell, he tipped his hat in her direction, entered the carriage and disappeared from view.

Elizabeth continued to peer out of the window while visions of her happily married life with Darcy continued to fill her head. In her heart, she knew as long as they were together their lives would be whole. A few minutes later, Sophia joined her and gathered the items which were left on the table. Moving away from the window, the two women made their way back to Elizabeth's bedchamber where they began to make preparations for another day with the dressmaker.

CHAPTER TWENTY-FIVE

INTERMEZZO

Longbourn
Mr. Bennet's Book Room
Saturday, 21 September 1811

"*M*r. Bennet, Hill said you wished to see me."

"Yes, yes, my dear. Please do come in and sit down. I have something of great import to discuss with you."

With moist palms and trembling hands, Mrs. Bennet entered. Although her relationship with her husband had vastly improved throughout the last two months, it was still a rare occasion to be invited into her husband's book room. Wondering if she might have done something to displease the man, Mrs. Bennet took out her hand-kerchief and began to wring it in her hands in an effort to remain calm.

"My dear, yesterday I received a letter from Lizzy which I have found to be a bit unsettling."

"Husband?" she fluttered. "Pray do not tell me she has gone on in her usual manner and offended Miss Darcy or even worse Lady Helmsley. I promise you, Mr. Bennet, I sent her very specific instructions requesting she regulate her wild behaviour while staying at Feversham House."

He arched an eyebrow. "Of that, I have no doubt. Fanny, Elizabeth did not write of any such offence."

Mrs. Bennet clasped her bosom and let out a sigh of relief. "Thank heaven." The woman momentarily closed her eyes and began fanning herself in relief.

Clearing his throat, Mr. Bennet interrupted her wool-gathering. "My dear, if I may, I would like to share with you the contents of Lizzy's letter."

"Why yes, of course, Mr. Bennet. I suppose she was only requesting some extra pin money or something of the sort."

He furrowed his brow. "If only it were the case. On the contrary, she writes something of an entirely *different* nature. Her letter concerns Mr. Darcy."

"Mr. Darcy?"

"Yes. Lizzy informs me of Mr. Darcy's intention to call here while he is in the neighbourhood. Indeed, I have already received and replied to a note from the man himself. We can expect to see him at no later than two o'clock this afternoon."

"Thank you for telling me. I suppose he means to accompany Mr. Bingley when he comes to visit our dear Jane. Husband, you are very sly teasing me in this manner. Of course, I shall be delighted to wait on both gentlemen, and I shall speak with Hill this instant about some refreshments." She rose to leave.

"Fanny, please remain. It is not what you think. Mr. Darcy comes alone."

"Alone?" She fretted. "Why ever would he come alone? What about Mr. Bingley?"

Mr. Bennet could see his wife's nerves were being tested. "May I offer you some wine, my dear?" He motioned for her to sit back down and then half-filled a glass.

"Mr. Bennet, I beg of you do not toy with me. Please tell me what else Lizzy has done. I must know the worst of it."

Handing her the glass, he spoke. "Ah yes, the worst of it.... I suppose you might say it all depends on one's point of view. For a man who has seen little of his beloved daughter in nearly nine months, the thought of losing her to the wilds of our northern country does not sit well. You, on the other hand, being the mother of said young woman, may take delight since a wealthy gentleman has offered his hand in marriage and will be seeking my permission."

"Mr. Bennet! Dear me, did I hear you correctly?" Her eyes widened as she began to take shallow breaths followed by several gulps of wine to calm her nerves. "Husband, we are saved! How kind of Mr. Darcy to bring us the news. A wealthy gentleman—oh, my dearest, dearest child," she fluttered. "I *knew* Lady Helmsley would introduce her to a man of means. My darling Lizzy will have such fine carriages and jewels. Mr. Bennet, it is essential we make arrangements for her wedding clothes while she is yet in Town. Pray excuse me. I must write to our sister Gardiner with my recommendations, since I cannot possibly attend to Lizzy with Mr. Bingley in the neighbourhood. Think of it, one daughter engaged and another practically just so. I shall go completely distract...."

"Mrs. Bennet," he boomed, halting her mid-sentence. "Though you would continue to speculate and prattle on over the marriageability of your two eldest and remove yourself to correspond over ribbons and lace, are you not in the least bit curious to learn the name of Lizzy's intended?"

"But ... but of course, Mr. Bennet." She tried to calm herself, resuming her seat. "I would very much like to know *all* of his particulars."

A wry smile slowly formed over Mr. Bennet's face as he waved the letter at his wife and blurted out, "My dear, the young man in question is none other than *Mr. Darcy.*"

"Mr. ... Darcy?" she managed to answer in a rather high pitched voice.

"Yes. Would you care to read it for yourself?" He handed his wife the letter. "Apparently, Mr. Darcy intends to come here seeking my permission—with preliminary settlement papers in hand, no less. What is more, the young man is not keen on a long engagement and

would like to marry Lizzy from Longbourn church as soon as everything is settled. I am assuming no later than the middle of October,
possibly earlier. That being the case, it appears you have precious little
time for wedding preparations, but perhaps it is for the best. The less I
hear about finery and what not, the better it will be for my peace
of mind."

"Oh, oh! Look here, Mr. Bennet." Her hand was shaking. "Mr.
Darcy has applied for a special licence. Why he is as good as a Lord. I
… I think I shall faint." Being too emotional to read any further, she
handed back the letter.

"No later than the middle of October you say? Oh dear, there is
much to be done and so little time. My poor nerves! I simply do not
understand why Lizzy did not insist on a longer engagement? What
was she thinking? Does she not realise it will take time for me to plan
the wedding breakfast and attend to all of the other arrangements?"
Suddenly Mrs. Bennet's face contorted, and her breath became
shallow.

"Please, please, Thomas, my salts, my salts." One hand was
outstretched while the other continued to blot her face and neck with
her handkerchief. "Thank … thank you." She inhaled deeply and
sighed. Before Mr. Bennet could ask if his wife needed any other
assistance, she suddenly shrieked and burst into a deluge of tears.

"Mrs. Bennet, now what is the matter?"

"Mr. Bennet," she sobbed. "I nearly ruined everything. I was so
intent on matching Lizzy with Mr. Collins when we were in Town.
Why even Lady Catherine approved the match. And when she boasted
of her own daughter being promised to Mr. Darcy, I never gave her
nephew a second thought where Lizzy was concerned. Instead, I was
angry at him for offending Mr. Collins in the middle of the dance.
With such an action, I should have suspected there was some
partiality on his part, but I thought…. I thought a man of such importance would only want Lizzy for his … his…. Oh, Thomas," she
wailed. "At the time, I was very insulting with what I said to Lizzy, and
if Mr. Darcy overheard any part of it, he shall *never* forgive me."

"My dear, please…."

"But, Mr. Bennet, do you not see? Had I not said such things and interfered, he may have already offered for her while we were yet in Town."

"Fanny, Mr. Darcy has declared himself to Lizzy, and the rest is in the past. During the last month you and Elizabeth have been on much better terms, and there is no need for this excessive emotion." He wiped his brow in frustration.

"Yes, Mr. Bennet." She sniffed, looking quite forlorn.

"There, there, all will be well, my dear." He patted her hand and smiled reassuringly. "Fanny, we have both made mistakes during our time together, but we are in the process of mending our ways. I regret I have not said this until now, but I want you to know how much I have appreciated your cooperation throughout these past two months of severe change. I know it has not been easy for you to adjust to my new directives."

"Truly, Mr. Bennet?"

"Yes, my dear, and to further show my appreciation, I have decided to suspend all studies with Mr. and Mrs. Holyoak for the next week or so. With Lizzy's wedding so close at hand, I imagine you will need at least one or two of our daughters to assist you with the preparations."

"Oh, the wedding!" Her hands flew to her mouth, going back to the reality of what would be required.

"Husband, I must speak with Hill and Mrs. Holyoak this very minute. However shall I manage the wedding in such a short time with Mr. Bingley here? Why, the wedding breakfast alone will take at least a week to plan. And, Mr. Bennet, what about her clothes? With a husband as rich as Mr. Darcy, Lizzy must be dressed in the very finest of gowns and accessories."

"My dear, I have great confidence in your abilities to plan a party. Your table has long been celebrated throughout the village. As for Lizzy's wedding clothes, it says here Lady Helmsley, Miss Darcy, and our sister Gardiner will all be assisting her. The only thing I insist upon is that you restrain yourself for the next several hours and do not begin to make a fuss until I have met with Mr. Darcy and formally given him my permission. I shall not allow you to fall back into your old ways and have the whole of Meryton in gossip before the man even sets foot in this house. Do you agree?"

"Yes, yes Mr. Bennet. Thank you. Thank you. Of course, I shall do as you ask. There is much for me to accomplish and so little time." Deep in thought, Mrs. Bennet began mumbling to herself as she quickly rose and left the room. "First, I shall need to confer with Hill, and then I must write to Lizzy and give her my advice about her wedding clothes and ask her if there is any particular dish Mr. Darcy is fond of. The girls will all need new dresses, and I simply must have...."

Sighing, Mr. Bennet poured himself another glass of wine and moved back to his desk where he picked up the letter. "Well, Lizzy, for once, you have made your mama very happy. Of course I would prefer a much longer engagement, but in the end, I shall relent and give him my permission. On the other hand, let me assure you, daughter, your young man will *not* have an easy time of it this afternoon." Chuckling, Mr. Bennet took his favourite queen from the chess board and contemplated how he might best Mr. Darcy in a game of wits to start with.

"Let me see.... Other than the more serious inquisition which I intend to give the young man during his initial declaration, I do believe I shall make a few other requests. Ah, if I am not mistaken, there is an assembly ball on Tuesday." Again he chuckled. "Perhaps it is time I put my youngest daughters and their newly acquired sense of decorum to the test. They have not attended a public function since we returned from Town. Surely Mr. Darcy would not object to dancing with two of the silliest girls in all of Hertfordshire." Clasping his hands together in mirth, he continued. "Then there is the dinner with my sister Phillips on Wednesday. I do believe Mrs. Bennet will insist on showing off her future son-in-law to some of the neighbourhood. Yes, that will do quite nicely to begin with." He chuckled.

"In truth, Lizzy, you have been gone far too long. If you think I shall be easily mollified by his violent profession of love or your generous praise of the man, you are mistaken. And although you have boasted of his fine library in an effort to soften me, I shall see Mr. Darcy *dutifully* earns my regard."

~ ♪ ~

Ferversham House - The Music Room
Thursday, 26 September 1811
The following week, late afternoon

Elizabeth sat peacefully by the window embroidering yet another handkerchief with Sweet Williams. She glanced over at Sophia and Rebecca who were diligently putting the finishing touches on her new gown and could not help but be pleased. The shimmery white dress, adorned with rose and emerald accents was a gift from Mrs. Gardiner and would be worn at a small engagement dinner to be given by Lady Jessica following Darcy's return.

For the present, all was quiet with the exception of Georgiana's beautiful music which filled the room. Elizabeth found it calming after a day filled with so much activity. Today was the first time she had gone anywhere since her injury. Nothing could compare to the enthusiasm both Lady Jessica and Georgiana showed for shopping during their outing. The women insisted Elizabeth needed many more accessories for her wedding clothes than were originally agreed upon, and noting their pleasure she could hardly refuse. They even managed to buy presents for all of her sisters and mother before making their way to Gunter's for afternoon tea.

Closing her eyes for a moment, Elizabeth's musings happily turned to Darcy. Tomorrow he would begin his journey back to Town and she would see him by early evening. Their week apart had gone quickly, but it did not ease the longing she felt when he was not by her side. The sound of his voice as he said her name, his kiss and the way he looked at her were forever rooted in her being. Smiling, Elizabeth retrieved Darcy's express from her pocket, wanting to read it again. It mattered not that she knew each and every word by heart. Simply holding his letter and gazing at his finely written hand gave her comfort.

My dearest Elizabeth,

Words alone can never express the depth of my love for you or how very much I miss your presence at this moment. You, my darling, embody all I hold dear, and the anticipation of being with you once again fills my every thought. How is it that my arms ache to feel you in their embrace and my lips long to taste the sweet nectar of your kiss? Even now my mind rings with the sound of your voice, and my heart is filled with joy and gratitude, knowing you will soon be my wife.

Since coming of age, I have been a servant to my own legacy, doing what was required of me in all areas but one. Although I had dreamed of one day taking a wife and starting my own family, I had never wanted a marriage of convenience and had long resisted the expecta-tions of society put forth on gentlemen in my position. I cannot help but smile when I recall the lovely young lady with the luminous emerald green eyes who unknowingly touched my heart on the first day of our acquaintance. I am thankful for the love which we share and for the prospect of living our lives together as man and wife.

To this end, I am happy to tell you your father has graciously given his consent and blessing for us to marry. As anticipated, I was able to meet with him on Saturday. After spending several hours bearing witness to his droll sense of humour, I am also pleased to report he agreed to my request for a short engagement. Once I return and we have decided upon a date for our wedding, I shall formally tell the rest of my family and put the announcement in the papers.

Meanwhile, I pray you are well and that your hand continues to heal quickly. My business with Bingley will be concluded on Friday morn-ing, and shortly thereafter I shall begin my journey back to Town and to you, my darling. You may expect me to join you at my cousin's house early Friday evening. Until then I am sending you all of my love and devotion.

Affectionately yours,
William

"Elizabeth." Georgiana interrupted Elizabeth's reverie. "I wonder if Mrs. Gardiner might bring your cousins with us to the Autumn Festival tomorrow. Did you not say there would be some amusements for children?"

"Yes, I did. I think there is to be a puppet show on the green as well as storytelling and several games of skill. Aunt Gardiner mentioned she would like to bring the girls and possibly the boys if my uncle is able to join us. We shall find out when they come for dinner this evening."

"I am so looking forward to it. Perhaps we can go again next week after William returns." Georgiana beamed.

Elizabeth rose and moved to the pianoforte where she took Georgiana's hands in her own. "I know we shall have a lovely time, and I suspect your brother will be delighted to escort us." The two continued on in conversation until they were interrupted by a servant who delivered a letter for Elizabeth.

"Ah, according to the direction, it seems my mother has written yet again this week." Elizabeth quickly read the letter, chuckling as she did so.

"Apparently, Mr. Bingley has decided to let Netherfield Park, and once his sisters are able to come down from the North, he will open the house. Of course, in my mother's eyes, this is practically a declaration for Jane. Poor Mr. Bingley, if he only knew the workings of Mama's mind." She smiled. "My mother can be rather enthusiastic when it comes to finding husbands for her daughters. Although my family is striving to improve in decorum, I only pray you will not be shocked by some of the goings on that often occur within our house. They all mean well, I assure you."

"Oh, Elizabeth, I could never think ill of them. I have little memory of my own mother and have never had a sister until you. I shall love all of my new family most dearly. You need not fear on my account."

"Georgiana, your goodness is overflowing, and I know they will in turn love you all the more. I dare say your time with us will be quite enjoyable. Now, considering my mother's eagerness, I had best answer her letter. Pray excuse me."

~ ♫ ~

The Kitchen
After dinner

"Miss Sally, just where do you think you are off to?" Cook stood shaking a large wooden spoon as an extension of her arm with her other hand resting on her hip. "These pots and pans are not going to wash themselves, girl."

"Beggin' yer pardon, Mrs. Coope, but Johnny down by th' mews 'as been feelin' poorly ov late. I thought 'e might fancy a little bi' ov somethin' from th' kitchen ta cheer 'im up." The young scullery maid held out some biscuits wrapped in a serving cloth.

"Johnny?" Cook tapped the long spoon on her thigh while glaring at Sally. "What about that clever one, George Wickersham? Is *he* not your beau?"

"Well ... I say no, ma'am. He got a new job an' I 'ave not seen 'im lately. He 'as been workin' wiv th' runners on Bow Street."

"Humph!" grumbled Cook. "I highly doubt it. If you ask me, I say good riddance to that lot. Men such as that George fellow only want one thing when it comes to a pretty lass, and Her Ladyship will not take kindly to scullery maids who are with child. Do you understand me?"

"Blimey, yes!"

"Good. Hurry on now and take Johnny his food. Then you come right back, girl. I want these pots cleaned by the time I finish copying out the menus for the rest of the week."

"Yes, Mrs. Coope." Sally smiled and rushed out of the kitchen.

~ ♪ ~

The Mews

If George Wickham paced the path outside of the mews much longer, he was certain he would wear through the thin soles of his boots. "What is taking the little wench so long?" he complained. "If she does not come soon, I shall have to find another means of getting the information I need. That blasted Frenchman will have my neck if I am late." Wickham picked up a few stones in the path and deliberately threw them at the fence in an effort to ease his frustration.

"This is *your* fault, *Master Fitzwilliam!* Had you not been so tenacious, I *never* would have been reduced to my current state of poverty. Ha! And to think old Darcy favoured *me* over you! Well, you have not heard the last of me, old friend! I promise you I shall get what I am due before leaving this miserable place." Having thrown the last of the stones, Wickham cursed under his breath and resumed his pacing.

"Sally, love, what took you so long?" His face softened as soon as he saw the girl.

"Well, I say, George, I 'ad ta make me excuses ta Mrs. Coope before I come out." Holding up the little bundle in her hand, Sally nervously swished from side to side, batting her eyes in the process. "The family 'ad guests, an' I 'ave ta get right back an' 'elp clean up or Cook 'll 'ave me 'ead."

"What guests?" he asked, ignoring her offering and pulling her into his arms where he promptly started kissing her pretty neck.

"I fink they be some relations ov Miss Darcy's friend. I 'ear they all be goin' ta Green Park on th' morrow fer th' fair."

"All of them? Miss Darcy too?"

"Lawd, yes. Miss Darcy an' all. Do ye fink ye might take me on me day off, George?"

That was all he needed to hear to complete his plans. George smiled seductively as he loosened the pins holding Sally's hair and continued his ministrations. "Anything for you, love."

Sally gave a little squeal of delight. "I be free on Wednesday. Will ye take me then?"

"Um-hum," he cooed. "And I would like it if you wore these." Taking some cheap beads from his pocket, Sally gasped when he dangled them in front of her face before placing them around her neck. "I picked these out just for you, my sweet. They sparkle like your pretty eyes." He grinned.

"George, no one ever gave me anythin' so fine. They must 'ave set ye back a might." She kissed him in return.

"Then will you wear them for me?"

"Blimey, I would do anythin' fer ye, George."

"Oh, of that I am certain." He let out a coarse laugh, then picked her up, and headed straight for the nearest pile of hay.

~ ♫ ~

Younge's Boarding House
Wapping, London's east end
Later that night

A stocky man dressed in black made his way to the top of a dimly lit staircase leading to the narrow second storey hall of 6 Prusom Street. The smell of cheap perfume was hardly enough to mask the odour of chamber pots which needed to be emptied or the stench of dead fish originating in the dock areas but a few blocks away.

For a man such as Monsieur Jacques Everard, however, these small annoyances meant little. Being a favoured agent of Monsieur Joseph Fouché, Minister of the Secret Police under Napoleon I, he had often risked his life doing Fouché's bidding throughout the course of the war. If anything, Everard was annoyed with having to enlist the services of an English deserter in order to accomplish his current assignment. Tapping twice on the door before entering, he was greeted by the very person he loathed.

"Ah, Everard, I have been waiting for you."

"Wickham," Everard acknowledged in his thick French accent. "How much longer before you are ready? It is getting late."

Hunching over a cracked mirror, Wickham was applying the finishing touches to his disguise. "I shall be but a few more minutes." Seeing Everard's reflection in the corner of the mirror, he smirked. "You should try this paste, Everard. If not for that offensive scar, you might make a rather fetching catch for the ladies."

Running his right thumb along the newly healed scar circling from his left eye to his ear, Everard growled, "I am not here to please your whores, you fool." Stepping closer, he quickly pulled a dagger from his boot and held it to Wickham's cheek. "You would be wise to concentrate on your business, or I shall have to make your pretty face look just as handsome as mine. N'est-ce-pas?"

Wickham confidently reached for the weapon and pushed it away from his face. "And you, Everard, would be wise to keep your distance with that thing. You cannot possibly pull this off without my assistance. N'est-ce-pas?" he mocked. Everard scowled replacing the dagger in his boot.

"That is much better. Needless to say, I shall expect full payment once I have returned with your *merchandise.*"

"You will have it, provided he is unharmed. My man will be watching and will assist when your prey is no longer aware of what is happening."

"Then he will see a master at work." Wickham stepped away from the dressing table and began donning his coat. "Furthermore, after I have made your delivery and have been paid, I shall no longer be available, should you again need my services. I have had a change of plans, and I intend to procure some *merchandise* of my own if I am to survive in Italy with more than the clothes on my back and your paltry payment."

"What is it you are saying, Wickham?" Everard stepped close enough for Wickham to smell his foul breath. "If you jeopardise my plans with your foolishness, you will go nowhere and will pay with your life."

Ignoring him, Wickham began straightening his cravat before buttoning his coat. "You worry too much, *my friend*. Although I intend to set my plan in motion, my transaction will not reach fruition until *after* you have set sail. Now hand me my hat, and I shall be off."

"Get it yourself, *mon ami*."

"As you wish."

CHAPTER TWENTY-SIX

COME TO THE FAIR

Green Park
The next day, late morning
Friday 27 September 1811

Feversham House, located in Kensington Park and situated less than one mile from Green Park, proved to be a convenient meeting place for Lady Helmsley and her party. Having assembled mid-morning, the little procession of three carriages transporting both guests and servants was now making its way down the avenue towards the fair. Colonel Fitzwilliam and Mr. Gardiner had planned to be in attendance, but both men were called away much earlier in the morning and had thus left their regrets. Fortunately, plans for the day's outing remained intact since Lord Helmsley and his father had also agreed to escort the merry group.

With her husband's absence, Mrs. Gardiner decided to leave the younger boys at home and make a day of it with her girls. Both Margaret and Grace were elated when Georgiana and Elizabeth joined them in the Gardiners' carriage for the short ride. The sisters were determined to behave as proper young ladies in front of Georgiana, their ideal of perfection.

"Miss Gardiner, Miss Grace," spoke Georgiana, unaware of their admiration. "Look here, I do believe there are some performers already assembled on the Green. If I am not mistaken, it sounds like they are singing madrigals." Margaret and Grace nervously giggled peering out of the window with curiosity.

and peered

"I wonder who they are supposed to be!" exclaimed Margaret in excitement. "They have the most beautiful dresses and so unlike any I have ever seen. Miss Darcy, I can see several more performers by the large tent. Their dresses are far more elegant, and they are wearing elaborate feathered masques. Do you know who they are?"

"They may be part of a group of dancers. Elizabeth, did you not say there would be demonstrations throughout the day?"

"Yes, I did." Elizabeth leaned forward to get a better look. "From the look of their clothing, I believe their group is called *Cortesía*, meaning courtesy in English. And if I remember correctly, they will be performing formalised court dances which were first popular during the time of King Henry the eighth.

Elizabeth continued to explain how this particular group would be dancing in front of a mock throne room where two actors were dressed as the King and Queen. In addition, the spectators in that area would be entertained by court jesters, jugglers, and strolling musicians. Beyond the throne room, one could also observe several athletic demonstrations including archery, caber tossing, fencing, and finally a mock jousting tournament.

saber?

When the carriage came to a halt, the occupants exited and assembled with the rest of Lady Helmsley's party, eager to enjoy the pleasures of the day. Stepping onto the Green, Elizabeth smiled with pride upon seeing the results of so many weeks of planning. The park appeared to have been transformed into a charming world of its own. It had everything from vendor carts and exhibit tents to a multitude of demonstrations which would delight the young and old. The magnificence of the palace, towering above the trees in the distance appeared as though it were giving credence to what was taking place below. Elizabeth could not have imagined a more perfect setting for the Autumn Festival.

As Lady Helmsley's little party visited the various displays and listened to the musical demonstrations over the next several hours, Georgiana became captivated by one instrument in particular. "Elizabeth, even though I have read about the dulcimer and actually saw one on display at the Royal Museum, I never dreamed we would have the opportunity to hear the instrument being played here in the park. Is it not lovely?"

"Indeed, the sound is quite similar to that of the harpsichord if I am not mistaken."

"So it is," Georgiana remarked. "Though in truth, I believe the instrument has more similarities to the pianoforte since it appears the strings are being hammered rather than plucked. Yet, from what I can discern by listening, the tuning is far different. I wonder if we might speak with one of the musicians and learn more."

"By all means, let us enquire."

During the course of the conversation, many of Georgiana's questions were answered. Much to her delight, she was told the dulcimers, along with several older styled instruments such as the lute and mandolin, were being sold in a nearby instrument tent. Before any inquiries could be made, however, Mrs. Gardiner approached the women and told the girls Lord Helmsley's father was beginning to tire. With the weather threating to take a turn for the worse, Lady Helmsley thought it would be better for her party to curtail their outing and walk back to the carriage area.

"Aunt," Elizabeth asked. "Would you mind if we stopped by the instrument tent for just a few minutes? Georgiana would like to make a purchase before leaving the park."

"I am sure it will be fine since His Lordship walks rather slowly. Unfortunately, it is likely to rain, and it would not do for either of you to get wet."

"We shall not be long."

"Very good. I shall go ahead with the girls and Mrs. Annesley and leave Sophia and Daniels to accompany you back to the carriage."

"Thank you, Aunt."

Entering the instrument tent, the women were greeted by an

elderly man of rather short stature who had a twinkle in his eye and spoke with a strong Scottish accent. "Kin ah help ye wi' somthin', lassies?"

"Yes, if you please," Georgiana answered. "I am interested in purchasing one of the dulcimers for I have never heard anything so lovely."

The man beamed with pride. "Ah, lassie, yer askin' th' right man. A'm Mr. Aaron Michael McKinney o' Glasgow, ' th' maker o' a' ye see 'ere. Ah say, folks hae bin playing instruments lik' these sin th' days o' King David his-self, an' ah would be happy ta share me knowledge wi' ye."

The kindly gentleman continued to talk and quickly captured Georgiana's undivided attention with some history of the instrument and tales of his homeland while instructing her how to tune the dulcimer and play a simple folk melody. Georgiana could not believe how easy it was for her to understand the workings of the instrument and would have spent more time with Mr. McKinney if not for the threat of bad weather. Even so, she assured the gentleman of her intention to return sometime during the next few days accompanied by her brother. As soon as the transaction was concluded and the directions were left where the dulcimer was to be delivered, the women said their goodbyes and began walking towards the carriages.

"Elizabeth, since Mr. McKinney will be staying in Town for some weeks, I am hoping William will be able to arrange a few lessons for me before we travel to Hertfordshire. Then when the gentleman makes his journey to the north, I thought we could invite him to stay on with us for a short time at Pemberley. Our estate is not so far out of the way and his visit would allow me to take more lessons."

"Georgiana, it would be a wonderful opportunity, and with your excellent knowledge of music, I doubt it would take long for you to become proficient."

"That is my wish." She beamed.

Minutes later, the women were startled by a loud burst of thunder, prompting Daniels to open the umbrella and the women to quicken their pace. With the sudden downpour of rain, visitors were now hastening to their carriages. Amidst the commotion, Elizabeth noticed an elderly gentleman who had collapsed to his knees on the Green and looked to be in some distress.

"Mr. Daniels, it appears that gentleman could use our help." The man was being attended by a woman who leaned on a cane and hovered over him with her umbrella. When they moved closer, the man suddenly began to clutch at his chest, prompting the woman to cry out in alarm.

"Oh, dear, what shall I do? What shall I do?" she wailed.

"Madam." Elizabeth called to the woman. "Please tell us how we may assist you."

"My husband has not been feeling well for the past half an hour," the elderly matron fretted while bending over the man. "We must get him to our carriage lest he perishes out here in this storm."

"Sir, do you think you can stand?" asked Elizabeth. He shook his head in the negative and began to cough. "Mr. Daniels, please go ahead to our party and bring back another footman to assist these people." Sophia took the umbrella from Daniels who promptly turned and ran in the direction of the carriages.

"He will not be long." Elizabeth leaned over to address the man. "Sir, please try to relax your shoulders and breathe more deeply if you can."

"Water, I need water," the man choked out.

"Sophia, please see if you can get a cup of water from one of the vendors for this gentleman."

"Yes, miss." Sophia passed the umbrella to Georgiana and rushed off. With the rain, most of the vendors had already closed their displays and were no longer in sight. It would not be easy for her to find water for the ailing man.

For the time being, Georgiana continued to hold the umbrella and watched as Elizabeth offered words of encouragement to the couple. When Daniels and Sophia were no longer in view, the older woman took a step back and forcibly grabbed Georgiana's arm, taking her by surprise. A small pistol was placed just below the side of her ribs.

"Miss Darcy, how *pleasant* it is to see you again." The woman's voice was bitter.

"Mrs. Younge!" Georgiana gasped, causing Elizabeth to look up. In an instant, the gentleman rose to his feet, took hold of Elizabeth's arm and pulled a dagger from his boot.

"If either of you do not wish to be harmed, you will both act as though nothing is amiss and come with us. Do you understand?" The women nodded in compliance. "Now!" he commanded.

Elizabeth desperately searched the vicinity for anyone who might come to their aid as she and Georgiana were being spirited from the park. With the storm intensifying, nearly everyone had already left. At first glance, she had not recognised the man who was holding them captive. But now, being so close in proximity, there was no mistaking this imposter was George Wickham.

~ ♫ ~

The umbrellas did little to keep Elizabeth and Georgiana dry with Wickham and Mrs. Younge hastening them across the green to the roadside where a shabby carriage was waiting. Soaking wet, the women were nearly pushed into a darkened vehicle where the shades were drawn. An unpleasant man wearing a patch over one eye whispered to Wickham in French before slamming the door shut. "Nous partons maintenant!" the Frenchman suddenly shouted in his gruff voice. The carriage immediately lurched and began navigating the slippery roads as fast as the weather would allow.

Mrs. Younge took to binding the women's hands and wrists while Wickham removed his wig and peeled off his external facial hair. Straightening his jacket, he righted his shoulders and smirked before addressing the object of his interest. "My, my, Georgiana," he finally spoke. "You certainly have changed since I last saw you. How is it you do not cower in fear like the little lost mouse I once knew you to be?" He laughed mockingly. Georgiana continued to sit tall and said nothing.

"What?! Am I no longer your *dear George*? Will you not give me one of your pretty smiles, my sweet?" Again he laughed. "Ah, it seems I have misjudged you after all. Let me see...." His gaze became repulsive while perusing her figure in his unabashed manner before lifting her chin with the tip of his dagger.

Jerking her head to the side, she spat, "Mr. Wickham, you disgust me!"

"Georgiana, this new defiance is so unlike you. How is it you never displayed this little streak of boldness when we were together at Ramsgate? In truth, I find it to my liking since a man such as me prefers a woman with spirit over a simpering little girl." For a moment, he looked inquisitively between the two women. "Could it be you have been influenced by the troublesome Miss Elizabeth Bennet, the woman who *claimed* to have no knowledge of the Darcys when we last spoke?"

"Mr. Wickham," Elizabeth interjected. "Can you not leave Miss Darcy be and put away your weapon? We are already at your mercy. Pray, what more do you want?"

"Ah, *what more*...." He drawled. "Why, to put it simply, Miss Bennet...." He sneered, all the while fingering the dagger. "I WANT MY DUE! If it was *not* for that meddling colonel, I could have at least continued on where I was in the militia until my prospects improved. As it is, I am sorely in need of funds, and I am determined to get them before I set sail."

"In my opinion," Elizabeth stated, refusing to be intimidated. "With regard to your present course in life, I believe all that will ever be *your due* is the gallows, or at the very least, prison. You are a *fool*, Mr. Wickham, if you think you will succeed in keeping us captive and claiming a ransom from our families. Colonel Fitzwilliam has eyes and ears everywhere, and I dare say you *will* be found out."

Replacing the dagger in his boot, Wickham boasted, "We shall see. Perhaps I, *too*, have many eyes and ears. And knowing Darcy, I can assure you he will have no objections in paying whatever ransom I should ask for his *lovely* little sister. As for you, Miss Bennet, you annoy me, and I think I would take great pleasure in selling you to the French." He boldly laughed. "Your father may be a country squire, but from what I learned in Meryton, I know he has little money at his disposal. Now that my associates have His Lordship under their protection, I suspect they will be willing to pay far more for you than your father could ever afford.

"His Lordship?!" Her eyes narrowed.

"Why, yes. Lord Wolverton, your lover. Surely His Lordship would gladly relinquish his secrets to the French if he thought you might be spared from being tortured in his stead."

"Mr. Wickham, you are mistaken if you think I hold any interest whatsoever where His Lordship is concerned. He has merely done business with my uncle, and there is nothing more between us." She glared at him. "I am *not*, nor have I ever been Lord Wolverton's *paramour*, and I seriously doubt your associates would pay so much as a farthing for my person."

"Silence! I am beginning to tire of your impertinence. My dear Althea, if you will be so kind as to blindfold our guests, I would like to continue on to our destination without further conversation."

With the blindfolds firmly in place, Elizabeth and Georgiana could no longer see anything within the dimly lit carriage. Oddly, Elizabeth had a sense of which direction they were heading. Having noted the sudden shift to the east upon leaving Green Park, and after hearing Wickham speak of the French and of transport, she assumed their destination to be somewhere close to the docks. Knowing Lord Wolverton was also a prisoner, Elizabeth suspected he was the reason why her uncle and Colonel Fitzwilliam had had a sudden change of plans and could not attend the fair. She only hoped the men would connect the two incidents and be able to affect a rescue. As much as she detested Lord Wolverton, Elizabeth knew it would be disastrous if he were taken to France. Hopefully, Wickham would not be able to make good on his threat where she was concerned.

On top of all these uncertainties, Elizabeth could not help but fear for Darcy. As soon as he reached Town and was apprised of the situation, she knew he would be consumed with worry. If only there was some way to let him know she and Georgiana were unharmed. Wickham had mentioned *ransom*, but he had given no indication as to *before he set sail*

what course of action he was planning to take or how soon he would contact Darcy with his demands. At present, Wickham obviously had no notion of their engagement. If it were the case, she knew his demands would be far greater.

With the storm intensifying, the carriage was forced to travel at a much slower pace. Both Elizabeth and Georgiana were jostled with each dip in the road and clung to each other for support as best they could. An hour later, the carriage slowly came to a halt. When Mrs. Younge removed their blindfolds and prompted them to depart from the carriage, Elizabeth could clearly see they were in at an area of Town which she had never been to. With so much uncertainty, both she and Georgiana would need to remain calm while dealing with Wickham and Mrs. Younge in this dangerous situation. In the meantime, she would do her best to protect her friend and prayed that the two of them would be able to find some means of escape if it were at all possible.

CHAPTER TWENTY-SEVEN

UNCERTAINTY

Darcy's Study
Much later the same evening

He howling wind and clattering sound of the rain pelting against the windowpanes only served to exasperate Darcy's sour mood while he waited for Colonel Fitzwilliam. From the time Lady Helmsley's express rider had intercepted his carriage with the alarming news of Elizabeth and Georgiana's disappearance, he had been ill at ease. Upon arriving back at Ferversham House, his frustrations had only increased as his relations could provide him with no further information.

"Blast!" he burst forth continuing to pace the length of the room. "Who could have done this, and *why* has there been no demand for a ransom? I should have been with them." Darcy paused at the window peering out into the darkness. "Bingley had little need of my counsel this morning. He had already settled on Netherfield Park and could easily have finalised the arrangements with the solicitor himself. Had I left yesterday, this crime *never* would have taken place." Darcy's unrelenting thoughts of guilt continued to torture him until he was distracted by the sound of someone speaking in the hallway. Moments later, Benson opened the door admitting Colonel Fitzwilliam who appeared exhausted. Without offering the slightest greeting or explanation, he walked to the liquor cabinet, poured himself an ample glass of brandy, and downed it before turning back to face his cousin.

"Richard, what the deuce is going on here?"

"Wolverton was taken early this morning."

"What!" Darcy roared. "You assured me Elizabeth was in no danger where that man was concerned, and now both she *and* my sister have been abducted on the very same day. I hardly call this a coincidence."

"I know, I know. At present, there is no solid proof to support the connection, but with the evidence we have collected thus far, my instincts tell me the same." The colonel poured himself another glass. "Let me start with Wolverton. As you can well imagine, His Lordship has been lying low after you marred his pretty face. Up until a few days ago, he kept to his townhouse with the exception of a few nightly excursions to various gaming parlours.

"Apparently while patronizing one such establishment, our illustrious Lord acquired a new friend, *Mr. Giles St. George* to be precise. On each successive night, the two men expanded their outings to include *private* parties if you understand my meaning. Unfortunately, last night's entertainment proved to be deceiving since all guests, save *one*, were drugged."

"Let me speculate. May I assume the *one* you are referring to was *St. George?*"

"Just so. My man was witness to St. George leaving with His Lordship in tow. They were joined by one other who spoke French. When Norris attempted to intervene, he was overpowered and rendered unconscious. He did, however, learn something of use during their confrontation. Norris discovered St. George was wearing a disguise which was designed to make him appear a much older man."

"A disguise?"

"Yes, apparently some additional facial hair and a wig."

"Why do I have a bad feeling about this St. George fellow? Richard, what is it you have yet to tell me?"

"From the information we have garnered with regards to Miss

Elizabeth and Georgiana, it seems one of their abductors wore a similar disguise."

"What!"

"Yes, my men discovered a witness who was quite helpful. A Mr. McKinney, from whom Georgiana made her final purchase, was privy to what happened. The elderly vendor described the man and woman who took the girls and insisted from the way they hurriedly left the park that the couple were much younger than they appeared. Being concerned, McKinney followed the group as best as he could. Though he was not able to assist, he clearly overheard the driver of the carriage shouting instructions in French when leaving the park and heading east."

"Good God, Richard! Assuming Elizabeth's and Georgiana's abduction *is* related to Wolverton's, all three might be taken out of the country before they can be found. Why, they may be aboard a ship even as we speak!"

"Easy, man. All is not lost. Though what you say could be true, at present, the docks are essentially closed. As it is, fierce winds and destructive waves along the shore have already swamped three vessels that we know of, possibly more. Some of my men have been working closely with Mr. Gardiner who has been invaluable with his contacts along the wharfs and with the Thames River Police.

"According to Gardiner, one merchant in particular has agreed to help us in lieu of having his business shut down because of questionable activities with illegal imports. Thus far, the man has given us a list of ships which are expected to come into port during the next few days carrying French goods. One Dutch ship flying under the guise of another flag is expected late tomorrow. Still, with the current storm, it is unlikely any ship will be able to dock or leave port in the near future, giving us some extra time."

"Richard, with Elizabeth and Georgiana in the middle of this mess, surely you must have more information. What of Ferversham House? Have all of the servants been questioned? Could there have been some disloyalty in that quarter? How else would these people have known the whereabouts of Elizabeth and my sister?"

"I did have them questioned and nothing out of the ordinary surfaced with the exception of a man who was seen visiting one of the kitchen maids on Thursday evening. His name is George Wickersham, and according to the young girl, he *did* happen to ask about the family, but only in passing. Apparently, the man works for the Runners although I highly doubt it. Earlier this evening, I sent a man to Bow Street to search him out."

"*George Wickersham* did you say? Do you not find it odd both *his* name and that of *St. George* bear resemblance to that of our old nemesis, *Wickham?* Not to mention, the man's accomplice at the park could have easily been Mrs. Younge!"

"Those, too, are my thoughts. Since deserting, his circumstances have no doubt been dire, and I am positive he would risk anything at this point. Wickham was sighted in Town shortly after leaving Meryton, but as of late, my sources have not come forth with any further information. One can only guess what he has been doing to have remained so well hidden. On the other hand, I do have a current file on Mrs. Younge. Several months ago, she let a boarding house, of sorts, in Wapping. More accurately, one might call it a second-rate brothel. To date, Wickham has not been seen coming or going from her establishment. Then again, if he were disguised, his activity may have been overlooked. To be on the safe side, I have increased my watchers in that area."

"Richard, Wapping is adjacent to the docks and would make the perfect location to secure Wolverton until they are ready to leave England. If the perpetrator of both crimes is indeed Wickham, Younge's boarding house might be the logical place to hold the prisoners. How long before we may expect any reports from your men?"

"The man who is investigating Wickersham with the Runners will go directly to the River Police with any information he garners. If something is amiss, he is instructed to contact me here. The same goes for my agents at Younge's house in Wapping. You and I shall meet with my father and Gardiner at Matlock House a little before first light. From there, we shall all proceed to the River Police. After convening with them and my aides, it will be far easier to decide on our next course of action."

"Very well, though I fear morning cannot come soon enough for my part. I only pray Elizabeth and Georgiana have not been harmed."

"Take heart, man. We shall find them. Now, if you do not object, I would like to indulge in a hot bath and try to sleep a few hours before we leave."

"Go right ahead. Your usual room is ready. I shall have hot water brought up for your convenience."

The colonel nodded and gave Darcy a brotherly hug. "Get some rest, Cousin."

~ ♫ ~

Younge's Boarding House

Ghostly shadows painted the greying walls of the dusty attic room where a dimly lit candle slowly burned on top of a small table. An uninviting bed was pushed up against the wall, and from the appearance of its tattered blanket, one could only surmise what undesirable creatures might lie beneath. The remaining furnishings were no more than two chairs and a single chamber pot. In the midst of all this, Elizabeth and Georgiana stood with their arms about each other, attempting to peer through the wooden slats of a boarded-up window.

"Do you see anything?" Georgiana whispered, still clinging to her friend.

"Regrettably, I do not. With this constant rain and darkness, it is impossible." Elizabeth placed both of her hands on one of the boards and gave it a hearty tug. "Nothing. These boards are firmly set, and I doubt we can loosen them without proper tools. At any rate, it is unlikely this window would provide a means of escape with us being on the third floor."

"I hate this place and do not understand why no one has come. Mrs. Younge said she would send a girl to see to our needs and bring us some dry clothes, but that was hours ago. Elizabeth, if you were not here, I do not know how I could endure it."

"Sweet one, you must continue to be brave. I am sure William and Colonel Fitzwilliam are looking for us and will not rest until we are rescued."

Georgiana wiped a tear from her cheek. "Forgive me. I did not mean to complain."

Elizabeth kissed her cheek. "When Mr. Wickham presents himself again, we must both remain calm and show no fear. I suggest we cooperate as best we can, saying as little as possible. I suspect he will require you to write a note to William. Thankfully, Mr. Wickham is not aware of my betrothal to your brother. If it were the case, I fear his demands would be far greater."

"I agree. He would never be satisfied with my fortune alone."

"From what was said in the carriage, it seems Mr. Wickham intends to leave the country as soon as he is able. Having taken our reticules and our jewellery, he is obviously desperate and in great need of immediate funds. I am so thankful he overlooked the chain around my neck with your mother's ring. We should try to hide it before he comes back. Georgiana, do you think you can secure it within the laces of my undergarments?"

"Oh, yes. Please turn around and I shall do it right away."

Elizabeth removed Lady Anne's ring from the place where it had been resting within her bodice and waited while Georgiana continued to loosen her laces. "Though I shall miss my grandmother's garnet cross, I could never forgive myself if this ring was taken as well. It is far too precious."

"After our father died, William showed me this ring along with some of our family jewels set aside for my coming out. At the time, William told me our mother had intended the ring for his bride. It was the same ring Papa gave to Mama when they first became engaged. Elizabeth, I am so very happy William chose you. Mr. Wickham must never touch this ring." Minutes later, the chain and ring were secured, and Elizabeth's dress was reassembled.

~ ♫ ~

The second floor hallway

"Althea, can you tell me how our guests are faring?" Wickham called out to Mrs. Younge while closing the door to his room.

"How would I know?" she answered with displeasure. Mrs. Younge had just come from the far end of the hall after consoling yet another of her girls who was disenchanted with the presence of the French. For a solid week, regular clients had been refused admittance to the house, and those women who agreed to service the French had not been paid.

"If you recall," she continued. "*You* are the one who holds the key. Perhaps you would like to see them *yourself*, and while you are at it, take Molly with you with some dry clothing and a bit of food. I would not wish *our guests* to take ill from neglect," she spat.

"My, my, we are irritable tonight."

"You would be too if you had those idiot Frenchmen watching your every move."

"Who is to say they are not? Go ahead, send your girl up. I shall unlock the door momentarily and return the key to you. It would not do for *Master Fitzwilliam* to become upset if he finds we did not treat his little princess accordingly," Wickham sneered.

"Speaking of Mr. Darcy, when do you intend to send a request for the ransom? We shall not be able to keep the women here for long. Your *French associates* tell me Monsieur Everard is angered. He says you have compromised his purpose by bringing them here, not to mention he has threatened to withhold payment for the use of the house when he leaves. George, I fear none of them are to be trusted."

"Let me handle Everard. For now, he is occupied with Wolverton. Once this blasted rain lets up and his ship is able to dock, His Lordship will be moved to the waterfront. At that time, I shall contact Darcy and put our plan into motion."

"Good, it will be none too soon for my part. If our plans fail and we are caught, it will be the end of us, George."

350

"Trust me." He stepped closer to her and whispered, "I know what I am about, my sweet. Before long, we shall have our money and be bound for Italy."

She smiled seductively. "May I assume you will stop by my room later?"

"You know me only too well." He kissed her soundly on the mouth, causing her to let out a low, raw laugh as they parted.

~ ♫ ~

Startled by the sound of a key rattling in the lock of the door, Elizabeth and Georgiana sat upright, straightening their damp clothing. Refusing to sleep in the bed, they had both been resting on the chairs with their arms and head draped over the table.

"My dear Georgiana, Miss Elizabeth Bennet. Why are you not sleeping in the bed? Are these accommodations not to your liking?" Though neither woman answered, Wickham was obviously amused and burst into laughter. Moving closer to Georgiana, he sneered. "My dear, with your brother repeatedly cheating me out of my due, I have had little choice but to live in such squalor as you now see. I wonder what your beloved father would think of my predicament. He always liked me, you know." Again he laughed. "Of course, with *your* help, it appears my prospects are about to change. I suspect Darcy has quite lost his mind by now with worry over what has happened to you and will willingly meet my price."

"Do you mean to say you have not even contacted my brother yet?"

He cocked his head to the side, reaching for her chin and tilting it upward. "The time is not yet ripe, my dear. I am sorry, Georgiana, but you will have to remain in this room a bit longer.

"As for you, Miss Bennet, your fate has yet to be determined. It all depends on *who* will pay the highest price for your release—the French, your uncle, or possibly even Darcy. Knowing you are the *particular* friend of his little darling, I suspect *he* will be the highest bidder in the end. For now, things will remain as they are. When I return, I shall have the two of you write letters stating my demands.

"Mrs. Younge will be sending in a girl to assist you. I insist you keep silent and do not interact with her under any circumstances." Just then, there was a knock on the open door.

"Here she is now. Come in, girl." A tall, slender girl wearing a worn dress and a scarf about her head came in carrying a modest tray of food and two plain muslin dresses.

"Molly, I shall lock the door and send Mrs. Younge up to let you out in about twenty minutes. Be quick about it."

"Aye, sir." Wickham left without further discussion.

Looking shyly at the two women, Molly placed the tray on the table and took a step back. "Beggin' yer pardon," she stammered with a trace of an Irish accent. "The Missus says yer clothes are wet an' … an' I should be helping ye change into these." She began first with Georgiana.

"Thank you for your assistance," Elizabeth offered. "Tell me, did I hear Mr. Wickham call you Molly?" Elizabeth asked trying to appear friendly.

"Aye, miss."

"Can you tell us where this place is?"

"I … I cannot say. The missus would be cross."

"Molly, I think you are a good girl, and we are in desperate need of your assistance. I am Miss Elizabeth Bennet, and this is my dear friend, Miss Georgiana Darcy. Her uncle, Lord Matlock, is a personal friend of the Prince Regent, and her cousin is Colonel Richard Fitzwilliam, the decorated war hero. We have been brought here against our will. I do not wish to see you get into trouble with Mrs. Younge, but I beg of you to please help us."

Molly furrowed her brow. "Ye say she is the cousin of Colonel Fitzwilliam, miss?"

"Yes, do you know of him?"

"Aye. Me brother, Michael, be serving under his command sum years back."

"He did?"

"Aye, miss. If it not be fer the good colonel, our Michael be left fer dead. When me brother was wounded, he lost his arm an' nearly died of fever. The colonel would not be leavin' him behind, an' after our Michael was brought home, the man himself comes to visit. There not be a kinder man than Colonel Fitzwilliam, miss."

"Yes, my cousin is truly the very best of men."

"Molly, is it possible you will help us then?" Elizabeth nearly begged.

"Aye. Me and mine would do whatever it takes to pay back the man who saved our Michael. But I must tell ye, all the while the French be here, none of us be leaving this place."

"Has not your family come to look for you?"

"No, miss. The missus sent word to me mather saying she be needing me and me little brother, Jimmy, to live here for some weeks. Me mather be none the wiser. The missus says the French will kill us all if any be leavin' from here before their business be finished. Me brother works out back, but even he be watched. I be talkin' with Jimmy an' we be thinkin' on how to help ye."

"I cannot thank you enough, Molly. You are very kind."

Moments later Mrs. Younge unlocked the door allowing Molly to leave. "Miss Darcy, Miss Bennet." She frowned. "I shall send Molly back in the morning to see to your needs and give this room a good cleaning." Without another word, Mrs. Younge swiftly left, locking the door behind her.

CHAPTER TWENTY-EIGHT

ESCAPE

Younge's Boarding House
Saturday, 28 September
The next day, early morning

*T*he rumble of thunder hummed in Elizabeth's ears, startling her from a restless sleep. All was dark now save for a faint light filtering through the slats of the boarded-up window. The lone candle had long burnt its last. Aching and stiff, Elizabeth warily lifted her head and pushed herself up from the rickety table where she had hunched next to Georgiana for most of the night. Slowly twisting her head from side to side, she rubbed the muscles in the back of her neck, hoping to release some of the prickly tension. After stretching a bit more, she rose and moved towards the window. The heavy rain, which had persisted throughout the night, continued to tap against the cracked glass on the other side of the wood. Touching the window casing, a cold trickle of water slipped through her fingers and onto the floor. Elizabeth silently prayed she and Georgiana would be delivered from this nightmare and that no harm would come to those who would be aiding in their rescue.

"Elizabeth," whispered Georgiana, her voice breaking as she spoke.

"Yes, sweet one."

"Are we truly here in this horrible place?"

"I am afraid so." Elizabeth helped Georgiana to sit up knowing she would also be stiff from their awkward sleeping positions. "It is morning, but I am not sure of the hour since the storm continues to rage."

"Pray, excuse me," Georgiana said, easing away from the table in order to use the chamber pot.

Turning her back to allow for more privacy, Elizabeth continued to speak. "The house is quiet now, but these walls are thin. Last night while you were sleeping, I heard two men arguing. One man was French and the other, I am sure, was Mr. Wickham."

"Could you make out any of what was said?"

"A little. The man who spoke in French was angry, and I understood him to say Mr. Wickham had compromised this location by bringing us here."

"Oh, dear."

"There was a scuffle during which I heard Wickham cry out in pain. Afterwards, I heard nothing more until the Frenchman stood outside of our door and ordered the guard to let no one enter with the exception of the girl who would see to our needs."

"Elizabeth, what shall we do? We know nothing of these men. At least with Mr. Wickham, we knew he sought a ransom from brother. I am so frightened."

"I know, dear one." Elizabeth held out her hand to Georgiana. "The uncertainty is daunting. Yet, we must try to be patient and hope Molly will be able to tell us more once she comes back."

~ ♫ ~

As soon as the door was unlocked, Molly entered carrying a candle and a clean chamber pot. Alarmingly, she was walking with a slight limp.

"Molly, what has happened?" Elizabeth whispered, taking the candle and placing it on the table.

"Tis nothing, miss. Last night when we be locked up, one of the guards pushed me, and I hurt me foot a bit."

Georgiana gasped.

"Twill be fine, miss."

"What of Mr. Wickham and Mrs. Younge?" Elizabeth enquired.

"The mister and missus has their hands bound up and be under lock and key along with the girls and everyone else. I be let out to see to yer needs and Jimmy to that of the French. Miss, they be moving His Lordship to the docks soon, well before the rain stops. Ye not be fretting. Me and Jimmy worked out how we can help." Molly leaned in closer as she continued to whisper. "The young miss had best change clothes with me and take me place. When the guard opens the door, no one will be the wiser and Jimmy will be helping her to get away. I was to go meself, but with this foot, I cannot. Miss, there not be much time so we best do it now."

Terror struck Georgiana's face as she realised what Molly was asking. "Elizabeth, I am not sure if I...."

"Georgiana, we have no choice, and I know you can do this. You and Molly are similar in size and once we hide your hair beneath her scarf, no one will recognise you as long as you keep your head down. Please, let us hurry." By the time Elizabeth finished speaking, Molly had already taken off her dress and shoes. She began helping with Georgiana's buttons and within minutes the girls had exchanged their clothes.

"Molly, how far are we from the Wharf Police?" Elizabeth asked while weaving Georgiana's hair into a braid.

"A little more than a mile, miss. From here it be a good six blocks to the wharf, and then it be a bit further on to the station."

"Do you think Miss Darcy can find it?" She asked tying the scarf around Georgiana's hair and then wrapping the tattered shawl about her shoulders.

"Jimmy will see to the miss. Ye are not to worry."

"Thank you." Elizabeth squeezed Molly's hand. "You and your brother are very courageous to risk your own safety by helping us. Dearest Georgiana, you must also embrace courage. It will be up to you to secure help for us. If there was any way I could go in your place, you know I would gladly do it."

Though trembling with fear, she nodded and answered, "Yes, I do."

Elizabeth hugged her and kissed her on the cheek. "Remember we are sisters."

Georgiana's eyes brightened. "Yes, and sisters always take care of one another. I shall not disappoint you, Elizabeth."

"I know you will not, sweet one."

"Miss, when ye knock on the door, the guard be opening it. Just take the pot an' go down to the end of the hall. Ye best act like yer foot is hurt so he not be the wiser. Take the stairs down to the bottom where me brother will be waiting. Jimmy be showing ye where to go and how to get away once ye dump the pot. He be staying behind and causing a stirring so as the guard will not be noticing. God speed, miss. The French be everywhere about this place."

Moments later, Georgiana knocked on the door where she stood holding her charge. The door was opened by a stout looking guard who took little notice, allowing her to pass through. The door swung shut and was relocked without any exchange of words. Listening to Georgiana hobble down the hallway, Elizabeth closed her eyes and prayed in earnest her dearest friend would be safe.

With each step Georgiana took, her heart seemed to beat faster. Shuffling along while feigning a limp, she prayed for strength. The trial she had faced following Wickham's deception was nothing in comparison to what she was about to do. Others depended on her and their lives were at risk. *If William were here, I know he would not hesitate. How many times have I heard him speak of our heritage and what we stand for? I AM a Darcy, and I vow I shall not falter.*

Having arrived at the end of the hall, Georgiana began to slowly traverse the narrow stairs which were difficult to see in near darkness. As she carried the chamber pot in one hand and felt along the wall with the other, her senses were assaulted with a stench so strong she might have cast up the contents of her stomach had she eaten anything before leaving the attic room. The thought of any person relieving themselves in the stairwell was revolting. The stairs were slippery and a bit irregular, but an even greater challenge was posed when Molly's large shoes threatened to slide off of her feet with each descending step. Georgiana swore if she survived this ordeal, never again would she take for granted what her servants did to ensure her personal comfort. Continuing, she did not stop until she reached the bottom of the stairs and heard the sound of a boy's voice.

"Over here, miss," he whispered from the shadows.

Georgiana walked in the direction of his voice until she nearly bumped into the dirty lad of no more than eight or nine years-of-age.

"Are you Jimmy?" she whispered.

"Aye, miss. We best be quick. The guard in the alley be waiting for this here mug of brew. I say, it be a mite early for drink, but with the storm and all, he be wanting it. After we go out, I be making sure the guard be looking the other way so as not to notice ye. Leave the pot behind the water barrels and squeeze between the buildings. Keep going till ye get to the other side. It be a wee bit narrow but ye can fit. There be a cart stuck in the mud near the opening. With all this rain, the guards not be seeing ye sneak out. Go left to the corner an' turn left again. It be about six blocks or maybe a little more to the docks. When ye get there, turn left again and follow the road along the river for seven or eight blocks till ye be coming on the wharf police. Ye cannot miss it for it be the tallest building on the street."

"Jimmy, you are so kind to assist me. I promise I shall send back help for all of you as soon as I possibly can. God bless you."

The boy looked at his feet in embarrassment. "We be proud to be helping ye, miss. The colonel, he saved me brother's life, and we be in his debt." Nodding, the boy opened the door and the two of them went out into the heavy rain.

A gust of wind caused Georgiana to nearly lose her balance as she pushed against it and made her way to the rain barrels. Her skirts became wet within seconds and clung to her legs making it difficult to walk. All the while, tiny particles of grit caught up in the wind stung the exposed flesh of her face and hands.

Standing next to the narrow opening between the two buildings, Georgiana quickly put down the chamber pot. Shielding her eyes from the rain, she looked back hoping to see if Jimmy had indeed distracted the guard. Nearly screaming out in horror, she witnessed the guard kicking the poor lad who had purposely tripped and spilled the drink in his effort to assist her. With tears in her eyes, Georgiana knew there was nothing she could do to help him. She had to escape or they all would be lost. Determined, Georgiana slipped her body between the two buildings and started to move sideways along the wall.

The space itself was narrow, and if she was not mistaken, it looked even tighter further down. Thank goodness her womanly figure was not any fuller than it was, for as she shuffled along the opening, her breasts became mashed against the offending wall. Moving in this fashion, there was little she could do when Molly's large shoes became dislodged from her feet. Much to her dismay, she could neither pick them up nor slip them back on.

Suddenly filled with panic, Georgiana wondered what would happen if she were to become permanently lodged within this narrow tomb, unable to move in either direction. With tears threatening to blur her vision, she momentarily closed her eyes and thought of Elizabeth who was depending on her. Forcing herself to continue on, Georgiana endured the pangs of sharp rocks and other debris lodged in the mud. Without the protection of shoes, her socks became sodden and eventually slipped from her feet. Even so, she willed herself to keep going and did not stop until she was but a few inches from the end of the two buildings.

Thankfully, it was as Jimmy had said. There, with its wheels lodged deep in mud, a large vendor cart had been stalled. For the present, several men were scurrying about the cart in an effort to remove some of the heavy crates and lighten its load. This would be her best chance to escape unnoticed by the Frenchmen who stood porter at the front door of the building. Slipping from her hiding place, Georgiana pulled the shawl around her head while hurrying from the building and around the corner without looking back.

Shielding her eyes as best she could from the wind and rain, she hoped to make her way to the wharf area without falling. The tender flesh of her bare feet had quickly become sore and scratched. Although she felt a little dizzy and was now shivering from the wet and cold, Georgiana was determined to ignore her present discomfort and continue on until she reached the end of the street. It was only after she turned the next corner that she stopped to rest.

Being so close to the waterfront, this area was now abandoned, and the road which was to take her to the wharf police appeared to be washed out. On the other side of the pilings, she could see large waves crashing against what was left of several small craft now submerged in the harbour area. If only there was someone nearby whom she could ask for help.

Before moving on, Georgiana peaked back around the corner of the building and looked down the street from where she had just come. To her surprise, she saw Jimmy running towards her. Waving at him, she felt an odd surge of relief when he finally arrived where she was standing.

"Jimmy, however did you manage to get away? I saw that horrible man kick you." She could see his shirt was torn and his eye was bloodied where it had begun to swell.

"I took me blows and played fer dead." He smiled. "Then I listened and watched. Miss, they be sending for the carriage, and then they be bringing down His Lordship." He frowned for a moment and continued, "I saw him earlier and he not be looking too good. I also be worried for the others. The French are a mean lot."

Georgiana's eyes grew wide thinking of the treachery they might inflict upon Elizabeth and the prisoners. "Jimmy, you had better go on ahead and leave me. The Wharf Police must be alerted at once. I shall only slow you down."

"No, miss, I not be leaving ye here. The good colonel would have none of it. As soon as we get past this here water it be not far, and then I be running ahead. Just follow me." Georgiana did as the boy asked and allowed him to lead her away from the flooded area and onto an adjacent street which had not been washed out.

~ ♫ ~

Darcy's Carriage

The wheels of the carriage continued to creak as Darcy's driver slowly traversed the heavily rutted roads on the east side of Town. It was to be expected with the continuation of such a heavy rain. Yet each time the vehicle sprung forward, the passengers inside were startled by the abrupt movement and had to steady themselves.

"Richard," Lord Matlock complained. "How much further is it to the station? Another jolt like the last one, and I am liable to lose what little I ate this morning."

"Father." The colonel chuckled. "You would never survive in the military. These roads are nothing compared to what our men on the continent experience on a daily basis."

Darcy glared at his uncle. "Just be glad we did not have to get out and walk after entering this stretch of road. Did you not notice how many stranded vehicles we have passed thus far? Considering the conditions, my man is doing admirably."

"Humph!"

"We should be there in another one or two blocks," Gardiner offered.

Very little more was said on the subject, and Darcy turned his head to the window ignoring the rest of their conversation. While he and the colonel left Darcy House well before dawn, after picking up Lord Matlock and Mr. Gardiner, travel had become tedious. Unable to sleep due to an overactive mind filled with worry for the safety of Elizabeth and Georgiana, Darcy now found himself aching and irritable.

Thus far, there had been no demand for a ransom, and it was no surprise when they received word that the Bow Street Runners had never heard of George Wickersham. Having that confirmation, Darcy instinctively knew Wickham was involved. *How could it be otherwise?* Hopefully, there would be more information to go on once they arrived at the station.

"Colonel, look here." Gardiner motioned as he peered through the carriage window. "There appears to be some commotion outside of the station." With the carriage slowly pulling to a halt, all four strained to see what was going on. It was impossible to get closer since the road directly in front of the building was flooded and cluttered with several small boats which had been hauled ashore.

"It looks like our men are getting ready to move out," spoke the colonel with alarm. "Something must have happened. Be quick." Colonel Fitzwilliam abruptly flung open the door and jumped from the carriage not waiting for the stairs to be let down. Splashing through standing water, he rushed to his aide who was issuing orders.

"Morris, what has happened?" He motioned to his man who followed him into the building.

"Colonel Fitzwilliam, the French have been spotted at 6 Prusom Street where two carriages were brought around to the rear of the building."

"Younge's boarding house. What of Lord Wolverton? Was he with them?"

"Up to now, he has not been seen by any of our men."

"Morris," Darcy interrupted. "Has there been any news of Miss Darcy or Miss Bennet?"

"Sorry, Mr. Darcy, we have no way of knowing if...."

"Let me pass! Let me pass!" All turned to watch as a young boy, ragged and soaked through, furiously thrashed and kicked struggling to make his way past the officer who held him back.

"I have to see the colonel!" he yelled. "They said he be here. The French are holding me sister an' the others, an' there be worse trouble unless ye help."

"Release him!" Colonel Fitzwilliam boomed. "I know this boy."

The boy ran towards the colonel and grabbed his hands. "Sir, we all be held prisoner by the French on Prusom Street. But I got away with the fine miss who is coming just outside. The French have His

Lordship, an' ye must hurry lest any harm comes to those who be prisoners in the house."

"Son, you are Tully's brother, are you not?"

"Aye, Colonel, sir. Michael Tully be me brother."

"Good lad. We are aware of the situation and some of our men have gone ahead to the house. The rest of us shall be leaving shortly. You are not to worry. Billings please see to it this young man is taken care of."

Before the colonel had finished speaking, Darcy bolted through the door and took to the street. *'The fine miss,' he said. Could it be Elizabeth or could it be Georgiana? Dear Lord, I pray no harm has come to either of them.*

Darcy strained to see if a single woman might be near the building or even a little further down the street. Several people were endeavouring to make their way through ankle deep water, but he could not tell if any of them were Elizabeth or Georgiana. Pulling his hat over his brow and the collar of his greatcoat up around his neck, Darcy set off in the direction of the boarding house. Not having gone far, to his great relief, he saw her. There, bedraggled and barely able to walk, was his precious sister.

"Georgiana, Georgiana," he called. "Georgie, it is me, William."

"William!" She burst into tears as he swept her up into his arms and began carrying her back to the station house.

"Dearest girl, I have you, and you are safe now." Seeing her bare feet, he had to stop himself from cursing in her presence. To think Georgiana had come all this way without shoes was enough to fill him with rage.

"Elizabeth...." Tears trickled down her face. "She is locked up on the third floor. It was Wickham who took us, and now the French have her along with the others at Mrs. Younge's house. I am so worried."

"I know and I promise you we shall get her back. Some of Richard's men should be at the house by now, and as soon as I am sure you will be looked after, I shall join them."

"William, did you see the boy?"

"Yes, he said you were out here on the street."

"His sister took my place so that I might escape. William, it was so awful. Please, please help them," she sobbed.

"Hush, hush, my brave dear girl. All will be well. You are not to worry." He cuddled Georgiana against his chest, and within minutes, they were back inside of the building. There, Darcy requested one of the attending women to look to Georgiana's needs. Next, he quickly penned a note to Lady Helmsley alerting her to the seriousness of the situation. It was sent on with one of his footman who was instructed to return with another carriage and a proper escort for his sister. Having reassured Georgiana one last time, Darcy quickly left the building, eager to join the others. *Wickham, this time you will not get off so easy. I vow you will pay dearly for what you have done!*

CHAPTER TWENTY-NINE

RESCUE

The same morning

*D*espite the wet and cold, Darcy knew he would not be able to endure the confines of a slow-moving carriage while Elizabeth's life was at risk. His unease demanded he take immediate action, and at that moment, riding on horseback suited him best.

Mounting a horse belonging to one of his cousin's men, Darcy was surprised when the young boy from the station house came running to his side. The colonel had insisted the lad stay behind. Despite his demands, the boy had ideas of his own.

"Please, sir, take me with ye. Me mather thinks I be looking after me sister, and I promise I be no trouble if there be fighting. I can run back to Prusom Street meself, but it be faster with ye on this horse. I be knowing in what room the other fine miss and me sister be kept, and I can help ye look fer them."

The pleading look in the boy's eyes touched Darcy's heart. He knew neither of them would be at ease until their loved ones were safe. Disregarding his better judgement, Darcy extended his hand. "Jimmy, is it?"

"Aye, sir, it is. I thank ye, sir." Jimmy spoke with energy as Darcy hoisted the lad up onto the horse.

"Let us go then. We shall find them together." With Jimmy seated in front of him, Darcy wrapped the flaps of his greatcoat around the young boy who was slight of build. Riding off as fast as the weather would allow, Darcy could not help but wonder what misfortunes had prompted Jimmy and his sister to seek employment from Mrs. Younge. Words alone would never be enough to express his gratitude for what this boy and his sister had done to help Georgiana escape. Without question, he would see to the needs of Jimmy and his family once this ordeal was over.

On horseback, it was only a matter of minutes before Darcy and the colonel's armed men were on Prusom Street bound for Younge's boarding house. Shockingly, they were not prepared for the chaos which pervaded the neighbourhood. The house was on fire and despite the heavy rain, black curls of smoke spewed forth from the windows, alerting all that the blaze inside was out of control. Here in the East End where poverty and crime prevailed, the building regulations introduced after the great fire of 1666 had never been enforced. The thatched roofs and close proximity of the buildings were ready kindling for any spark. If the fire was not contained, the entire block could perish in the flames.

With the first sign of fire, one of Colonel Fitzwilliam's watchers had run from building to building, alerting the inhabitants and spreading the word to gather buckets to form a water brigade. Given the location of the neighbourhood, the poor shop owners had limited access to modern hand-powered fire pumps, which meant the locals had to put out the flames as best as they could.

Amidst the growing crowd of people, the colonel's men had broken through the front door of the boarding house, attempting to free those who were locked inside. Alarmingly, by the time the people on the first and second floors had been unbound and led to safety, the flames and thick smoke had engulfed the stairwells, making it impossible to reach the attic floor where Elizabeth and Molly were now trapped.

A cold chill enveloped Darcy's being as he and Jimmy dismounted the horse and hurried through the area where the victims were being helped. Several bore evidence of minor burns on their skin while others persisted in violent coughing from the smoke they had inhaled. Much to their dismay, Elizabeth and Molly were not to be found.

"Darcy," Colonel Fitzwilliam shouted through the chaos. "Wickham and Mrs. Younge have escaped. Some of the girls who worked for Younge said those two have not been seen since my men untied everyone and helped them to safety."

"Richard, I brought Jimmy with me. Neither of us has been able to find Elizabeth or his sister. The boy is still looking."

"Take heart, man. She has to be here. I wish I could help, but I must be off. It seems the French did not get far. One of their carriage wheels cracked in the mud, and they are attempting to flee with His Lordship on horseback. I am taking my best men with me to intercept them now and have left word for Father and Gardiner, who should be here shortly. Wish me luck, Cousin!"

"Godspeed!"

Looking to the third floor where Jimmy had said Elizabeth and his sister were being held prisoner, Darcy was sure they were still trapped in the building. With the raging flames now consuming the lower floor of the structure, it was impossible for anyone to enter from below. He would need to find an alternate way to reach them. Quickly searching the area for something which might be of use, he spied a coil of rope on one of the abandoned wagons. Taking it in hand, Darcy hurried to the entrance of the building adjacent to the boarding house. On entering, he nearly collided with Jimmy, who was running in his direction.

"Sir," he panted. "This way! They still be in the attic room. I heard their cries from out back and called up to them. With the storm, they not be hearing me. There be a set of stairs leading up to the third floor of this house. We be reaching their room from the roof, but the window be boarded, and we be in need of something strong to break it open."

Seeing an old coal shovel stored near the back door, Darcy took it

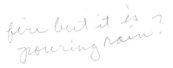
fine but it is pouring rain?

in hand. "Let us make haste. I fear we have not a moment to lose." The two rushed through the back door and climbed the wet stairs to the third floor.

Unlike the boarding house, the adjacent building contained a porch area which ran the length of the third floor. The porch itself was only a few feet higher than the edge of the attic roof of the boarding house. Darcy removed his coats and with little effort, dropped down from the porch and onto the roof. Hurriedly tying one end of the rope to the corner post of the porch and the other around his waist, he insisted Jimmy stay back until he had safely traversed the roof and secured the other end of the rope. As expected, the roof was unstable and nearly gave way in places under Darcy's weight. Edging closer, he fought to keep his balance on the slippery thatches now oozing smoke from the fire below.

"Elizabeth, Elizabeth!" Darcy shouted repeatedly. "Elizabeth, can you hear me?" There was no answer. "Elizabeth!" he shouted again.

"William, we are in here," Elizabeth called through the slats of the window. "Hurry, William, the room is filling with smoke." The sound of their coughing was unsettling.

"Move away from the window!" Darcy shouted before breaking the cracked glass with the end of the shovel. As soon as the glass was cleared, he used the butt of the handle like a hammer and began pounding on the end of one of the boards until the nails gave way and he could work it loose. From there, Elizabeth and Molly took hold of the wood and pulled it back from the window as he continued to loosen more boards. With the opening becoming larger, a stream of smoke quickly poured forth causing Darcy's eyes to water and prompting him to work faster. At last, the opening was large enough for him to climb through.

"Elizabeth," he coughed, clasping her to his chest. "We must be quick. The roof will not last long." Untying the rope around his waist, he said, "We need something stable to secure this end to."

"The bed!" Elizabeth and Molly cried together. All three quickly pushed the bed next to the window where Darcy tied the rope to the frame.

"William, did Georgiana get away?" Elizabeth managed to ask although her flow of speech was interrupted by coughing.

"Yes, she is safe."

"Thank God."

Once the bed was braced against the wall and the rope was taut, Darcy helped the women out of the window and onto the slanted rooftop. At Elizabeth's insistence, Molly went first. Holding onto the rope and Darcy's hand for balance, she carefully traversed the distance until she was met by Jimmy who continued to help her to safety. Returning for Elizabeth who had taken a few steps on her own, Darcy firmly grasped her hand and prayed that they would make it to the other side of the roof before it gave way. As soon as they reached the neighbouring building, Darcy climbed onto the porch. Straddling the rail, he gripped Elizabeth's outstretched arms and pulled her onto the platform and into his embrace. Moments later, the boarding house roof collapsed with a loud crash allowing flames and billowing smoke to burst forth through the opening.

"Stand back!" Darcy shouted as the women screamed in alarm.

"Sir, look! The fire be spreading to the side of *this* building," Jimmy pointed.

"Let us be quick, son, and take the women to safety," Darcy grabbed his coats as he hurried everyone along the planks of the warped porch and down the back stairs.

"Jimmy," Darcy called out when they neared the bottom. "I would like both you and Molly to ride with us in my carriage when we leave this area. Would that be acceptable, young man?"

"Aye, sir. Me and Molly be honoured." The boy beamed.

"If we become separated in the crowd, rest assured Miss Elizabeth and I shall not leave without you. My carriage is quite large and bears the Darcy crest. Any of Colonel Fitzwilliam's men will be able to direct you if need be. We shall follow in a moment."

"Thank ye, sir." Jimmy took Molly by the hand to lead her through the building and out into the street.

As soon as they left, Darcy pulled Elizabeth away from the doorway and into his embrace. "My love," he whispered kissing nearly every inch of her face before settling upon her mouth. "If I had lost either you or Georgiana today I.... The two of you mean everything to me."

"William, I prayed you would come for me, and you did. I love you so very much." Tears misted in her eyes as she looked up into his and gently cupped his cheek with her hand.

Turning his face to kiss her palm, he then clasped her hand and pulled it firmly to his breast. "My darling Elizabeth, I love you with all of my heart, and I never wish to be parted from you again. Though I mean no disrespect to your family, I beg of you to put my mind at ease and consent to become my wife as soon as it may be arranged.

"Your wishes are mine." She smiled reassuringly. "I promise I shall write to Papa this very day and send our request by express."

Unable to hold back his desires, Darcy began kissing Elizabeth with a hunger which could no longer be denied. As he deepened his kiss, she willingly responded in kind until their passions left them both unsteady and short of breath. Picking up his belongings, Darcy lovingly wrapped his jacket securely around Elizabeth's shoulders and pushed several wet curls away from her face. After kissing the tip of her nose, he reclaimed her mouth for one final kiss before taking her hand and leading her through the building.

~ ♫ ~

Unknown to Darcy, a lone man observed all that had taken place within the confines of the alley during the past hour. Having nearly been killed in the burning building and then soaked through from the storm, one George Wickham had decided to remain hidden while contemplating his next course of action. Looking up to the building from which he had just escaped, he could scarcely believe his eyes when he saw his old adversary. There, nearly crawling across the roof of the building was Fitzwilliam Darcy making his way to the boarded up window so that he might rescue his sister.

For one fleeting moment, Wickham had actually considered attempting the rescue himself. He desperately needed the ransom money if he was yet to flee England and set sail for Italy. In the end, the mere thought of losing his life in the process proved not enough to take the risk. If only he had not bungled her abduction—not to mention losing what little money he had in the fire.

Wickham watched in silence as Darcy broke through the window and helped the women to climb out. The man was suddenly left aghast when he realised Darcy's sister was nowhere to be seen. Without question, he, George Wickham, had been duped. Georgiana Darcy had escaped and the other woman with Miss Elizabeth Bennet was none other than the serving girl, Molly.

Recovering from the shock, he frowned with indignation. *Why would Fitzwilliam waste his time on Miss Bennet and a mere serving girl, unless....* Fuming with anger, he nearly leapt from his hiding place when he saw Darcy embrace and kiss Elizabeth. *Fitzwilliam Darcy is in love with that country chit! How could I have been so blind? She was with Georgiana NOT because they were friends, but because of HIM! Blast! If only I had known. I could have left the accursed French and demanded far more than what I would have gotten for Georgiana. What a fool! How many times must I be cheated in my dealings with that man?*

Reaching in his pocket, he pulled out a single cameo brooch. Wondering how much it might bring, he replaced it in his pocket for safe keeping. It was obviously not one of Georgiana's better pieces, but even so, it was the only thing of value he had left to his name. Georgiana's rings and the garnet cross belonging to Elizabeth had been lost somewhere in the burning building. He wondered if this one piece of jewellery would be enough to get him to Italy, or if he would have to try his luck at the gaming tables before setting sail. Being a deserter and traitor, he knew there was no possibility of his remaining in England without risking the chance of facing the gallows. In addition, he had the threat of what Darcy and Colonel Fitzwilliam might do to him if they were to catch him.

Wickham spat on the ground watching Darcy and Elizabeth conclude their display of affection. For the moment, Italy would have to wait. With the storm, it was not possible at any cost. *What I need is a stiff drink and someone to warm my bed, and I know just the place to find them both. She may not be handsome, but not far from here there is a widow who would gladly keep me for a day or two. Thank God I still have my charm and good looks to see me through.* Laughing to himself, he quickly rallied and left the area, knowing he could easily forget his misfortunes for the next few days in the arms of a willing woman and some strong drink.

~ ♫ ~

Darcy and Elizabeth emerged from the building where people from the bucket brigade were dousing the smouldering wall with water. From there, they made their way into the overly crowded street where several local residents were fighting to save their belongings from would-be looters.

"This place is not safe," Darcy called out. Hurrying Elizabeth towards his carriage, he could see Jimmy and Molly waiting within. Both Lord Matlock and Mr. Gardiner stood off to the side speaking with one of Colonel Fitzwilliam's aides. When Gardiner noticed his niece, he excused himself and ran towards the couple with a huge smile on his face.

"Lizzy, thank God you are unharmed, my dear." He pulled her into his embrace and kissed her on the forehead. "Mr. Darcy, I owe you a huge debt of gratitude." Releasing Elizabeth, Gardiner continued, "Wolverton has been recovered, and all of the French have been apprehended with the exception of their leader, Monsieur Everard. Please continue on and take Lizzy out of this rain. Lord Matlock and I shall join you directly."

After Darcy and Elizabeth were finally seated in the carriage, Darcy extended his hand to the boy. "Jimmy, I cannot begin to thank you enough for what you and your sister have done for my family today. The two of you were very brave in the face of death."

"We be honoured to help, sir," Jimmy stated. "Our brother, Michael, be dead on the field of battle if it not be fer Colonel Fitzwilliam. We did what our Michael would want us to do." The boy beamed with pride.

"I would like to meet your brother, Jimmy. And in return for your generosity, I intend to help your family. Both of you will be taken care of and provided with food and a warm bed for tonight. As soon as you are settled, I shall send a messenger to your mother informing her of what has taken place here. On the morrow, it is my intention to accompany you to your home and offer her my personal thanks. Since Mrs. Younge's boarding house is no more, I would also like to propose to your mother that the two of you come to work for me at my townhouse."

"Thank ye, sir. Me mather an' all me family be grateful, sir."

"As am I, son. I am in your debt."

Minutes later, Lord Matlock and Mr. Gardiner entered the carriage. The storm had finally begun to ease, but with unrest threatening to take over the street, Darcy was anxious to depart. It would take nearly half an hour before his driver was able to leave the confines of Prusom Street, and almost another hour before the carriage would reach Ferversham House. Neither his uncle nor Gardiner chose to divulge more specific information concerning what had taken place, yet Darcy suspected they were fairly satisfied with how things had turned out. For much of the ride back to Ferversham House, Darcy sat quietly with Elizabeth's hand securely clasped within his own. Although the horror of the day would not easily be erased from his thoughts, the two women who mattered most in his life had been spared, and for that, he would be eternally grateful.

CHAPTER THIRTY

ALL WILL BE WELL

Ferversham House
The same afternoon

*L*ady Jessica's servants had been on high alert ever since receiving the first of Darcy's messages including a request summoning his personal physician. As soon as his carriage arrived back at the townhouse, its occupants were escorted inside where a multitude of servants waited to assist. Upon seeing Elizabeth's dishevelled appearance, Lady Jessica took immediate charge of her guest's care, insisting she be given a hot bath and readied for Mr. Mitchell's examination.

After seeing the physician, Elizabeth was advised to rest. Before doing so, however, she insisted on discussing her change of wedding plans with Lady Jessica. Then she needed to pen a letter to her father which would be sent by express along with one from her uncle. By the time Elizabeth retired, the fatigue she had been fighting quickly took over leaving her asleep within minutes.

As for Darcy, the man had not slept since returning to Town on the previous day and was equally if not more exhausted. Still, with nearly losing both Elizabeth and Georgiana, he could not abide returning to his own home. Knowing he would not feel at ease unless he remained close by, Darcy chose to spend the night at Ferversham House. Before retiring, he was invited to join Lady Jessica and the viscount in their private sitting room for a late night drink. There, the events of the day were shared in greater detail. To his relief, talking through some of what had taken place seemed to ease his mind. His cousins were very supportive and Lady Jessica assured him both Elizabeth and Georgiana would both be feeling much better by morning.

Having said goodnight, Darcy ambled through the long hall of the family wing towards his own room. After two arduous days of stress and worry, he was so very tired. He only prayed that sleep would come quickly. Pausing outside of Georgiana's room, he listened to make sure all was well before proceeding on to Elizabeth's. There, he silently placed his hands on her door and leaned his forehead against the cool wood. Thank God he had not lost either of them today. Despite reassurances from his cousin, he fervently prayed all would be well.

"William…. William…."

It was Elizabeth frantically calling his name and jolting his mind from drowsiness to high alert. Forsaking all propriety, he pushed open the door and rushed to her bedside where he immediately pulled her into his arms and offered comfort.

"William," she choked out, desperately clinging to him, half asleep. "The fire…. I could not breathe."

"Shh, shh my love…. I am here. It was only a dream. Nothing can harm you now. You are safe." Continuing to hold her in his arms, he tenderly kissed her forehead and caressed her back as he whispered endearing words of love. Moments later, she was asleep. Gently laying Elizabeth on the bed so as not to wake her, Darcy pulled the blankets about her shoulders and lovingly brushed the side of her cheek with his fingertips.

"Fitzwilliam," Lady Jessica whispered. She, too, had heard Elizabeth's cries and had hurried to her room along with Sophia. "I shall sit with her for a while. It is not proper for you to be in here like this. You *must* return to your room before her reputation is severely tarnished."

"I know." He looked back at Elizabeth with great concern. "But ... will you not send for me if she calls out again?"

"Yes." Lady Jessica smiled and kissed him on the cheek. "Against my better judgement, I will. You need not worry so. Though her life was in peril today, Elizabeth is a strong and healthy young woman. The two of you have much to look forward to. Now, you should get some rest. Your Elizabeth will be fine."

~ ♫ ~

29 September 1811
Sunday, the next morning

After being comforted by Darcy, Elizabeth experienced a restful sleep for the remainder of the night. Waking early, she asked Sophia to quickly help her dress so as not to miss him before he left with the Tully children. A short time later, Elizabeth felt presentable and left her room eager to begin her day. Wanting to send a basket of food and basic necessities to the family, she first set off in search of the house-keeper. Once her request was made, Elizabeth went on to the dining area where she was pleasantly greeted by Darcy and Colonel Fitzwilliam.

"Good morning," Elizabeth replied with a cheerful smile, although she barely acknowledged the colonel with her address since her eyes were solely fixed on Darcy who quickly rose from his chair and moved to her side.

"I did not expect to see you this early, my love. May I get you a cup of hot tea and perhaps something to eat?" Darcy led her to the sofa and lovingly placed a pillow behind her back for comfort.

"Thank you, William. Some tea would be lovely." Her voice was a bit irritated from the effects of the smoke, and she could not help but let out a slight cough.

"I trust you slept better as the night went on." He finished preparing the tea and joined her on the sofa.

"Yes, I did, thank you."

"Richard has decided to accompany me to the Tully house this morning. He says the family's circumstances are dire."

"Oh dear."

"It is true, Miss Elizabeth. I spoke with Jimmy earlier this morning, and it seems Mr. Tully had not been well for some time and died last winter. It is no wonder the children were forced to seek employment."

"And at such a place." She shook her head in dismay. "The boarding house was disgusting. But, Colonel, what news is there of the older brother? Is he not able to help in some way?"

"With one arm, the man is certainly at a disadvantage, and I suspect his opportunities have been limited to little more than odd jobs."

"I feared as much. William, before coming here, I asked the housekeeper if a basket could be prepared for you to take to the family. Considering their unfortunate situation, I am sure it will be welcomed."

"You need not worry." He squeezed her hand. "Knowing what Jimmy and Molly did to help you and Georgiana, I shall see to it their family is never again in want."

"I am glad of it. Thank you."

"Richard, would you please check on the basket? I wish to speak with Elizabeth before we leave."

"Indeed!" He chuckled. "I can tell when my presence is not wanted. I shall see to it and send for the children." The colonel gave a quick bow and exited the room, closing the door as he did so.

"Your cousin is very kind to allow us a few minutes alone." She held out her hands. "I cannot help it, but after yesterday, I find myself longing to be near you."

"Oh, my sweetest love." He kissed her hand and gently touched her face with his fingertips. "I would give anything to take away the pain you and Georgiana have suffered. To think I nearly lost you both." He pulled her to his chest. "Yet, here you are in my arms, and soon we shall marry. God has blessed us, Elizabeth." Despite the need for proper decorum and the possibility of a servant entering at any moment, Darcy continued to hold her and tenderly kissed her where they sat.

"My darling, I love you so very much. I only wish I did not have to leave you today, but it cannot be helped. After Richard and I have taken care of the Tully children, I need to spend a few hours at Darcy House. Hopefully, I shall return by mid-afternoon. Will you wait for me in the library?"

"Yes, happily." She beamed.

"There is something I wish to give you, and I think that room will offer us the most privacy."

"I shall be waiting."

Darcy kissed her one final time, and together they left the dining area. On reaching the foyer, Elizabeth was able to offer her sincere gratitude to the Tully children once again. Taking their hands, she promised she would see them very soon.

~ ♫ ~

The Library
Mid-afternoon

Elizabeth stationed herself at the library window, just as she had done little more than a week prior. Patiently awaiting the return of her beloved William, fond memories of their last time alone in this room brought a smile to her face.

In light of what she had experienced during the past two days, those memories were now more precious to her than ever. Though determined not to dwell on the horror of those events, at this moment, Elizabeth still longed for his comfort. She wanted nothing more than to be held close by the man she loved and for him to kiss away the ugliness still threatening to disturb her peace.

Gazing out of the window, Elizabeth was thankful to finally see blue skies and billowy clouds overhead. With the worst of last night's storm dissipating into an early morning drizzle, the afternoon air was now filled with a gentle breeze and the warmth of an autumn sun. She only hoped the roads would be passible on the morrow since her father's return express indicated the Bennets would set out for Town at that time. Unfolding his letter, she proceeded to read it again, pleased he had given his permission for her and William to marry in a few days.

My dear Lizzy,

Needless to say, I was shocked in receiving not one but two letters of an alarming nature from yourself and my brother Gardiner. Daughter, it grieves me to think you might have perished in the fire had it not been for Mr. Darcy's determination and bravery. I am grateful you are well and pray you are not suffering any ill effects from a prolonged exposure to the deadly smoke.

As to the matter of your abduction by Mr. Wickham, that shocking aspect of your ordeal has not been revealed to the rest of the family. I agree there would be no benefit in further alarming your mother or sisters with such distressing information. Let us hope Mr. Wickham will be apprehended and punished accordingly. What he did was unconscionable.

Now, with regard to your request for an earlier wedding date, I fully comprehend why Mr. Darcy wishes to marry you sooner than we originally agreed. Considering all the two of you have endured, I shall abide by his request. Knowing he risked his own life to rescue you from the fire, the man will forever have my undying gratitude, and I shall be pleased to call him son.

I have informed your mother of the change in plans, and we both agree Wednesday, 2 October will be acceptable. That being said, there is one thing I would like to propose. Since we shall not be hosting the wedding here, may I suggest you and Mr. Darcy consider extending your visit to Longbourn for at least a few more days? I know your mama would take great delight in showing you off to the neighbour-

hood before you travel to the north. And frankly, after such a long separation, I, too, would enjoy your company.

With regard to any further disappointment your mother may be feeling, I must say the letter of consolation sent by Lady Helmsley along with your personal note has greatly improved her spirits. Per Lady Helmsley's request, you will find a list of Mrs. Bennet's recommendations for the wedding breakfast. In truth, your mother is quite beside herself knowing a titled peer will be hosting the breakfast in addition to your engagement dinner on Monday evening. Thank goodness I shall not have to accompany all of you on Her Ladyship's proposed shopping tour of Bond Street on Tuesday morning. Instead, I have decided to take up Mr. Darcy's previous offer to avail myself of his library whenever I am in Town. If your young man has not the constitution for shopping, please inform him he will be most welcome to join me for the duration.

Lastly, I trust you will extend my gratitude to Her Ladyship for the kindness she has bestowed upon you and our family. I must admit Lady Helmsley has been exceedingly gracious in offering to house ALL of your sisters during our stay. Be assured the younger two will receive thorough instructions from the Holyoaks before we depart. Even though they have yet to master every aspect of their tutelage, I think you will notice a considerable improvement in their deportment. Our time in Town may prove to be an excellent opportunity to find out if they are able to retain any of what they have been taught thus far. If their behaviour does not regress, I may possibly allow them to resume regular attendance at the local assembly balls when we return home.

We shall leave Longbourn on Monday morning with our expected arrival being sometime in the early afternoon, providing there are no serious delays with the roads. After four hours or so in a confined carriage, I dare say I shall be quite happy to deliver all of your sisters

to Ferversham House before proceeding on to Gracechurch Street. I
shall leave you now, my dear. Please give my sincerest regard to
Mr. Darcy.

Papa

why still hidden?

Refolding the letter, Elizabeth placed it on the table and resumed
her vigil at the window. Touching the place where her ring remained
hidden within the bodice of her dress, she knew it would not be long
before it would be given a new home upon her finger.

~ ♫ ~

Not more than a quarter of an hour had passed before Darcy's
carriage pulled up in front of the house. "William," Elizabeth said with
delight. She watched him exit the vehicle and approach the house
carrying several more of the beautiful gardenia flowers in hand. "My,
with all of the branches you have recently cut, it is a wonder those
poor plants are still alive." She giggled to herself in anticipation of
receiving his treasured gift.

Within minutes, Darcy removed his coat and hat and entered the
library with the flowers still in hand. "Elizabeth, you look lovely this
afternoon." He smiled broadly handing all but one flower to Sophia
who took the bouquet and discretely left the room.

"I trust you were able to rest while I was away?"

"Yes, I did. Thank you. With the family remaining in their rooms
for most of the day, the house has been fairly quiet. Georgiana did not
awaken until late morning and was feeling far better. She will join us
for dinner along with your cousins."

"Good." He nodded. "Your voice sounds much clearer this afternoon, and since I have yet to hear you cough, may I assume you are
experiencing less discomfort?"

"I still feel a little tightness in my chest, but it is really nothing.
Soon after you left this morning, a footman bearing one of Aunt

Gardiner's herbal remedies arrived. The elixir was soothing and I find much of the uneasiness I was experiencing has dissipated."

"I am pleased to hear it. While I was at Darcy House, I found the gardenia bushes had produced several more blossoms. I thought they would cheer your day and could not resist cutting a few more branches." She took the flower he offered.

"William, the smell is heavenly, and having you here again cheers my day immeasurably."

Darcy pulled her into his embrace. "Hearing you say so, my love, cheers mine as well." He kissed her tenderly. "Please, let us sit. I have something to show you."

"And I have something to show you! My father has written and has given his consent for us to marry on Wednesday."

"Elizabeth!" In his exuberance, Darcy picked her up and twirled her around causing her to giggle.

"William, put me down. Supposing someone comes in here."

"Let them come, for on Wednesday I shall be a married man, and you, my dearest, loveliest Elizabeth, will be Mrs. Fitzwilliam Darcy."

"Mrs. Darcy," she quietly said, her eyes misting. "I like the sound of that very much."

"As do I." Carrying Elizabeth to the couch, Darcy sat with her resting upon his lap. Not able to resist kissing her with the same fiery passion which they had shared when alone in the alley, he did not release her lips for several minutes.

"William," she whispered his name, almost gasping for air. Her head was light and her eyes glazed.

"Forgive me." He panted. "There is no excuse for my behaviour. For my part, it seems Wednesday cannot come soon enough."

"You are forgiven even though it appears I am a willing partner in your crime." She arched an eyebrow and playfully kissed Darcy on the cheek before slipping from his lap to sit beside him on the sofa.

Not able to resist her little tease, Darcy gave her a quick kiss in return and took her hand. "Elizabeth." He smiled lovingly. "I have brought you something else which belonged to my mother. But first, if I may, I would like to place her ring upon your finger." Elizabeth *now it's not hidden?*

clasped her hand to her breast where the precious ring lay hidden. Holding his gaze, she slowly pulled the chain from the bodice of her dress.

"Allow me."

Turning her back to him, Elizabeth could feel his breath upon her neck as his fingers gently touched her exposed flesh. She could not help but close her eyes, revelling in the sensation of his caresses as he did so.

"You are so very beautiful, my love." Darcy whispered and then softly kissed her neck before undoing the clasp and removing the chain. "The ring is warm," he remarked. To her surprise, he quickly dropped on one knee and continuing to hold her hand, commenced his addresses. "My dearest Elizabeth, will you do me the greatest honour of becoming my wife?"

"Yes, my love, I shall. With all of my heart, I am yours."

Darcy slipped his mother's ring on Elizabeth's finger and gazed into her shining eyes. "Elizabeth, you have made me the happiest of men. I pledge to you my eternal love and shall do everything within my power to make our life together a happy one."

"William, I *am* happy and I love you so dearly." They kissed again.

Darcy took delight in examining how perfect the ring looked on Elizabeth's finger. After kissing her hand, he took two elongated boxes from the pocket of his jacket. As she opened the first box, he said, "My father gave this emerald necklace to my mother shortly after they became engaged. She in turn gave it to me before she died, asking that I present it to my intended. I thought perhaps you might like to wear it tomorrow night at our engagement dinner."

"William." Elizabeth could barely contain her emotions. "It is so very beautiful, and knowing your mother meant it for me makes it all the more precious. I shall be proud to wear this in her honour. It will look stunning with the new gown Aunt Gardiner had made for me to wear at our party. Dare I look in the second box?"

"By all means. These were worn by Mama on the day my parents married."

Elizabeth carefully opened the second box, unsure of what to expect. "Pearls!" she exclaimed, holding them up. "Oh! And look! There are earrings to match. I love them and shall wear them on our wedding day just as your dear mama did." She kissed him in return. "William, I cannot thank you enough for sharing these with me."

At Darcy's insistence, Elizabeth tried on both of her necklaces, a task which proved to be very appealing since it was interspersed with more kisses and teasing banter. Next, they shared Mr. Bennet's letter and discussed how they could easily alter their plans and spend more time at Longbourn before travelling on to Pemberley. Darcy then proceeded to speak of his visit with the Tully family.

"Elizabeth, their living conditions were far worse than I anticipated. Even Richard said he did not remember their dwelling being so very poor."

"I am so sorry to hear it. If not for them, Georgiana and I...."

"I know. You are not to worry, my love. Their needs will be met. I should never allow them to continue on in their present state." He held her hand. "I have already written to my solicitor requesting he find a more suitable dwelling for the family. It will be in Mr. Wilcox's hands on the morrow. In addition, Richard has promised to secure a job in the war office for the elder son, Michael. While the young man has lost much of his left arm, his right is perfectly functional. From speaking with him, I found he has a keen mind. With his knowledge of the war and having served on the continent, Richard thinks the man could be employed as a military aide despite his disability."

"When Jane and I assisted the wounded soldiers with the *Correspondence Hours* at the hospital, we came upon many young men who were in a similar situation. At the time, Aunt Gardiner suggested we form another committee to help these men find some type of meaningful employment. Since we are no longer active with Lady Matlock's charity, I am not sure what progress has been made on their behalf."

"If you like, I shall ask my solicitor to make some inquiries."

"It would please me very much."

"Consider it done." He kissed her hand. "Now, tell me, what have you worked out for Jimmy and Molly?"

"They are exceptional children." He smiled. "Their mother was beside herself to learn of their good deeds. For now, they will both work at Darcy House. After Molly is trained in the ways of a proper maid, she may be of greater use here at Ferversham House. Once the viscount assumes his father's place in Parliament, this house will be far more active and will be in need of additional servants. I shall speak with Lady Jessica later today and settle the matter between us."

"And Jimmy?"

"Yes, Jimmy.... I confess I am very fond of the lad. He has proved himself to be a brave little boy and one who is fiercely loyal to his family. He is resourceful and very intelligent. To begin with, he will be assigned to the mews. I do, however, intend for him to spend part of his time learning how to read and write. I have a man who will work with him on a daily basis. As soon as he becomes proficient and has mastered his numbers, I shall sponsor him in an apprenticeship of some sort. Possibly with your Uncle Gardiner if he is amenable."

"William, I thank you with all of my heart for assisting this family. You are giving the Tullys a chance to improve their lives, and I could not be more pleased."

"My darling, it is nothing when compared to what I might have lost if you and Georgiana had been more seriously harmed. I owe their family much more than I shall ever be able to repay."

"We both do."

"Now, my love, may I interest you in a short walk?"

"Yes, please. Pray, what do you have in mind?"

"Well, with the pathways remaining a bit wet after the storm, I thought we might take a short turn about the solarium."

"How delightful!"

"Let us go now." He held out his arm. "With the afternoon sunlight, the solarium will prove to be quite pleasant."

CHAPTER THIRTY-ONE

TWO SHALL BECOME ONE

Ferversham House
1 October 1811
Late Tuesday evening

*E*lizabeth sat in her room sorting through a few personal items which would be transported to Darcy House in the morning along with the last of her trunks. The lively chatter and giggles emanating from Georgiana's rooms just down the hall warmed her heart. The dear girl was nearly beside herself after learning Lady Jessica had invited all of Elizabeth's sisters to reside at Ferversham House for the duration of their stay in Town.

On the first afternoon of their arrival, Georgiana eagerly invited the women to her rooms with the intent of giving them gifts. For Jane, she had chosen a beautiful Persian scarf and a matching silk fan while Mary was presented with some new sheets of music and a pair of kid gloves. Kitty and Lydia could not imagine what Georgiana had purchased for them and were overjoyed when she brought forth large hat boxes containing new bonnets and matching reticules of the latest fashion.

"La, Miss Darcy!" exclaimed Lydia trying on her bonnet. "How ever did you know I favoured pink? Does it not suit me?"

"Indeed, I am glad you like it. And please, all of you … do call me Georgiana. You have no idea how happy I am to claim you as my new sisters."

To Georgiana's delight, the girls had also purchased some small gifts for her from some of their favourite shops in Meryton. She had never expected such kindness and was overjoyed. Her desire to experience a sisterly bond with women of her own age had finally become a reality.

Elizabeth had missed being with her sisters and was pleased to see Lydia and Kitty in particular had made a good deal of progress since they were last in Town. With the exception of one little setback on Monday evening prior to her engagement dinner, they had behaved remarkably well. Their misadventure happened to involve Colonel Fitzwilliam who drew their immediate attention having arrived at Ferversham House dressed in his regimentals. Previously, the two youngest Bennet sisters had been thoroughly instructed by Mrs. Holyoak on the necessity of proper decorum when in the presence of officers. In this instance, however, the temptation proved to be too great.

"Colonel Fitzwilliam." Lydia implored. "My sister and I noticed the scar on your chin and were wondering how you happened to come by it. Was it in battle?" she asked somewhat breathless with the thought.

"Miss Lydia, my time in Portugal was perilous indeed!" He feigned a grimace while slowly rubbing his fingers along the side of his jaw where the scar was most obvious.

"Oh, do tell us," Lydia pleaded, giving off a little nervous giggle. "The men of the Militia Regiment who are quartered in Meryton are so very dull and have nothing of a heroic nature to report."

"Very well." He took a stoic pose and began his little tale with a sense of drama. "The injury took place during my second tour of duty on the continent. We had been fighting for days, and at one point, the enemy was so thick that none of us knew if we should survive. In one last attempt to rally, my men followed me into the brink where we fought hand to hand in combat until our foe was defeated. This souvenir came from the tip of one of

Napoleon's finest as he tried to escape our onslaught. With regard to the rest, I shall say no more of the matter for I would not wish to disturb the sensibilities of any young lady by continuing my discourse."

After hearing Colonel Fitzwilliam's account, Lydia and Kitty clasped their hands together and nearly squealed before promptly swooning on the nearest sofa. The colonel, taken by surprise, sought immediate assistance for the young ladies. Even with the administering of smelling salts, however, the two silly girls did not revive until Mr. Bennet intervened with the threat of having them removed to Gracechurch Street. Fortunately, the incident occurred well before Lady Jessica's other guests had arrived and received little notice from anyone with the exception of Elizabeth's immediate family. To her astonishment, once Mr. Bennet had intervened, the girls took it upon themselves to apologise to Colonel Fitzwilliam. From that time and throughout the remainder of the evening, both Lydia and Kitty behaved like proper young ladies.

Moving to her dresser, Elizabeth opened her jewellery box which had yet to be packed. "Mama," she sighed. Carefully examining Mrs. Bennet's gift, her mind was now filled with yet another memory.

"Lizzy, I wish to speak with you in private," Mrs. Bennet whispered, not wishing those who were seated in Lady Helmsley's drawing room to overhear.

"Mama, will you not come to my room? It is quiet there, and I would like to show you Lady Anne's pearls."

"Oh yes, my dear, your room will be just the place."

Elizabeth had hoped her mother was not planning to tell her of the wedding night since she had already faced those somewhat embarrassing yet informative moments with Mrs. Gardiner. "Come, Mama." Elizabeth took her mother's arm and led her to the bedroom.

"My, this room is lovely!" She looked about the room taking note of the furnishings and touching certain decorative items. "Lady Jessica has been most gracious in hosting you as Miss Darcy's guest. And the view is quite pleasant, is it not?"

"Yes, it is, indeed. Mama, please be seated. Would you care for anything? I would be happy to ring for a glass of wine or whatever else you may desire."

"No, no, I am fine." Mrs. Bennet smoothed her dress and took a seat on

the sofa where she momentarily patted her chest in an effort to calm her nerves.

"Lizzy, I must say I was given quite a fright when your father told me of your near demise in the fire. I cannot even begin to describe to you the fluttering and palpitations I experienced during the shock of it all. Why, to think I might never have seen you again."

"Mama...." Elizabeth held her mother's hand. "Please, do not distress yourself. All is well now."

"Yes, yes, I know. Still, learning the truth of what happened gave me pause. Throughout your years, I realise I have been known to show preference for Lydia and Jane. Today, however, I wanted you to know how very much I love you and how proud of you I truly am."

"Oh, Mama." Elizabeth kissed her mother on the cheek. "I love you too and have never doubted your love. I am sorry for those times when I have been a source of anguish for you. Please forgive me."

Overcome with emotion, Mrs. Bennet burst into tears. It was several minutes later that she felt composed enough to continue. "Lizzy, there is something more I wish to speak of. Your father told me you were saddened by the loss of Grandmamma Bennet's garnet cross."

"Yes, it was a keepsake which I had hoped to one day share with my own daughter."

"Before your father and I married, she gave me a similar necklace. It has been many years since I have worn it. I only remembered having it after learning of your loss." Taking a small velvet pouch from her pocket, she handed it to Elizabeth and said, "I have decided to give you my necklace in its stead."

"Mama!" Elizabeth was touched as she opened the pouch and took out the simple garnet cross bearing one small diamond chip in the centre. "This is lovely and not so unlike the necklace which Grandmamma gave to me. I shall always treasure it." She wrapped her arms around her mother kissing her once again.

"I, too, thought you might one day give this to your daughter although I do urge you to give Mr. Darcy his heir first."

"Mama, please do not worry on that account. There is no entailment on

Pemberley, and William assures me he will not be disappointed with daughters."

"I am glad to hear of it though I caution you to heed my advice. A great man like Mr. Darcy will surely want a son."

"Yes, Mama."

"Now, with your wedding taking place on the morrow, is there anything you would care to ask me regarding the marriage bed? Your aunt informed me she has already spoken with you about such matters. Even so, I am willing to address any further concerns you may have."

"Mama, I shall be fine. Aunt Gardiner was very thorough." She blushed.

"I am glad to hear of it. Perhaps only a slight review will be necessary."

Elizabeth chuckled to herself remembering the satisfied look on her mother's face after imparting her *advice.* Although she was a little nervous about what was to take place on her wedding night, she looked forward to starting her married life with Darcy and to someday giving him a child.

A short time later, Jane lightly tapped on the door interrupting her thoughts. "Lizzy, may I come in?"

"Why yes, of course, please join me." She motioned to the bed. "I was hoping you would come. With my wedding tomorrow, this will be our last chance to talk as we used to."

Jane took a seat at the end of the bed, curling her legs beneath her dressing gown. "Our sisters have invaded Georgiana's rooms once again and will no doubt be there for some time." The younger Bennet girls and Georgiana had been inseparable since their arrival.

"So I have heard."

"Lydia and Kitty are looking through her closet of accessories while Mary and Georgiana are attempting to play a song on the dulcimer. It is such an unusual instrument."

"Yes, very."

"Lizzy, I was wondering about the gentleman who delivered it. Did Georgiana not say he was from Scotland?"

"Yes, he is." Elizabeth smiled. "Mr. McKinney is also the maker of the instrument."

"Ah, I see."

"We met him at the Autumn Festival, which is where Georgiana made her purchase. He is a fine old craftsman who was selling a variety of stringed instruments. Georgiana heard the dulcimer being played on the Green and was immediately taken with it. William has since engaged Mr. McKinney's services to instruct Georgiana on the instrument before we leave Town and travel to Hertfordshire. After we go to Pemberley, Mr. McKinney will spend a month with us before making his final journey to Edinburgh where he resides."

"I overheard Georgiana telling Mary as much. She invited our sister to stay on at Ferversham House when our family returns to Longbourn on Monday. Georgiana wishes Mary to partake in the lessons with Mr. McKinney."

"Mary must be delighted. It seems the two of them are getting along very well."

"They are. Lizzy," Jane spoke quietly. "I would like to know if there is something more to the incident with the fire which we are not aware of. When Mr. McKinney delivered the instrument this afternoon, I distinctly overheard him say the word *abduction* while he and Georgiana were conversing."

"I shall tell you Jane, but it would be best if our mother and sisters knew nothing of what I am about to say."

"I understand."

Elizabeth proceeded to relate some of the events of her ordeal although she did not describe them in great detail for fear of upsetting her sister's sensibilities. Even so, Jane was horrified to learn what Elizabeth and Georgiana had endured. "Oh, Lizzy, I had no idea you were being held prisoner. You might have died had it not been for Mr. Darcy coming to your rescue." Tears misted in her eyes. "Now I understand why Papa allowed you to change the wedding plans and marry here tomorrow. I shall be forever grateful to my new brother for saving you."

"Jane, I have never met a finer man, and I shall do everything within my power to see to his happiness. I love him so very much."

"I have not the slightest doubt the two of you will be very happy. If

I could but find a man who is half as good as your dear Mr. Darcy, I would be truly blessed."

"Perhaps you will," Elizabeth teased. "According to Mama, Mr. Bingley holds great promise. Not to mention he was very attentive to you at my engagement dinner and then again earlier today when the gentlemen joined us at Gunter's for tea." The two sisters giggled.

"I do like him very much. I suppose one can only hope."

"From what William says, the man is smitten."

"Lizzy." Jane blushed profusely. "You must not tease me so. I am honoured by Mr. Bingley's attentions, but when we saw him in Hertfordshire, he was pleasant to many young ladies in the neighbourhood. In the end, he may choose to fix his attentions elsewhere."

Elizabeth reached for Jane's hands. "My dear sister, if Mr. Bingley does not ask you for a courtship, then he is a very foolish young man and does *not* deserve you. Furthermore, considering he is William's good friend, I know for certain my intended would *never* choose to be closely associated with a man who was a fool. Therefore, the matter is practically settled." Elizabeth sat tall, giving Jane a smug look until the two broke into more giggles.

"Lizzy, my dearest sister, I am surely going to miss your teasing."

"Yes, tis a great pity I shall have no other choice but to share my more *unusual* qualities with William and Georgiana. I only pray they will somehow survive." Again they laughed. "We shall vow to be diligent correspondents, and before you know it, it will be December, and all of us shall be together again at Pemberley."

"Yes, at Pemberley."

~ ♫ ~

Darcy House
The same evening

Darcy sat with his chair pushed back and his feet propped up on his desk. Having tossed his coat to the side and loosened his cravat, he held a small glass of brandy in one hand and a shiny gold band bearing several brilliant emeralds in the other. The ring had been commissioned for Elizabeth, and on the morrow, he would lovingly place it upon her finger. From that day forward, she would not be parted from him again. "Elizabeth, my darling, as long as I am able, you will never want, and I shall love you until my dying breath."

Placing his glass on the desk top, Darcy returned the ring to his breast pocket and removed Elizabeth's handkerchief which held her lock of hair. Slowly wrapping the long curl around his finger, he remembered how his desires had been ignited by such a simple yet intimate act of cutting it from the rest of her beautiful tresses. Smiling to himself, he could not help but imagine how it would feel to run his fingers through her loosened hair on their wedding night. From the kisses he had stolen, he knew Elizabeth to be a passionate woman, and he looked forward to unlocking the treasure his beloved embodied. "Tomorrow, my love…. Tomorrow we shall become one."

Breaking his reverie, Darcy recognised the heavy footsteps of Colonel Fitzwilliam striding through the hallway. Although his cousin was to stand up with him at the wedding, he had not anticipated seeing him at this late hour. Rising he greeted his cousin who quickly walked through the door. "Richard, what brings you here? I did not expect to see you before morning."

"I was taking care of a little unfinished business at the office and thought I would stop by with the latest news of Wickham."

"Wickham! What? Has he been found?"

"In a way." The colonel let out a sardonic laugh and proceeded to pour himself a drink.

"You might say he has been *found* by the French. According to my sources, Monsieur Everard boarded a Dutch ship early this morning with Mr. Wickham in tow. Regrettably, we did not receive the information until well after the ship had set sail for Holland. Unless they are apprehended at sea, it is unlikely they will be caught once they reach land."

"I cannot believe Wickham is no longer on British soil and not made to face trial here." Darcy shook his head in disgust.

"Personally, I would not want to be in his shoes with *Monsieur*

Everard as my jailor. I suspect he will either be drowned at sea or will have to face *Madame Guillotine* when the two of them return to France."

"To think Wickham was once a favourite of my father."

"Yes. Uncle James gave him the opportunity to make something of himself, as did you. But ... in the end, his choices were poor."

"Father would have been gravely disappointed." He sighed.

"True. So, tell me, Cousin, are you ready to give up the life of a single man on the morrow?"

Darcy raised a brow. "Need you even ask?"

The colonel let out a hearty chuckle. "No, I suppose not. Miss Elizabeth is perfect for you, and I shall take delight in seeing how long it takes her to reform your taciturn ways."

Darcy returned his tease with a playful glower. "Richard, you do realise at some point this business with the French will be finished. Unless you see fit to find a suitable wife by your own merits, you will no doubt be subject to the machinations of your mother."

"Heaven forbid." He threw his hands up in the air with boisterous laughter. "Knowing Mother, I am sure she will gladly take up my case. Why, I would not be surprised to find she has already made a list of eligible women for me to choose from." He chuckled. "Frankly, I cannot begin to think of marriage while I still have my commission. For now, I shall simply take delight in observing your marital bliss from afar and hope to be named godfather to your first born."

Darcy grasped the colonel's hand. "I shall hold you to it, Cousin, and may you someday be as fortunate as I."

~ ♫ ~

Church of Saint George
Wednesday, 2 October 1811

On the following day, a few friends and immediate relations of the Darcy and Bennet families assembled for an early morning service at the Parish Church of Saint George in Hanover Square. The Anglican

Church with its ornate interior was quite large when compared with the simpler structure in the village of Meryton. While it could have easily accommodated several hundred guests, in this particular case, there were no more than thirty or so in attendance.

Standing quietly in the back of the church, Elizabeth lightly touched the delicate petals of her bridal bouquet as she waited for her father who was currently speaking with Mr. Gardiner. Jane and Mrs. Gardiner had finished straightening the back of her dress and were now adjusting the long, thin veil of lace which hung from a stunning pearl and diamond wedding tiara belonging to Lady Jessica.

Lifting her bouquet, Elizabeth closed her eyes and inhaled the luscious scent of the last of the gardenia flowers. They had been delivered by one of Darcy's footmen during the wee hours of the morning. Smiling to herself, she was sure her beloved William had slept as little as she in anticipation of this glorious day.

"Elizabeth, I have never seen a bride lovelier than you," complimented Mrs. Gardiner as soon as she and Jane were finished. "I do believe Mr. Darcy will be very pleased."

"Thank you." She squeezed her aunt's hands in appreciation. "The dress which you and Lady Jessica ordered turned out to be far more elegant than anything I could have ever imagined. Lady Anne's pearls are perfect, and the lace veil is exquisite."

"Luckily, I had the presence of mind to put it aside before the French embargo was enacted. I have never seen lace of such fine quality, and Lady Jessica says this type of thing is quite popular on the continent nowadays."

"I shall be very careful not to damage it so Jane may also use it on her wedding day."

"Lizzy." Jane blushed. "A simple bonnet will suffice, should I be so fortunate."

Elizabeth squeezed her sister's hand. "My dearest sister, I am sure you, too, will marry for love, and you must never doubt it." Minutes later, Mr. Bennet and Mr. Gardiner made their appearance.

"My dear," Mr. Bennet addressed Elizabeth. "Margaret and Grace have finished spreading their rose petals on the carpet, and the minister has indicated he is ready to begin the ceremony. Everyone is seated, and I believe a certain young man is anxiously awaiting your arrival. From the look on his face, I suspect the colonel will need to restrain the poor fellow from meeting you half way down the aisle if we do not begin soon." He chuckled and encouraged the Gardiners to go ahead to their seats. They were followed by Jane who began her procession to the front of the church where she took her place as the maid of honour.

"Lizzy," spoke Mr. Bennet. "I always knew this day would come. Today you are making your old papa a very proud and happy man. I could not have given you to anyone finer than my new son."

"Thank you, Papa."

With misty eyes, Mr. Bennet kissed his precious daughter on the cheek and wrapped her arm about his. He patted her hand, and they began walking down the long red carpet leading to the front of the church where Elizabeth's future waited with the man she loved. As father and daughter continued down the aisle, the organ music increased in volume announcing their presence to those who were in attendance.

An early morning rain had long ceased, and the church was now bathed in a rainbow of colour from sunlight filtering through the stained glass windows and into the sanctuary. All eyes were turned in the bride's direction, but Elizabeth saw only her dear William. Moments later, Elizabeth and Mr. Bennet reached the front of the church. After placing another chaste kiss on his daughter's cheek, he gave her hand to Darcy who nodded at his new father-in-law in acceptance. Following a brief sermonette and the recitation of the vows, the wedding band was placed upon Elizabeth's finger. The ceremony was thus concluded by the minister who proclaimed Mr. and Mrs. Fitzwilliam Darcy to be husband and wife.

Darcy was not one to publicly display his affection, but to the astonishment of those who knew him well, he kissed his wife for all to see. Walking hand and hand back down the aisle and into the foyer, they were greeted by tears of joy and words of congratulations from the well-wishers. As soon as the signing of the register and a few other formalities were concluded, Darcy led Elizabeth to the bridal carriage which departed immediately for Ferversham House.

The wedding breakfast was expected to host no less than one hundred guests. During the course of the party, the guests were invited to assemble in the ballroom for music and dancing. For Darcy and Elizabeth, this was not an unwelcome addition since the only time they had danced together was on the eve of the disastrous Military Ball. Now, with those unpleasant memories far behind them and being newly wedded, the couple delighted in being able to do so once again.

"Mrs. Darcy, have I told you how very beautiful you look today?" Darcy whispered as they came together for the first time.

"I do seem to recall something of the sort. Perhaps you should tell me again," Elizabeth teased. They passed each other once more before coming around and joining hands.

"*Perhaps* I should rather say I am madly in love with you, my dearest, loveliest Elizabeth. In truth, I do have much more to say, but those words are for your ears alone and shall not be spoken in a crowded ballroom."

"Mr. Darcy." Elizabeth blushed, never having heard him speak so boldly in public. "I will look forward to our next conversation on the subject." She playfully arched a brow in his direction causing him to smile brilliantly without reserve.

Following their set, Elizabeth and Darcy declined to dance any further since there were many more guests whom they wished to greet. Later, when the musicians paused to take their allotted break, Lady Jessica announced that Elizabeth and Georgiana had planned to entertain the guests with two beautiful love songs. It so happened they were the same songs performed by the women at her farewell party for Miss Paradis.

Unlike the setting for Lady Jessica's party, here at the wedding breakfast, there was no question in anyone's mind who Elizabeth was singing for. At the conclusion, there was nary a dry eye and once the audience began to applaud, Darcy went to her side. Bowing over her hand, he tenderly kissed her fingertips and softly spoke, "My love, on today of all days, you have given me a gift which I shall always cherish." Lifting her hand to his breast and clasping it between his own hands he continued, "The melody of your heart is here, singing within my own, now and forever. How I love you, my darling."

~ ♫ ~

Not long after, the wedding breakfast came to a conclusion, and the well-wishers gathered as the newly wedded couple boarded the carriage and left for Darcy House where they would spend their first days together as man and wife. Having assisted Elizabeth into the carriage, Darcy boarded taking a seat at her side. Bringing her hand to his lips, he tenderly kissed it before placing another kiss on her lips. "My darling, how is it I am so blessed to have you in my life? At this moment, I am the very happiest of men."

"And I am the happiest of women." She touched his cheek. "As your wife, I promise I shall do everything within my power to see you always remain so."

"Elizabeth...."

Minutes later, the carriage arrived at Darcy House where the newly wedded couple were greeted by the many servants who had formed two lines at the front entrance. There, they graciously welcomed their master and new mistress who proceeded into the house. Intending to remove to their chambers, Darcy informed his butler and the housekeeper to make sure they were not disturbed. Dinner had been arranged for seven o'clock and was to be served unattended by candlelight in their private sitting room. Arriving on the second floor where the family rooms were located, Darcy lifted Elizabeth into his arms and spun around, causing her to giggle.

"Finally, I have you to myself, Mrs. Darcy." He kissed her passionately on the lips. "If I am not too bold, may I request we remove to *my* room?"

"*Your* room, Mr. Darcy?" She playfully arched an eyebrow as her eyes lit up with mischief. "Sir, I am at your leisure, and I believe your preference will suit me very well."

Darcy immediately opened the door and did not put Elizabeth down until they had crossed the threshold and he had locked the door behind them. Though no servants were in the room, someone had opened a beautiful mechanical music box which was playing a lovely waltz. He allowed her feet to touch the floor but remained with his arms about her waist as she looked with awe about her husband's bed chamber.

The room itself was much larger than what she had envisioned, and she instinctively knew Darcy had taken great pains to make it inviting. The curtains had been drawn and there was a log burning in the fireplace for warmth. The room had been lit with candles and rose petals had been scattered about the floor and on the counterpane leaving a fragrant smell. A bottle of wine and two glasses sat on a low table along with some fruit and other light refreshments. Off to the side, she noticed a woman's dressing-table where several of her personal items, including brushes and combs were arranged and ready for her use. Blushing, she saw that even her nightwear had been laid out on the end of the large bed, no doubt by Sophia, who must have helped prepare the room for her arrival.

"William, I am…. I never expected…. Everything is so…." Turning around in his embrace, Elizabeth found her feeble efforts at speech interrupted by an ardent kiss.

"I trust you are not disappointed, my love," he tenderly offered. "If I have in any way displeased or offended you with my preparations, I shall call your maid and return here as soon as you are ready. Or if you prefer to dress in your own room, I shall understand." His look was hopeful though his words were unsure.

"William, I do not wish to leave, and I would prefer it if you stayed and assisted me." She lovingly smiled, lightly touching the side of his face with her fingertips. "I shall do quite well with your help, my husband. Everything you have arranged is perfect."

"My dearest love." He kissed her without restraint. "I have dreamt of this for so long. Today we shall become one, and I shall cherish and love you for all of my days."

"And I, you, my William."

So thus it was Darcy and Elizabeth became one in mind and body on this blessed second day of October, in the year of our Lord, 1811. Never again were they to be unduly parted from one another for they were destined to live out the melody of their lives in harmony and in love.

CHAPTER THIRTY-TWO

OUR FUTURE

Pemberley
Not Quite a Year Later

*G*olden hues of sunlight glimmered across the walls of the study where Darcy had been working for the last hour. While his dear wife slept, he was anxious to finish his correspondence so he might devote the rest of his afternoon to her pleasure. Now that Elizabeth was heavy with child and near her confinement, she easily tired and needed more rest.

During the past month, it had become commonplace for Darcy to put off his work in lieu of spending time in Elizabeth's company. The well-being of his wife and their unborn child took precedence above all else, and he vowed to personally see to her every need despite her protests.

"William," she would say. *"I dearly love your attention, but I am hardly a delicate flower about to wither. Women were made to birth children."* She would laugh, trying to tease him out of his serious mood. *"My mother thrives to this very day, and she gave birth to five healthy daughters as you well know!"*

Even with her playful mocking, Darcy knew Elizabeth's words to be true. Yet the man could not help but worry as there had been much sorrow associated with his mother's confinements.

Finishing the last of his letters, Darcy quickly sealed them and put his writing materials away. He then proceeded to remove the upper right hand drawer from the desk. Stretching his arm the entire length of the opening, he felt for the latch to a hidden compartment only known to himself and his father. With the tips of his fingers, Darcy unfastened the latch and retrieved an item which had rested undisturbed for the past twelve years. "Ah!" he exclaimed with eagerness pulling forth a thin ribbon of green velvet attached to a solitary key. Tarnished from neglect, Darcy took out a small oilcloth from the middle drawer and began to rub the key with vigour.

The key itself, long and slender, was very plain. Upon first seeing it, one would not have given it any notice whatsoever. Still, this particular key held many treasured memories for Darcy since it was the means of unlocking a room which had been one of his mother's favourites. After her death, his father had bitterly shut up the room, forbidding anyone to ever enter it again. Today, however, Fitzwilliam Darcy intended to defy those wishes.

Behind the locked doors, a small greenhouse had been added to the far side of the conservatory. The *Nature Room*, as it was called, was commissioned by his father and gifted to Lady Anne for her studies early on in their marriage. In that special place, young Fitzwilliam had spent many happy hours assisting his mother while she completed drawings and made entries in her journals.

Having polished the old key as best he could, Darcy tightly clasped it in his hand and quickly left the study. Within seconds, he reached the wooden door to the locked room. Carefully placing the key in the lock, he manoeuvred it until he was able to feel the bolt give way.

With the door being closed for so many years, it was now stiff and creaked with age when Darcy pushed it open. A musty stench permeated the air, and he momentarily held his breath in revulsion. The room itself appeared dark and uninviting for the windows were covered with vines and dirt, obstructing the natural light. Returning to the conservatory to retrieve a candelabrum, he hastily lit the candles and came back to the dreary chamber in order to survey the damage caused by years of neglect.

Setting the candelabrum on a dusty table, Darcy could easily see this room would need a thorough cleaning and much renovation before bringing Elizabeth in to view it. Most of his mother's equipment had been stored in two large cupboards, but the hinges on one of the doors had come loose, leaving its contents subject to the mercy of layered dust and cobwebs. In addition to the deterioration of the woven collection baskets, it appeared most of the metal apparatuses and colanders were severely rusted. Even the holding boxes once used to study small reptiles and insects were no longer serviceable. In his mind, this room would have been better served as a tribute to her memory rather than a symbolic tomb.

With the anticipated birth of their child, Darcy had planned to revive some of the traditions he had shared with his mother in this room. Determined to implement the necessary steps to restore everything to its former glory, he knew the room could again be a place of joy and discovery for his own children.

Taking one last look about before leaving, Darcy's gaze settled on another table where Lady Anne often sat making her notations. To his astonishment, one of her journals lay open on the dusty surface. Removing a handkerchief from his pocket, Darcy began to carefully wipe the fragile pages now yellowed and curled around the edges. *Father, why did you not store this away in the library with her other journals?*

Gingerly turning the pages to see what his mother had been working on, he discovered the journal had nothing whatsoever to do with her studies. Lady Anne had been drawing a book for his sister, just as she had done for him when he was a young boy. This particular book had several sketches of Georgiana from the time she was an infant until the last unfinished drawing. Here a little girl probably no more than three years-of-age sat upon a cushion playing with a baby kitten. Her expression was happy, and as she cuddled the little creature, Darcy could not help but be moved by the images he saw. He wondered if there was any way he could have the drawings restored for Georgiana. It would give his sister great pleasure to have this special connection to their mother.

Carefully picking up the tattered book, Darcy left the Nature Room and carried it back into his study where he would keep it until he was able to have it sent out for repair. Putting down the book and taking up a miniature of his mother, he studied it for several minutes. In his eyes, she was beautiful, and her expression was one filled with love and kindness. *If only you had not died so young.*

Suddenly gripped with fear for the well-being of his wife and unborn child, Darcy felt his chest tighten and his breath quicken. "Elizabeth," he half-choked aloud. Striding from the study and heading through the library to the staircase, Darcy took the stairs two at a time and did not stop until he reached the door of their shared room. Attempting to calm his breathing, he momentarily paused before entering. Hearing no noticeable sound, he quietly turned the knob and pushed the door open.

The curtains around the windows had been let down to keep out the light, yet he could easily see the bed where she rested. With her hair loosened and a simple shawl about her shoulders, his wife lay sleeping. Her legs and feet were tucked beneath her gown, and she rested curled up on her left side while her right hand caressed the swell of her stomach. Never had anyone looked so peaceful or beautiful in this state, he thought, continuing to gaze.

Gripped again with the same fear which had overtaken him in the study, Darcy became alarmed when he could not discern his wife's breathing. With a rising sense of panic, he quickly approached their bed. Kneeling at her side, he touched her hand before letting out the breath he unknowingly held. Relieved to feel the warmth of her flesh beneath his touch, he muttered, "Thank God."

Suppressing silent tears and feeling a bit foolish for anticipating the worst, he unreservedly admitted he had allowed himself to be consumed with worry. Elizabeth was healthy, and he knew he needed to embrace her sentiments, trusting she and their child would be well throughout her confinement. It would not do to let the sorrow and fear of the past take him away from the happiness he could be sharing with his wife during this blessed time in their lives.

"My darling," he whispered. "Please forgive me. From this moment, I vow I shall do better."

Releasing her hand and stepping to the other side of the bed, he quietly removed his coat and boots. Undoing his cravat and rolling up his sleeves, Darcy slid his body onto the bed and moulded it to hers. Smelling the sweet fragrance of her hair and feeling the softness of her curves, he gently kissed her neck and lowered his head to the pillows.

"William," she murmured, having sensed him in her sleep.

"Yes, my love, I am here."

Placing his large hand over her small one, he could feel the slight movement of their child as she snuggled against him, resuming her sleep. Contented, Darcy himself drifted off into slumber, finally trusting all would be well.

~ ♫ ~

During the following days and weeks, Darcy remained true to his pledge. His mood had lightened considerably, and he was finally able to resume his duties without the self-imposed strain he had been experiencing when his worries had taken over his sense of reason. With Elizabeth's confinement nearly upon her, it was clear she had been feeling more uncomfortable with each passing day. Not only were her days and nights restless, but she had been plagued with lower back pains.

Although her feet were a little swollen, Elizabeth's greatest relief came when she was walking. Sensing his wife's need for an outing, Darcy had proposed taking the phaeton to the pond where they could enjoy a picnic together and stroll leisurely about the grounds. As of late, the temperatures had been cool for mid-August. Today, on the other hand, the air was pleasant and the skies were clear, perfect for their afternoon excursion. Darcy had instructed the cook to make up the basket with light foods favoured by Elizabeth. In addition, he brought along a book of poetry with the intention of reading to her while she rested after their walk.

"William, I could not have asked for a lovelier afternoon," Elizabeth commented as they strolled towards the stone bench overlooking the pond. "The picnic was delightful, and the walk was precisely what I needed to release some of the achiness I have been feeling of late."

"I am glad of it," he said pulling her into an embrace and kissing her tenderly before helping her to sit. With her hand firmly placed in his, she slowly lowered herself to the bench.

"My … I never dreamed it would take so much effort to sit when carrying our child. In thinking over my situation, I have come to realise that I would not be having nearly so much difficulty if it was not for you, Mr. Darcy," she teased, continuing to rub the swell of her stomach with her free hand.

"You would place the blame on me, Mrs. Darcy? I seem to recall you were a very willing participant in the conception of our child." He feigned a scowl at her playfulness.

"Yes, I would," she said turning up her nose and crossing her arms as best she could. "If you were not such a great, tall fellow, I am convinced our child would be considerably smaller, thus making it easier for me to get up and down from *wherever* I chose to sit."

He laughed with abandon. "Then again, perhaps our child is not so very big at all," he bantered in return. Pulling Elizabeth's hand free in order to place a kiss upon her fingers, he continued, "Have you never considered the possibility of carrying twins?"

"William, what are you saying?" She snatched back her hand, nearly panicking with the thought.

"Elizabeth, my love, I did not mean to alarm you." He smoothed her brow with his thumb and kissed her nose. "My darling, there has *never* been a report of twins in either the Darcy or the Fitzwilliam families. And since there has never been such an occurrence in your family, I believe we are fairly safe on that account. Please forgive me."

"Your apology is accepted." She visibly relaxed, leaning into him as they continued to sit and enjoy the view. "It is so lovely here. I can imagine your mother spending many hours in this very spot with her journals."

"And so she did. My father had this bench placed here for her use. Mama would draw while I collected various specimens and made notes in my own journals. Later we would discuss the drawings and evaluate our findings together. She was an excellent teacher and I learned much from her." He smiled in remembrance. "Someday I shall take great pleasure in sharing those same experiences with *our* child. This babe you carry is our future." Darcy gently covered his wife's hand with his and warmly kissed her. To his surprise, his ministrations were interrupted when he felt the babe move beneath their joined hands with more force than he had felt on previous occasions.

"Oh my," Elizabeth tensed. "It appears our son wishes to make his presence known." They removed their hands and stared at the protrusion remaining beneath her thin dress.

"Elizabeth, does it not hurt?" Darcy gently pushed on the bulge which in turn pushed back causing him to frown.

"William, it is only his foot. Can you not recognise the shape of it?"

"Why yes, I suppose so, but it is so large."

"My dear husband, did I not earlier give you my thoughts concerning the nature of our child? I realise I can no longer see my feet, but the last time I could, I distinctly remember them being fairly small. This foot is *not* small. Therefore, our child decidedly takes after *you*." The two of them chuckled together until Elizabeth was jolted with a sharp spasm.

"Oh dear," she frowned, quickly moving her hand to the lower part of her abdomen and rubbing the area until the pain eased. "It seems our son does not care for this discussion."

"Elizabeth, I should get you back to the house."

"Yes, please."

Rising with Darcy's assistance, Elizabeth nearly lost her balance when she experienced yet another sharp pain. At that moment, a warm liquid began to trickle down her legs where it pooled at her feet. "William, our son...." She panicked. "I thought there would be more warning before the waters broke."

"All will be well, my darling." Lifting Elizabeth into his arms, Darcy carried her the short distance to the phaeton and called for the attending footman to run back to the house and alert Mrs. Reynolds. The trusted housekeeper would need to send for the midwife as well as the local physician who Darcy insisted must be present at the birth.

Progress to the house was slow with Elizabeth experiencing yet another strong pain and urging Darcy to stop. Doing so, he lovingly rubbed her lower back and encouraged her to breathe deeply while they waited for the discomfort to subside.

"William, I know it is not proper, but will you come to me once I am settled in my room?"

"Of course, my love, I shall do whatever you desire."

"Aunt Gardiner says it is important for me to walk during the first hours of my confinement. Both she and the midwife have insisted it will help the babe and speed the birthing process. I fear these few pains have left me feeling rather weak, and I do not know how I shall manage without your help."

"You are not to worry, Elizabeth. If it is your wish, I shall walk with you, and if need be, I shall stay by your side through it all."

"I *do* wish it."

Lightly snapping the reins of the carriage, Darcy continued on to the house with Elizabeth leaning into him for support. Encouraging her to relax, she closed her eyes and did not open them again until they arrived at the house. Determined not to let his own anxiety show, he forced himself to remain calm, knowing steadiness and reassurance was what his wife most needed from him at this point in time.

With Mrs. Reynolds having been informed of Elizabeth's condition, the servants were ready to take over as soon as the Darcys arrived back at the house. Darcy insisted on carrying his wife up the stairs to her bedchamber himself where she was promptly assisted with her clothes and basic necessities in anticipation of their child's birth. Contrary to the rules of British Propriety for the upper class in this situation, once the maids had finished assisting Elizabeth, Darcy was readmitted to her room. Not even the admonition of his trusted long-time housekeeper, Mrs. Reynolds, could dissuade Darcy from attending his wife during her confinement.

Elizabeth's pains continued well into the night and it was not until nearly midnight that she had progressed far enough to begin pushing. Even though she had been steadfast throughout, at one point, she could not help but blurt out through gritted teeth, "William, your son is being very stubborn. I would never think of behaving in such a manner to my dear mama."

"You need not worry, Elizabeth. I shall have a hearty talk with the little fellow after he makes his presence known."

"Be sure you do," she chided in all seriousness.

With each new push, Darcy continued to encourage his wife, and soon the babe's head had crowned. With just a few more pushes, the little one was finally expelled, and his cry was heard.

"Mr. and Mrs. Darcy," the physician announced. "You have a son."

"William," Elizabeth sobbed through tears of joy. "Please, let me see him." The babe had yet to be cleaned, but once the cord was severed, the midwife wrapped the child in a soft blanket and handed him to his father.

"Elizabeth, he is a handsome little fellow, is he not?" Darcy said placing their child in his wife's outstretched arms.

"Yes, he is perfect." She touched his matted hair and wiped some of the mucus from his wrinkled face. The child was lean and long and his little hand proved to be very strong as he tightly gripped her finger.

"Mrs. Darcy," the midwife kindly spoke. "It is time to clean the babe now. And, sir, it would be best if you stepped out while we take care of Mrs. Darcy."

"Of course." Turning to Elizabeth, he kissed her forehead and whispered, "I shall return to you very soon, my darling wife. In the meantime, I will visit with Georgiana and share our good news. I love you both so very much."

"We love you, too, William."

~ ♫ ~

When Darcy stepped out of the room, he found Georgiana waiting in the hallway with anticipation. He suspected she had been pacing outside of her room for some time, for upon seeing him, she ran directly into his outstretched arms.

"William.... I was so worried. I heard the babe cry, and then there was nothing. The maids were rushing in and out of the room so quickly and I was not able to find out what had happened. Please, tell me all is well."

"You need not worry, sweet one." He touched her tear-stained face. "Elizabeth is fine, and we have a healthy son."

"A son? Oh, William, you have an heir!" She could not help but shed her tears anew. "I am so very happy. You have given me the most excellent sister, and now I have a nephew! Brother, our family is complete."

"Yes, my darling sister, we are truly blessed. Come, shall we not go back to your rooms where it is warmer? It may be yet another hour before I am able to join Elizabeth. If you like, I could sit with you, or if you prefer, you may go on to bed and see Elizabeth and your nephew tomorrow."

"Thank you, William, but you need not stay with me. Knowing Elizabeth and the babe are well gives me the reassurance I need to sleep peacefully. I shall see them tomorrow after everyone has rested."

"Goodnight then, Georgiana." He lovingly kissed her forehead.

"Goodnight, Brother. Please tell Elizabeth I love her."

"I shall."

~ ♪ ~

Darcy quietly entered the bedchamber where Elizabeth lay sleeping with their precious child swaddled in her arm. The room had been cleared, and all was as it should be. The maid, who had been attending his wife, nodded and removed herself to the next room where she would stay until she was needed. Placing a vase of flowers on the table, Darcy took the vacated chair next to the bed and simply smiled allowing silent tears of gratitude to trickle down his cheeks.

Not quite a year ago, he had joyfully married Elizabeth, and they had joined as man and wife. Today, she had given birth to their son. At this moment, he could want for no finer gift.

Gently touching his son's dark hair, Darcy wrapped a single auburn curl around his little finger and marvelled at its softness. He then touched his fat little cheeks and could not help but chuckle to himself when the babe pursed his lips together and made a wee gurgling sound as though to suckle his mother's breast. What could be sweeter than the sight of his wife and child together in this setting? The vision they presented would be forever etched within his mind. After lightly kissing Elizabeth's forehead so as not to wake her, Darcy leaned back in the chair. Contented, he closed his eyes and drifted off into a peaceful sleep.

EPILOGUE

Ten years later

During the course of their marriage, Fitzwilliam and Elizabeth Darcy were revered throughout the neighbourhood for their good works and affability to the poor. They were esteemed by all and often referred to as the proud parents of four handsome children. Four years after the birth of Bennet James Fitzwilliam Darcy, their second son Daniel Richard was born. A few years later, the family was blessed with a little girl, Anna Elizabeth, and then another son, Alexander Charles. With so many children, the halls of Pemberley were no longer quiet but had become lively with much joy and laughter.

All four children, though quite different from one another, were unconditionally loved by their parents. That being said, it was only natural for Bennet to be fawned over and spoiled prior to the arrival of his younger brothers and sister. Darcy had always looked forward to being a parent, yet the experience fulfilled his expectations far beyond what he could ever have imagined.

Bennet was intelligent beyond his years and from a very young age had been eager for knowledge. "Papa is my teacher, and I want to learn everything that *he* knows," the boy would say with pride. And so it was in his father's company the child thrived. Bennet was inquisitive and his natural curiosity challenged Darcy to go beyond what was traditionally expected of a parent. As Bennet grew older, it was not uncommon for both father and son to spend hours at a time in each other's company while pursuing a given task.

Daniel, the Darcys' second child, held a special place in his parent's heart for far different reasons. Young Daniel took after Darcy not only in looks but in disposition. The shyness and reserve exhibited by the young boy was not unfamiliar to his father. With Daniel idolizing Bennet, both parents took great care not to let the boy feel insecure in the shadow of his more confident older brother.

Next came little Anna. Being the only girl, it was difficult for her parents not to dote on her. She was a loving child who could charm either Darcy or Elizabeth with a giggle or a simple smile. Having large expressive blue eyes and curly golden locks of hair, this child resembled Georgiana when she was of a similar age. In observing Darcy with his daughter one could easily see it was little Anna who warmed his heart beyond measure.

"Papa, I love you so much," she would say as she snuggled into his neck and placed soft kisses on his cheek.

"I love you too, little one."

"Papa, Aunt Georgie taught me and Dolly a new song when she came to play with us. We have been practicing every day, just like she told us to. Please, Papa, may we sing it for you?"

"Why, yes, my little songbird." He would chuckle in delight. "I would dearly love to hear you and Dolly sing."

The Darcys' fourth child, two-year-old Alexander, was an observant lad and, like his older brother, very confident. The little boy was determined to be included in the activities of the older children, and whenever they played games or ventured out of doors, he did not want to be left behind. Even on days when Elizabeth took him to visit the school room, he would happily sit at the little desk which would one day be his and ask his mama to help him learn.

"I am a big boy," he would say with a beguiling smile on his face.

"Yes, you are, Alexander," Elizabeth would reply while running her fingers through his dark curly hair and kissing his forehead. She would then bring him his supplies, and the two would draw or look at picture books until he tired.

No matter how busy Darcy was with the running of the estate, his wife and children took precedence. Each day he insisted they all spend time together, whether it was on an outing to the pond, reading in the Library, or simply enjoying tea in the Conservatory, just as he had done with his own parents. When his time permitted, he would often plan a short tour of the countryside or a visit to the Lakes for the entire family. Then, every summer he and Elizabeth would host a month-long house party where their extended families could reacquaint themselves.

Jane and Bingley had married the year after the Darcys and gave birth to a son followed later by two daughters. Following the Bingleys' marriage, Lydia married a military officer and now had three girls. Kitty, who was expected to follow in Lydia's footsteps, surprised the family by marrying her Uncle Philips' young solicitor the following year. With him, she gave birth to a girl and a boy. Mary was the only sister who never married. Not long after Elizabeth's wedding, she removed to Town where she took up residence with the Gardiners. It was there Mary formed an attachment to a military surgeon who was a personal friend of Mrs. Gardiner's brother, the apothecary. They had planned to marry after the war ended, but sadly, Mary's intended was killed in June of 1813 during the Battle of Victoria. Following his death, Mary returned to Longbourn so she might be of assistance to her parents during their ageing years.

Georgiana remained with the Darcys for some time even though she experienced two seasons in Town. Interestingly, her heart was not so easily touched, nor was she inclined to be a part of the political atmosphere surrounding the eligible gentlemen whom she had been introduced to by her cousins, the Helmsleys, or by Lord and Lady Matlock. Returning to Derbyshire, she later married a landed gentleman and had two children. She had always wanted to remain close to her brother and sister, and being that her husband's estate was no more than a few hours from Pemberley, their families saw each other often.

Darcy's cousin, Colonel Fitzwilliam, never did return to active duty but remained in service to the *Secret Guard* of the Crown for the duration of the war. Despite his mother's protests, he married a lovely widow with two boys. His wife's departed husband had also been a second son and a close friend of the colonel's from their days together at university. Upon resigning his commission, the former colonel happily moved his family to reside in Derbyshire at the estate which had been given to him by his father. A year later, he and his wife were blessed with yet another son.

The Darcy family had indeed prospered in circumstance and happiness over the years. Yet, the master of Pemberley never took for granted all that he had been given. Unknown to even Elizabeth, Darcy kept his father's miniature of George Wickham secured within his desk drawer. Although Wickham had never been heard of again, his likeness served to remind Darcy of what he had nearly lost on one horrifying day in Wapping. Elizabeth was his life, his joy, and to think he might never have fully known her love or seen the faces of each of their precious children was unfathomable. He was grateful. He was humbled. His life was full for he had been blessed beyond all measure. The master of Pemberley was truly a happy man.

~Finis~

NOTE TO THE READER

Dear Reader,

Thank you so much for reading my second offering to the world of Jane Austen Fanfiction. Below you will find an excerpt taken from my first published novelette, *A Very Merry Mix-up,* and a short preview of *A Holiday to Remember* which will be available later in 2018.

Sincerely,
Jennifer Redlarczyk ♫

A VERY MERRY MIX-UP: A PRIDE AND PREJUDICE NOVELETTE ~ PREVIEW

A VERY MERRY MIX-UP: A PRIDE AND PREJUDICE
NOVELETTE ~ PREVIEW

*J*t all began when Fitzwilliam Darcy and his cousin Colonel Richard Fitzwilliam stopped at the posting station in Bromley on their way to Rosings Park for their annual visit. Looking for some diversion, the good colonel happened upon a local Romani woman who was selling her people's treasured *Moon Wine*. Find out what happens to some of our favourite Jane Austen characters when her advice is ignored in *A Very Merry Mix-up*.

FROM CHAPTER ONE

1 April 1811
All Fool's Day
Kent

Fitzwilliam Darcy yawned and stretched, squinting as the early morning light flickered through the partially opened curtains of his bedroom window. For some unknown reason, he had not slept well.

Bleary-eyed and wondering if the potent wine he had drunk on the previous evening had been the cause, he slowly rolled over intending to stay in bed a bit longer. To his chagrin, his senses were alerted when his hand met with the soft, warm body of a woman.

"Good God! Who are you?" he bellowed, startling the woman who was sharing his bed.

The woman's breath nearly caught in her throat when she turned over and saw who was by her side. "WHAT, may I ask, are YOU doing in MY bed?" Quickly pulling the sheets up to her neckline, she continued. "I demand you leave THIS INSTANT!"

"You are.... You are Mrs. Collins!" he shouted in distress.

"Mrs. Collins!" she shouted back. "Sir, you are mad! I am your cousin, Elizabeth Bennet, and I DO believe my dear friend Charlotte will NOT be happy when I tell her of your indiscretion."

"MY indiscretion?! Madam, you are in MY bed!"

Quickly rising, Darcy felt a little unsteady and found it necessary to hold on to the bed post while searching for his robe. Catching a glimpse of himself in the mirror, he staggered closer to the glass and groaned in disbelief. Slowly rubbing his stubby fingers across his ruddy cheeks and through his oily hair, he wondered if he had indeed gone mad. Wiping those same fingers on the front of his nightshirt, he could not help but feel his flabby chest and the protrusion of his round stomach through the cloth. Grasping the reality of his predicament, Darcy stared at himself with revulsion.

"Merciful Heaven!" he thundered, turning back to the woman. "It is me, Fitzwilliam Darcy, in the body of that idiot rector! If you are Miss Elizabeth Bennet, as you claim, I fear we have both become the victims of some cruel joke. Will you not come and look for yourself?"

Picking up Charlotte's dressing gown and quickly wrapping it around herself, Elizabeth guardedly went to the mirror as he requested. "Mr. Darcy?" She paled, realizing what he said was true. "How ... how could this have happened?"

"I do not know," he said momentarily pinching his brow in hope of staving off a sudden headache. "But ... I have a feeling Colonel Fitzwilliam may have some answers. I suspect *this misfortune* has something to do with the wine which he offered us following dinner."

"The wine?"

"Yes," he nearly hissed. "Did you not feel a little strange after drinking it?"

"I did, but I thought it was nothing more than the warmth of the room created by the burning logs which were piled high for Miss de Bourgh's comfort."

"At the time, my thoughts were the same as yours." He scowled. "In retrospect, I am more inclined to believe it was *not* the heat, but rather the wine which we consumed. The *good colonel* insisted on buying that particular bottle from an old woman who was selling it out of the posting station at Bromley on our journey here. While I have never been one to embrace superstitions, in this instance perhaps I should have paid more attention. I vaguely remember overhearing the woman cautioning my cousin when it came to drinking the wine and making wishes during a full moon."

"Oh, dear," Elizabeth murmured more to herself than to Darcy. "Yesterday evening, the moon *was* full, and the last thing I remember was wishing I could see you...." Gasping, she took a step back not wanting to say more.

"What!" he demanded.

"Forgive me." She tried to remain calm. "You are always so fastidious in your appearance, Mr. Darcy. I ... I merely wondered what it would be like to see you in ... in a more unkempt state. I promise you, I would never wish to see any man exchange places with Mr. Collins. That would be too cruel, indeed. Pray, sir, did you not make a wish of your own to have ended up in this predicament with me?" Her eyes suddenly grew wide realizing the truth of what Mr. Darcy's stares must have meant all along. *It must have been admiration and not simply to find fault.*

Clearing his throat, Darcy stated, "It matters not what I wished for, Madam. More importantly, we need to find out who else was affected by the wine and what course of action can be taken to rectify this dilemma."

"Yes, of course." Her face coloured. "Mr. Darcy, you will find Mr. Collins' room through the door just behind you. It would be best if you took your leave now. I should like to dress and find out if Charlotte has taken my place."

"I beg your pardon. Forgive me, I was not thinking. I should not be here and shall leave you at once." His face reddened at the impropriety of his appearance and the situation he found himself in.

"I shall await your arrival downstairs. For now, it would be best if we do nothing to alert the servants of the changes which have taken place. Meanwhile, I shall send a note to my cousin asking him to come directly." Darcy abruptly left the room feeling very unsettled.

A HOLIDAY TO REMEMBER ~ PREVIEW

$\mathcal{W}$illiam Darcy and Elizabeth Bennet had an unfortunate encounter at a summer music festival in Chicago where unpleasant words were exchanged and tempers flared. What happens when their paths cross again in December? Will their animosity continue or will their reunion turn out to be *A Holiday to Remember!* Coming in December of 2018, a modern novella inspired by Jane Austen's Pride and Prejudice.

FROM CHAPTER ONE

Meryton Academy for the Performing Arts, Choir room
Monday, 4 December
Present day

"Liz Bennet! Please tell me I didn't hear what I just thought I heard!" Charlotte Lucas burst through the door and marched straight to the keyboard where Elizabeth was working out the final arrangements for *A Holiday to Remember*—part of the school's final showcase before the winter break.

"Char, I have no idea what you're talking about, and I'm kind of on a deadline here. Uh … you do remember I have a major rehearsal at six?" She arched a questioning eyebrow in her friend's direction before pencilling the last of the chords on the master lead sheet.

"Right, but for *your* information, Mr. Billy Collins just told everyone in the teacher's lounge he has a big date with *you* on New Year's Eve. He *says* he's escorting you to the Pemberley Foundation's charity gala at Forest Ridge. What gives? Don't those tickets start at five hundred a pop? Not to mention any woman who would dare to go out with that nutter would have to be a marble short."

Elizabeth stopped what she was doing and burst into laughter. "Char, do you honestly think BC would actually shell out *that* kind of money just to have a date with *me?* The man is so tight he probably wouldn't even spend five dollars on his own mother. As it turns out, the Choralteens were asked to perform at the party. They're doing the opening act right after dessert and since Reeves will be out of town, I'm making do with *Billy-boy* for my sound guy. You're welcome to join us if you don't have a date. I can always use an extra chaperone. Plus after the kids leave, we're invited to stay and enjoy the rest of the party. There's going to be a live band, dancing, loads of food and some kind of a silent auction. It could be fun, even without dates."

"Sorry, Liz. As a matter of fact, I *do* have a date." Charlotte straightened up and fluttered her eyelashes in jest. "And … as much as I should like to hob knob with the *rich and famous*, Brexton Denny is taking *me* to the Signature Room to celebrate the New Year. Who knows, this might turn out to be *my* Holiday to Remember, if you don't mind me borrowing the title from your medley."

"Go right ahead. The Signature Room is pretty impressive. Is there any chance your Mr. Denny might finally be getting serious?"

"Not to my knowledge. Still, there's no way I'm going to pass up a date with a buff trainer from the fitness club, fireworks over Lake Michigan, and a kiss at midnight."

"*A kiss at midnight.*" Elizabeth sighed kind of dreamy-eyed. "Aunt Mady says being kissed at midnight is *magical* and I believe her, not that I've ever been kissed at midnight to test the theory."

"Girl, you are such a romantic. I could never be like you. Listen, if you need an escort, you can always ask my brother. I know Johnny isn't ideal, but he's okay in a pinch. On second thought, what about the cute drummer from the music store? Didn't you go out with him a couple of times? Maybe you can take him."

"*George Wickham?* I think not! And *no,* we *never* dated. Char, your memory fails you. I offered to sing backup for that smooth talker's band at Lollapalooza back in early August and was only helping him out in a pinch. Believe me; *dating* was *not* part of the chord chart. Besides, I'm hardly interested in a fly-by-night drummer or any free-lance musician for that matter. Not to mention, I'm definitely consid-ering adding your brother to the list. If Johnny stands me up for one more transmission or any other mechanical failure, the man is toast. As it turns out, I'm thinking of handing him his marching papers after he escorts me to the holiday party being given by Jane's new boyfriend. Who knows, I may follow my sister's lead and use the professional dating service where she met Charles."

"Are you serious?"

"Uh-huh. Jane's boyfriend is one special guy. He's so considerate and has a great sense of humour. Plus he brings her flowers and takes her to concerts, out to dinner, company functions, yada, yada…. It was Charles Bingley who recommended my kids for the Pemberley gig. He's one of the corporate lawyers who works for the foundation and submitted our PR materials to the marketing director. Mr. Reynolds thinks our *Holiday to Remember* medley will be perfect for their New Year's Eve charity gala."

"It's bound to be a hit. The Choralteens are already looking pretty good, and you still have until next Thursday to put it all together for the showcase. Speaking of the gala, I hear the CEO of Darcy Enter-prises is pretty *hot*." Charlotte wiggled her eyebrows as if in the know. "*William Darcy* has been in *all* of the tabloids lately. They say he's kind of a mystery man. Aside from being gorgeous, it appears he is very private, possibly somewhat of a recluse or even a workaholic type if you know what I mean. I wonder if *he'll* be there."

"*William Darcy?*" Elizabeth frowned. "His sister, Georgiana, was studying piano with Aunt Mady at the music store until…." Her voice trailed off. "Are you sure he's connected to the foundation? Mr. Reynolds never mentioned him."

"Small world! According to Google, the foundation is run by Darcy Enterprises." Glancing at the wall clock, Charlotte changed the subject. "Listen, the bell is about to ring so I better get a move on to my advanced ballet class. Do you still need help tonight with choreography for the opening number?"

"Char, I'd really appreciate it since I'm going to have my hands full with the pit orchestra. If you can take over while we run through my new arrangements, it would mean one less thing for me to juggle at practice."

"No problem. I'll be there. Catch you later."

"Thanks."

After Charlotte left, Elizabeth rushed over to her laptop and googled William Darcy, CEO of Darcy Enterprises. "I can't believe it. It *is* him! Well, Mr. Darcy, your Mr. Reynolds booked us. How was *he* to know you never wanted to see me again?" She shrugged her shoulders. "I guess we'll just have to make the most of it, won't we?"

ABOUT THE AUTHOR

Jennifer Redlarczyk

I am a private music instructor living in Crown Point, Indiana where I teach voice, violin and piano and work as an adjunct music professor at Purdue University Northwest in Hammond, Indiana. As a teen, I was introduced to Jane Austen by my mother who loved old books, old movies and old songs. In the summer of 2011, I stumbled upon Jane Austen Fanfiction at a Barnes and Noble store and became obsessed with this genre. From there, I met several talented JAFF authors and devoted readers who were active on social media and eventually became a moderator for the private JAFF forum, DarcyandLizzy.com. It was there that I first tried my hand at writing short stories. I have the greatest appreciation for the creative world of Jane Austen Fanfiction and am thrilled to be a part of the JAFF community. You can find me at: DarcyandLizzy.com, Facebook, Twitter, Pinterest, and YouTube. On my Pinterest page you will find inspiration pictures for each chapter of Darcy's Melody, and on my YouTube channel you can listen to my recordings of all of Lizzy's songs.

Jennifer Redlarczyk (Jen Red) ♫

Made in the USA
Columbia, SC
26 August 2018